ALSO BY ÀNNA McPARTLIN

Pack Up the Moon

Apart from the Crowd

As Sure as the Sun

Available from Downtown Press

alexandra, gone

gone

Anna McPartlin

DOWNTOWN PRESS
New York London Toronto Sydney

Downtown Press
A Division of Simon & Schuster, Inc.
1230 Avenue of the Americas
New York, NY 10020

Originally published in Ireland in 2009 by Poolbeg Press, Ltd.

First Downtown Press trade paperback edition April 2010

DOWNTOWN PRESS and colophon are trademarks of Simon & Schuster, Inc.

For information about special discounts for bulk purchases, please contact Simon & Schuster Special Sales at 1-866-506-1949 or business@simonandschuster.com.

The Simon & Schuster Speakers Bureau can bring authors to your live event. For more information or to book an event contact the Simon & Schuster Speakers Bureau at 1-866-248-3049 or visit our website at www.simonspeakers.com.

Designed by Akasha Archer

Manufactured in the United States of America

10   9   8   7   6   5   4   3   2   1

Library of Congress Cataloging-in-Publication Data

McPartlin, Anna, 1972–
    Alexandra, gone / Anna McPartlin.—1st Downtown Press trade pbk. ed.
        p. cm.
    1. Disappeared persons' spouses—Fiction. 2. Loss (Psychology)—Fiction.
3. Rock music fans—Fiction. 4. Friendship—Fiction. 5. Psychological fiction.
6. Domestic fiction. I. Title.
PR6113.C585A79 2010
823'.92—dc22

2009039262

ISBN 978-1-4391-2333-1
ISBN 978-1-4391-6920-9 (ebook)

For Donal, and for all the fans of Jack

Note on the Author

Anna McPartlin's first book, *Pack Up the Moon,* was published by Poolbeg in January 2006. Since then Anna has written two more novels, *Apart from the Crowd* and *As Sure as the Sun,* also published by Poolbeg. Her books have been published in Ireland, Germany, America, the United Kingdom, and Australia. She has also written a drama for TV3 and is currently working on a film script. Anna lives in Dublin with her husband, Donal; their cat, Maggie; and their dogs, Harriet and Trudy.

Acknowledgments

The first time I heard Jack Lukeman sing, we were both teen-agers. His voice was as big then as it is now, and it's something I'll never forget. He was a kid and he could silence a room full of adults with just one bar of "Summertime." I've witnessed his talent and career unfold over the past twenty years, and some of my best times have been hanging out with one or all of the Jack camp. I was there in the beginning, when Jack led the Black Romantics and they played night after night in the Da Club. I took my turn selling the first album, *Wax*, during the intermis-sion. Once or twice I was roped into carrying gear through the streets of Dublin heading for 38 South Circular Road, which was the Jack base camp for all of the nineties. So many demos were recorded there; so many people lived there on and off: Jack in the back flat, David in the front, Martin upstairs. There was always something going on. Football, EU canned meats, comedy gigs, phone calls to and from America in the middle of the night, drums, bass, vocals, drinking, smoking, laughing. When I think about the nineties I think about 38 SCR, and it always makes me smile. The first time I conceived the smallest kernel of the idea for *Alexandra, Gone* was while standing on a balcony with Martin, looking down at the crowd at a sellout show. Onstage Jack was singing and doing his thing, but it was the crowd that captured my imagination. They were in awe, transfixed and completely silent. I made a joke to Martin that we should set up a church, the Church of Jack, and make some real money. The image stayed with me, and over the years, seeing a lot of the same faces come to show after show, the idea of fans becoming friends wouldn't let go. I spoke to Jack, Martin, and David about the idea for this book as early as two years ago, and not only were they really supportive but they gave me carte blanche to incorporate all of Jack's material. I'm so grateful to them for trusting me not to f##k up. If you read this book and your interest in Jack Lukeman is piqued, his website is www.jacklukeman.com. I hope you enjoy his music as much as I do.

So to all in the Jack camp, beginning of course with Jack Lukeman, thank you for the songs and the laughter over the past twentysomething years. Martin Clancy, you are and always will be one of my best friends and I'll be forever grateful for the day you walked into my world. David Constantine, that night in Northumberland Road, me on crutches, the meter out of coins, and a lunatic screaming the words "I've gone blind"—that was our Vietnam. I love you, man! Myra Clancy, you rock, and Patricia Clancy, I can honestly say there isn't one of us you haven't mothered at some point. Thank you.

I also thank Ken Browne. When my husband introduced us fifteen years ago, Ken was a guitar player in a rock band. We lost contact and didn't see him for years, and when we reconnected we discovered that he had transformed into an incredible artist. He, like me, is inspired by music and uses it in his work. He's energetic, with the ability to say more in a minute then some say in a lifetime. He's deeply passionate about his work, and when I'm around him he reminds me how lucky we are to be in a position to be creative and to do the things we love doing. (When my pal Enda reads this he will yawn and make an unseemly gesture with his right hand. Apologies, Enda, I'm finished; the luvvy has left the room.) I asked Ken if I could pick his brain for this book and also asked if I could include him. He was kind enough not only to grant me my wish but also to act excited about it. So thanks again for your enthusiasm, exuberance, and the beautiful painting that rests on my sitting-room wall. For anyone who wishes to view the works I mention in the book, his website is www.kenbrowneart.com.

I thank all my other pals whom I've mentioned in the three other books, my family, and everyone at Poolbeg, especially Paula Campbell and Gaye Shortland, Valerie Kerins for being as good a PR agent as she is a friend, and Faith O'Grady, my ever-patient agent. I thank Rowohlt Germany, Pocket Books USA, and Penguin UK for all their support and hard work on my behalf. I thank my husband for his love, support, and kindness, and finally, I thank anyone who has taken the time to read these acknowledgments!

1

"Universe"

Oh nothing lasts forever,
you can cry a million rivers,
you can rage it ain't no sin
but it won't change a thing,
'cos nothing lasts forever.

Jack L, *Universe*

Alexandra

June 21, 2007

Tom,
When you are shopping can you pick up the following:
Bread
Milk x 2
Water x 4
Spaghetti

Mince (Lean! Make sure it's lean and not the stuff they call lean and charge half price, because it's not lean. I want lean cut right in front of you and I don't care how much it costs.)

Tin of tomatoes
Basil
Garlic
Wine, if you don't still have a case or two in the office, and make sure it's not Shiraz. I'm really sick of Shiraz.

If you want dessert pick something up.
I'm meeting Sherri in Dalkey for a quick drink at 5. She has the Jack Lukeman tickets so I took money from the kitty to pay for them. I'm taking a ticket for you so if you don't want to go, text me. I'll be home around 7:30. Your aunt called. She's thinking about coming to Dublin next weekend. Try and talk her out of it. I'm exhausted and can't handle running around after her for 48 hours straight. Your aunt is on cocaine. I'm not messing. An intervention is needed.
Oh, and dishwashing liquid. And will you please call someone to get the dishwasher fixed?
OK see you later.
Love you,
Alexandra

P.S. When somebody close to you dies, move seats.
God, I love Jimmy Carr.

Alexandra laughed and put her note up on the fridge and held it in position with her favorite magnet, a fat, grinning pig rubbing his tummy. She was damp and sweaty, having run five miles, which was a record, and she was extremely pleased. She unclipped her iPod from her tracksuit, placed it on the counter, and headed upstairs to the shower. There she sang Rihanna's "Umbrella" and did a little dance move before rinsing shampoo out of her hair. Forty-five minutes later she walked down the stairs with her shoulder-length glossy chestnut hair perfectly coiffed. She was wearing her favorite black trousers and a black fitted blouse complete with a large bow. She stopped at the hall mirror and applied lipstick and then rooted some lip gloss out of her handbag and applied that too. She stared at herself in the mirror for a moment or two, sighed, and mumbled something about Angelina Jolie crapping her pants. She smiled at her own joke while putting on her jacket. She picked up her handbag and walked out the door.

Alexandra walked along her own street and waved at Mrs. Murphy from No. 14. Mrs. Murphy was busy sweeping her step, but she waved and called out that it was a lovely day. Alexandra smiled and told her it was perfect. She waited for the DART and listened to a man talk about cruelty to animals to Joe Duffy on Joe's radio show *Liveline*. It was too sad, so she switched from her radio to her music collection and stopped humming along to James Morrison's "Last Goodbye" only when she realized that three pimpled teenagers were laughing and pointing at her. She stuck out her tongue and grinned at them, and they laughed again. She sat on the train next to a man in his fifties. He asked her to wake him at Tara Street Station if he fell asleep, explaining that there was something about moving trains that always made him sleep. She assured him she would wake him, and true to his word he was snoring less than five minutes later. Coming up to Tara Street, she tapped his arm gently; nevertheless, he woke with a start. He thanked her once he regained his senses and made his way off the train. He forgot his bag and so she ran after him and handed it to him, and he was grateful, but she was in a hurry to get back on the train, so she just waved and ran.

The woman sitting opposite her grinned and nodded. "My own dad would forget his head," she said.

Alexandra smiled at her. "He was sweet."

The woman nodded again. Alexandra got off the train in Dalkey. The woman got off at the same station, but neither made eye contact.

Alexandra made her way through the station and out into the sunshine. She continued straight onto the main street and took the left at the end of the street, after that she took a right and then another left, and after that Alexandra was gone.

Elle

Sunday, December 31, 1989

Dear Universe,

Please don't send a fiery ball of hellfire comet thing to kill us all. I'm only eight so if I die now I won't get to do anything that I really want to. Miss Sullivan thinks that I could be an artist. If I'm dead I can't paint and I love painting and living. Margaret Nolan says that everyone thinks that we're going to be nuked in 1999 but the real truth is that a flaming ball of death is going to crash into earth at the stroke of midnight tonight. She sits next to me in class and sometimes smells like a hospital. Her dad's a scientist and he told her so she has a good chance of being right. She's already given her pocket money to the poor and says I should do the same so that when our time comes God will think we're decent enough sorts and let us into heaven. I forgot to go to the church to put money in the poor box because I got carried away working on a painting of my family dying in dancing fire. Jane says I'm a depressing little cow. She's always in a bad mood lately. Mum says it's because she's a teenager, she's fighting with her boyfriend, and she's got fat. She thinks being eight is the same as being slow but I know Jane is pregnant because they shout about it all the time. I'm not slow and I'm not deaf either. I feel sorry for the baby because if we all die tonight it will never have known life but then again maybe that's for the best.

OK, here are my promises to you if we make it past midnight.

1. *I'll be good.*
2. *I'll do what my mum tells me to.*
3. *I won't swear.*
4. *I won't tell any lies unless my mum asks me to (see promise 2).*
5. *I'll be nicer to Jane.*
6. *I'll paint every day.*
7. *I'll help Jane take care of Mum a bit more. (I can't help all the time—see promise 6.)*
8. *I'll give my pocket money to the poor tomorrow morning.*
9. *I'll be nice to Jane's baby because I've a feeling I might be the only one.*
10. *I won't listen to anything Margaret Nolan has to say again.*

And, Universe, if we do all die in fire tonight, thanks for nothing.

Yours,

Elle Moore

XXX

That was the first letter Elle Moore wrote to the Universe, and once it was written she folded it and put it into an old shortbread tin. After her supper, she tied her long brown hair in a knot and dressed in her brand-new Christmas coat, hat, and gloves, and her sister Jane's favorite tie-dye fringed scarf. She made her way down toward the right-hand side of the long garden, where she dug a hole between her mother's roses and the graves of four dead gerbils—Jimmy, Jessica, Judy, and Jeffrey. Once the tin was placed in the hole and its earth returned, she made a promise to herself that if she did live past midnight on that thirty-first of December in 1989, the following year she'd retrieve her letter and replace it with another. Little did she know back then that Elle Moore would continue to write letters to the Universe every New Year's Eve for the next eighteen years.

Jane

"May 5, 1990

"Dear Mrs. Moore,

"I am writing to you today about my concerns regarding your daughter Jane. I have attempted to reach out to Jane on a number of occasions in recent times but to no avail. As you are well aware, I have also attempted to communicate with your good self, but that too has proved difficult/nigh on impossible. Therefore, I am now left with no choice but to write this letter.

"It is clear to the teaching staff and to the student body that Jane is in the latter stages of pregnancy and so it is now urgent that we speak. Jane's schoolwork and attendance suffered immeasurably last term, and as a Leaving Cert student she now faces her mock examinations unprepared and with motherhood imminent. Jane seems to be incapable of coming to terms with her condition, as it would appear are you, but we in St. Peter's cannot simply stand by and act like nothing is happening to this seventeen-year-old girl.

"I urge you, Mrs. Moore, to phone me or to come in to the school and meet with me at any time convenient for you. I cannot allow this silence to continue any longer, and so if we do not hear from you within the next week we will be forced to ask your daughter not to return to school until such time as communication has been reestablished.

"Over the years, Jane and I have had our disagreements. Her flagrant disregard for our rules regarding smoking on school premises and the Irish stew incident that led to a fire in the home economics room are only two of the episodes I could mention. As you are aware, we've butted heads on many more occasions, especially when she came to school with purple hair or indeed during her thankfully short-lived Cure-inspired Gothic phase. This school has a zero-tolerance policy when it comes to the presentation of its students, but I must admit, though exasperated by her opposition and having to endure debate on many occasions, she conveyed her points ably and with admirable passion. The reason I mention this is that although our relationship as principal and student is checkered, I feel it necessary to make it clear that Jane is a very clever girl, bright and articulate, and I have often thought that this girl could do anything she set her mind to, and in twenty years I have thought that only a handful of times. I am worried for her, Mrs. Moore. She has lost her sparkle and her fight. The girl I knew and, despite our differences, have a great fondness for has all but disappeared.

"Teenage pregnancy is terrible and absolutely not to be encouraged, but support is not the same as encouragement, and with support Jane could continue her studies and fulfill her ambitions. Surely it is not the end for a girl such as Jane?

"Please come and speak to me for Jane's sake. Don't leave me with no option but to expel such a talented young girl from our school.

"Kindest regards,
"Amanda Reynolds
"Principal Amanda Reynolds"

Jane finished reading the letter aloud and blew her blond fringe out of her eyes while waiting for her best friend's response. Alexandra twirled her chestnut hair around her finger and stared at it in silence.

After a few seconds she shrugged. "Jesus, who knew Reynolds had a heart?"

Jane felt like crying because her principal had responded to her crisis pregnancy with far more kindness and understanding than her own mother, who had one tantrum after another since Jane's condition was revealed months previously. During her latest tantrum she took the time to mention how much money she had pissed into the wind by sending Jane to private school and told Jane in no uncertain terms that her education was over because only a bloody childless spinster like Amanda Reynolds could possibly think that having a baby at seventeen didn't mean an end to an academic career. She slammed the door on exiting the room, not once but twice for effect.

On that afternoon and for the first time Jane truly acknowledged the predicament she was in and how badly wrong her life had gone. She realized that she would miss her principal and she would miss school and the opportunity to go to college. She'd miss her friends, who except for Alexandra had drifted away during her pregnancy, and she'd miss Dominic even though he was avoiding her and was completely ignoring the fact that she was carrying his child. She could see through his schoolyard bravado and recognized his pained expression and haunted look, and she loved him.

Following an argument with Dominic's parents, who had dared to imply that Jane was a little whore, her mother had made it clear that if she saw him anywhere near their property she'd attack him with a shovel, and Jane's mother did not make threats of violence lightly. Once when Jane was seven a man had come to their door. He was buying and selling antiques. Her mother said she wasn't interested but he spied an antique table in the hall. He put his foot in the door and attempted to change her mind about doing business. She reiterated that she had no interest and told him if he didn't remove his foot from her door she would hurt him. He laughed at her. "No can do," he said, and his foot remained in the door. She counted down aloud from five to zero. He continued to push his foot farther into her hallway, all the while grinning stupidly at her. It was clear to Jane's mother that this man believed her to be a stupid, incapable woman and that she would not or could not keep her promise. When she got to zero, she calmly reached for an umbrella that she kept by the door and, releasing the door, shoved the umbrella with full force into his stomach. Startled, he bent forward, clutching his midriff. She then bopped him on the head, not once or twice but three times. He fell backward; she smiled politely, said good day to him, and left him winded and slightly dazed on her doorstep. Jane remembered the incident well because she had stood at the window watching the man sit on the step for what seemed like a long time before he was capable of getting up. Her mother had joined her just as he was leaving. "Good riddance," she'd said with a genuine smile. "You know, Janey, there is nothing quite like giving a smug arrogant cock like him a good dig to cheer up an otherwise gray day." Jane knew that if her mother had enjoyed giving that cock a dig because he put his foot in her doorway, she would definitely enjoy slapping Dominic in the face with a shovel for putting his cock in her daughter.

After Alexandra had read the letter a few more times and lamented with Jane over her mother being a bigger bitch than Alexis on *Dynasty*, she opened the first of six cans of Ritz. Later, when Jane was drunk on one can and Alexandra was on her third, Jane compared her and Dominic's plight to that of Romeo and Juliet. Alexandra expunged Jane's fanciful theory in an instant.

"It's like this, Janey," she said. "Romeo didn't get Juliet up the pole and then dump her at a disco."

"I know, but his parents made him give me up and—"

"And anyway," Alexandra said with drunken authority, "as bad as your situation is with Dominic, you don't want to be anything like Romeo and Juliet because Romeo and Juliet is a shit love story. Romeo was a shallow slut, Juliet was pathetic and needy, their families were killing each other, and they were in love one stupid day before they were married and then dead. Romeo and Juliet weren't star-crossed lovers, they were white trash."

"When you put it that way," Jane said sadly.

"Can you believe Miss Hobbs only gave me a C in English? I may not be able to spell 'apothecary,' but I have insight. That woman doesn't know her ass from her elbow."

Then Alexandra threw up in Jane's wastebasket.

After that they talked about how Jane could win Dominic back, but neither came up with a workable solution, and so they agreed that Jane should just wait it out.

"As far as I'm concerned he's just a cock artist, but I know you love him, so it will work out," Alexandra said.

"He's more than a cock artist," Jane said.

"I disagree," Alexandra said, burping Ritz.

"He's the one," Jane said.

Alexandra sighed and tapped her can. "He'll come back,

Janey. He'll see you in school every day and he'll miss you. Just give it some time." She stopped in time to throw up again, wiped her mouth, and sighed. "That's better. What I was I saying?"

" 'Just give it some time,' " Jane said.

"Exactly. And anyway you still have me."

"I know."

"You will always have me."

"I know."

"Even if I get Science in Cork because, let's face it, I'm not going to get into UCD, you still have me."

"I'll miss you," Jane said.

"You won't have to," Alexandra promised. "I'll be home every other weekend, and you can come and stay with me."

"I'll have a baby."

"Leave it with your mum."

"She's made it clear she's not a babysitter."

"She's such a cow."

"Yeah, she is."

"I love you, Jane."

"I love you too, Alex."

They were interrupted by Jane's mother, who was even drunker than Alexandra and determined to fight.

"Go home, Alexandra."

"I'm going home."

"So go!"

"I'm going."

"So get out!"

"Jesus, what's wrong with you, woman? Can't you see I'm trying to get up?"

Jane helped her friend into a standing position.

"See," Alexandra said with arms outstretched, "I'm off!" She weaved through the corridor and walked out the front door. She turned to say good-bye, but Jane's mother slammed the door in her face.

Jane's mother turned to her. "She's not welcome here anymore."

"She's my best friend."

"Yeah, well, kiss your best friend good-bye."

That was the last time Alexandra was in Jane's house. Jane gave birth to a son two weeks later and, although they maintained a friendship for four months after that, when Jane became a mother and Alexandra went to college in Cork, they lost contact. Over the next seventeen years Jane often thought of her friend, and she missed her.

Leslie

June 5, 1996

Dear Jim,

It's time to talk about Leslie. We both know she's stubborn and cut off, and we both know why. When I'm gone you'll be all she has left in this world and I know it's a big ask, but please look out for her.

We've talked about you remarrying, and you know I want you to find someone to love and to love you. I want you to have a great new life that doesn't include overcrowded hospitals, dismissive doctors, overworked nurses, and cancer. I want you to find someone strong and healthy, someone you can go on an adventure with, someone you can make love to, someone who doesn't cause you anguish and pain. Every time I see your face it hurts because for the first time I see that in loving you I've been selfish and I understand why Leslie is the way she is.

Leslie is a better person than me. I know you're probably guffawing at that as you read, but it's true. She's watched her entire family die of cancer, and when we were both diagnosed with the dodgy gene after Nora's death she made the decision not to cause pain to others the way Nora caused pain to John and Sarah and I'm causing pain to you. Before cancer she was smart and funny, kind and caring, and she still is to me. Without her care I wouldn't have coped. I know sometimes she calls you names, but trust me, she knows you're not a monkey so when she calls you an ass picker, ignore it and be kind.

I thought she was being defeatist. I thought that we'd suffered enough as a family and that we'd both survive. So I made plans and fell in love and for a while we had a great life but then that dodgy gene kicked in. Now I see you look almost as ill as I feel, and I realize that my sister Leslie knew exactly what she was doing when she broke up with Simon and all but closed off. I watched her disappear from her own life. I thought she was insane back then, but it makes sense now. She put the pain of others before her own. She watched John and Sarah suffer after Nora, and she'll watch you suffering after me, and although she pretends not to like you, she does, and it will hurt her and it will also confirm for her that she is right to remain alone waiting for a diagnosis that may never come.

I'm her last family and friend. She hasn't even let herself get to know her niece, and so when I'm gone she'll have no one and that haunts me. Please go and live your life but all that I ask is that every now and again, no matter how rude or uninviting she may seem, call her, talk to her, be her friend even if she fails to be yours, because she has been there for me, for Mum, for Dad and Nora, and I can't stand the idea that after everything she's been through she should live or die alone.

I know I say it all the time and in all my little notes and letters about this and that, but time is running out and I need you to know that it's been a privilege to be your wife. And although I feel selfish for all the pain I've caused you, I know I've brought happiness too, so hang on to that and forgive me because even knowing what I know now I'd love and marry you again. I suppose Leslie would say I was a selfish pig, but I can die with that.

Yours,

Imelda

Imelda Sheehan died at eight o'clock on the morning of July 12, 1996. She was twenty-five years old. Her husband, Jim, was by her side and holding her right hand, and sitting on the opposite side of the bed and holding her left hand was her sister Leslie. They both felt her slip away at exactly the same time. For Leslie it was familiar: the ocean of grief inside her swelled and rose, but she knew what to do, and so she remained still and allowed the pain to wash over her. For Jim it was so shocking: one second his wife was alive and battling to breathe, the next she was dead and silent. He let Imelda's hand go and stood up quickly, so quickly that he nearly fell. He steadied and hugged himself. He stood in the corner of the room as the doctor and nurses approached to confirm time of death. Leslie sat with her dead sister Imelda, holding her hand for as long as they would allow her. Jim cried, and his parents, brothers, and friends made a fuss over him. Leslie sat alone and frozen. She knew the physical pain that made her heart feel like it was about to explode and her ears ring until she feared they'd bleed would dissipate in time, just as the tide would turn and with it Imelda would drift farther and farther away until she was a distant memory and it only served to make her loss greater. Leslie had just turned twenty-seven.

Jim asked Leslie to read at the funeral, but she refused. He asked her to sit beside him in the first pew when she'd attempted to sit at the back of the church. She told him she didn't want to shake hands with the people whose hands she had shaken so many times before, but Jim was not taking no for an answer, and so she found herself sitting beside her brother-in-law with a heavy heart and an all-too-familiar swollen hand from those whose earnest sympathy ensured they squeezed too tight.

When the priest asked if anyone would like to speak, Leslie stood up. This surprised her and those around her, especially Jim, who couldn't even get her to agree to a reading. She found herself standing without reason. The priest asked her to come forward, but her legs refused to comply with his request, and so he waited and the congregation waited, and Jim nudged her and asked if she was all right. *What the hell am I doing?* she asked herself as she started to move toward the altar, but once she was at the altar and standing in front of a microphone the words came easily.

"I am the last of the five Sheehans," she said. "Four days ago there were two of us—me, the middle child; and Imelda, the baby of the family. I should have been next, and not just because I was older but because Imelda was the strong one, the one who embraced life regardless and without fear. Over the years she's run five marathons in aid of cancer. I didn't even walk for cancer, not even once—mostly I'll avoid even standing if I can." She stopped to take a breath. There was a hint of a titter from the crowd. "She fell in love and married Jim, and she always planned to have kids. Imelda always made plans, and that's what I admired about her most, because even when she was diagnosed with the same cancer that had killed our grandmother, our mother, father, and sister, she still made plans. She froze her eggs and they bought a house, and when she wasn't in chemo she traveled. Even when she knew her life was coming to the end, she still made plans. Little plans that don't mean much to most, like 'Tonight we'll reminisce about the summer we spent in Kerry' or 'Tomorrow when the sun comes out we'll sit in the hospital grounds and watch the people come and go and make up stories about who and what they are.' She even planned her own funeral. She knew exactly what she wanted—the kind of casket, the flowers, the priest, the prayers, the attendees. She asked me once if I would speak at her funeral and I said no. I'm sorry, Imelda, of course I'll speak for you. I just was scared that I wouldn't know what to say and I didn't want to let you down. So I'll just end by saying this: I miss my dad, my mum, my sister Nora, and now I miss my sister Imelda, and I'm so sorry because it should have been me, but I will see you all again and soon."

Leslie's voice was cracking, her eyes were streaming, and her nose was running. She walked toward her seat, and once she'd accepted a tissue from Jim she sat with her head in her hands, attempting to regain composure but finding it almost impossible to do so. Back then her hair was still jet-black, she was slim, and although she was not a natural beauty, she was striking. The people sitting in pews behind her felt nothing but pity for this young woman who was merely waiting for her turn to die. Later, by the side of the grave, she watched Jim grieve, and if there was something she could have said to make him feel better she would have said it, but there wasn't, so she stood in silence waiting for the day to end so that she could disappear behind her closed door and wait for the inevitable. It never occurred to her that she'd still be waiting for the inevitable twelve years later.

Tom

August 25, 2007

Transcript of *Liveline* radio show with Joe Duffy

"I have a Tom Kavanagh on the line. Tom, are you there?"

"I am, Joe."

"Tom, you are trying to find your lovely wife, Alexandra."

"Yes, Joe."

"She went missing on the twenty-first of June this year?"

"It was Thursday, the twenty-first of June."

"Tell us about it, Tom."

"I don't know where to start. She was last seen in Dalkey and now she's gone."

"Okay, okay, all right. How about you tell us a little about her?"

"She's funny, she's giddy, she's kind, she's friendly, she's fussy, she's lovely, Joe." *Caller becomes emotional.*

"The police have managed to retrace her steps as far as Dalkey. Can you tell us about that?"

"She left the house in Clontarf around two p.m. She said hello to a neighbor who verified the time. She walked to the train station, and three teenagers who were there came forward to say that they witnessed her getting on the train. She's also captured on CCTV footage on the platform at Tara Street at three thirty, but she got back on the train. After the train stations were canvassed, a woman came forward and identified her as getting off the train in Dalkey. She was captured on CCTV footage again there but after that . . ." *Caller becomes emotional.*

"And after that?"

"She was gone. She's just gone."

"Ah God, that's desperate. What time was that?"

"It was approximately four p.m."

"And where were you?"

"I was working. We were finishing a project in Blackrock."

"It says here you're a builder."

"I am."

"So when did you realize that she was missing?"

"I was supposed to be home by four. I had promised to make dinner because Alexandra was meeting her friend Sherri to collect tickets for a gig from her. She had left a note saying she'd be home by seven thirty. But I was delayed on site. I didn't get in until nine p.m."

"When did you raise the alarm, Tom?"

"The next morning, Joe." *Caller becomes emotional.* "I thought she'd stayed out with Sherri or maybe she was pissed off that I didn't get home in time to make the dinner so went out again. I was exhausted so I fell asleep."

"That's understandable. What age is Alexandra?"

"She's thirty-six. She has chestnut-brown hair, shoulder length. She was wearing black trousers and a black blouse with a bow on it. She had a black fitted jacket on. She's very attractive, the kind of person you'd remember if you'd seen her." *Caller becomes emotional.*

"And she went missing on ..."

"Thursday, the twenty-first of June this year."

"And did she have any mental issues, Tom?"

"No, Joe. She was a very happy, well-adjusted, normal woman. She was normal, Joe, ordinary."

"Okay, okay." *Joe sighs.* "I'm going to ask the obvious, Tom, so forgive me. Is there any chance she took herself into the water?"

"No. No. She wasn't suicidal, and the coast guard searched it and the police divers, and there were plenty of people on the beach that day and no one saw her."

"Okay, I had to ask. I'm sorry for your trouble, Tom. I hope that maybe someone listening remembers something."

"And, Joe?"

"Yes, Tom?"

"I'll be at Dalkey train station handing out flyers later this evening and I'll be doing the same at a Jack Lukeman gig on Dame Street next Friday."

"Why there, Tom?"

"She was a big fan, Joe. She never missed a show." *Caller becomes emotional.*

"And he's very popular; lots of people from all counties will be there."

"It's as good a place as any to get the word out, Joe."

"God love you, Tom. I sympathize. Good luck to you. We'll put Alexandra's details on the website, and if you could send in a photo we'll post it."

"I will, and thanks for taking the call."

"And if anyone has information on Alexandra Kavanagh, who went missing on the twenty-first of June 2007, would they contact Clontarf Garda Station, and the inspector in charge of the investigation is Des Martin. Right, we'll be back after these ads."

Tom put down the phone and turned to Breda, his mother-in-law. She was sitting at the kitchen table, looking frail and small. She smiled at him through tears.

"You did very well, love," she said.

"You should have left this phone number," Eamonn said while pacing. Eamonn was Alexandra's older brother, and he and Tom had never really been close. Alexandra's disappearance had served to widen the divide between them. "And you should have said that she was upset about not getting pregnant."

"Nothing to do with anything," Tom said. "She was fine, happy."

"You just didn't want to see it!" Eamonn shouted. "It was tearing her apart and you didn't see it!"

"Take that back, Eamonn," Tom said, walking toward Eamonn.

Eamonn in his mind was begging Tom to punch him. *Take a swing, I dare you!*

Breda called out to the two boys, "Stop it, both of you!"

Alexandra's father stood up from his chair outside on the patio. He put his cigarette out and came inside.

"Go home now," he said to Eamonn and Tom. "Go home before you both say and do things you'll regret."

Eamonn and Tom both nodded and apologized. Breda was crying again. She looked at Tom, who had aged ten years in ten weeks. His black hair was almost entirely gray; his once-sparkly blue eyes were tired and circled by shadowed skin. He had been so persnickety about the way he looked that Alexandra's family, especially Eamonn, had often joked about her marrying a metrosexual. His suits were always the best, dry-cleaned after one wearing and fitting precisely. His hair was professionally cut, and his face was perfectly clean. Off-site, Tom didn't look like a builder; he looked like a banker. He was wealthy, and although he wasn't extravagant, he left those around him in no doubt about his standing. Breda noticed his suit was now too big, his hair was a mess, and he hadn't shaved in weeks. He was a shadow of the man he used to be, as she was a shadow of the woman and mother she once was. She recognized his suffering, as it mirrored her own, and she wanted her son, whose anger was more intense than his pain, to stop hurting her already mortally wounded son-in-law. She promised herself she would talk to Eamonn when she found the strength to deal with his quarrelsome nature.

When Tom was leaving, she hugged him, and he could feel every bone in her back. She whispered into his ear, "She's still with us, I can feel it. God will take care of her—she's not alone because God is there beside her."

Tom nodded. "Try and eat, Breda."

Tom sat in his car for a minute or two and was still there when Eamonn came out of the house. Eamonn walked over to the car window and knocked on it. Tom rolled it down.

"I don't care what the police say," Eamonn said. "I don't care what my mother says. It's your fault. I blame you." He turned and walked to his own car and drove away, leaving Tom sitting in Alexandra's parents' driveway crying like a baby.

Oh God, please, please, where is she? Bring her home to me, please, please, bring her home! I'm so sorry for everything I've done. Forgive me and bring her home.

Alexandra had then been missing nine weeks and two days.

2

All the shapes in the dark are playing with your heart,
fear is always near.
It'll never set you free, it'll never let you be,
once you let it in all the fun begins,
'cos fear is all you'll breathe.

Jack L & the Black Romantics, *Wax*

October 2007

The night was damp and overcast. Jane had thought twice about whether she actually wanted to go out. It had been a long and tiring day, but she had promised her younger sister, Elle, and Elle did not handle disappointment well. The gig had been due to start at nine. It was just after ten. They had missed the supporting act, and Jack Lukeman would already be onstage. The venue didn't have a car park, and because of a lack of inner-city knowledge and a pathological fear of driving the wrong way up one-way streets, Jane had parked the car miles away. They were already late and so were forced to run from the car park to the venue, and just as they turned the first corner the rain came tumbling down. Neither sister had an umbrella. Elle had a hood, but as she ran it insisted on falling back off her head. She held it tight around her face and continued to run, with Jane doing her best to keep up in heels and praying she wouldn't break an ankle.

At the door they fumbled for their tickets and, once they had presented them to the bouncer with the build of a silverback gorilla and the manner of a brick, he waved them through.

"Move," he said.

"Charming," Elle said, and Jane widened her eyes and tightened her mouth, which signaled to Elle to shut up.

They passed a disheveled man who was considerably drier than they were. He was standing behind the box office and between the lifts and the stairs. He handed them each a flyer with a picture of a woman on it.

"If you see her, there's a number you can contact me at," he said.

Neither of them looked at the flyer because they could hear Jack singing "Don't Fall in Love." Elle spotted the lift. "We're in the gods, let's get the lift."

"I hate the lift."

"We're missing the show." Elle pouted.

Jane sighed, and Elle knew that she had gotten her way. She pressed the button for the lift just as the silverback charmer looked at his watch and started to close the main doors. A woman in a full-length plastic see-through raincoat that was pulled tight around her face and knotted with a toggle under her chin pushed her ticket against the window and her foot in the doorway. The bouncer considered whether to let her in or to attempt to amputate her foot for a second or two before he opened it, took her ticket, and allowed her to enter.

Elle smiled as the walking condom approached her. *Well, that's one way of keeping dry.* The human condom ignored the leaflet man's attempt to hand her a flyer and stood behind Jane, who was busy mentally preparing to encase herself in a small space. *Don't freak out. It will all be over in seconds.* The silverback charmer bolted the front door. The leaflet man packed away his remaining leaflets into a briefcase and stood behind Elle, waiting for the lift. The red light appeared over the doors and they heard a *ding*. Elle was first in, followed by the human condom and the leaflet man. Jane was frozen, but only for a second. When she realized that her sister and the two strange strangers were staring at her, she made her legs move toward them to avoid embarrassment. The doors closed, and Jane breathed in and out slowly and surely. *Ten seconds and it will be over. Count back to one. Ten . . . nine . . .*

Elle could hear Jack singing clearly: *"Don't fall in love with the girls around here, you give them your heart they soon disappear."* She sang along quietly: *"They come from country towns and live on Crescent Street and all that they share are the secrets they keep."*

Jane counted in her head: *. . . five . . . four . . .*

Elle became slightly louder as the song was reaching its conclusion, *"La, la, la, la, la, la, la!"*

The human condom and the leaflet man stared forward, ignoring the tone-deaf girl who was compromising their enjoyment of the song by obscuring Jack L with her off-key wailing. Jane continued to breathe and count: *. . . three . . . two . . .*

The lights went off. The lift ground to a stop with such a jolt that all four passengers automatically braced themselves. Jane stopped counting, Elle stopped wailing, and outside the music stopped playing. Only Jack L continued to sing. He finished the last line of the song without mike or music. The crowd cheered and roared, and Elle found herself staring from her sister, whose legs had gone from under her and who was suddenly sitting on the floor, to the human condom hanging on to the rail, to the leaflet man who seemed to be holding on to his briefcase for dear life. Outside the crowd was still roaring, and it was all so strange, and she liked it.

"What's going on?" she asked with a grin spreading across her face. "Do you think it's a fire?"

Jane's breathing was becoming shallower and faster, and so she was in no position to respond. The leaflet man shook his head before telling her that if there was a fire, the alarm would ring. The human condom undid her toggle and pulled her see-through raincoat from her head to reveal short black hair streaked with gray and sprinkled with white.

"It's a power cut," she said, "probably the damn weather. I knew I shouldn't come out tonight, but I just wouldn't listen to myself." She took off her coat and rolled it up and put it into her oversized bag and sat on the floor next to Jane, who was trying her best not to hyperventilate. "Is she okay?" the leaflet man asked Elle, referring to Jane.

"She's got a thing about lifts," Elle said. "Hang in there, Janey." She squatted and brushed her sister's wet blond hair from her face. "It won't be long now."

For some reason the human condom found it necessary to correct her. "Actually, it could be hours."

Jane grabbed Elle's hand and squeezed it hard.

Elle looked at the human condom and shook her head. "Not cool, Condom. Not cool at all."

The human condom and the leaflet man stared at her quizzically, and both wondered if they had heard her correctly, but their musings were interrupted by a man using a loudspeaker to address the audience.

Jane looked around the lift, wide-eyed. "What's happening out there?" she asked breathlessly.

"Shush," the condom said, placing her finger to her lips.

Onstage, Jack L and his band stood back, allowing the manager of the venue to fix his handheld microphone before making a second attempt to speak to the crowd without the loud screeching he'd nearly deafened himself with on his first attempt. The crowd was mumbling and shuffling and waiting for him to get off stage. Jack began to bounce behind him, and the audience laughed. The manager was taking too long to get the mike working, and Jack was in performance mode. He bounded across the stage like a puppy and threw his arm around the manager, who was now red-faced and fumbling. The man was scared. He was scared because Jack was well known for being as unpredictable as he was energetic and as mischievous as he was hypnotic. He prayed he wouldn't be the butt of one of the singer's jokes and sighed with relief when he got the mike working well enough so that it screeched only intermittently.

He explained that the entire street was experiencing a blackout. He wasn't aware how long the problem would last, and he apologized because for some reason the backup generator wasn't working as it should.

Back in the lift, the human condom's ear was to the door.

"What?" Elle said.

"As I said, it's a blackout."

"So what now?" Elle asked.

"Shush," she said, "and I'll tell you."

Onstage, the manager assured the audience he had someone working on it and that if the generator didn't kick in within the next ten minutes they could have their money back, but they booed him and that was when Jack took the mike from him. Jack was fired up and ready to play, and electricity was not something he was short of. He paced the stage like a caged panther before placing the mike to his mouth.

"I'm not ready to leave," he said, and the crowd roared its approval.

Jack would often be described as anything from sexy to forbidding, one commentator even going so far as to describe him as the result of a struggle between a vampire and a wolfman. That night his mood and demeanor could only be described as a hybrid of Jack Nicholson's malevolent Joker and Johnny Depp's playful pirate.

Jack bounded toward the side of the stage. In the blink of an eye he had scaled the wall and was hanging out of the balcony.

"So are we going to do this?" he shouted. The audience screamed to signal it was. His dark arched eyebrows rose, his big wide grin appeared, and he jumped back onto the stage from the considerable height. "Let's do it, then!" he said, and the crowd roared. He handed the mike to the manager, who was still standing on the stage and staring at the wall the singer had seemingly walked up, his mouth slightly agape. Jack patted him on the back. The manager walked offstage, thinking that he was going to have to put a sign up in the dressing rooms asking artists not to walk on the walls, while ruminating as to how the man had managed it.

Jack pushed his hand through his shock of thick black hair, then turned to his guitar player and unplugged his guitar, and the crowd roared. The roadie handed the guitarist an acoustic guitar, and he fixed it around his neck. Jack looked toward the drummer, who took out his brushes and held them high.

The crowd roared again.

In the lift, the four captives wondered what was going on.

"He's not going to play, is he?" Jane said between deep breaths.

"I think he is," Elle said.

Onstage, Jack nodded and leaned into the guitar player and said something unheard. The guitar player picked out the familiar chords to "Move On," and Jack opened his mouth and his haunting, mythical voice emerged as clearly as though it was still amplified, and in that second he silenced the crowd.

And as soon as he began to sing, inside the lift his voice resonated as though he was in there with them.

"Ah Jesus, I love this song!" the condom said, punching the lift door. She slumped to the floor, leaving leaflet man as the only one still standing.

Makes no difference who you are, love will find you, yeah,
Opera or movie star, love will find your path.
All the money in the world won't save you from that.
All the beauty in the world you can't just cover your tracks . . .

The audience joined in for the chorus:

And if you move on it will keep up
And if you jump town you know you'll be found.

"Should we make some noise?" Elle asked after a minute or two of the group sitting in silence save for Jane's panting and Jack's singing.

"The bouncer will realize we're in the lift," the leaflet man said, hoping that the bouncer was slightly more conscientious than his earlier encounter with him had suggested.

"The silverback?" Elle snorted. "Fat chance."

"She's right," the condom said. "He was probably too busy picking fleas out of his ass to notice us getting in."

Elle laughed, clearly entertained by the condom's crudity and her ability to pick up on and run with the primate theme. Leaflet man looked at the doors and decided to try to force them apart. He couldn't get his fingers between them, though, and when he'd established that none of the women carried a crowbar or anything remotely like a crowbar in her handbag, he started to bang on the doors instead, which shook the lift, and that in turn made Jane pant harder, shake, and cry.

"Breathe, Janey," Elle said. "You're all right, everything is fine."

Jane wasn't fine. She was experiencing chest pain and fighting the urge to run through the wall.

"If you don't stop shaking the lift, that woman is going to have a full-on panic attack if she's not already having one," the condom said to the leaflet man.

He turned and looked at Jane's ghastly face. He stopped shaking the lift and sat down.

"I'm sorry," he said.

Jane tried to smile at him but she couldn't breathe, never mind smile.

"Does anyone have a paper bag?" Elle asked.

The condom said no immediately, but leaflet man checked his briefcase.

"No," he said, "but try this." He took out a large poster and fashioned it into a sort of paper bag. He handed it to Elle, who placed it around Jane's nose and mouth and once again instructed her to breathe. It didn't work. Jane pulled the poster away from her mouth and held it tightly against her chest, then lay down on the floor, cursing herself for wearing white linen, which was now rain-soaked and filthy.

Oh my God, I'm going to catch a flesh-eating disease from this floor. Oh sweet God, whatever happens, let my face be last to go. I don't want my child saying good-bye to an open wound. Good-bye, Kurt, Mum loves you. Good-bye, Dominic, you're a selfish bastard, a waster, and an ass. God, I love you. Why can't you love me? Good-bye, Mother, you are a bitch in your heart but I don't hate you so that's something. Good-bye, Elle, focus on your career and stop doing stupid things and you'll be fine without me.

Elle viewed her sister prostrate on the floor, rubbing her chest, sweating profusely, and breathing at a rate that couldn't be good for a person. Jane had often talked about the possibility of this happening when Elle had bullied her into getting into a lift, but she'd never actually experienced it before, and aside from the paper-bag idea, Elle had no clue what to do.

"What can I do?" she asked Jane, who was busy watching herself float up toward the ceiling. *At least I'm off the floor.*

The condom made a *hah* sound and stood up and then repositioned herself on the other side of Jane, making the leaflet man move over in the process. She took Jane's hand from Elle because Jane's other hand was holding the poster against her chest.

"You are having a panic attack. You are not dying. No one dies from panic attacks," the condom said.

Jane stopped floating and returned to her body and the floor.

"You can deal with this. Just let it happen and it will pass," the condom said, and Jane listened and believed her. "It's okay to feel anxious. You'll be okay."

Jane's breathing slowed, and for the next ten minutes the condom repeated the mantras and Jane began to feel normal again. By the time Elle and the leaflet man had all but lost the will to live, she was able to sit up, and once her breathing was controlled enough to allow for speech, she thanked the condom.

"I'm Jane."

"Leslie," the condom replied.

"Elle," Elle said. "That was extremely impressive. Are you a doctor?"

"No."

"Do you suffer from panic attacks?" Elle asked.

"No."

"So how did you know what to say?" Elle asked, refusing to be put off by Leslie's monosyllabic answers.

"My sister used to suffer from them."

"Used to?" Elle said. "She got over them?" She looked from Leslie to Jane and was about to put her thumbs up.

"She died," Leslie said, and Jane's cheeks once again lost color, "but not from a panic attack." She smiled at Jane, who nodded gratefully and sighed.

Elle focused on the leaflet man, who was sitting quietly in the corner. "So what's your name?"

"Tom." He turned to Jane. "Sorry about earlier. I shouldn't have rocked the boat, so to speak."

Jane smiled at him. "It's fine. I'm just being silly."

Onstage, Jack had been talking and the audience was laughing. He began to sing "Taste of Fall" a cappella.

Take me back to your old ma's place
where the bedspring squeaks and your body shakes
and I lose myself before the morning takes me home.
Love me in the doorway I'll love you on the stairs . . .

Elle started to snap her fingers. "I love this song."

Leslie also loved the song. *Please, please don't sing it and kill it.*

Jane straightened a little and decided to sit on her bag.

"It's a bit late to be thinking about ruining your suit, Jane," Elle said while still snapping.

"I know." Jane sighed, looking at the filthy floor. "I'm going to need a tetanus shot after this."

Elle noticed Leslie moving to the music, and Jack was heading for the chorus. "Sing it with me, Leslie!" she said.

"No," said Leslie.

"Is 'no' your very favorite word?" Elle asked.

"No."

Elle laughed. *I like you.* "Come on, I know you want to."

And Leslie did want to and if she didn't she'd have to listen to Elle murder it anyway. So when the chorus hit, she found herself in a lift singing with a total stranger. *This is not me, but I like it.*

> *Oh come on down while we're in full bloom*
> *It's a big bright night, let's howl at the moon.*

Tom laughed at the women, and even Jane forgot her anxiety for a moment or two to enjoy the sight of her sister and Leslie howling.

> *Whoa come on down we're in full bloom,*
> *Howl at the, howl at the, howl at the moon.*

They howled and howled, and by the end they weren't half bad.

"Hello? Is anyone there?"

Tom stood up and pressed his hand against the door. "Hello."

"How many are in there?" the voice asked.

"Four of us," Tom said.

"Okay, sir, we hope to have the generator up and running soon."

"Thanks," Tom said.

"Is everyone okay?" the voice asked.

"We're fine," Tom said, looking at Jane, who nodded to signal she was feeling better.

Before the man got a chance to ask another question, Jack began singing "Georgie Boy," and the whole audience was singing along, drowning out the lone voice.

Tom sat back down.

Jane finally loosened her grip on the poster that was crumpled against her chest. She opened it and saw a picture of a woman she recognized. She was older than Jane remembered her, but she was unmistakable. "Alex? Alexandra Walsh?"

Tom stared at Jane. "You know her?"

"I used to."

"They were best friends," Elle said, "but then my sister got pregnant at seventeen and Alexandra disappeared. So maybe not best friends after all."

"Elle," Jane said in a tone that meant *shut up*. "She's missing?" she asked Tom.

"Since June."

"My God, that's terrible!" Jane was genuinely upset. She raised her shaking hand to her mouth. "I'm so sorry."

Elle took the leaflet out of her pocket and looked at it. "I'm sorry. I shouldn't have said she disappeared. Sometimes I'm an ass. It's genetic—you'd have to meet my mother to understand."

Tom attempted to smile at her, to assure her that she was forgiven.

"What happened?" Jane asked.

"She went to Dalkey and vanished."

"As in gone?" Elle said.

"Gone."

"Is it possible she . . . hurt herself?" Leslie asked.

"No," Tom said firmly, "it's not."

"I know it's been a long time, but I agree with Tom. That just doesn't sound like the girl I knew." Jane sighed and shook her head. Her eyes filled, but she didn't cry.

"What do the police say?" Leslie asked.

"They say they're doing the best they can. They've been very good to us really."

"How's Breda?" Jane asked, referring to Alexandra's mother.

"Devastated, completely and utterly devastated."

"I'm so sorry," Jane said. "Breda was always so kind to me. When I had my son she knitted him a blue blanket. He didn't go anywhere without that blanket for years."

"I remember that. He called it 'manky,'" Elle said.

"We were trying for a baby for a long time," said Tom. "Alexandra gave up work after Christmas hoping it would help . . ." He trailed off as if he'd already said too much. Alexandra would kill him if she knew he was talking about their private life to strangers, even if she had been friends with one of them when she was young. And already so much of their private life had been laid bare.

"It's a nightmare," Leslie said. "An absolute nightmare."

"She was wearing black trousers, a black blouse with a bow, and black boots," Tom said, repeating the information he had repeated so many times before. "She took her handbag. She never really kept a lot of cash on her, but she hasn't used her cards since. She was fine that morning, in good humor—she had planned to meet her friend Sherri in Dalkey at five. She was fine."

Suddenly Elle felt the urge to cry, but she couldn't because it would have been deeply inappropriate, and yet it was becoming harder to fight the tears. She stayed silent and breathed in and out much like her sister had earlier. The full enormity of Alexandra's disappearance and Tom's desolation was causing her actual physical pain.

"I'd like to help you," Jane said to Tom. "I know we're strangers, but if there is something I can do?"

Tom shook his head. "That's kind of you, but I just don't know how you can help."

"We'll think of something," Elle said, and she looked at Leslie, who stared at her blankly.

"What?" Leslie said, after enduring Elle's stare for what seemed like an eternity.

"Aren't you going to help?" Elle said.

"I wish I could," Leslie said, "but if the police can't, I can't, and unfortunately neither can either of you."

"I disagree," Jane said. "I'd rather try than stand by and do nothing."

"Well, good luck," Leslie said, and she meant it.

"Leslie's right," Tom said, moved by the two women's kindness, "but thank you."

"We're going to help whether you like it or not," Elle said. "Besides, you look like you could do with some direction. Handing out leaflets at a gig? What's that all about?"

"If you can think of something better, I'd be happy to give it a go."

"I'll put my thinking cap on," Elle said. "I take it postings in Dalkey are taken care of?"

"Yes."

"Right. I had to ask."

After that Jane reminisced about Alexandra making others

laugh. She told them about the time Alexandra had insisted that they sneak out of her parents' house during a sleepover. They had to get out of a second-story window, jump down onto the extension, and shimmy down the pipe, and when they finally made it to the ground without killing themselves and were busy high-fiving, they failed to notice Alexandra's father standing on the porch having watched their every move. When he made himself known to them, Alexandra stuck out her arms in front of her and, zombielike, she walked toward her dad, pretending she was sleepwalking.

"And what did you do?" Tom asked.

"I wet myself," Jane admitted, "but Alexandra kept up the act until her dad laughed, and once he did we were off the hook. She could always get out of anything."

"What about the time she stayed with us, and Mum caught you both drinking her stash of wine?" Elle said.

"Rose threatened to call the police," Jane said.

"Rose is our mother," Elle clarified for the group.

"But Alexandra told her that she'd call the police because our sitting-room carpet was a crime against taste."

"Mum nearly lost it," Elle said. "I could hear her screaming from where I was in my bed, but Alexandra didn't care."

"Alexandra was too drunk to care," Jane said. "She called Rose an old lush and challenged her to a drinking competition." She started to laugh. "I've never seen Rose turn purple before or since." Jane laughed some more before falling silent. "Rose walked away. Of course I got it in the neck for the next couple of weeks, but it didn't matter because Alexandra had got the best of the old bat. That kept me going for years."

"Again, you'd have to know our mother," Elle said.

"She did talk about you," Tom said to Jane, having remembered some of Alexandra's stories involving the girl who dropped off the grid after having a baby. Alexandra had felt guilty about losing the friendship with Jane. She had talked about reconnecting with her but never found the will or the time.

Leslie was smiling. "She sounds interesting."

"She is," Tom said. "She's amazing." He fell silent, and his mind traveled to the dark place, and the weight of his worry permeated the small space.

His sadness was overwhelming, and Elle became desperate to change the vibe. "What about you, Leslie, do you have a story to tell?"

"No," Leslie said, and she smiled because during their short acquaintance she had come to realize that Elle was not the kind of person to take no for an answer.

"Liar," Elle said. "Everyone has a story."

They fell into silence again, lost in their own thoughts. Tom was still lost in the hell he'd created in his head. Jane's mind took her into the past before Kurt, when she and Alexandra were making plans to travel the world. Elle was busy working out what she could do to make everything better.

"I could set up a website," Leslie said. "We could go viral."

"Now you're talking!" Elle said, and she clapped.

"I've no idea what 'going viral' means," Jane said, "but I like the sound of it."

"Jane?" Elle said. "When is my next exhibition?"

"First week in February."

"How soon could we do another one?"

"What have you got in mind?" Jane asked.

"Faces." Elle grinned. "How about I paint the faces of missing people, a collection of twelve to include Alexandra. I could start as soon as I've finished this last painting for February."

"I could definitely get media attention," said Jane.

"Good," Elle said. "Let's do it."

After seventeen weeks and two days of hopelessness, recrimination, confusion, frustration, fear, and suffering, three strangers opened their hearts to Tom, and they were kind enough to pretend they didn't notice when he cried.

3

"Can't Get Bitter"

It's so easy to be cynical, you just turn on your TV screen
and everyone tells you who you should be.
When I feel stupid, disenchanted,
those pretty flowers that he planted,
the pollen comes floating down the breeze.

Jack L, *Broken Songs*

December 2007

It was just after eleven on the morning of New Year's Eve and Elle was standing at the back of her garden, knotting her long brown hair before picking up the shovel from the ground. Her ritual had changed from late evening to late morning many years previously on account of it getting in the way of her social life.

Jane emerged from the big house and made her way down the patio steps and toward her sister, who was unaware of her and busy staring into the middle distance. Jane often noticed Elle staring at something unseen by anyone else, but she was sure that whatever it was her sister was looking at, it was real and interesting to her. *Weirdo.*

"Morning, soldier," she said affectionately while patting her sister's back before crossing her arms, hugging herself tightly, and waiting for the ceremony to commence.

Elle saluted Jane while holding the shovel in one hand and a cigarette between her lips. Jane waited for Elle to begin shoveling dirt, but Elle was slow to start.

"What are you waiting for?"

Elle dropped the shovel and walked backward toward their mother's rosebushes. "I'm just double-checking. I know the spot should be five feet from Mum's rosebushes and eight feet from Jeffrey's grave, but five feet from Mum's rosebushes appears to be only six feet from the bloody grave."

She began walking forward toe to heel and counting.

"But those aren't proper feet," Jane said. "As in twelve inches, one foot."

"I'm not taking about 'proper' feet—I'm talking about *my* feet," Elle said.

The recount was the same. Elle was displeased.

"Well, does it make a difference? Just dig a bigger hole," Jane said.

"Can't," Elle said, circling the point where she believed her box to be buried. "Last year I nearly lopped off Jeffrey's head."

Jane laughed. "Jeffrey died when you were six."

"So?"

"So that was twenty years ago."

Elle pretended to be confused. "What's your point?"

Jane spelled it out. "Jeffrey's head is long gone."

"I'm telling you it was Jeffrey."

"Not Jessica, Judy, or Jimmy?" Jane asked, laughing.

"Definitely Jeffrey," Elle said before counting her steps again. After a third recount she was utterly baffled. "It should be five feet from Mum's roses and eight feet from Jeffrey's head, so how the hell did the garden lose two feet all of a sudden?"

"Maybe it's the shoes you're wearing," Jane said helpfully.

Elle considered this and took off her shoes. In socks she re-counted and bizarrely gained one foot. *Christ, no wonder my toes look like stumps.*

"You need to get your feet seen to," Jane said, staring at her sister's hammertoes.

"Will do," Elle said, nodding and flexing them, hoping they would stretch back into toe shape. They didn't.

"And you need to give up wearing high heels."

"Won't do," Elle said before refocusing on the ground.

After another minute or two of standing around and arguing over the lost foot, she carefully shoveled out dirt, retrieved the old biscuit tin, and walked the short distance to her small cottage situated at the very back of the long garden with Jane in tow. They headed into the kitchen. Jane made coffee while Elle battled to open the rusty old tin.

"You need a new tin."

"No way. It's this vessel or no vessel. It's all about tradition, Jane," Elle argued before screaming "Bollocks!" after nearly losing her middle finger to a sharp end of the rusted vessel.

A few minutes passed before the coffee was made, the tin was open, the girls were sitting opposite each other, and Elle was reading silently. Elle always read the letter silently while sipping her coffee before reading aloud the parts she was happy to share. Elle laughed, and Jane smiled although she didn't know what she was smiling at, and it was always at this point in the procedure that she remembered that sometimes she didn't like what she heard. Elle put down the letter and nodded to herself with a sheepish grin.

"Well?" Jane asked a tad nervously.

Elle began reading:

"Sunday, December 31, 2006

"Dear Universe,

"What in the name of fuck is wrong with you? . . ."

"Strong start." Jane laughed.

Elle read on:

"The icecaps are melting, the ozone is burning, and species are actually dying out, the golden toad gone, the West African black rhino gone, the baiji dolphin gone . . ."

She took a breath long enough for Jane to interject, "God, that's awful!" Jane was referring to the demise of the baiji dolphin. She didn't give a shit about the toad or the rhino. "Do you remember when I took Kurt to Kerry for a week and we swam with a dolphin? He was only nine then and it seems like just yesterday."

"Did you swim with a baiji dolphin, Jane?"

"No, a regular one."

"Well, then, it's not really relevant, is it?" Elle resumed her place in the text.

"The Pyrenean ibex, gone . . ."

"What's a Pyrenean ibex?"

Elle thought about it for a minute before shaking her head. "I've no idea."

"Did you Google 'extinct species' before writing your letter?" Jane asked in a tone that approached condescension.

"Of course I did. I'm not a bloody zoologist."

"I just don't understand your insatiable need to Google depressing subject matters."

"Because they're important. We may not know what a Pyrenean ibex is, but I can assure you its extinction will have a fundamental effect on the delicate balance of its ecosystem and vice versa."

"Do you even know what you're talking about?" Jane asked.

"Not entirely," Elle admitted, "but it doesn't mean I'm wrong."

"Well, it sure as Shinola doesn't mean you're right either."

"Can I read this letter or not?" Elle asked, and Jane nodded, allowing her to proceed.

"Why aren't you fighting? I'm doing my bit. I recycle, I turn the lights off, I don't even own a TV, but you don't even seem to care that this world, which is a really big part of you, is dying. I know it's not your fault. I know it's ours but we are trying and we'll try harder so stop being such a fucking asshole and adapt or at least bloody try to . . ."

Elle looked up at Jane. "Wow, I was really pissed off with the Universe," she said, and Jane nodded. Elle sniffed and drained her coffee cup before finding her place in the letter, while Jane stood up and started to make more coffee.

"And as for this so-called Celtic tiger, I wish it would die . . ."

Jane placed the coffeepot on the counter with a bang. "Bite your tongue," she ordered. "This so-called Celtic tiger is part of the reason you can charge forty-five K a painting."

"Yeah, well, I was over it last New Year's and I'm still over it this New Year's," Elle said. She read on a little, silently, while her sister busied herself rinsing out their cups.

"Okay. My promises for 2007." She looked at her sister. "Please reserve your comments until the end."

Jane grinned, steadied herself, and nodded her head in

agreement. She placed a fresh cup of black coffee in front of Elle and sat opposite her.

"*1. I will learn to play the piano. 2. I'll donate the proceeds of my next painting to War Child. 3. I'll paint by candlelight. 4. I'll try to help Jane more with Mum. 5. I'll get pregnant . . .*"

Jane gasped. Elle shook her head and sighed a little. "Did I get pregnant in '07?" she asked.

"Not unless there's something you're not telling me."

"There isn't," Elle said, before admitting it was a desire that had passed and that she had no intention of getting pregnant in '08 either. She resumed reading.

"*6. I'll be nicer to Jane . . .*"

"You're always nice to Jane," Jane said, smiling.

"I said no talking," Elle said sternly.

Jane nodded and pulled her index finger and thumb across her lips to indicate that she was zipping her lip.

"*7. I'll take Vincent to China . . .*"

Elle stopped reading for a second and both women reflected on what had happened the previous June while Elle and her boyfriend Vincent were in China, but it was far too painful for either woman to discuss or rehash, and so Elle moved on.

"*8. I'll grow my own vegetables . . .*"

She stopped and smiled at Jane, who was still ruminating on China, but when Elle's eyes met hers, Jane brightened.

"You made a complete mess of that," Jane said, remembering the amount of money, time, and effort Elle had put into growing her own vegetables to end up with nothing bar one crop of pretty poor-tasting potatoes and carrots that looked like they'd been shipped in from Chernobyl, never mind the damage she'd done to the patch of land closest to their mother's gardenias.

Elle laughed. "Remember Mum's face?"

" 'What the fock has happened to my garden?' " Jane said, mimicking her mother's faux-posh accent. It was a funny memory and a good distraction from China.

"9. I'll start a pension fund . . ."

"You already have a pension fund. I set it up ten years ago."

"Oh good. 'Cause I didn't start one. Right, *ten*," Elle said, and she bit her lip.

"What?" Jane asked.

"You might have a problem with this one."

"What?" Jane asked again, becoming quite nervous. "What did you do?"

Elle cleared her throat.

"10. I'll take Kurt skydiving."

Jane jumped up and pointed at her sister. "Oh no, you didn't!" Actual tears were springing into her eyes. "You didn't push my child out of a plane!"

"Of course I didn't push him," Jane said soothingly. "The qualified instructor pushed him."

Jane's mouth was open but no sound was coming out.

"He loved it and he's fine and it's over." Elle was wishing she had kept number ten to herself.

"When?" Jane managed to ask.

"End of April, for his birthday."

"Seventeen-year-olds need parental consent."

"Yeah, I gave that," Elle said, holding up her hand.

"How could you give parental consent seeing as you are not his parent and there is less than nine years between you?" Jane asked through gritted teeth.

"I must look older than my years."

Jane walked to the door.

Elle called after her, "Please don't be annoyed!" But Jane *was* annoyed, and now Elle was sorry.

"You can't just do whatever you want to do, Elle."

"I know. I'm sorry. He'd been begging me for years, and I did hold out until he was seventeen."

Jane shook her head. "I'm really pissed off with you."

"I know. Sorry."

Jane opened Elle's sliding door.

Elle shouted after her, "So are you still going to that party with Tom?"

Jane turned to face her younger sister. "Yes," she said, and she sighed. "Are you coming?" she asked hopefully.

"I'd rather be dead. Anyway, Vincent is taking me out."

"You could bring Vincent," Jane said with hope in her voice.

"It's New Year's Eve and you're spending it with the family of a missing friend whom you haven't known since you were seventeen." Elle shook her head. "You have got to learn how to say no."

"I couldn't. Breda asked Tom if I'd come and—"

"And she knitted that bloody blanket. Jesus, Jane!"

"Right. I'm going." Jane turned to walk away.

"Happy New Year!"

"Happy New Year," Jane responded, "and, Elle, don't think that because I want you at that party it means I'm not really pissed off, because I am."

Elle's intercom buzzed just as Jane closed her door. She picked up the receiver and a man told her that he was standing outside the main gate with flowers. She buzzed him in and told him where to find her. She reopened the door and waved to him as he made his way down the garden.

"Elle Moore?"

"That's me."

She signed for the flowers and closed the door. She smelled her flowers and smiled. She opened the card, and her smile quickly faded.

Elle,

    Like the song says, I want you, I need you, but let's face it, I'm never going to love you. We've had four good years so let's start '08 with a clean slate.

Yours,

Vincent

Elle's legs turned to jelly, her ears began to burn, and her stomach tightened so much that there was no room for her breakfast. She ran to the toilet and threw up, and then she sat on the bathroom floor and gazed at the note with a sense of disbelief that was overwhelming.

For six years running, Jane had joined Elle at the back of their garden to retrieve her letter to the Universe, and for six years running Jane had discovered something she didn't want to know. And yet, though her sister had taken her son skydiving even after she had expressly forbidden it and she was so annoyed she could spit, she knew she would partake in her sister's reading again. Five years ago, after a particularly nasty surprise involving her sister and an intended sexual encounter with a prostitute named Cora, it occurred to her that she should dig up Elle's letter to the Universe every January and read it to get a heads-up on what Elle had planned for the year ahead, but Jane was terrible at espionage, as had been proved seventeen years previously when she had managed to conceal her pregnancy from her mother for only two hours.

"What's wrong with you?"

"Nothing."

"Oh my God, you're pregnant!"

If she dug up the letter, Elle would find out and she'd never trust Jane again, so she couldn't risk it even though she often stood on the spot that was five feet from her mother's rosebushes and between six and eight feet from Jeffrey's head and was sorely tempted.

For instance, there was the year that Elle promised the Universe she'd give money to Comic Relief. She watched the show, got drunk, and pledged a hundred grand. Jane had argued that although people all over the world were in need, Elle didn't know if she'd sell another painting that year and although Ricky Gervais was funny he wasn't that fucking funny. Elle had laughed and called her mean, but it was Jane who paid Elle's bills when she'd squandered all her money by June and was waiting for three months for that next big check. There was the year she promised to rescue a dog and ended up rescuing ten dogs from different pounds across Dublin. Two weeks and two tons of dog shit later, it became apparent to all but Elle that she couldn't care for them. It fell to Jane to rehouse them, and Elle took to her bed for two weeks mourning the dogs she couldn't seem to remember to care for. There was the year she decided to run a marathon and forgot to practice. She made it twenty miles before she collapsed, suffering the effects of exhaustion and a speed overdose. Elle had felt that it was perfectly acceptable to take speed to run a marathon, going so far as to query the doctor as to how in the hell he thought she'd make it without speed. All of these incidents had caused Jane to deliberate on risking Elle's wrath, but then she conceded that even if she knew of Elle's plans in advance there would be no way of stopping her, as she was a law unto herself. Their mother said it was her creative nature that drove her to extremes and that neither she nor Jane could ever hope to understand the things that drove her. Jane and her mother didn't agree on much, but they agreed on that. Elle was a genius, and everyone knew that genius was close to madness, and so as long as Elle painted the most beautiful and inspired paintings, she would be indulged.

Jane opened the back door, and before she got inside and had time to close it her mother was calling her through the intercom that linked her kitchen with her mother's kitchen in the basement apartment downstairs.

"Jane? Jane? Jane? Jane, it's your mother! Jane! Jane! Jane, have you gone deaf? I know you're there. I saw you come out of Elle's cottage. Jane, Jane, will you please answer me for God's sake!"

Jane wondered how many times a day her mother shouted through the intercom and abused an empty room. She pressed the button. "I'm here."

"Are you planning on starving me?"

"To be fair, Rose, I've heard that drowning is faster and less cruel."

"I want eggs, scrambled, dry and fluffy. Not wet and slimy. If I see slime I'll throw up."

"I'll be down in five minutes."

"I'm hungry now."

"Oh fine. I'll go ahead and pull a plate of scrambled eggs, dry and fluffy, from my rectum then, shall I?"

"No need for vulgarity, Jane. You weren't born in a barn."

Kurt entered the kitchen in time to witness Jane give the intercom the finger. "Whatever she wants, I'm not doing it," he said.

"Oh yes you are," Jane said in a voice that her son recognized as his mother meaning business. The look that twisted her face suggested he was in big trouble.

"What?" he asked, trying to work out what he'd been caught doing.

"Skydiving, Kurt?"

"I'm going to kill Elle!" He flopped onto the chair and pulled his hood over his head, covering his blond curls, and pressed his hands to his ears.

"Skydiving. You know how I feel about skydiving. I said no. Every time you asked me I said no. No means no. It doesn't mean maybe, it doesn't mean I'll think about it, and it sure as Shinola doesn't mean go behind Mum's back with Elle!"

"Mum, please stop saying 'sure as Shinola.' It sounds retarded. The expression is 'You don't know shit from Shinola.'"

"I don't give a shit if it is, and that's not the point."

"You said it the other day in front of Paul, and he thought you'd hit your head."

"Really, I don't give a Shinola. You cannot get away with deliberately disobeying my rules."

"Ah Mum, back off. It was last April. It's done, over, it was a laugh, it was safe, and nobody died."

"Well, you can forget about tonight."

"You can't stop me from going out on New Year's Eve!" he said with scorn.

"No, probably not, but I can withhold funds."

Kurt pushed his hood back off his head. "You can't do that. I've promised Irene."

"Tough."

"I can't believe you're doing this to me on New Year's Eve!" he shouted before storming out of the kitchen.

"Yeah, well, believe it, and you'd better storm back here in ten minutes flat to bring Rose's eggs to her or you're going to be poor for all of January!"

"I hate you!" Kurt screamed at his mother.

"I hate you too!" Jane screamed back while breaking two eggs into a bowl.

Ten minutes later Kurt stormed in, picked up the plate of eggs, and stormed out without a word.

Although Jane's authority had been briefly undermined, her power was restored, she was fifty euros richer, and she had managed to avoid Rose, so her mood brightened considerably.

Kurt made his way down the steps to his grandmother's basement flat with the tray in one hand, fishing for the key with his other. Inside, the place smelled of air freshener, cigars, and wine, making his eyes water a little. In the small hall he nearly tripped over a stack of unsolicited mail that she kept piled up against the wall. It was stacked so high that the pile kept falling over. He had once asked her why she kept it, and she had told him that she was waiting for a member of the Green Party to call at her door so that she could throw the paper at him, douse him in alcohol, and then set him alight. She had been drunk at the time and so Kurt had hoped she was joking. He opened the door to the sitting room, and his grandmother sat up straight in her chair.

Her face broke into a smile. Kurt's relationship with his grandmother was far different from what he had with his mother. She idolized her grandson and saved all her grace for him. He laid the tray on the table that she kept near the big chair that dominated the room. The chair was referred to as the "throne" by her daughters, and she spent most of her time sitting in it. No one dared sit on Rose's chair—not her daughters, not her friends, not visiting dignitaries, and not even her grandson, who was one of the very few people Rose actually liked. While poking at her eggs, she asked after Jane, and he lied and told her she felt fluish.

"Well, then, she may stay away—I prefer you anyway," she said, smiling and winking. She sampled her eggs and made a face to suggest that she was less than impressed. She always made that face. Usually it was for Jane's benefit, but as it had become habit she did it whether Jane was there or not. She sniffed the plate.

"Just eat the eggs," Kurt said.

Rose took a forkful and popped it into her mouth, rubbed her tummy, and made a "yum" sound. Kurt laughed.

"How's Irene?" she asked.

"She's good," he said, and he sat down. "Better; she'll be fine."

His grandmother nodded and winked at him. "Of course she will. So her father's an ass. She has you, doesn't she? So, is your mother still determined to go to the Walsh household tonight with Alexandra's husband?"

"She's dreading it."

"Of course she's dreading it. The Walshes have always and ever been complete lunatics. Alexandra was the cheekiest pup I ever met. The mother is one of those holier-than-thou types, the father hasn't done a real day's work since the seventies, and as for her brother, Eamonn, that little snot was trying to get into your mother's pants when she was thirteen!" She stopped and took a breath. "And anyway she has no business there—the family is grieving the loss of a child."

"She's missing, not dead," Kurt reminded his grandmother.

"Of course she's dead," Rose said. "She's Valley-of-the-Dead dead."

"You don't know that."

"I know this: if someone vanishes without a trace in this day and age, she is buried somewhere, and it's usually someone closest to her who's done the burying. For all we know, your mother's next."

Kurt laughed at his gran. "Now I know where Elle gets her imagination."

"Mark my words. Your mother is getting herself involved in something very bloody sinister there." She pushed the remaining food on her plate to the side and put down her fork. "I'm finished."

Kurt told his grandmother about his run-in with his mother, expressing how annoyed he was that she was punishing him for something he had done eight months previously. For once his grandmother was on his mother's side; she felt that anyone who jumped out of a perfectly good plane deserved to be crippled for life. Having said that, she felt that Jane's withdrawal of funds was an overreaction, bearing in mind what night it was.

"How much do you need?" she asked.

"Seventy?" Kurt said, knowing full well he was pressing his luck.

"Fifty it is," she responded.

Rose took fifty euros out of her handbag and handed it to him.

"Cheers, Gran!"

She waved him away. He left the basement flat, and she watched him through her window as he turned on his iPod, searched for some noise, pressed Play, and walked down the street while probably deafening himself. *Kids are mad*, she thought. Then she picked up the open bottle of red wine that was resting against her chair. She drained her teacup of tea and poured in the wine. She took a sip and smiled. *Happy New Year, Rose.*

4

"So Far Gone"

I'm so far gone that it seems like home to me.
I'm so far gone, have I lost my way or am I free?

Jack L, *Universe*

It was just after eight thirty on New Year's Eve when Leslie got off the train, returning from the family bungalow she owned in the country. Her apartment was located conveniently beside the train station, so she wheeled her suitcase past all those queuing for a taxi, turned the corner, and she was home.

In the lift, she heard crashing and banging, and it became louder the closer she got to her floor. She exited and walked toward a bunch of five people whom she recognized as neighbors. They were blocking the way, so she mumbled "Excuse me." They didn't notice, as they were wrapped up in what was going on around the corner. It was then that Leslie noticed a fireman. He was standing in front of the group as though he was there to hold them back. Leslie couldn't smell any fire. She said "Excuse me" again, but this time the banging was louder.

One of the girls whom she recognized but didn't know turned to her and looked her up and down. "Oh shit," she said, "she's here!"

Leslie wasn't one for pleasantries, but the girl's response to her arrival was slightly shocking. The others turned and gaped at her. The fireman called to his buddies.

"Lads, it's a false alarm!"

The gaping neighbors parted and she was allowed to walk through them with her case rolling behind her. She rounded the corner to be met by two firemen standing in the space where she used to have a front door.

"What the hell?" she asked.

"It's my fault," the girl who had uttered "shit" in response to her arrival said. "I haven't heard your music in a few days, and there was a smell."

A fireman walked through the doorway. "Well, the good news is we have no dead body; the bad news is the cat has shit all over the place."

"I was down in the country," Leslie said, a little shocked at the scene.

"I'm really sorry," the girl said, to the fireman as opposed to Leslie. "She rarely leaves the apartment," she went on, her tone sliding from apologetic to accusatory, "and for the past few days no music, and then that awful smell."

"You smelled cat shit and you thought I was dead?" Leslie said in a voice that was laced with contempt and disbelief.

The girl turned to face her with her hands raised in the air. "Look, I was just being a good neighbor. You hear about these people left to rot all the time, and to be fair I don't know what death smells like."

"Well, it doesn't smell like cat shit—and what do you mean 'these people'?"

"Well," the girl said, becoming a little uncomfortable, "loners."

Leslie stood dumbfounded.

"She thought you'd killed yourself," a random man said.

The girl nudged him and mouthed the words "shut" and "up."

"Well," he said, directing his speech toward the firemen, "everyone knows that New Year's Eve is a big night for suicides."

"Am I going to get charged for this call out?" the girl asked.

"Don't give them your name, Deborah!" the man said.

"Brilliant, Damien," she said, walking away and shaking her head. "Thanks for that."

The firemen gathered their gear; the five people disappeared.

Leslie entered her doorless apartment and sat on her sofa, and her cat, who had apparently recovered from her gastrointestinal malady, jumped on her lap, and together they surveyed the pile of cat shit matted into her carpet near her electric fire. Then the realization of how she was perceived in her building hit Leslie like a ton of bricks. *I'm the crazy loner cat lady who drops dead and rots in her apartment.* The irony was not lost on her, as she had only recently rejoined the society she had shunned for so long.

A mere two months before this night, Leslie had been sitting in a chair opposite her oncologist. He was the oncologist who had cared for her mother and both her sisters through their cancer. He had also been testing Leslie twice a year for more than twenty years. He was smiling.

"Good news," he said. "You are clean as a whistle."

"Right," Leslie said. "Fine. Thanks." She stood up to leave.

"What's wrong with you?" he asked.

"Nothing. Apparently I'm clean as a whistle."

"You sound disappointed."

She sat. "Well, would it be odd if I said I was?"

"Very odd."

"I'm sick of waiting," she said. "I'm sick of waiting for this stupid ticktocking time bomb to go off."

"Oh," he said, and he nodded. "I see."

"The truth is, when Imelda died, I stopped living." She hunched her shoulders. "Now I'm a woman about to turn forty with a cat for company. I thought I'd be well dead by now, yet here I am, alive and lonely." She smiled at her doctor to assure him she wasn't going to cry. He must have been shocked at her revelation, possibly the most she'd ever said to him.

"You know that you might never get cancer," he said. "But a lot has changed in recent years, and although I'm not a huge advocate of preventative surgery, I can give you some brochures."

She looked at him. "We talked about this years ago. You were adamant it was just self-mutilation."

"A lot has changed," he repeated, "and, besides, I might have thought differently if I had known how you were feeling or if you'd given even the slightest indication of the effect this worry was having on your life."

"How could it not?" She stared at him and asked abruptly, "Are you talking about a double mastectomy?"

"Yes. And in your case I'd recommend a full hysterectomy also, for peace of mind."

"Wow," she said. "Jesus. Holy crap." She nodded. "Give me the information."

This new prospect was daunting, but even as Leslie pulled out of the hospital car park she had made up her mind. *I'm going to do it.*

It was around that time that Leslie had also decided she'd had enough of being lonely, and she had tentatively stepped back out into the world. As she was a Web designer who worked from home, she decided instead to rent an office in a building in town.

She had yet to move on this, but the plan was in place. As she had no friends, she decided to visit museums and art galleries so that, even if she was alone, at least she would be outside and partaking in life.

It would be a slow road back, but thanks to that night stuck in a lift, not as slow as she had first envisioned. Elle had become a fixture in her world over the past two months, and to a lesser extent Tom and Jane. She had created a website for Alexandra and was in contact with Tom with updates, and Jane filled her in on how the exhibition idea was coming along so that she could blog about it.

But Elle wanted more than her help. Elle wanted her friendship, and although it was unnatural to Leslie to be a friend to a woman half her age, she had become fond of Elle early on.

So the fact that she had so recently ventured back into the world and actually made friends meant that the comments from her annoying neighbor really bugged her.

"I'm not a loner, Deborah!" she shouted at the wall. "I have friends. I go out. I have a life."

Someone coughed. It was the caretaker. "Sorry to disturb you," he said.

"It's fine," she said. "I was just talking to the wall."

"I'm here to fix the door."

"Okay." She nodded. "Please forgive the smell. I'm about to clean."

"Will do," he said, and he got to work.

Much later and after a new door had been hastily fitted by the caretaker, Leslie poured a glass of wine, picked up her phone, and dialed a number she hadn't dialed in over ten years.

"Hello?"

"Jim?"

"This is Jim."

"Hi, it's Leslie Sheehan."

"Leslie. Jesus. I can't believe it's you!"

"I know. It's odd. I hope I'm not intruding."

"No, I'm just sitting in."

"Me too."

"Happy New Year, by the way!"

"Happy New Year."

"So what made you call after all this time?" he asked.

"I don't know . . . well, it sounds stupid."

"You're sick?"

"No, no, not sick," she said. "I'm thinking about having preventative surgery, actually."

"I think you should," he said without missing a beat.

"Wow."

"If Imelda had had that choice I know she would have done it."

"That's what I thought."

"Are you scared?"

"No."

"Have you got anyone in your life?"

"No."

"Do you want me to be there for you?"

Leslie couldn't believe it. She hadn't spoken to Jim in so many years and before that she had usually been rude or standoffish.

"That is really kind of you," she said, "but no."

"So why have you called?"

"I just wanted to hear your voice," she said, and she laughed a little. "People are mad, aren't they?"

Jim laughed. "Yes, Leslie, people are mad."

After that she asked him how he was and what he was doing

and if he'd ever remarried. He was fine, doing well, and no, he hadn't. He'd been seeing a Russian woman for a year, but she'd returned to Russia when her father died six months earlier.

They spoke for about fifteen minutes, and before she hung up she promised to call him to arrange to go out for a drink.

"You see, Deborah! I'm going out for a drink, with a man, very soon!" she shouted at the wall once more. "I am not Crazy Dead Cat Lady, not today and not tomorrow!"

The cat stared at her from her freshly washed and pine-scented bed. Leslie looked at her watch. It was only nine, so she opened her computer and watched three episodes of *Desperate Housewives* season one before hitting the hay around eleven thirty.

"Yeah, happy New Year, Deborah, and up yours!"

Tom beeped the horn, and Jane appeared within seconds. She ignored her mother's face pressed to the basement window when she turned to close the gate. Tom had gotten out and opened her door. She thanked him and buckled up while he made his way around to his side of the car. He got in and thanked her for agreeing to come to the Walshes with him, explaining how awkward it was since Alexandra disappeared. She wondered why he put himself through it, and he admitted to having a soft spot for Alexandra's mother, Breda.

They got to the house just after nine, and Alexandra's younger sister, Kate, opened the door. She hugged Tom and said a polite hello to Jane. Kate vaguely remembered Jane. The last time she had seen her she had probably been no older than ten. They entered the hallway, and it was as though Jane had stepped back through time. The carpet was brown with red diamonds, the telephone table still had two yellow telephone books under it, and the walls were still dotted with holiday photos from the seventies and eighties and at least three of them included her. She was ushered quickly into the sitting room.

There, sitting on the green velvet chair by the window, was Breda. The chair was the same, but Breda had aged well beyond her years. Having begun her family at a young age, Breda couldn't have been any older than sixty-five, but she looked ninety. Her face was wizened and her tall frame shriveled. Her hair was white and cropped. Her hands, clasped and holding rosary beads, were so thin they were transparent, revealing blue and purple veins and knuckles that appeared knotted.

She smiled and held out her hand. Jane took it and felt a little weak.

"Jane Moore," said Breda, shaking her head, "you've grown into such a beautiful woman."

"Thank you, Breda. It's lovely to see you again."

"And Tom tells me you've been so good helping him find my Alexandra."

"I'm only setting up a benefit to highlight her case and the Missing of Ireland." Jane was embarrassed and wished she was in a position to do more.

"You were always such a lovely girl. Alexandra will be so pleased to have you in her life again." She was crying, but her tears were silent.

Jane noticed Eamonn enter the room from the corner of her eye, but Breda still had a firm grip on her hand, and she felt Breda deserved her full attention.

"Still so blond," said Breda, and she flipped some of Jane's shoulder-length hair.

"I have some help these days," Jane said.

"Do you remember Alexandra's hair?"

Jane nodded.

"She had the richest chestnut hair, thick and glossy," said her mother. "It was just above her shoulders when we saw her last, but the police say it could have changed now. I hope it hasn't. She had the most beautiful hair."

"Mam," Eamonn said, "Jane doesn't want to hear that."

Jane turned to Eamonn and nodded hello. "It's fine," she said. "I understand."

Breda let go of Jane's hand. "You should get a drink." She looked at Tom, who was still standing at the door. "Tom, you should get Jane a drink."

Tom took Jane into the kitchen, where Kate and her husband, Owen, Eamonn's wife, Frankie, and Alexandra's father, Ben, were standing around the counter. Frankie welcomed Tom with a hug and Ben nodded to him. Kate offered him a drink, but Tom said he'd make it himself.

Ben shook Jane's hand and thanked her for coming. "It's great to see you. How's that boy of yours?"

"He's fine. He's seventeen."

"My God, time passes quickly. It seems like only yesterday yourself and herself were giving us a run for our money."

Jane grinned. Although Ben was older than his wife, he still managed to look ten years younger. He sported a full head of gray hair and he rubbed at the gray stubble on his chin. He was heavier than he had been years before. She remembered him as being fit and sportive, but those days were long gone. His shirt buttons strained over his paunch, and when he'd approached her he walked with a limp.

Some neighbors arrived and sat in the sitting room with Breda. The house seemed full and empty at the same time. Tom handed Jane a glass of red wine. Tony Bennett was playing on the stereo. No one talked about the fact that Alexandra was gone. They referred to her often and included her in stories about the past, which was where it seemed her parents now resided. Tom talked with his in-laws' neighbors and Frankie and Owen, but it was difficult not to notice the coldness between him and Alexandra's brother and father. He spent some time with Breda, who hugged him warmly and whispered something in his ear.

Half an hour before midnight he found Jane in the hallway studying a picture on the wall.

"That was taken on a day out in Bray in 1983," she said. "It was such a hot day, the beach was mobbed, and we'd run into the arcade and onto the bumper cars just to cool down. Alexandra ate so much cotton candy she puked pink all the way home."

Tom looked at the picture and recognized Jane. Her hair was so blond it was almost white, and it was braided to her waist. She was hugging Alexandra, whose rich, wavy chestnut hair shone in the sun. Both girls were facing the camera and grinning so hard they had dimples. He shook his head. "It's a funny old world," he said, but nobody was laughing.

Midnight came and went and the new year was celebrated. As soon as the clock struck one, Tom and Jane made their excuses and left.

In the car, Jane asked Tom about his relationship with Alexandra's family.

"Ben and Eamonn need someone to blame," he said.

"Why you?"

"Why not me? She was my wife."

"And what about Breda?"

"Breda blames herself."

"And you?"

"It depends on the day."

When they got to Jane's house, he thanked her once more for coming. "It meant so much to Breda."

She nodded and told him that she'd be in touch the following week with an update about the benefit. He nodded, and she got out of the car. She closed the gate behind her and waved, and she made her way up the steps of her house. She could hear Bing Crosby's voice singing "You Are My Sunshine," punctuated by laughter and chatter, coming from her mother's basement flat. She didn't stop to say hello. Instead she went inside, took off her shoes that were pretty but painful, poured herself a whiskey, and took it to bed.

When the clock turned midnight Elle raised her bottle and toasted the sky. She spun around the beach in bare feet with a bottle of vodka pressed closely to her chest. When she stopped spinning, she fell on her ass, still managing to hold on to the bottle. She got up as quickly as a drunkard can and sprayed some alcohol on the fire so that the flames danced higher and higher. The car engine had already exploded, and so now she and a homeless man who called himself Buns watched the shell burn out. She sat beside the old man and clinked her bottle against his.

"Happy New Year, Buns!"

"Happy New Year, my dear!"

They sat in silence listening to the flames crackle and the low hush of the sea as it swept in and out. Elle lit a cigarette and passed it to Buns. He refused with a wave of his hands. "Those things will kill you."

She laughed a little. "Sleeping on a pavement in December will kill you quicker."

"Ah well, it's January now, so roll on spring!" He took a slug from the bottle of vodka the strange girl had bought for him. "Vincent must be a right bastard," he said after a minute or two.

"Depends on who you ask," she said, getting up and dancing around again.

"How much would you say that car cost?" he asked.

"Around forty grand." She could have answered with precise figures if she had wished, as she had bought him the car.

"Jesus. He'll be sorry he messed with you."

She smiled. "That's the hope."

They both heard the police sirens. Buns drained his bottle before the cops could take his booze off him. Elle continued to dance to the music she could hear in her head. The police approached them cautiously, but Elle smiled and waved them over as though they were at a party and she was asking them to join in. Once they had established that Elle had stolen her ex-boyfriend's car and burned it out, they put her and Buns, who happily claimed himself as a willing accessory, in the back of the police car. Buns was delighted that he would have at least a night inside, or even two if he was lucky, because he'd seen the weather forecast in the window of Dixon's electrical shop and it was set to fall below zero. Elle was focused on the sights, sounds, and smells around her. Everything seemed so vivid; she was giddy, high on revenge and adventure. The city moved quickly past the window and the siren pealed, not because there was an emergency but just to get through the drunkards on the streets. The car smelled of disinfectant, and she breathed in deeply. Buns smelled of something else entirely, a little sweat, a little oil, a little damp, and a little puke, and still she inhaled and smiled as though it was the sweetest of perfume.

"I've never been in a jail cell," she said, excited by the notion. "I've always wondered about it."

The female officer looked over her shoulder. "Well, you won't have to wonder anymore."

"True." Elle smiled.

Jane woke with a start. Kurt was standing above her with his hand on her shoulder, shaking her. "Mum, Mum, Mum!"

She bolted upright. "Kurt?" She looked at the clock beside her bed: four ten a.m. "What the hell?"

"It's Elle. She's been arrested."

Jane stared blankly at her son; the words coming from his mouth seemed to lose meaning. "Excuse me?"

"Sit up," he ordered, and she noticed he was slurring, but at that moment her drunken teenage son was the least of her worries.

"Did you say 'arrested?'" she asked, silently praying she'd misheard him.

He nodded.

She swung her legs around and sat at the edge of the bed and held her head in her hands. "Oh for fuck's sake," she said before she sighed a sigh that seemed to come from her very core. "Where is she?"

"Clontarf."

"Clontarf," she repeated, and got out of bed. "And why not? Clontarf is as good as anyplace to get arrested."

Jane talked to herself and bumped into things while trying to locate something to wear. She said "ouch" twice and "for fhu" a number of times before Kurt took his leave so that she could get dressed.

Jane entered the sitting room in search of her handbag. Kurt and his girlfriend, Irene, were lying on the sofa together listening to music.

"Hi, Jane," Irene said with a big grin that suggested she had imbibed one too many alcopops.

"Hi, Irene," she said to the grinning teen. "Does your mother know where you are?"

"She's in Venice," Irene said, slurring a little.

"Nice."

"Not really," Irene said. "She found out that Dad was sleeping with some woman he met on the Internet, and she's gone over there to spend as much of his money as possible before kicking him out of the house."

"Oh my God, that's awful," Jane said, truly shocked and momentarily forgetting her sister was in a jail cell. "Are you okay?"

"I'm fine." Irene waved her hands dismissively.

"Well, if things get a bit rough at home you can always come and stay here—in the spare room, not Kurt's."

"Ah Jane, that is so nice of you, thank you." She burped. "Excuse you!" she said, pointing at Jane before she burst out laughing. Kurt laughed too.

Jane raised her eyes to heaven and grabbed her bag, but before she left she stood in front of the two drunk teenagers wagging her finger. "No sex in here, no sex in your room, no sex in this entire house. And don't think I won't know, because I will know." She left the room.

Irene looked at Kurt and wagged her finger. "And yet she didn't cop to the fact that we've just done it on this sofa."

Jane could hear Kurt and Irene laugh as she left the house. *Of course they're laughing. It's four in the morning, they're seventeen, drunk, and awake, and they've probably had more sex in the past five hours than I've had in two years.*

At the police station, Jane waited for more than two hours before she even got to speak to someone. It was then that she was informed that her sister faced possible charges of theft and arson. Jane closed her eyes and didn't speak for what seemed to be the longest time. The policeman queried whether she was all right.

"I hate my life," she said.

"I know the feeling."

She sat in the waiting area for another hour. She was freezing and tired and so pissed off that she actually wanted to weep. The man beside her smelled of feet and the woman opposite stared at her in a manner that suggested she might wish to hurt her. Jane would have loved to be bold enough to square up to the stranger and demand an explanation as to what she wanted, but she didn't have the balls. *The story of my life,* she thought while keeping her head hung low to avoid her aggressive opposite's gaze.

Elle appeared a little after eight o'clock. She was yawning and stretching. She grinned when she saw Jane, who in turn stood up, grabbed her sister's arm, and dragged her out of the station.

"Do not grin, do not speak, do not even bollocking whimper!" she ordered Elle, who seemed to be veering between alarm and amusement. "I am cold and tired and I've just about had it up to here. So just shut up."

"Okay," Elle agreed.

They sat into the car. Jane started the engine.

"Can I smoke?" Elle asked.

"Shut up," Jane said.

"I'll take that as a yes then," Elle said, lighting up.

Jane drove in silence. Elle smoked and stared out the window. When they were less than a mile from their house, Jane pulled the car to the side of the road and parked. She turned to her sister and began the rant she had practiced while sitting in the station and attempting to avoid being head-butted.

"You have done some unbelievable things in your time—stupid,

stupid things that have left me wide-eyed and openmouthed. But my God, this one has really topped the lot. You burned out Vincent's car? No, hold on, you *stole*, then you burned out, Vincent's car? What is wrong with you? How insane does a person have to be?" She noticed tears streaming from Elle's eyes, and they silenced her.

Elle took the card out of her pocket and passed it to Jane. Jane read it aloud.

" '*Elle, like the song says, I want you, I need you, but let's face it, I'm never going to love you.*' " She faced her sister, who was still crying. "Like the song says?" She looked back at the page. "Let's face it?" She shook her head. "Oh, Elle!"

She pitied her sister because even though Vincent was a pig, Elle loved him deeply. "Let's face it," Jane repeated, "he's obviously back on drugs."

Elle didn't respond.

Jane handed the card back to Elle, whose nose was now running. She took some tissue from her pocket and wiped Elle's nose and then hugged her. "It's all right, Elle, we'll sort it all out." But she knew there was nothing she could do.

Elle shook her head. "He's really gone this time, Janey." Then she sobbed on her sister's shoulder until her tears ran dry.

5

"Authentic Fake"

Pillows bursting at the seams,
feathers floating like dreams,
naked on the wooden floor,
night porters banging at the door,
and we just turn the music up.

Jack L, *Broken Songs*

January 2008

Although it was cold, the sky was blue and there wasn't a cloud in sight. Jane particularly favored cold dry days, and they were so few and far between. She wasn't a fan of central heating, as it made her skin itchy and dry. She liked a nip in the air and couldn't understand when her son complained that he was cold, because she had spent so much money on clothes for him to wear and yet he had the audacity to stand in front of her in a T-shirt and boxer shorts wondering what it would take for her to put on some heat. The kitchen was warm because she had spent the morning baking. Kurt came in, rubbing his hands together and blowing into them for effect.

"Put on a sweater and jeans," she said with her back to him.

"Who's coming?" he asked, ignoring her and putting on the kettle.

"Tom and Leslie."

"Oh them." He made a face.

" 'Oh them,' " she repeated, amused. "What's wrong with them?"

"He's haunted and she's a bit of a freak," he said, spooning coffee into a cup. "Oh, and Gran thinks he's a murderer."

"Oh for God's sake, stop listening to that twisted woman!"

"Well, you can't say it hasn't crossed your mind."

"I can say it hasn't crossed my mind," she replied. "Alexandra disappeared when Tom was at work, and he has witnesses."

"So it has crossed your mind, but you're satisfied with his alibi." Kurt pointed his spoon at his mother.

"Fine." She put her hands up. "I'm satisfied by his alibi."

"Lots of people have good alibis, and then those alibis turn out to be crap."

"Kurt," Jane said, "please stop calling Mammy's new friend a murderer."

Kurt laughed a little. "Okay, but be careful—you don't want to be a Nicky Pelley to his Joe O'Reilly." He poured boiling water into the cup and then gripped it tightly. "God, Mum, it's freezing in here."

He went to his room to sit at his computer with his duvet strategically wrapped around his body and arms while his hands remained uncovered and unencumbered. Jane remained in the kitchen cleaning the spilled coffee grounds from the counter while keeping an eye on the oven and clock.

This would be the third time Leslie and Tom had come to her house to discuss their project's progress. Elle had been there both times before, but she was taking her breakup with Vincent pretty hard and so when Jane spotted her GONE FISHING sign on her door earlier that morning, she knew it meant that Elle might be gone a week or a month. She wasn't sure how she was going to break this news to Tom.

Tom had become incredibly excited at the last meeting when Elle had revealed the painting she had done of Alexandra. He had previously given Elle a box of photos of his wife, and she'd gone through all of Jane's from when Alexandra was younger, and after spending a week looking at the woman's face, she spent another week working on capturing it. According to Tom, Jane, and even Leslie, she had done so beautifully.

"I made her look sad," Elle said. "I hope you don't mind because I know she is a happy sort, but I think she needed to look sad."

"I don't mind—she's beautiful," Tom said, staring at the painting that leaned against Jane's kitchen wall. "How did you do that? How did you make her look lost?"

Elle stared at the face she had come to know so well and hunched her shoulders. "I don't know."

Tom bit the side of his mouth so hard there was an indent in his cheek. He nodded and looked at Elle. "You're incredible."

Elle loved it when people complimented her. She'd blush and say she hated it, but her heart would flutter, her pulse would race, and for a moment she'd feel a great high that she'd come down from all too soon.

Leslie had created a fantastic website—www.findingalexandra .com—that incorporated Alexandra's most recent photos and a map of her last movements. She'd even managed to attach the CCTV footage from Tara Street and Dalkey DART stations. She created a blog space for Tom to update if and when he wanted and a chat room for anyone who wanted to post a comment, and of course there was an e-mail address for anyone with information. Tom was overwhelmed, especially when Leslie revealed the link to Jack Lukeman's website, and when she clicked on Jack's site there was a link to Finding Alexandra. Tom was dumbfounded. Jack's website even mentioned Alexandra and asked his visitors to check out the Finding Alexandra site to see if they had seen her.

"How?" Tom asked.

"I designed Jack's site."

"Wow, that's fantastic. Absolutely fantastic."

"And you said you couldn't help!" Elle teased.

"Well, I'm glad you're happy," Leslie said, a little pleased with herself.

"How did you get Jack to agree?" Jane asked.

"Alexandra's a Jack fan, and I got Myra in his office to agree, and once she agreed it was pretty much done and, by the by, they asked if there was anything else that they could do."

"You are shitting me!" Elle said.

"No," Leslie said. "And I'm not sure I even know or care to know what shitting a person is."

"Of course there's something else they can do," Jane said suddenly.

"Yeah," Elle said, beating Jane to it. "Jack can sing at the Missing Exhibition opening."

"It would make the PR a cinch," Jane said.

"I'll talk to Myra," Leslie said.

Tom didn't know what to say. He was bowled over. In the few short weeks he had known these three women, his search for his wife had taken on a whole new life, and he was so grateful that he found it hard to express it.

Jane smiled at him when he became tongue-tied and slightly teary. "We'll find her," she promised.

Now, less than a month later, her promise appeared slightly premature if not a tad arrogant. Elle was missing in action, and that meant she wasn't painting, and if she wasn't painting the exhibition might not happen in April as had been planned, and if the exhibition didn't happen in April Jack wouldn't be available to play at it again until after he'd finished with the European festivals in September, and he was key to publicity. She had tried to call Elle, but to no avail. GONE FISHING meant no contact.

Jane felt sick about having to disappoint Tom and Leslie after all the work Leslie had put into promoting the exhibition on the website, and she wasn't even sure if she should tell them. *Maybe I'll give it a week,* she thought. *I'll give it a week and see what happens and then, if I have to tell them and break Tom's heart, I'll do it. Damn it, Elle, this is no time for your selfish crap. Come home.*

Leslie was the first to arrive. Jane opened the door, and Leslie pointed to the basement and asked if Jane knew who the old woman was.

"My mother."

Leslie nodded. "Oh," she said. "She has Tom."

"Sweet Jesus! There's coffee made. I'll be a minute." Jane took off down the front steps like a hare before Leslie could even respond.

Tom was sitting in a chair opposite her mother when she burst into the room as though she was a gangbuster.

Rose was swirling liquid in her mug, and Jane prayed it was tea. Tom was silent and had his hands clasped and resting on his knee.

"What has she said?" Jane asked Tom.

"I asked him if he'd killed his wife," Rose said. "I further inquired whether or not he had any intention of killing you."

"Oh God." Jane sighed and closed her eyes for a moment to compose herself.

"I said no on both counts," Tom said, and thankfully he seemed a little amused.

"You see, Jane," Rose said, "we are only having a nice quiet chat. There's no need to run down here like your anus is on fire."

Tom laughed a little.

"Tom," Jane said, "time to leave."

Tom stood up.

"Rose, I'll talk to you later," Jane said.

Tom said good-bye to Rose and followed Jane out into Rose's small hallway, where he managed to kick over her stack of unsolicited mail. He stooped to pile it all back together, and before Jane could tell him to ignore the mess and move on, her mother shouted from her sitting room.

"And Tom dear!"

"Yes?" He moved back to the doorway.

"If my daughter happens to go missing, you'll die roaring. I'll make sure of it," she said in an airy and sweet tone as though she was promising to take him out to dinner.

"I understand."

"I'm so sorry," Jane apologized as she drew him away from the door and slammed it shut. "I really am so very sorry."

"It's fine," Tom said.

"You need locking up!" she screamed at her mother through the closed sitting-room door. She opened Rose's front door, and Tom followed her into the cold air. He was both a little miffed and a little entertained.

Jane was pissed off. "Sorry you had to witness that."

"It's fine," he said. "Worth it. After all, without you and Elle I'd still be handing out leaflets at gigs."

Oh God, Elle! Come home for Christ's sake, just come home!

Jane smiled at Tom and pretended everything was okay. He followed her up the steps and into the house and to the kitchen, where Leslie was hugging her cup of coffee.

"Is the heating broken?" she asked.

"I'll just put it on." Jane went into the hall and turned on the heat.

Kurt heard the familiar clicking and came out of his bedroom dressed in his duvet. "Oh yeah, Mum, you'll put on the heat for visitors but not your only son. Nice."

Jane ignored her son, and after taking a detour into her bedroom to quickly smear her face with moisturizer for extra-dry skin, she made her way back to the kitchen in time to hear Leslie inform Tom that the hits on the Finding Alexandra site had increased by seventy percent since they'd linked up with Jack Lukeman's site.

Jane offered them a choice of carrot cake, chocolate log, or coffee cupcakes and brewed fresh coffee, and once they'd munched on cake and complimented Jane on her baking skills, Leslie revealed that before she'd left her apartment she'd received an e-mail from someone who believed that she'd spotted Alexandra at a Jack Lukeman gig in London the previous week.

"I think it's important not to get excited," Leslie warned, producing a printout of the e-mail. "It could have been anyone."

"But it could have been Alexandra," Tom said. "Please read it." He lowered his head so that he could focus on the floor.

Leslie began to read:

"Hi, my name is Michelle Radley. I work at the Pigalle Club in London. Last month Jack Lukeman was playing. It was a busy night, two of the girls were off sick, and the toilet attendant didn't show up. There was a young girl who'd had too much to drink and she was getting sick in the toilets. I was called in to help her but the club was so busy I couldn't really stay with her. So a woman who looked exactly like the one in your picture said that she would. We talked for a minute or two. She said her name was Alex. She really did look like the woman in your picture, but she was thinner and her hair was shorter. When I returned to the toilet, she and the sick girl were gone. My phone number is 20 77326531 if you want to talk about it. Jack Lukeman is returning to play a show on Saturday, March 1, and I'll be working so I'll watch out for her. If you would like to give me a telephone number, I could phone you if she returns. Regards, Michelle."

Leslie looked at Tom, who was still staring at the floor. She looked at Jane, who was wiping her hands on a tea towel for a little longer than necessary.

"This could be it," Jane said, and she threw the towel on the counter.

"It's her," Tom said.

"Hang on," Leslie said, "hang on one second. This is a thin, short-haired woman who just looks like Alexandra."

"She called herself Alex," Jane said.

"But Tom told us she hasn't called herself Alex since she was a teenager," Leslie said.

"But helping some drunken girl in the toilet is something she'd do," Tom said.

"It's something a lot of people would do," Leslie said. "I really think it's important not to get ahead of ourselves here. We should just pass the information on to the police and let them handle it."

Tom looked up from the floor. "I'm going to London for the show."

"I'll come with you," Jane said.

"Really?" he asked.

"Absolutely." *It's the least I can do considering my sister has gone AWOL.*

"Oh for God's sake," Leslie said. "You pair haven't listened to one word I've said."

"We have," Tom said. "Look, Leslie, I will pass on the e-mail to the police, but I can't just leave it at that. We're so close!"

"But you might not be," Leslie said.

"But we might be," Jane said.

"I give up!" Leslie got up and cut herself another slice of carrot cake even though she'd been watching what she ate since Elle had sat her down in a coffee shop the week before Christmas and told her that not only did she need her hair dyed and styled and a complete new wardrobe, but she also needed to lose a minimum of six pounds. When Leslie had argued that she was happy the way she was, Elle was having none of it and asked her new friend one simple question: "Do you ever want to have sex again?"

Leslie had thought about this question for a long time before answering, because she really wasn't sure. It had been so long since she'd had sex with anything that wasn't battery operated that it seemed like it might be a little too much work. After serious consideration, during which time Elle had managed to finish her cappuccino, order another one, go to the loo, and send two text messages, she had admitted that yes, she probably would like to have sex again in her lifetime.

"Well then," Elle said, pointing to Leslie's head and moving her finger downward toward her toes, "sort yourself out."

"I'm not that bad!" Leslie argued.

Elle agreed that she wasn't that bad, going so far as to comment that in fact for a woman in her early forties she looked quite good.

"Thanks a lot," Leslie said, once again wondering why she was allowing herself to be friends with a girl in her twenties.

Elle smiled at her and, after rummaging through her bag for a few minutes, took out a bent card that was covered in bag dirt. She cleaned it off and straightened it out and handed it to Leslie. "That's my hairdresser. She'll take care of you."

After thinking about it for a week, Leslie had decided to get her hair done but had put it off until after Christmas to avoid the crowds. Her appointment was for later that afternoon. She halved the slice of cake and then ate half of the half because since Elle had mentioned her thickened midriff she'd become conscious of it.

"Where is Elle?" she asked after pinching some crumbs together and popping them in her mouth.

"Working," Jane lied.

"I'm really looking forward to her exhibition in two weeks," Leslie said. "Elle showed me some of the paintings last time we were here, and they are stunning and just a little bit frightening. Love them."

"Yeah," Jane said, "she's a genius." She said this while nodding. *Stop nodding, Jane.*

"Would it be okay if I called in on her for just a moment before we leave?" Leslie asked.

"No," Jane said, "I'm sorry. She's just really busy with the exhibition pieces."

"But I thought she had finished those paintings," Tom said. "Is she working on the Missing Exhibition already? I thought you were still waiting for permission from the families."

"No, she still has some work to do for this upcoming show—she's a perfectionist. And we are still waiting for permission from the families, although that man missing from Clare, Joe something, his family has come back and would love to be involved." *Oh Christ, I hope she comes home in time for the show in two weeks.*

"Okay," Leslie said, "I'll call her later."

"Fine," Jane said, "but don't be surprised if she doesn't answer. When she's in the zone the whole world could be collapsing around her and she wouldn't notice."

"Right," Leslie said, and sensing Jane was nervous she let it go at that. "Probably better to leave her be."

Jane nodded enthusiastically. *Stop nodding, Jane.*

Tom left soon after. He had promised to go online to book the tickets and accommodation for the London gig and insisted on paying for it. Jane had then insisted that they both take home slices of carrot cake, chocolate log, and a biscuit cake she spotted in the fridge that she'd made two days previously and forgotten about.

Tom hugged both women before he left. "Thank you," he said, "thank you. Thank you. Thank you." He sighed and smiled, then turned and walked down the steps, leaving Leslie and Jane standing together at the door. They waved to him as he drove off.

When he was out of sight, Leslie turned to Jane. "So what's really going on with Elle?"

For somebody who didn't spend a lot of time with people, she was incredibly intuitive.

"You'd better come back in," Jane said.

Jane brewed another pot of coffee and began by telling Leslie about Elle's New Year's Eve and Vincent's note.

"Good God," Leslie said. "Could she go to prison for that?"

"I have to meet that sniveling little snot Vincent next week to sort out compensation. Basically if we buy him a new car he won't press charges, and if he doesn't press charges hopefully the DPP won't either."

" '*I want you, I need you, but let's face it, I'm never going to love you,*' " Leslie repeated, shaking her head in disbelief. "Just when I thought it was safe to go back in the water."

Jane explained her sister's inexplicable passion for the man who had mistreated her from the day they met and how, having an inexplicable passion of her own for the father of her child, she understood and sympathized with her sister's misguided love.

"You can't choose whom you love," she said.

Leslie thought about it and it made her crave more cake. After that, Jane explained that whenever things got on top of Elle she would hang the GONE FISHING sign on her front door. This signaled that she needed peace and quiet, time away from everything and everyone, and until she was ready to face the world again she would be off the radar. Leslie was aghast that Elle would just disappear like that and couldn't understand why Jane indulged her.

"That's extremely selfish," she said. "What if you need her?"

"I leave a voice message and hope she picks it up," she admitted before dismissing Leslie's concerns, noting she was simply happy that Elle gave her a clear indication of what she was up to so she didn't have to worry. Although of course she did worry, but not as much as she would if Elle disappeared without warning.

It took Leslie a few minutes to realize the significance of Elle's latest fishing trip, and it became clear only when Jane recounted the time two years earlier when she had failed to return for two months.

"Will she paint while she's away?" Leslie asked.

"She hasn't before," Jane admitted.

"But the Missing Exhibition is scheduled for April!"

"She'll be home, it's important, she'll get it done," Jane said, but Leslie could tell she wasn't convinced.

"And if she doesn't?"

"Well, we'll just have to find Alexandra in a club in March," Jane said, and she knew her proposal sounded weak.

"It's not her," Leslie said, "and even if it was it doesn't mean she's going to turn up in the same place again."

"Don't be so negative."

"Can't help it—it's my default setting," Leslie said, and smiled.

"Elle will come home," Jane said. "Hopefully in time to deliver twelve stunning paintings, and if not we'll sort it out. I'll sort it out."

"I should warn the Jack camp."

"No, don't say anything, please just give it a week! Let's get over this exhibition first and then we can worry about what happens in April."

Leslie nodded and asked Jane how she would cope if Elle didn't turn up for her own exhibition.

"Actually, sometimes it works out better," Jane admitted. "In case you hadn't noticed, my sister can be a bit of a handful."

Leslie had noticed, and so the conversation ended there. It was too late to get her hair done, so she phoned the hairdresser to reschedule while enjoying a brisk walk through the park to negate at least some of the cake she'd inhaled at Jane's.

Tom's business was suffering and not just because he'd lost interest in it. His company had finished a large development in South Dublin in mid-2007, and he'd been looking for more land since then, but planning was getting tougher and, if he were to be honest, the houses in the development he'd just finished hadn't been as quick to sell as those in the previous two. He had decided to bide his time and wait for the right project, and then Alexandra had disappeared and after that the only thing he'd been looking for was her. He'd lost most of his building staff in the second quarter of '07, retaining only a few men for snagging. The plumbers and electricians he'd contracted had moved on to work with others, and by the time he'd gotten stuck in a lift his company had been reduced to himself and Jeanette in the office. It was quite clear that the business was dead, and Jeanette received her severance pay a week later. The risk-taking and swagger that were needed to build and preside over the successful business he'd built from nothing had left with Alexandra, and in an environment where growth rates were falling and the clouds of economic recession were gathering, Tom Kavanagh had simply lost his nerve. After ten years of blood, sweat, and tears, when the doors of his company finally closed on Christmas week, Tom walked away without even looking back once. Tom's only focus was finding his wife. He spent hours online on his wife's website, blogging and adding pictures just as Leslie had shown him. He looked at missing sites every day and made calls to shelters all over Ireland and the UK and sent them e-mails attached with pictures of Alexandra's face. He ensured that Interpol had all his wife's details and insisted on following up on every tiny piece of information the police were investigating and was so hands-on that in the end his liaison officer, Patricia Lowe, had to tell him in no uncertain terms to back off. He still handed out flyers and tacked them to mailboxes and trees.

When he wasn't searching, he visited with Breda and told her about all the things people were doing to get Alexandra back.

"You're a good man," she'd say, "and we will get her back."

Breda was sure that Alexandra was alive and well and just a little lost, and she knew this because she'd prayed to God to keep Alexandra safe and in sixty-odd years God had yet to let her down. Tom hadn't believed in God until his wife disappeared, but afterward he found his mother-in-law's trust and hope comforting.

"She's not alone, Tom," she said over and over. "She's never alone."

Alexandra's father didn't talk about God or anything at all. Instead he sat in the garden and smoked one Marlboro after another. In the evenings he went out to the pub with his friends and they talked about football and politics and the state of the world and anything but his missing daughter because every time he thought about her his guts twisted, his head ached, and his heart threatened to stop dead.

Tom always made it his business to go into the garden and say a few words to Ben, and Ben was polite but a little cold in his response.

"How are you doing?" Tom would ask.

"Fine."

"It's freezing out here. Are you sure you wouldn't be better off inside?"

"I'm fine."

"Breda seems good today."

"She's fine."

"Can I do anything?"

"You're doing all you can."

"I'm sorry."

Tom would end every short interlude with his father-in-law with the words "I'm sorry," and every time Ben nodded and said nothing at all.

• • •

In the car on the way home from Jane's, Tom wondered whether or not he should call his in-laws with the good news, but then he thought better of it. He'd wait, and maybe in March he'd be bringing his wife home. He knew in his heart that Leslie was right to be cautious, and he knew that the likelihood of finding Alexandra in a club in London was a million to one, but he didn't care because a million to one was better odds than a million to none.

Tom had never been much of a drinker, but since his wife vanished he drank every night because he couldn't sleep without being intoxicated, and even then he was restless, kicking and sometimes yelling out. When Tom didn't drink, he'd lie in bed afraid to close his eyes for fear that he'd go to the dark place. The scenarios were always different and yet they were the same: his wife was hurt, she needed him, and he wasn't there. In one Alexandra was tied up and dirty. She was facedown on the floor and her arms were twisted behind her back. Her face was streaked with dirt, blood, and tears, she had a hole in her head that was caked in blood, and she was crying out, calling his name, and over her a shadow loomed, a monster playing with a knife, and Alexandra would beg Tom to find her before the monster cut into her again. In another he'd see her in a tiny, windowless room with concrete walls and a black steel door with a tiny flap at the bottom. She was in the corner hugging the wall, and there was nothing but silence and a tray still full of slop that Alexandra couldn't eat, and she was so thin her bones stood out, and she'd call to him and tell him that if he didn't find her soon she'd be gone. There was the one where she was drugged and tied to a bed and men were coming and going, screwing her, and her head would roll and her red raw eyes would call to him to save her, but he couldn't because he couldn't see where she was. He'd claw at his face and hit the side of his head, and he'd roar and bawl and scream and rock until he was so tired that all he could do was lie so very still and stare at her smiling picture hanging on the wall. And with each night that passed, he'd live another and more twisted and painful nightmare.

Since Tom's secretary, Jeanette, had lost her job three weeks earlier she had called on him several times on the pretext of checking up on him. The first time he was drunk and wearing what appeared to be uncomfortably snug tracksuit bottoms.

"I didn't know you even owned a tracksuit."

"I don't. They're Alexandra's."

"Why?"

"I wanted to walk a mile in her shoes, but they didn't fit."

"How drunk are you?"

"Very."

She'd come into his house and run a bath, and when he refused to get into the bath she insisted, and her insistence and freakish upper-body strength ensured that ten minutes later he was soaking in bath oils while she ran around and cleaned his kitchen and sitting room of take-out cartons and empty bottles. He'd fallen asleep and she woke him, and when he realized that he was naked and in the bath he became embarrassed, but she made light of it and handed him a towel.

"I've seen worse on-site," she said, and she wasn't lying, having caught a plasterer taking a dump behind a tree, and when she closed her eyes she could still see ass hair and excrement. She'd also walked in on the bricklayer Barry Brady receiving a blow job on his lunch hour, not once but twice, and he was a pig about it, winking at her and asking if she wanted to join in, and even thinking about it made her want to go back in time and punch him.

Tom asked her to leave the bathroom while he covered

himself up, and he briefly wondered how to dissuade her from coming to his house again.

Jeanette had worked for Tom for four years, and she'd developed a crush on him within a week of her joining his company, and of course he knew it. Before Alexandra went missing, Tom was warm and funny. He was the kind of man and boss who didn't need to feel that he was superior to those working for him. He'd drop a cup of coffee on her desk as he was passing, always remembering how she took it—no milk, one sugar—and every now and then he'd bring her something sweet. It wasn't just her—he did it for the others too. In fact, when she thought about it, for a man who ran a profitable company he spent a lot of time making coffee. He would listen to her when she spoke, and he'd tell her what a great job she was doing. He wasn't available back then, he wasn't even looking for sex. More was the pity, because Jeanette would have done him on the photocopier week one if he'd asked her.

At least that's what she'd told her pals Lily and Davey in the pub the night before she'd decided to visit him at his home that first time.

"Uncomfortable," Davey said, "and technically impossible. He'd be the one doing you, and you'd only be leaning on it. But I suppose you could say that you'd invited him to do you *over* the photocopier."

"Shut up, Davey!" Lily said.

"I was only saying."

"Yeah, well, don't say. Go on, Jeanette, you'd have done him on the photocopier week one . . ."

"Well, that was it, really."

Lily punched Davey in the arm. "You always do that! Interrupt someone when she's saying something interesting just to say something totally boring, throwing off the person who actually has something to say!" She punched him again.

Davey rubbed his arm and then said something interesting. "Okay then, elephant in the room: he offed his missus."

Jeanette didn't believe it possible. "No way."

"Of course he did. Nobody just disappears."

"People disappear all the time, faggot!" Lily said.

Jeanette shook her head. "Nothing could make me believe that he did anything to her."

"Well, my advice to you is to stay away until we know that for sure," Davey said.

Lily nodded her agreement. "He has a point. Better safe than headless in a suitcase floating down the Dodder."

Jeanette had no intention of staying away, and even though the sparkle in Tom's eye had been replaced with a terrible sadness, God help poor Jeanette, she fell deeper in love.

She waited for Tom to emerge from the bathroom, and when he did and he was clean and his house was clean and there was real food cooking in his oven and she was talking about the job interview she'd just had and looking for some music, he felt normal and calm, and it was nice, if only for a while. When he sobered up, she poured some wine, and they sat together and ate. When they'd polished off the bottle and were halfway through the second, and after she'd served a dessert that neither of them ate, she gazed at him across the table and slowly and hesitantly took his hand in hers.

"What more can I do?" she asked. While retaining his hand, she walked around the table and sat on a chair at his side, and now he was facing her with his hand still in hers, and her other hand was sliding up his thigh. His pulse raced, and her heart was racing too, and she asked him again, "What can I do?" and he was staring into her face and eyes, and the kitchen fell away as he reached for the back of her head and pulled her into him, and they kissed.

The next night in the pub she reenacted it for Lily and Davey.

"Jesus, that's like in a film," Lily said.

"Exactly like in a film," Jeanette said. And she believed herself.

Davey was less impressed. "You're playing with fire." But he was ignored.

"What happened then?" Lily asked.

Tom had pulled Jeanette onto the floor, and they kissed and her pants were off before she could say, "Take my pants off," and his were around his ankles and he was on top of her and inside her, and their tops were still on and it was over quickly, which was a good thing because the tiles were freezing. When he was done, she could see his regret and shame, and so she acted fast before he could ask her to leave and file their encounter under "mistake." They both pulled up their pants. She took two cigarettes out of her bag and lit both of them. She asked him to sit next to her on the floor. He complied out of a combination of guilt and a genuine desire for a cigarette, despite having been off them for five years.

When he was sitting and puffing, she straddled him.

"I know what you're thinking," she said.

"I doubt it," Tom had said.

"You're thinking, 'Jeanette is a nice girl and I'm grateful for the tumble, which was badly needed, but how the hell do I get her out of here without making her cry?'"

He shook his head, and she smiled. "Something like that," he admitted.

"I like you," she said.

"I'm a mess."

"I know." She shook her head. "I'm not blind."

"I'm married."

"She's not here."

"Please go home," he said, and she knew she'd spoken out of turn.

"Okay." She nodded. "I'm sorry." And she *was* sorry. She was sorry he was so sad, and she was sorry for poor Alexandra, and she was sorry for herself because although she was desperate for him to love her, she knew he never would. *I had to try,* she thought as she closed the door behind her.

"Jesus, you could have waited," Davey said the next night.

"He's right," Lily agreed.

Jeanette knew she'd blown it, so a phone call from Tom came as a shock. He phoned her from his car on his way back from Jane's.

"Tom?"

"Good news," he said. "I have a lead on Alexandra. It's not much, but it's something."

"Oh that's great," she said, brightening. "I hope it works out." She meant it.

"Look, I wanted to apologize for that night," he said. "I should never have done that."

Jeanette thought about how kind he was to call. After all, she had preyed on him—he had been vulnerable, lost, and drunk, and she'd seduced him. *God, I love you.* "It wasn't you, it was me," she said, "and I appreciate you apologizing, but you've nothing to apologize for."

"I wasn't that drunk."

Jeanette's heart leaped a little.

"Could we be friends?" he asked.

"Yeah," she said, "I'd love that."

"Would you like to come over tonight?"

"I'd love to."

When she put the phone down, she jumped around the place, because even if Tom genuinely thought that he was looking for a friend, he wasn't, and he might be naïve enough to think the night would end with a kiss on the cheek, but she wasn't.

I need to shave. Whoohoooooooooo!

Jeanette arrived soaked to the skin. It had been raining on and off since six o'clock, and she had left her second umbrella in a month on the bus. Tom opened the door, smiling. She shook herself off in the hall before noticing that he was wearing an apron.

"What's going on?" she asked, following him into the kitchen.

"I cooked." He grabbed a pot holder and a large fork, opened the oven door, and turned a roasting leg of lamb.

"I can see that," she said, sitting at his counter while he opened some wine. She poured it into two glasses and handed him one.

He clinked his glass against hers. "I'm going to find her," he said.

"Alexandra?"

"No—Amelia Earhart," he said, and he grinned the way he used to grin before he lost his wife.

She wondered who Amelia Earhart was while he tended to the vegetables.

Jeanette drank until her wineglass was empty, then held out the glass for some more. Tom topped it off.

"I've met these women," he said, "and they're amazing, they're helping me. I don't even know them."

"That's weird. Why?"

"Jane was Alexandra's best friend years ago when they were

kids, and her sister, Elle, is an artist and she's going to do an exhibition. She's painting the faces of missing people. She's already painted Alexandra and it's really beautiful. And Leslie, she's set up an incredible website, and they've got Jack Lukeman on board and now this lead in London—"

"Jack Lukeman the singer? What is he? A part-time private eye?" She was being sarcastic, and although Tom noticed, he didn't care.

"No, he's going to sing at the exhibition. Jane says it will increase media interest."

"Well, it sounds like you've got a lot of new friends, so why did you call me?"

"I missed you."

He wasn't lying. He had become very fond of Jeanette during the four years they had worked together, and if he was really honest with himself he missed the attention she gave him. He missed feeling like a man, a sexual being, and even though he promised himself that he would never allow what had happened before to happen again, it was nice to be around someone who was attracted to him. Tom missed many things about his wife, and one of the things he missed most was being wanted.

"I missed you too," she said, and in her head she was singing, *"Here comes the bride, all dressed in white . . ."*

Later, after they'd indulged in passionate sex, the kind of sex that Jeanette had always suspected Tom was capable of, they lay there in silence and darkness just breathing.

"What are you thinking?" she asked.

"It's blissfully quiet in here," he said, pointing to his head.

She smiled at him and leaned over and kissed his cheek. "You're welcome," she said.

She went into the bathroom to take a shower, and he

reminisced about the last time he had lain in bed and listened to the shower running; his wife had been singing "I Can't Stand the Rain" and attempting a very bad impression of Tina Turner. Tom closed his eyes, just as he had done when he was having sex, and for the second time that night he pretended the woman who had been in his bed and was now in his shower was his wife, and for the first time in thirty weeks and one day, Tom slept peacefully.

6

"Little Man"

Take the world off your shoulders,
little man, little man, little man.

Jack L, *Universe*

February 2008

Elle had been lying in bed for twenty days. Ten days after New Year's Eve she had taken a taxi to a hotel in Kildare. When she arrived, someone took her bag out of the car as she paid the fare. She signed her name on the form the receptionist handed her, took her key, and followed the man with her bag up to the third floor and into her room. She tipped him, and he left. She undressed, put a DO NOT DISTURB sign on the door, and got into bed with the curtains drawn, and the only time she had gotten out of bed in those twenty days was to pee, apart from the times the maids came in. They knocked every second or third day, and she'd get out of her bed and sit on the toilet while they cleaned the room, and when they were finished she'd get back into bed while they cleaned the bathroom. Some days she ate something small, and some days she didn't eat at all. The television remained off, and days and nights blended into one. Some days she was numb and without any kind of coherent thought; other days her mind raced so much that her head hurt and she felt the need to put pressure on her ears. Her phone remained off. There were days she cried rivers; other days she simply breathed in and out, in and out, in and out, each breath becoming more and more laborious until every cell in her body hurt, so that even lifting her arm became almost impossible.

The manager knocked on her door after she'd refused the maids access for the sixth day in a row. He waited for a response but was met with silence, and so he knocked again but either she was ignoring him or she was sleeping, so he knocked louder a third time and in her head and for the second time she screamed at him to go away. As the general manager didn't read minds, he made the decision to enter the room. He was accompanied by one of the receptionists to ensure that there was no misunderstanding as to the intention of his visit. He entered slowly with the girl following. Elle was lying on her side. He called out to her. She remained still. The girl seemed to be of a nervous disposition, so the general manager smiled at her to assure her everything was fine. He walked around the side of the bed, and Elle's eyes were open and staring. She was pale and, because the blankets were tucked under her neck, it was unclear whether or not she was breathing. The girl mistook her for a corpse and screamed. Elle moved her eyes to focus on the screaming girl, whose nervous disposition had been long ago blamed on her twin brother, who had often chased her while pretending to be a zombie. Seeing the corpse's eyes move sent her over the deep end, and so she screamed again loudly and ran out of the room and down the hall and stairs and out the front door of the hotel, leaving the general manager alone and decidedly uncomfortable. *Thanks for nothing, Sheena.*

"Are you all right, Miss Moore?" he asked.

"How many times have I told you to leave me alone today?"

"None."

"Are you deaf?"

"I'm not deaf."

"I just told you to leave me alone at least twice if not three times."

The general manager decided not to argue. "Is there someone I can call?"

Elle slowly raised herself up in the bed; the blanket dropped, revealing her naked breasts. The general manager turned red and looked away.

"If I wanted you to call someone I would have asked you to call someone," she said, letting the blanket rest at her waist.

The general manager turned from red to a funny purple color. He covered his eyes because he could still see her in the mirror and she knew he could still see her because she was watching him through that same mirror.

"Do you like what you see?" she asked.

"Sorry?" he said in a voice that had gone up one octave.

"My tits," she said. "Do you like them?"

The general manager did like them. She had a lovely rounded, pert, full pair of tits, but there was no way in the world he was going to say that, and he wasn't going to tell her he didn't like them either, so instead he did what any man in his right mind would do: he ignored the question.

"I'm sorry to disturb you," he said, "but we need to know that you are okay."

"Now you know."

"If there's anything we can do for you . . ."

"You can go away."

He nodded and left the room.

She lay back down, tucking the blanket up around her chin, and lay perfectly still in absolute darkness.

When capable of coherent thought, Elle reminisced about all the things about Vincent she had loved. His face: she had fallen in love with his face the first time she saw him across a crowded bar. It was a strong and pretty face, and he had an old man's eyes—deep, dark, chocolate eyes nestled behind lush eyelashes so thick and long that any woman or drag act would sell themselves for them. His curly brown hair: she loved that it was always messy and sexy and soft and loved putting her hands through it, playing with it. She loved his height: he was taller than her but not too tall, and they could always kiss comfortably even on the rare occasion she wore flats. She loved his hands: soft and manicured and always perfectly clean. She loved the things he did with his hands and how those hands made her feel. His laugh: when he laughed his eyes leaked water and he threw back his head and slapped his thigh, and it was a throaty and giddy giggly laugh that encouraged her to join in. His mind: she missed him reading passages out of newspapers and books to her, she missed watching him read his books and the way he screwed up his face when fully concentrating and bit at his thumb before turning the page. Vincent was never without a book, and all his jackets had pockets big enough to hold at least one. She missed the poetry that loving him had brought into her life. She missed the fights where they'd scream and roar at each other, where she'd smash a plate and he'd stamp his foot and punch the wall. She missed making up, ripping at each other's clothes and the heat between them and the way he often bit her lip and the feel of him inside her, his rhythm and the way he looked at her afterward when they lay still and sticky. She missed herself: the silly, giddy part of her that she shared only with him.

He had tried to end it in China, and deep down she had known that he loved what she represented rather than who she was. He was an out-of-work model studying design at night, and she was a successful artist, and with success came a lifestyle he had become accustomed to and, in a small town like Dublin, Elle was a big fish, ensuring minor celebrity status and entrance to every VIP room in the city. Vincent loved the champagne lifestyle, not Elle. He had never loved Elle, as the note said. He had wanted her, she had always been certain of that, he most definitely had needed her as she had paid for his lifestyle for years, but he was never going to love her no matter what she did to keep him. China had been a reprieve, and ever since she'd been waiting for the other shoe to drop.

Elle's love had died, and it was all she could do to keep breathing.

The hairdresser put her hands through Leslie's short crop, and when Leslie confirmed that she had cut her own hair for quite a few years, the hairdresser admitted that the thought had certainly crossed her mind and then called over a fellow professional so that they could confer on what was the best course of action to minimize the damage Leslie had done.

"God almighty, did you use a bowl?" the other woman said.

"No."

"Well, you may as well have. I've seen Trappist monks with better hair."

"What's your name?" Leslie asked.

"Sophie."

"Well, Sophie, if I wanted to be insulted I'd sing for Simon Cowell. As it is, I just want my hair restyled."

"Fine," Sophie said curtly.

"And Sophie?"

"Yes?"

"No talking."

"So you don't want me to tell you what we're going to do?"

Leslie could tell that Sophie wanted to slap her.

"After that," she said.

The first woman walked away, leaving Sophie to it. Sophie explained to Leslie that she could no longer get away with black hair because of her age and the pallor of her skin, but she could give her a nice copper tone. Leslie was fine with that. Sophie called over two young girls, Esther and Julie, and explained what she wanted them to do. Then she walked away and they got to work. As instructed, they didn't address Leslie. Instead they chatted about an apartment block that had gone up near the salon and whether or not one of them should buy a one-bed apartment in the inner city with her boyfriend, Joseph, for €390,000, especially as it was possible only with a 100 percent mortgage.

"You should just go for it," Esther said.

"Yeah, I mean, what have I got to lose?" Julie said.

"Are you insane?" Leslie asked, and the two girls looked at her in the mirror.

"What do you mean?" Julie asked.

"How long have you been with Joseph?"

"A year."

"What age are you?"

"Twenty-one. I'll be twenty-two in April."

"What rate are you buying your mortgage at?"

"Don't know."

"How much will you be paying back per month?"

"No clue."

"What's your rush?"

"I need to get on the property ladder."

"You're twenty-one. You've got another ten years to get on the property ladder."

"Yeah, well, I want to do it now."

"Look, it's none of my business, but around here, well, let's be honest, it's a dump. You don't want to pay three hundred and ninety K for a one-bed apartment in a dump, especially when you're paying back a one hundred percent mortgage, no doubt on a noncompetitive rate, and with a boy you've been with for only one year. It's madness."

"It's not a kip around here," Julie said indignantly. "I grew up around here. My ma lives around the corner."

"What happens if you can't afford the mortgage?"

"But we can."

"What happens if mortgage rates go up and you can't afford the mortgage?"

"We're going for a fixed mortgage," Julie said, delighted she could answer at least one of the annoying woman's questions.

"What if you lose your job?" Leslie asked.

"I'm not going to," Julie said, looking around uncomfortably.

"What if you split up with your boyfriend?"

"We're happy."

"Happy now, but in six months' time, with a ridiculously large mortgage to pay, in an apartment the size of a box of matches, you might not be. In fact, if I was a betting woman I'd put a hundred euros on it not lasting the year."

Julie started to cry.

"What is wrong with you?" Esther asked, and she took Julie into the break room.

Sophie reappeared and silently resumed dyeing Leslie's hair.

"Is Julie okay?" Leslie asked. "I was only trying to help."

"No talking," Sophie said.

Leslie nodded her head. *Fair enough.*

When the dye was finally washed out after what seemed like an eternity, the girl who'd originally consulted with her returned with scissors in hand. She worked quickly and silently, and Leslie relaxed. She blow-dried it and fixed it with a little gel. Then she stood back, and Leslie looked at herself.

Despite being forty and having a few age spots on her face and chest, she still had a tight jawline and protruding cheekbones, and the copper worked against her brown eyes and the short elfin style suited her facial features. The girl was smiling. Some other girls, not Julie, came over and all agreed they had done a fantastic job, and Leslie agreed.

Not bad. Not bad at all.

Bolstered by her new look, she stopped at a makeup counter in Brown Thomas. The girl did her makeup while highlighting to her what she was doing and using to cover up her troublesome areas. She'd asked for something natural, and the girl did as instructed: dark eyes, light lips, flawless skin. By the end of it she looked and felt like a new woman and was so impressed she ended up spending more than €200 on the products the girl recommended despite knowing that she was never going to be able to re-create the look at home.

It was after five. She decided to grab something quick to eat upstairs in BT's before she headed to the pub where Jim would be waiting. When she'd invited Jim to Elle's opening she'd felt good about it, but now that the time had come she felt slightly regretful. It had been so long since she'd seen him, a lifetime had passed, and they had never really been that close to begin with. *What the hell am I at?* she asked herself as she queued for a table.

Jane spent the day running around. She started by picking up boxes of wine at the wine merchant's. She dropped the wine off at the catering company and then went to the gallery and hung the paintings. After that she went to a music shop and picked up some music she deemed appropriate for the theme of Elle's exhibition. As the theme was Angels and Demons, most of whom were copulating, the music she picked was a mix of metal and classical.

After that she got her hair done, and after that she returned to the gallery to set out tables and to load the CD player. When the place was spic-and-span, the paintings secure on the walls, and the tables ready for the caterer, she drove home to shower and change.

She heard Kurt laugh in the kitchen, and then she heard Dominic's voice, and then he was laughing too, and she couldn't remember the last time she and her son had laughed together. She entered the kitchen, and Dominic stood up and surveyed her before hugging her.

"You look great."

She smiled and told him he didn't look so bad himself. She inquired as to what was so funny, but neither her son nor his father was willing to share the joke. *In-joke bastards.*

"Are you hungry?" Dominic asked.

"I'm not cooking for you. I'm too busy."

"I know. Kurt told me you have the exhibition tonight, so I brought pizza."

"Ah, thanks but no, I'll just have a coffee."

Kurt checked the pizza, which was heating in the oven. It was ready, and he plated up. Dominic and Kurt ate their pizza, and Jane drank her coffee.

"So Elle's gone fishing?" Dominic said.

"Afraid so. Still, it's probably for the best. I've heard a rumor that Pat Hogan is coming."

"Who's Pat Hogan?" Kurt said with his mouth full.

"Don't talk with a full mouth," she said. "He's a critic Elle threatened to stab when she was at art college."

"Yeah, well, that wasn't yesterday," said Dominic. "I'm sure it's all forgotten."

"No. It's funny—he loves her work but, my God, she hates him."

"Dad, tell Mum about your new bike," Kurt said, and then he opened his mouth wide to show his mother that his mouth had been empty of food before he had spoken.

"Funny," she said. "What's this about a bike?"

Dominic was grinning like a Cheshire cat. "It's a Harley."

"A road king," Kurt said.

"Black cherry."

"And black pearl."

"It's a real beaut."

"I'd swap my dick for one," Kurt said.

Dominic laughed and Jane covered her ears and smiled.

"How's Bella?" Jane asked.

"She's not talking to me," Dominic said.

"Because you're a selfish prick who nearly killed himself on a motorbike a year ago and, having promised faithfully that you would never get on a bike again, you've gone behind her back and bought a Harley?"

"Got it in one."

"Jesus, Dominic, what is wrong with you?"

He grinned at her. "Ah, come on, Janey, Bella's already giving me hell. Can't you just be happy for me?"

She smiled at him. "Okay, I'll be happy for you. Congratulations on your new bike. Please don't cripple or kill yourself."

"Ah, thanks for worrying."

"I'm not."

"You are." He winked at her.

She smiled and blushed a little. *Oh grow up, Jane.*

"Jane, Jane, Jane? Are you there? Jane?" Rose's voice came over the intercom.

Dominic stood up and pressed the button. "Hi, Rose."

"Who let you in?" Rose asked.

"My son." Dominic smiled.

"I want Jane."

"I'm sorry. Jane is currently not available. Is there something I can do for you?"

"You can go back under the rock you've climbed out from."

"I miss you too, Rose."

"I want Jane."

Jane stood up and pushed Dominic out of the way. "Yes, Rose."

"Have you heard from Elle?"

"No."

Rose hung up.

Dominic turned to Jane. "So are you going to invite me to this shindig or what?"

"Don't you have a home to go to?"

"Maybe tomorrow when she's cooled down."

"Nice one, Dad. I'll make up the spare room," Kurt said.

Dominic reached into his pocket, took out a twenty-euro

note, and handed it to him. Kurt pocketed the money and headed out the door and toward the spare room.

"You don't mind?" Dominic said.

"I don't seem to have a choice." But she was smiling, indicating that she didn't mind. In fact, it was obvious she was really happy.

Get a grip, Jane, he married someone else, she thought as she made her way up to the shower.

Leslie walked into the bar, and despite the fact that it had been at least ten years since she'd seen him, she recognized him immediately. His head was down and he was reading a newspaper, and when she tapped him on the shoulder he managed to appear slightly surprised that she'd shown up. He stood, and he was shorter than she remembered. They hugged awkwardly.

"You're taller than I remember," he said.

"Heels," she said, and she pointed to her brand-new black wedge heels.

"Jeepers, the last time I saw you, you wore nothing but sneakers."

She didn't tell him that this was the first time in years she had worn anything but MBTs, which basically were posh sneakers that made her work harder when she walked.

They sat down, and he asked her if she wanted a drink, and she said a white wine would be lovely, and he went to get one, and she was alone waiting for him to come back, and her heart was racing and her palms were sweating. He had aged around the eyes, and he'd shaved his head. He was thinner than she remembered, but he still had his dimples, the ones that had made Imelda go weak at the knees, and that warm smile she had loved so much.

What do we talk about? I hope I don't make him cry. That last time

I saw him I made him cry. Why did I do that? What's wrong with me?

As it turned out, they had little trouble finding things to talk about. He came back with her wine and she asked him what he had been reading, and he told her and they talked about it, and then they moved on to books, and they shared a taste in books and so that gave them at least another hour of great conversation. Neither liked the cinema, so they discussed why they didn't like it and then Leslie attempted to persuade Jim of the benefits of broadband. She couldn't believe he was not yet converted.

"So you've never sent an e-mail?"

"No."

"That's amazing."

"Is it?"

"And you've never surfed the Net?"

"I wouldn't even know how to. Besides, I don't have the knees for it." He laughed at his own joke.

"If only that were funny, Jim." She shook her head. "You're a dinosaur, my friend."

"Sorry, I'll try to do better." He smiled. She had called him a friend. Imelda would be happy.

"What about you?" he asked. "Still thinking about surgery?"

She nodded. "I've been to three specialists since we last spoke, and I'm doing it."

It was strange that Jim was the only one she had told, but then again, it wasn't that strange. After all, who would understand better than he? She was hardly going to tell her new friends, and she didn't have anyone else in her life.

"When?" he asked.

"July. The first of July." She nodded. "That's the date they've given me."

"It's going to be hard. You're going to need help."

"I'm going from the hospital to a hospice," she said, smiling. "It's a really nice place. It's going to be fine. I'm a big girl."

"You're not as strong as you think you are. They're going to take your womb and your breasts"—he hunched his shoulders—"and that's not fine."

For the first time since Leslie had decided on surgery she felt her eyes fill. It had been such a relief to think that she would no longer be burdened by an imaginary time bomb ticking loudly in her head. She would be free, and that was bigger than a pair of breasts and a womb she was almost done with anyway. And still, those words and the way Jim said it—"They're going to take your womb and your breasts"—struck her; she'd never really let herself focus on that before. A fat tear dropped from her eyelid onto her cheek and slid down to her chin. She stopped it with her hand before it made its way to her neck.

Jim saw her single tear and made no apology for causing it. He needed her to understand the gravity of what she was doing because, although he agreed with her decision, knowing her of old it had occurred to him early on that she wouldn't allow herself to think or talk about the pain it caused her. They sat in silence and sipped their drinks.

After a while Leslie looked Jim in the eye. "Do you remember your wedding day?"

"Like it was yesterday."

"Imelda insisted I be bridesmaid, and even though I kicked and screamed she got her way. She made me wear peach, which is a color I detest, and the hairdresser piled my hair so high on my head that I looked like Marge Simpson."

"I remember." He smiled at the memory.

"We got dressed together, we got our makeup done together, we drank a glass of champagne, and we laughed at my dress even though she swore that she loved it. We talked about the future and all the babies she was going to have."

"Oh, don't," he said, and he closed his eyes.

"I wrote her a poem, and she laughed so hard she held her ribs." She smiled at the memory. " *Imelda sighed, Imelda cried, the day she met Jim the Ride / He was short, she was tall, he took her up against the wall.*' " She thought for a second. " *'She had style, he had wit, he really thought he was the shit!*' " She laughed a little. "I can't remember . . ."

" *'Love is blind, that's what they say, it must be, it's her wedding day!*' " Jim said, grinning.

"I can't believe you remembered!" Leslie laughed.

"She repeated it often enough."

"Yeah, well, I'm no poet laureate, but you must admit it has a kind of bawdy charm even if I do say so myself," she said. "And after the church we all walked through a wood to the reception, and it was such a hot day—do you remember how blue the sky was?"

"Not a cloud in the sky."

"And the band played all the best songs and we all danced all night."

"It was a great day."

"It was my sister's wedding, and I can honestly say it was my best day. They may be taking my breasts and my womb, but for the first time I feel like I have a chance of having my own best day."

Jim nodded and raised his glass and she raised hers.

"I'll drink to that!" he said, and they clinked glasses. "And, Leslie, when you need someone, and you will, promise you'll call me."

"Why?"

"Because of a promise I made a long time ago."

"Okay, I will."

On the walk to the gallery they talked about relationships, and Jim told Leslie about the women who had been in his life after Imelda. There was Mary, a librarian from Meath. She was a fan of musicals and Shakespeare, and according to Jim she was passive-aggressive. They had lasted eight months, but it had been only a year after Imelda, and although she was a great cook and looked like a slightly chunkier and seriously paler Sophia Loren, his heart hadn't been in it. Then there was Angela. She was funny, smart, attractive, and kind. She also had a psycho ex-husband and four kids under the age of ten so, after he'd been punched in the face on the street and warned to leave her alone or he'd be joining his wife in the ground, he had decided he needed space. She and the kids had moved to the UK a month later and he hadn't heard from her since. Then the Russian woman he had told her about on their first phone call.

"I really thought we might have a future," he said. "So what about you?"

Leslie laughed as he followed her across the street.

"Well?" he said.

"No one."

"No one! In ten years there has been no one?"

"Eighteen years, but who's counting?"

"Simon was your last relationship?" Jim was aghast and wasn't too shy to reveal his astonishment. He slowed his pace and took her arm. "I know nuns who get more action than you."

"That's funny, because my hairdresser knew some Trappist monks with better haircuts. Coming up short against religious orders seems to be the theme of the day."

"I like your hair," he said.

She smiled. "Thanks."

They entered the gallery and were met by Jane, who was surprisingly calm and collected despite her sister's absence. Leslie introduced her to Jim, and they shook hands, and Jane complimented Leslie on looking stunning, which embarrassed her, and then she insisted they have a glass of wine and some savory snacks. The place was packed with people, and many were crowded around the paintings, so they decided to wait until the herd thinned. They sipped wine and chatted in the corner. Jane was doing a lovely job playing host. She was polite and pleasant to the three critics who came, and she made time for all five collectors who had been supporters of Elle's since the beginning of her career. She made excuses for Elle and no one seemed to mind particularly, apart from the photographer, who was clearly high on cocaine and annoyed that he hadn't been informed of Elle's absence, despite the fact that plenty of other minor celebrities were there ready to pose for him.

"This is a joke," he said to Jane. "Where the fuck is she?"

"Freddie," Jane said, "you're not Herb Ritts. Take photos, hand them in to the media desks, and shut up."

"That's my girl!" Dominic said from over Jane's shoulder. He was on his third glass of wine and was thoroughly enjoying his night.

Freddie stormed off and started to push a TV presenter and a rugby player together, pointing at them and shouting for them to move this way and that. They complied, and he moved on and pushed three blond socialites back against a wall. Jane made a mental note never to use him again.

Dominic put his arm around her, "Nice event," he said. "Good wine, good food, good music, and who could have guessed Metallica would work so well sandwiched in between Beethoven and Bach?"

"It's Rachmaninoff and Chopin."

He nodded and leaned in to whisper in her ear, "And who could have guessed Metallica would work so well sandwiched in between Rachmaninoff and Chopin? You say tomato—"

"Get off!" She pushed him away playfully.

Leslie appeared with Jim, and Jane made the introductions.

Jane had filled Dominic in on Alexandra's extraordinary disappearance and what they were doing to find her as they were driving to the gallery. He had been really shocked to hear the news—he had been friends with her before he had gotten Jane pregnant and dumped her at a disco, but after that Alexandra hadn't had any time for him even if Jane had. The last time he'd seen her had been just before she moved to Cork to go to college. His son had been two months old and he hadn't seen him yet. She had pushed a picture of Kurt onto his chest and told him to look at it. She had told him it was his son and he should be ashamed. He still had the photo, and he had been ashamed, but still it would be another four years before he'd have the courage to knock on Jane's door to visit with his child.

Dominic smiled at Leslie and told her that she was doing a really good thing in helping to find Alexandra. "She was a great girl," he said.

Later, when all the people had gone and Dominic and Jane were alone, he helped her clear tables and box up the unused glasses.

"I missed so much," he said out of nowhere.

"So much of what?" Jane asked, too tired to try to work out what was going on in his head.

"Of Kurt."

"Oh," she said, and she sighed. "Yes, you did."

"I was such an asshole."

"You still are."

She was smiling, so he knew she was playing with him.

"I regret every day I wasn't around."

"Well, at least you got to have a life."

"I really left you in it," he admitted. "If I could go back . . ."

"You'd do exactly the same thing."

"Don't say that, Janey."

"You know, I don't think Kurt even remembers a time when you weren't a part of his life."

"But you do," Dominic said.

Jane didn't want to talk about it, so she got busy sweeping the floor.

"For a girl forced out of school, you've done an amazing job here," he said.

"Thanks."

"And, for the record, I would change it if I could just so I could stop you from naming our kid after a heroin addict with a death wish."

Jane laughed. "That was unfortunate."

Jane drove, and Dominic fiddled with the CD player.

"Dido, no. Dixie Chicks, no and no. James Morrison, shoot me. Ray LaMontagne—Jesus, Jane. Jack Lukeman . . . remember that night?" He grinned.

"Yes, I remember." She blushed a little and laughed.

Dominic flicked along until he hit track 12. The track kicked off with a bass drum kicking. Dominic and Jane fell into silence, and she drove through the dark streets intermittently lit by fluorescent lights of different shapes and colors. The car was warm, and outside the rain came tumbling down. She turned on the windshield wipers, and Jack L began to sing.

Take me to the edge of town, watch the evening veil come down,
I'll tell you all my hopes and dreams, hold your
tongue 'cos I believe
For me there will be only one, yeah for me there will be only one.

Dominic turned in his seat so that he could watch Jane. She saw him staring from the corner of her eye, and his gaze made her both happy and uncomfortable.

I'll take you to the silver well, make a wish, I'll cast a spell
That you'll remain here by my side, childlike thoughts
I cannot hide
For me there will be only one, yeah for me there will be only one.

"Stop staring," she said.
"Can't help it. I'm remembering that night."
"Well, stop remembering."
"Can't."
"You're married."
"Memories are allowed."
"I wish you'd stop." She was becoming more uncomfortable.
"Sorry," he said. "Inappropriate." He turned to face the road.

Until stars come showering down, till the seven seas engulf
this town . . .

Jane turned off the CD player and they drove the rest of the way to her house in silence.

Elle arrived home two days after her exhibition had opened. She walked through the side gate that led to her little cottage at the end of the garden. Her mother was tending to her witch hazels. She called out to Elle, and Elle stopped and turned toward her. Rose stood up slowly and took off her gloves. She pointed to the garden furniture and Elle sat. Rose joined her. They were both wearing heavy coats, but Rose could tell that her daughter had lost a lot of weight.

"Did you have a good time?" Rose asked.

"Brilliant."

"Jane was worried."

"Jane worries too much."

"That's what I told her. We all need to escape every now and then, don't we?"

"We do."

"And you're happy to be home now?" Rose asked.

Elle laughed a little. "And what about you, Mum?"

"I'm as good as can be expected."

"And Jane?"

"She's fine. Dominic's been sniffing around."

"Bored with the new wife already," Elle said, and her mother nodded.

"You know what that means, don't you?" said Rose. "Poor Janey will no doubt make a fool of herself again."

"Well, if anyone knows about being a fool, I do," Elle said.

"Vincent is the fool, and if I ever see him again he'll be a fool without a penis," said Rose.

Elle got up. "It's cold."

"That's winter for you."

"I'm going inside now."

"Me too."

Elle walked toward her cottage and took down the GONE FISHING sign. Her mother called after her, and she turned to face her.

"Good to have you home."

Elle smiled at her mother, then entered her home. Rose

picked up her garden shears and walked down to the basement and to the promise of a nice glass of hot whiskey. She took a large gulp, and when her eyes filled with tears she wiped them away and finished the glass. *Please don't frighten me like that again.*

When darkness had descended and Jane noticed the light on in Elle's cottage, she ran through the garden and up the path that led to Elle's door. She knocked before opening it slowly and creeping inside. Elle was in her sitting room, cuddled up on the sofa, music playing in the background.

Jane sat beside her.

"Hi, Jane."

"Hi, Elle."

"How was the opening?"

"We sold the lot."

"Good. Sorry I didn't make it."

"It's okay. Actually, it made my job a lot easier."

"Oh good. Did you miss me?"

"I did."

"I'm sorry for setting Vincent's car on fire, I'm sorry for all of it."

"I took care of it."

"I know. You always do." She sighed. "Sorry."

"It's okay." Jane smiled at her sister. "I'm glad you're home. You look tired."

"I'm exhausted."

Jane took Elle by the hand and lifted her off the sofa; then, arm in arm, they walked to the bedroom, where Jane tucked her sister into bed.

"You fall asleep now, and when you get up I'll make you your favorite breakfast."

"I love you, Jane."

"I love you too, girly girl." Jane turned out the light and left Elle cuddled up under her duvet.

Jane always called Elle "girly girl" when she was being affectionate. It was a term she'd given Elle when she was a toddler and Jane was a teen. Their father had died suddenly, their mother was on medication, and so Jane had cared for her sister. She'd pick up after her, play with her, feed her, and put her to bed. She'd read her stories and tell her things about their dad.

"Where is he, Janey?"

"He's in heaven, girly girl."

"Where's heaven?"

"Far away up there in the sky."

"Daddy doesn't like heights, Janey." Elle remembered the day their dad had gotten dizzy and fallen from a ladder while trying to retrieve her ball from the eaves.

"It's okay," Jane explained. "He likes heaven."

"Why?"

"Because it's great."

"Why is it great?"

"Because God's there."

"So?"

"God is really cool. Everybody wants to be with God."

"I don't. I'd rather be here with you," Elle had said.

And Jane had been a mother to her sister since then.

7

"Chocolate Eyes"

Ran out of hope, ran out of faith,
ran out of milk about quarter past eight
I gave up on dreams and regrets,
well, I quit smoking but not cigarettes.

Jack L, *Broken Songs*

March 2008

When Elle woke up in Leslie's house in the country to the sound of birds, strangely they were loud, angry, and without melody. She sat up and rubbed her eyes and looked toward the open window, and sitting on the windowsill were two crows screeching at each other. She got out of bed, stretched, and closed the window, and so engrossed were they in their dispute that her actions went unnoticed.

She could hear Leslie pottering in the kitchen. She had the radio on and was listening to two DJs make a crank call to some unsuspecting dentist. The house was a bungalow, the guest bedroom was next door to the kitchen, and the walls were paper thin, so Elle's bed might as well have been placed in the center of the kitchen.

She pulled on her dressing gown and joined Leslie, who was kneeling on the counter by the sink and cleaning the window.

Elle poured herself coffee and picked up a croissant from the basket in the center of the table. She nibbled and drank while Leslie filled her in on the plan for the day.

When Leslie's father died, he had left the house to her mother; when she died, she had left it to her three girls; when Nora died, the house had become Imelda's and Leslie's; and when Imelda died, the house had become Leslie's alone. She had maintained it over the years, and although she traveled to it about every eight weeks, she rarely stayed more than two days because the echoes of a tragic past haunted the place. This was the first time since Imelda's passing that she had stayed longer than two days, and with Elle for company she was actually enjoying herself. Elle had been working hard on the exhibition since she had returned from her break, and when Leslie mentioned that she had to make a trip to check on her family home, Elle had begged to be allowed to join her, as a change of scenery would inspire and invigorate her. She had been working hard to make up for lost time, and Leslie could see that painting the faces of the Missing was taking a toll on Elle. She seemed to be quietly absorbing their tragedies, and the pain, suffering, hope, and hopelessness imbued in her work was also imbued in her. She was quieter than when they had first met, and she seemed older. All the energy was gone, and in the few months they had known each other Elle had gone from being a playful puppy to an old sleepy girl content to sit on the porch.

As it turned out, the town was playing host to a weeklong

traditional music festival, which initially served only to annoy Leslie. But the first night, they walked into town and ate in a restaurant that Leslie hadn't visited in ten years, and they enjoyed a pleasant time eating pasta, drinking wine, and listening to a young man play piano accompanied by a girl on the violin and a boy on guitar. Neither woman was a fan of traditional music, and this little group was less thud-thumping, toe-tapping, feet-of-flames, old-school Irish and more New Age folk, mellow and enchanting. The music had elevated Elle into a happy place, and since then her mood had continued to lift ever so slowly but noticeably. As part of the festival, every restaurant, bar, park, and street corner was playing host to musicians of all ages, and because their first evening had been such a success, Elle and Leslie had gotten into the spirit of the event and by day three were really enjoying themselves. Leslie's long self-imposed seclusion and newfound joie de vivre meant that every day there was a great new discovery, or rediscovery, to be made. An old woodland that she had played in as a child was a beautiful place to walk and talk, and the new coffee shop that served take-out hot chocolate to sip and hug as they walked made it even more pleasant. Leslie had forgotten how beautiful her little town was. She'd forgotten the way the sky looked through the trees and how the light hit the water in the evenings and how friendly the people were when she actually engaged with them.

"So what's the plan for today?" Elle asked between nibbles.

Leslie turned and smiled at her, took off one of her gloves, and scratched her nose.

"Well," she said, "I was thinking we'd get in the car and drive to the coast this morning, and we can have lunch at this little pub that Simon and I used to go to—it has the best fish in the country. Then we could get back here around five and eat here or go out, depending on how you feel, and then Mahons is playing host to an interesting-sounding band from Westport."

"Sounds good. I'll just get showered and dressed and we can go."

Leslie nodded, put her glove back on, and resumed cleaning the window.

Elle nibbled on her croissant as she walked back to her room. She picked up her bag and headed down the hall into the bathroom, stripped, and got into the shower, and it was while the water was tapping at her head that she realized that a weight was lifting and she could feel her heart begin to soar.

Having spent a lovely if finger-numbingly cold morning walking along the coastline, Elle and Leslie stopped off at the pub for their fish lunch. Elle ordered the salmon and Leslie a fish platter, and when Elle saw it she was sorry she had ordered the salmon, but there was plenty, and so the women shared the assortment of fish before them and Elle agreed it was the best fish she'd ever tasted. Elle asked Leslie to tell her a little about Simon, and Leslie argued that her relationship with him had been so long ago that it was hard to remember much of it.

"You must remember it!" Elle said.

"There was so much going on back then." Leslie was referring to the sickness that had completely overtaken her world for so long.

"What did he look like?" Elle said, pushing for an answer.

"He was tall and thin and he had big blue eyes the size of saucers, his hair was sandy and he had freckles."

"Was he nice?" Elle asked.

"He was very nice. He was bright and kind and he put up with a lot from me."

"Did he love you?"

Leslie sighed and thought about it for a moment. "Yes," she said, and she remembered the day eighteen years earlier when she had just turned twenty-two, her sister Nora was dying, and she'd just been diagnosed with the cancer gene.

Simon had been waiting for her when she came out of the doctor's office. He was pale and his big blue eyes were glassy. She walked up to him and he stood up from the chair he'd been sitting on. She sat down because her legs could no longer carry her and tugged at his hand, and he sat again and faced her and she didn't have to tell him because her face said it all. He put his face in his hands and wept right there in the middle of the waiting area. Listening to the pain that was so evident in every wail and cry, she knew that she couldn't put him through watching a slow and painful death. And so right there in hospital chairs she ended their three-year relationship. Even when he attempted to contact her intermittently for six months and although she missed him more than she could say, she was steadfast in her decision, and deep down knew that Simon was grateful.

"I think you're brave," Elle said.

"Thanks. Most would say I was stupid."

"Bravery and stupidity are the same thing. It just depends on the outcome, and it's not over yet."

"No, I suppose it isn't."

She thought about telling Elle about her plans to have surgery in July, but decided against it because they were having such a lovely day and she didn't want to think about it too much. *Another time. I'll tell her another time.* And as she was thinking that, Elle's face changed and Leslie turned to see what she was staring at. A tall man with curly brown hair and big brown eyes was standing with a blond woman she recognized from somewhere but whom she couldn't recall in that moment. He was wide-eyed and staring back, obviously uncomfortable and unsure, and Leslie watched Elle maintain eye contact with this man and this man hesitatingly make his way toward her, leaving the blonde at the bar.

"Elle," he said, and Leslie detected a shudder in his voice.

Elle didn't have to introduce him. Leslie knew it was the prick who had broken her new friend's heart.

"Vincent," Elle said.

"How weird is this?" He raised his hands in the air. "Of all the gin joints in all the towns."

"Funny old world," she said. "How've you been, Vincent?"

"Good. You?"

"Great," she said, but it was unconvincing. Neither of them mentioned the car-burning incident and subsequent payoff. The blonde remained at the bar.

"This is Leslie," Elle said, looking beyond his shoulder at the blonde. "Who's your friend?"

Vincent turned to the blonde and called her over with a nod of his head. She approached slowly and stood slightly behind him.

"This is Caroline."

Caroline smiled. She seemed familiar, but Elle couldn't work out how she knew her face.

"Nice to meet you," Caroline said nervously. "I love your work."

"Thanks," Elle said. "Do I know you?"

"I'm an actress."

Elle nodded. "Of course you are," she said, and she looked at Vincent and shook her head. She remembered where she'd seen her before. It had been at one of her own exhibitions. The photographer had made them stand together for a press shot. That exhibition had been just before China.

Vincent attempted to disguise a gulp by clearing his throat. "We should go," he said to Caroline, who seemed more than happy to move on.

"You should have gone a long time ago," Elle said.

Vincent nodded and grabbed Caroline's arm and escorted her out of the lovely pub that served the best fish in Ireland before they'd even had a chance to look at the menu.

Leslie looked at Elle, who seemed lost in thought.

"Are you okay?"

"I'm more than okay," Elle said, and she sighed and grinned a little.

"You are?"

"He was screwing her all that time."

"And that's okay?"

Elle nodded. "It must be, because I can't seem to make myself care."

Leslie smiled at her young friend and squeezed her hand, and Elle's heart soared just a little higher.

Rose had been throwing up all week. She was steadfast in her refusal to seek medical attention, but eventually when Jane witnessed her doubled over in severe pain holding her stomach and throwing up in her kitchen wastebasket, she'd had enough of her mother's stubbornness and made the call to their family GP. Jane was flying out to London for the Jack Lukeman gig that evening.

Dr. Griffin arrived at ten as promised and a very grateful Jane, knowing he hated making house calls, especially to her mother, met him on the steps of her home. Together they made their way to the basement apartment.

"How's she behaving?" he asked.

"Same as ever."

"Still experiencing mood swings?"

"Dr. Griffin, what you call her mood swings, we call her personality."

Jane smiled, but Dr. Griffin just shook his head. He'd been the Moore family's practitioner for well over thirty years, and he really cared for the girls and Kurt, but Rose Moore was his worst nightmare. Jane opened the door, and he braced himself and followed her inside.

Rose was in the sitting room, asleep on the chair. Jane and Dr. Griffin looked at each other, both silently acknowledging that it was time to wake the beast.

Jane approached gingerly. She slowly and gently laid her hand on her mother's arm and shook it ever so slightly. "Rose."

Rose stirred a little; Jane backed off.

Rose's eyes opened, and she focused on her daughter and the doctor. "What?"

"Rose, I'm here to give you a checkup," Dr. Griffin said.

"Did I ask you to come?"

"No," he said before sighing audibly.

"Well, then."

"Rose, you are sick," Jane said in her most forceful tone, "and I'm not going to let you rot down here, so let the doctor examine you."

"How charming of you, Jane, but you are forgetting about a little thing called free will, and if I am rotting and I wish to continue doing so, that is my business and my business alone."

"Don't make me hold you down, old woman," said Jane.

"You can try."

Jane seemed serious, but so did her mother, and despite her

age and illness, Dr. Griffin was sure that she'd put up a good fight.

"Okay, ladies," he said, holding his hand in the air. "Rose, please just let me examine you. I won't take longer than three minutes."

"You have two," she said.

A minute later, Dr. Griffin was pressing on Rose's stomach and she was trying not to scream, but one press too many and she couldn't help but grab his ear and drag him off her. He called out, and Jane extricated his ear from her mother's closed claw. He stumbled back, rubbing his reddened and bruised earlobe.

Rose then grabbed Jane's hand and squeezed it as hard as she could and pulled her in close. "Don't you dare bring that man in here without my permission again!" she hissed. Tears sprang into Jane's eyes. Rose let go and Jane backed away, rubbing her hand much like Dr. Griffin had his ear.

Dr. Griffin packed up his bag before turning to Rose. "Your stomach is inflamed, and that's what's causing the pain and vomiting. I've no doubt you are suffering from recurrent diarrhea and possible pancreatitis. And I know for sure that however uncomfortable you are now, it will only get worse."

"Well, thank you for your medical opinion, Dr. Griffin. You know where the door is."

"Stop drinking, Rose," Dr. Griffin said. "If you don't, you will die."

"I'm an old woman, Doctor. It would be incredibly focking odd if I didn't die. Don't you think?"

Rose loved to curse. She loved to pepper the word "fuck" into her sentences when she deemed it appropriate. However, her accent ensured that it sounded like she was saying "fock," "focker," "focking," or "focked." She liked that it meant she was devilish enough to curse but not coarse enough for it to be instantly recognizable.

Jane and Dr. Griffin left her alone. She flicked on the TV and took a bottle of wine and an unwashed glass from the cabinet beside her chair. She unscrewed the cap and poured the wine into the wineglass. She took a sip and rested the glass back on top of the cabinet, all the while mumbling to herself. "Stop drinking or you'll die. Who does he think he is? I'm seventy-one years old and I haven't died yet, more's the focking pity."

Dr. Griffin followed Jane up the steps and into the main house. In the kitchen she made him tea, and for the one hundredth time he went through the kind of gastrointestinal damage her mother was doing to herself.

"What can I do?" Jane asked.

"Ban the booze," he suggested as though it was his first time.

A frustrated Jane shouted, "I can't! She's got her own money, she's perfectly capable of buying her own booze, and she's got friends who bring her presents of booze. They don't think she has a problem; she doesn't think she has a problem. My sister seems to think that just because she's not in bars or clubs doing shots till four a.m. I'm insane to even suggest she has a problem, and my son thinks she's hilarious. When she falls asleep with the heater on, it's old age; when she falls in the shower, it's her arthritis; and when I dare to address the problem, I'm deemed to be hysterical at best and a 'focking' bitch at worst!"

Dr. Griffin laughed a little at Jane's impression of the way her mother said "fucking" before becoming serious again. "Rose has been a functioning alcoholic for over thirty years, but time is running out and her body is slowly giving up."

Jane absentmindedly scooped out sugar from the bowl, then poured it back in. "I'm doing my best."

"I know."

"Can I have her committed?"

"Your mother isn't mentally ill."

"I know that, you know that, but how long would it take for them to realize that?"

Dr. Griffin grinned. They sat in silence for a minute or two, drinking tea.

"It's simple, Jane. If she doesn't stop soon, her health will deteriorate to a point where she will have to be hospitalized, and then she will be forced into sobriety. Whether or not it's too late to save her is anyone's guess."

"Sorry about your ear," Jane said, changing the subject.

"Does Rose behave violently toward you a lot?"

"No," Jane said, laughing the matter off. "I think you inspired the violence."

"Well, if it gets too much you'll let me know."

Jane nodded. "It's a pity, because when she's in good form she's almost fun to be around."

"I'll take your word for it." Dr. Griffin stood and fixed his jacket to signal his desire to exit. It had been a long time since he'd seen the pleasant side of Rose Moore. In fact, he could pinpoint the year: it had been the spring of 1983, three months before she had called him to the house to declare her husband dead.

Jane waved the doctor off and closed the door. She tried to take off her ring, but following her mother's attack her finger had swollen, making its removal difficult.

The phone rang, and it was Tom wanting to know if she

wished to share a taxi to the airport. She agreed because she was running late and wouldn't have time to park the car in the long-term car park. The gig was a late show. They had decided not to fly out until six that evening, which was a blessing because she still had a full day's work ahead of her.

A meeting she had with an artist by the name of Ken Browne ran late. She was really impressed by his work and energy, and they ended up talking for a long time, sharing stories over coffee. His bright blue eyes shone as he spoke about his latest painting, and he rubbed his bald head and smiled a wide smile that seemed to take over his rugged features. He had been in a rock band for years, and it was written all over his face. He was an accomplished guitar player, and he told her stories about his adventures on the road and talked about how he incorporated music into his artwork. They spent a very enjoyable two hours together, and by the end of their meeting they had agreed that he would show his work in her gallery in July. Kurt appeared in the gallery just after lunch with a packed bag and announced he was staying with Irene for the weekend. Irene's mother was on another post-breakup holiday and, as her dad was too busy boffing his new girlfriend to be interested in Irene, Kurt felt a responsibility to care for her.

"No way," said Jane.

"Mum, I'm going."

"You and Irene are not staying there unsupervised."

"I'm seventeen."

"No way, no way!" she shouted. She always repeated herself and shouted when she couldn't think of something else to say.

"She's upset. I'm not leaving her," he said calmly.

Jane calmed down. "So bring her to ours."

"What's the difference? You're going to London."

"Your grandmother's here."

Kurt started to laugh. "You're serious?"

"It's better than nothing."

"Where's Elle?"

"She's gone down to the country with Leslie for a few days."

"Mum, why don't you admit that you need me to care for Gran and not the other way around?"

"That's not it. She's perfectly capable of looking after herself for two days." She was lying, and there was a list of things she wanted him to do for his grandmother burning a hole in her pocket.

"Why don't you just tell the truth?" he said.

She didn't know why she felt it necessary to lie except that maybe she didn't want her son to feel obliged to care for her mother the way she did. And now her son had caught her in a silly and unnecessary lie and it embarrassed her, so she dismissed him angrily. "Fine, Kurt, go off with your girlfriend! Do your own bloody thing!"

"Fine. I will."

He walked out of the gallery, leaving her to stew.

What is wrong with me? Why couldn't I have said, 'Son, I need your help this weekend'? How hard is that? It's not hard at all. Jesus Christ, Jane.

She then had to sort her mother's prescriptions and pick up some take-out menus and cash. When she finally returned to her mother's it was ten minutes before Tom was due to turn up in the taxi.

Rose was displeased. "It's a bit bloody late to be thinking about me now," she said.

Jane ignored her and put the menus on the coffee table beside her.

Rose picked one up. "Jane?" she asked innocently. "Am I Chinese?"

"Don't start, Rose."

"Because I don't look Chinese, I don't speak the language, the only paddy I know is a person, and it will be a cold focking day in hell before I eat anything commonly described as flied lice."

"That's racist."

"That's fact."

"You're a pig."

Rose held up the menu. "Well, then, maybe it's my year." She picked up the other menu. "Indian?"

"I'm leaving," Jane said.

"Oh yes, I'll have an order of dead babies dumped in a river, followed by some Kama Sutra with a side order of shitting in the streets."

"Stop now, you insane old hag! Eat chips for two days for all I care! Don't forget your medication, and all the numbers you could possibly need are on the fridge."

"Fine, go off and enjoy yourself, leave a sick old woman on her own!"

"Thanks, Rose, I will. Try not to die before I get back," Jane said with a grin because two could play the old woman's game.

Rose licked her teeth. She always licked her teeth when she wanted to hide a smile.

"Is that because you don't want to deal with the smell?" she asked.

"If I didn't want to deal with the smell I would have turfed you out years ago."

Jane walked out the door and Rose broke into a smile. *Touché, Janey, touché.*

• • •

Tom had checked them in online, so they ran through the airport and joined the queue at the gate. He bought two coffees from a vendor, and they managed two sips each before their row number was called. An air hostess made a no-no gesture at the coffee with her hand and tut-tutted them. Neither Tom nor Jane had the will to argue with her, so they handed over their full cups of coffee and walked through the gate and onto the plane in silence. Once seated, Tom took the opportunity once again to thank Jane for coming, and she responded that he was most welcome for the third time that evening and possibly the fortieth time since they had decided on the trip.

Tom was nervous. He didn't know what to do with his hands and he kept shifting in the seat. He had cut his hair and manicured his nails, and he'd bought a suit that fitted him. He had shaved and he looked handsome—probably the way he had looked before Alexandra vanished, or at least close to it.

Jane was worried that all this effort and hope would not be rewarded. She knew they were clutching at straws, and although she appeared outwardly positive for the sake of Tom's sanity, she worried that she might have contributed to him having false hope. Now that they were actually flying to London to attend a Jack Lukeman gig in the hope of spotting someone named Alex with a passing resemblance to Alexandra, it seemed more than desperate, it seemed mad.

"The hotel is really close to the club," Tom said.

"Great."

"Just a walk away."

"Fantastic."

"We could just eat in the hotel if you like?"

"Lovely."

"Or we could go out. I'm sure there's a place between the hotel and the club. I just don't want to move too far away."

"The hotel is perfect."

"Oh okay."

"Nice suit," Jane said after a pause.

Tom nodded. "I thought I'd better make an effort if I'm going to see my girl."

"It's unlikely, Tom, you know that it's unlikely." She wanted to cry for him.

"I do. Still, you never know."

"Yeah."

He closed his eyes and she read her magazine and they didn't speak another word for the rest of the flight.

The plane landed on time, and Tom and Jane quickly found a taxi to take them to their hotel. They split in the lobby and agreed to meet half an hour later. Jane showered and changed while Tom paced his hotel room over and over again, counting down the minutes until he might see Alexandra again.

They met in the hotel restaurant. Jane ordered steak and salad; Tom ordered the same, but he only picked at it. Jane tried to allay his anxiety with idle chat. Since his encounter with Rose, Tom had developed sympathy for Jane and had become her sounding board. She told him about the incident with the doctor, which entertained him, and of course Rose's reaction to the take-out menus made him laugh out loud. Jane laughed too, because her mother was always funny from a distance. She told him about Kurt and their stupid fight and berated herself for being a bad mother. Tom disagreed and told her that she was a great mother, but then he hadn't witnessed the fight she'd had with her son when he was sixteen and he wanted to leave school to join the army after watching *Black Hawk Down* twenty-five times in the space of a week. He had approached her while she was working on her computer at the kitchen table, and he'd sat opposite her and folded his arms, and when Kurt folded his arms it indicated he meant to talk business. She'd looked up and asked him what he wanted, and he'd told her straight out as if he was asking for the price of a CD that he wanted permission to join the army. She had laughed it off at first, but it soon became apparent that he wasn't joking. Jane said no. Kurt refused to accept no for an answer, and their argument spiraled so out of control that Kurt called his mother the *c* word and stormed out of the kitchen, slammed the door, walked into his bedroom, slammed that door and locked it, and put his music on blaring. His mother, shocked by his language and red-faced from roaring, stomped down the hall and banged and kicked at his locked door, calling him a disrespectful little bastard. He screamed *I hate you* and she screamed *I hate you* back and managed to calm herself down only after she'd kicked a hole through the door and broken her small toe. Tom hadn't been witness to the time she'd left the child in a pram outside a shop and didn't notice that she'd left him behind until she got home and her mother inquired as to his whereabouts. He hadn't been there when Kurt was six and a kid aged eight started to bully him in the schoolyard. Kurt had confided in Rose rather than in her, and when Rose told her, instead of taking her mother's advice to back off, she barged into the school and grabbed the bully by the neck and threatened to break his legs if he ever touched her son again. It was obviously the worst move she could have made because there was a schoolyard full of witnesses, including a teacher and a visiting nun, and of course the child's parents threatened action against her, and following a meeting with the headmistress it became apparent that the best course of action in light of Jane's aggression toward a minor would be if she pulled Kurt out of the school altogether.

"You got him expelled when he was six?" Tom said, and he laughed.

"Mortified," she said. "But when Rose told me, I just saw red."

"I can't believe you attacked an eight-year-old."

"Well, I had to do something. Rose told Kurt to wait till the kid had his back to him and then beat him around the head with his bag."

"That doesn't sound like the worst idea."

"She told him to put a brick in it."

Tom laughed again. "I'm sorry for laughing, but that's insane."

"I have made so many mistakes with Kurt it's a wonder he's not a little psycho."

"You were so young having him," Tom reminded her.

"Yeah." She nodded. "And my example was Rose."

"My God, that's true. It's a wonder *you're* not a little psycho."

"It's possible I am," she said.

"I'll bear that in mind."

Tom's mind was momentarily distracted from finding Alexandra, and then it was time to head to the club, and his mind wandered away from Jane again, and silence resumed as they walked to the place that held one of Tom's last hopes.

Michelle met them at the box office. She ushered them inside and was wondering how they wished their search to proceed.

"It's a big club," she pointed out, "but I've put the flyers on the bulletin board and all the staff have been given her picture."

They had discussed it earlier.

"I'd like to sit close to the ladies', if I could?" Tom said.

"And I'll sit at the bar," Jane said.

"Look, we've got a pretty comprehensive security system,"

said Michelle. "Every part of this place is on camera. I could introduce you to Graham—he's our security guard. I've spoken to him and he's happy for you to join him in his office."

"That would be amazing," Tom said.

"Good." Michelle was only too happy to help.

She brought them to a room where a large man in his fifties sat. In front of him were small TV screens, each one capturing a part of the club. He turned and greeted them, and Michelle went off to get two more chairs while Graham pointed out each camera and where it was positioned.

"Box office, main door, back door, side entrance, hallway, main stairs, bar, bar till—you won't need to focus on that—stage, audience; that breaks into three here, here, and here," he said, pointing to three separate TV screens, all of which depicted empty chairs and tables. "That one is the balcony and so is that, and over here is the dressing-room area—obviously we don't have a camera in the actual dressing rooms, but it's the dressing-room hallway that leads here to backstage, stage right, and stage left, and that's it."

Michelle returned with two chairs. She placed them on either side of Graham.

Then Michelle left them, but before she did she crossed her fingers.

"Thank you," Tom said. "You've no idea."

She nodded and closed the door behind her.

"What happens if I see her?" Tom asked.

"You run," Graham said. "Michelle has given me your number so that I can call you if I see her again and guide you through the club on the phone."

"That's great," Tom said. "That's really unbelievably great. Isn't that great, Jane?"

Jane nodded and walked over to the counter and made coffee

for the three of them as the lads stared at the many screens. First the box office and the main entrance. They watched, and as people flowed through, Graham pointed out that he could zoom in on anyone who sparked Tom's interest, and while Jane's back was turned he provided Tom with an example by zooming in on a woman's large breasts.

They watched face after face as they flowed in through the doors and halls and spread into the various parts of the club. The place filled up quickly, and so each one took turns monitoring a set of cameras. Graham had posted Alexandra's picture on the wall in front of him for purposes of recognition. The club became louder as the chatter grew and people moved to and from their seats to the toilets and to the bar and servers began serving at the round tables where groups were drinking, laughing, and talking. Jane thought how funny it was to have this perspective, to watch people who were unaware they were being watched. She watched one woman lift and separate her breasts when her partner left to go to the toilet; then Jane followed him down the hall and witnessed him turn to watch a pretty girl walk past him. Another guy waited for his date to go to the bar before he picked his nose, examined it, and flicked it across the room. She pointed at the camera and made a sound suggesting she was appalled. Graham just nodded. "People are disgusting," he said. She saw so many brunettes, but none of them had the rich glossy hair she remembered her friend having. Every now and then her heart rate would increase because she spotted someone who just might be Alexandra, but Graham would zoom in and her heart rate would slow and Tom would momentarily close his eyes and bow his head for the second or two required to pull himself together.

Jack L and his band emerged from the dressing room two

minutes before they were due onstage. Jack was dressed in a black suit and red shirt; he ran his hand through his hair and took a drink from his bottle of water. The bass player slapped him on the back and he grinned at him, that familiar troublemaker grin that Jane recognized. The door of the dressing room stayed open for a second or two before someone inside closed it. The band walked down the hall and out of range only to be picked up on the next camera that focused on backstage. Onstage, the lights rose and danced on the rich velvet curtain. The drummer sat behind his drums, the guitar player picked up his guitar and placed it around his neck, the piano player made herself comfortable, and they started to play while Jack bounced with guitar in hand stage right on a separate screen. Tom watched the crowd as they clapped and cheered, and some people stood and some stamped their feet, and the curtain rose and Jack walked onstage. The crowd went mad, he bowed and grinned, and he raised his hand, the band started up, the show began, and Alexandra was nowhere to be seen.

They continued to scan each and every face while Jack sang and told stories and shared a joke with the guitar player, and time passed so quickly, and then the gig was almost over.

Jack returned to the stage to sing his encore, and just as Graham turned to offer his sympathy to Tom, Jane noticed a woman with short brunette hair and Alexandra's face emerge from Jack's dressing room. She pointed and called out to Tom, and he and Graham saw the woman. Tom shot up and Graham zoomed in, and Tom started running and Graham shouted for him to turn left at the box office and he did, but the hallway was empty. Jane ran after Tom. Graham phoned Tom's number and directed him to the side entrance, and Tom followed his advice and ran through the club, navigating through people who were up on their feet and dancing to "Boys and Girls," with Jane hot on his heels. He made it outside to an alleyway. The woman had her back to him and was talking to a man with a backstage pass around his neck, and Tom called out to her.

"Alexandra!"

She turned, and for a split second he thought it was her and seeing her took his breath away, and then she walked toward him and the closer she got the less she looked like his wife because the expression on her face was not an expression he'd ever seen before.

"Can I help you?" she said in an English accent.

Tom couldn't do anything but shake his head. "No," he said, "you can't help me."

And then he was on his knees and weeping uncontrollably.

Jane stood behind him, staring at the woman who looked so much like her friend on camera but in person and close up seemed shockingly different. *We're so stupid. Of course it wasn't her. It was never going to be her.*

The woman was unsure how to react. The man with the laminate moved to stand beside her, and they both found themselves staring at the man who was on his knees and crying.

"Where is she? Where is she? Where is she? Where is she? Where is she?"

Jane knelt and took his hands, and then she pulled him to her and hugged him close.

"Where is she, Jane?" he whispered. "Where's my girl?"

"I don't know," she said, rubbing his head like she used to rub Kurt's when he was young enough to be soothed rather than revolted by her touch, "but we will find her."

Michelle, tipped off by Graham, who was watching the sad

scene on-screen, appeared and took the English Alex inside, where she explained the tragic circumstances the crying man had found himself in. The English Alex was dreadfully sorry to hear of the man's plight and more than a little freaked at the likeness between her and the picture of the missing woman. She explained that she worked for Jack's UK distribution company and made her excuses as she had somewhere to be and was gone before at last Jane came in with Tom, whose disappointment had turned into mild shock.

Back in his hotel room, Jane insisted that Tom have a strong brandy to calm his nerves.

He was berating himself for having believed it possible to find Alexandra at a gig in London and saying how stupid it was of him to think that his wife would be in Jack L's dressing room—after all, the Jack camp had been so good about helping him. That woman was not just thinner, she was rail thin, and she was taller, and despite sharing similarities, up close she was nothing like his wife. He had been fooling himself.

His liaison officer, Trish, had said as much the last time she had visited to update him on the investigation surrounding his wife's disappearance. Their unit had analyzed the CCTV footage that Michelle had passed on and found that it wasn't a match. He had argued with her that computers were not gods and he knew his wife's face. She had been patient with him and was always kind, but she was adamant that he needed to let go of the notion of finding his wife in a London club.

"I can't let go," he said. "I have to find her."

His liaison officer had left soon after, and he had promptly blocked out the information she'd just given him because more and more his mind was visiting the dark place and he desperately needed hope.

As he sat, drinking brandy, that conversation came back to haunt him. He apologized to Jane for wasting her time and for breaking down in the alleyway. He assured her he would pay to clean the oil stains from her coat as a result of her sitting on the ground and rocking him like a baby for ten minutes.

She told him he should get some sleep. She kissed his cheek and said they would keep looking.

He held her hand and looked into her eyes and bit his lip. "Tell me something about her."

So she told him about a time when her best friend, Alexandra, was a little girl, maybe eleven or twelve, and stole an ice cream from the local shop. She spent a second or two choosing the one she wanted, placed it under her coat, and made her way outside, and when the shopkeeper ran outside after her, calling on her to stop, she turned to him, calmly took out the ice cream from inside her coat pocket, and handed it to him. Then she smiled and congratulated him on catching her.

"No flies on you, Mr. Dunne, no flies at all!" Alexandra said.

Mr. Dunne was taken aback, especially when she pointed out that two days earlier while he had been away from the shop and his wife had been behind the counter, she'd stolen a bar of chocolate without any fear of capture. She took the bar of chocolate from her pocket and handed it to him.

"I practically dangled it under her nose," she said to Mr. Dunne, who was now decidedly confused. "To be fair to her, the shop was busy, but Mr. Dunne, you can never be too careful, shoplifters are everywhere."

"I'll mention it to her," he said, still unsure what was going on.

"You're welcome," she said, and she walked down the road.

Mr. Dunne stared from her to the chocolate bar and to his wife, who was busy serving a customer. *What the hell just happened?*

Alexandra made it around the corner to where Jane was waiting, and as soon as she was sure that Mr. Dunne could no longer see her, she burst into tears. Once she'd recovered sufficiently to walk home, Alexandra promised Jane she would never again engage in a criminal act. But although she had scared the pants off herself and was down a bar of chocolate, the encounter was not a total loss because Alexandra learned something very powerful that day: any lie delivered with confidence and conviction is believable no matter how ridiculous the circumstance. This self-awareness had really worked in their favor when they were caught stealing while on holiday with Alexandra's parents in Mayo a year later.

"And what about you?" Tom asked. "Did you just wait to see if she'd get away with it before you had a go?"

"Oh no! I'd successfully stolen three Mars bars from a shop two doors down. It was one of those bars that she gave back to Mr. Dunne."

He laughed a little. "So what did you learn?"

"That the hand is quicker than an old woman's one good eye."

When Jane was content that she'd cheered Tom up a little, she bade him good night.

"Thanks," he said. "I don't know what I'd do without you."

He walked to the door with her and watched her go down the corridor to her room, and she could feel his eyes on her back and she smiled at him when she turned to place her key card in the door. She disappeared into her room, and Tom entered his and opened the minibar again and starting drinking, and when he saw he'd received three calls from Jeanette, he turned his phone to silent.

• • •

When Jane's taxi pulled up to her house, her son opened the front door, walked down the steps, met her at the gate, and took her suitcase from her hand.

"Sorry, Mum," he said. "I should have helped out with Gran."

Jane was taken aback and unsure what to say. Instead she just hugged him tight, and when he was in her grasp she took the opportunity to kiss his cheek.

"Mum!" he moaned. As they walked up the steps together he put his arm around her shoulders. "I have something to tell you," he said.

"I'm listening."

"Irene's here."

"And?"

"She's needs a place to stay."

"What's going on?"

"There's no food in her house."

"Okay."

"Really?"

"Really. Just make sure she lets her mother know."

"She would if she could reach her."

"Are you hungry?" Jane said.

"We're starving."

"Okay. Give me five minutes and I'll get busy."

Irene appeared in the sitting-room doorway.

"Hi, Jane," she said shyly.

Jane walked over to Irene, hugged her, and kissed her on the forehead. "Welcome."

Irene brightened. "Thanks, Jane, you rock."

"Yes, I do," she said, "and you're in the spare room."

"I know, I know, don't have sex, not here, not there, not anywhere," Irene said in a voice that mimicked Jane.

Kurt laughed and Jane nodded. "Exactly."

Jane went to her bedroom and sat on the bed and took a minute to allow the events of the weekend to wash over her, and then she took time to be grateful for her life, as hard as it sometimes was. *I'm one of the lucky ones.*

8

I looked behind the cooker,
sofa and the sink,
got down on my knees
and looked under the fridge
but I can't find love.

Jack L, *Metropolis Blue*

April 2008

Dominic had never been very good at relationships. In his thirty-six years on the planet, his longest relationship had been three years. He'd married Bella six months after he'd ended a disastrous but very passionate affair with a dancer called Heidi. She had been twenty-three and liked to take E or alternatively acid on the weekends. He hadn't bothered to take E in his teens and twenties with his peers, and so he was damned if he was going to do it in his thirties. He'd witnessed a guy in college attempt to hack off his own foot with a wooden spoon while screaming that the eagles had landed after a particularly bad acid trip, so that was out. Besides, as a respectable bank manager, the last thing in the world he wanted was to be found in a club in Dublin drunk and bouncing off the walls or screaming bloody murder while attempting to land himself on the moon. Heidi resented that he didn't share her interests, and he found it difficult to live with someone who was in a bad mood from Sunday morning to Tuesday night. So class A drugs were blamed for the demise of their relationship. They had fought and she had ordered him out of her flat, and he told her he would not be back and she was happy with that, further promising that if she saw him anywhere near her place again she'd call the police. He pointed out that calling the police would obviously be a bad idea, considering she lived with a drug dealer named Seth and spent half her time either going up or coming down. He walked from her flat to his car and drove to Jane's house, and she made him dinner and provided a shoulder to cry on, because even though Heidi drove him crazy he would miss her. Jane was a great listener. She was always there for him, even though when she'd needed him most he hadn't been there for her.

Dominic often regretted the choices he had made at seventeen, but there was a part of him that was also secretly grateful. If he and Jane had married like Rose had demanded at the time, they wouldn't have made it. He would never have gone to university. If he hadn't gone to university, he wouldn't have an extremely well-paid and cushy job in a top bank, and he certainly wouldn't be living the luxury lifestyle he'd become accustomed to. He could have kissed good-bye his cars and his house in Ballsbridge and his chalet in France and the five apartments he was earning high rents from in an exclusive development in Blackrock. God knows where he'd be, because when he was seventeen his parents had warned him in no uncertain terms that if he didn't go to university and get a degree and follow in his father's footsteps, he was on his own. At the time he was a kid, confused and scared, and although he was high on a drug called love, the reality of becoming a father sobered him up fast. His parents had insisted he stay away from the girl, who they believed had become pregnant on purpose to trap him. When their offer of financial support on the condition that Jane keep away from their son was rejected by the madwoman who had reared her, they were happy to wash their hands entirely of the girl and child. They were adamant that if Dominic didn't want to pay for university himself, he would never speak to the girl again. He didn't want to pay for college himself. He wanted the same free ride that his two older brothers had enjoyed. He wanted the cool apartment he could share with his two best friends, Mint and Brick. He wanted to experience the college lifestyle, the parties, the girls, the clubs, the drinks, the sport, the late nights, the crap food, and mostly the freedom from a life lived under the watchful eye of his strict parents. He easily acquiesced to their demands, and afterward, when Jane tried to talk to him, he ignored her. When she took the hint and stayed away, he watched her grow under her uniform, and although he ignored her it was hard to ignore the terrible sadness in her eyes because she wasn't given a choice. All that ambition that burned so brightly in her would be lost, and all Dominic wanted to do was run away because Dominic, like their principal, Amanda Reynolds, knew that Jane could have achieved whatever she wanted. She could hold a full-scale conversation with Alexandra during math class, and if the teacher tried to make an example out of her by asking her to explain the theorem on the blackboard, she could do so without even so much as a second's thought. Alexandra, on the other hand, would stand and make up something so preposterous that the whole class would burst out laughing; she'd take a bow and sit, leaving the teacher too busy trying to regain control over his class to bother correcting her for not paying attention. Jane barely opened a book and yet she maintained a B average. She could have been an A student with the greatest of ease but deliberately maintained her B average because she didn't want to be associated with the class nerds. She too had been desperate to go to university, and she'd applied to the same colleges as Alexandra, and although it would mean being apart from Dominic, she had secretly hoped that they would both get Cork because then she would get to leave home. Dominic was sorry for Jane and he wanted the best for her because she was cool and they'd had the best two years together, but he was far too selfish to risk his own future to tell her.

Four years after his son was born, Dominic had graduated from college. He had experienced all the things that came with college life, he was on a good starting salary with the bank of his choice, and his parents didn't own him anymore. He walked up the steps of his old girlfriend's house on the day of their child's fourth birthday. He carried a gift in his hand. Passing balloons tied to the railings, he stopped at the front door and took a moment to collect himself before knocking. He was perfectly prepared for the door to be slammed in his face, but it wasn't. Jane opened it with their son on her hip, and even though he'd walked up the pathway and knocked on her door, seeing her and his son was a shock to him. He tried to raise a smile, but was ashamed and embarrassed, and so he lifted up the gift and held it out. She looked from him to the gift and then to her son, and she opened the door a little more and invited him in. Thirteen years later, Dominic still couldn't work out why Jane had found it so easy to forgive him.

The first time they had slept together again was the night of Kurt's Holy Communion. Kurt was seven, and in the three years Dominic had been a father to Kurt, he and Jane had become close confidants and friends. He was there, dressed in a suit with video camera in hand, when his son came down the stairs dressed in his own little Mini-Me suit and wearing his rosette pinned to his chest. Kurt was embarrassed and hated his suit and begged Jane to gel back his blond curls, but there was no way that was happening, so after a minitantrum at the bottom of the stairs, which was later edited out, they made their way to the church together as a family. Dominic drove, Jane sat in the front, and Kurt sat between his auntie Elle, who was sixteen and going through her Siouxsie and the Banshees "craving for a raw love" phase, and Rose, who kicked the back of Dominic's seat twice, claiming it was an accident and pretending to be completely horrified that her daughter could possibly think it was anything else.

"I was merely crossing my legs, Jane, and if this car wasn't the size of half a can of beans I'd be able to do so without nearly losing a knee."

Afterward they met up with his parents in a posh restaurant in Dublin city center, and despite Rose getting completely twisted before the main course was even served and in spite of Dominic's parents' coldness, Kurt was happy to be surrounded by the people he loved, because back then Jane and Dominic were the center of his universe and Elle was the coolest person he knew. Dominic stayed well after Kurt had been put to bed. Together they opened a bottle of wine and toasted their son's big day. They weren't even through the first glass when Dominic was taking Jane to her bedroom, the same one that she had snuck him into eight years earlier, and they both crept as silently as they could because at that time Rose still lived in the main house, and although she was in a drunken stupor, neither Dominic nor Jane wanted to risk waking her and receiving her wrath. Once Jane's door was closed and locked, they kissed and touched, and they were naked within minutes and lying together on the same bed that their son was conceived in, except this time Jane had the coil fitted and Dominic was wearing a condom. Dominic snuck out a few hours later.

The next day he had phoned. He was regretful and hopeful that their actions the previous night wouldn't ruin the fantastic friendship they'd built. Jane had promised him that nothing would change, and when he hung up he was relieved that once again Jane Moore had proved herself to be so cool. Of course, he didn't witness her brokenhearted and lying facedown on her bedroom floor crying for hours, nor did he have any idea how much she had hoped that he'd give their relationship a chance, because for Jane what could be better than a happy ending with the man she loved and the father of her child?

The second time they had sex again was after Jane's twenty-seventh birthday. Dominic had been seeing two women but it was early days in their relationships as neither had yet allowed him access to her bedroom. Jane had broken up with an artist she'd dated for six months. They were incredibly drunk, and if Jane had not woken up on top of Dominic, neither of them would have remembered actually having sex. This was rectified the following night when Dominic brought flowers and chocolates to once again apologize for his pesky penis. Jane opened a bottle of wine, and half an hour after Dominic's apology they were once again in bed together. For the next year they often got together when Dominic was between relationships or Jane was lonely or having a hard time dealing with her mother, her sister, or their son. By that stage their relationship was firmly in the friends-with-benefits zone, which suited Dominic completely, and Jane seemed happy to make the best of it. Then it stopped when Dominic met Gina at a conference held in the Gresham Hotel. She was a country girl, accomplished, nice to Jane and kind to Kurt. They lasted for three years, and Jane was sure they'd marry, but when Gina demanded a ring, Dominic walked away and found himself in Jane's bed once more. And so their sexual history had continued until the last time they'd had sex—the night he'd split with the tripped-out Heidi.

A week later he had arrived to Kurt's fifteenth birthday with his new girlfriend, Bella, and one month later they were engaged. Dominic and Jane hadn't slept together since, and after the night in the car when he'd clearly attempted to seduce her, Jane felt more than a little awkward around him, and so his insistence that she invite him to Elle's Missing Exhibition made her extremely uncomfortable, especially in light of Kurt's recent admission that things were weird at his dad's house.

Elle felt like a new woman since her weekend away with Leslie. She had continued to work for hours every day, laboring over each face as though re-creating it in the presence of God. When the collection of twelve was completed, two of her old art school contemporaries arrived at her cottage to view the works. Fiona and Lori arrived together and Elle greeted them warmly, hugging Fiona and then Lori, and when Lori pointed out that they hadn't seen her since before Christmas she explained that she had been working very hard. They complained that she hadn't bothered to turn up to her last exhibition and she apologized for her absence, telling them that she'd come down with the flu.

She made coffee before the unveiling, and Fiona admitted that they'd heard the gossip that Vincent had ended the relationship and that she'd burned out his car.

Lori laughed a little. "He deserved it," she said.

"Elle," Fiona said, "he's a user, always was and always will be."

Elle poured the coffee. "So what's the story about the blonde?" she asked. "Caroline. I bumped into them recently."

"She's an actress on that stupid drama shot in the UK. What's it called?" Fiona asked Lori.

"Can't remember, but I've heard that she strips every second episode," she replied.

"So now he's living off her," Elle said, and she grinned. "Lucky girl. Until another source of income takes his fancy."

Lori and Fiona looked at each other, and Lori made a face.

Fiona turned to Elle. "He married her," she said.

"What?" Elle said. "No! It's only been five minutes. No way! Really?"

"Sorry," Lori said.

Elle was in shock. "He married her."

"Last week," Fiona said. "In a registry office, and the afters were in the Four Seasons."

"It's featured in this week's *VIP* magazine," Lori said. "Can you believe that? The only thing important about him is the person he's sleeping with."

Elle brushed it off, telling her two friends that she wished Vincent and Caroline the best, and then changed the subject. After talking some more they followed her to the studio, and they were both impressed with her work, going as far as to say it would be her best show yet.

"I feel like crying," Lori said, looking across the twelve faces, including Alexandra's, whose slight smile made her ache inside.

"It's genius," Fiona said, "and it's such a great concept."

Now that Elle was finished with her latest project, the girls would accept no excuses and insisted she join them at a party after the exhibition the next night. They left soon after, and Elle sat at her baby grand piano that took up half her sitting room and played some notes and decided that it was time she got back in the game.

Jane appeared later that afternoon, and they packed up the paintings together. Elle told her about Vincent, and Jane called him some names and wished ill health upon him, but Elle was determined to be over him and so her bitching seemed unnecessary. After Jane left, Elle got into a bath and soaked for a glorious hour. When she grew bored she got out and lathered herself in the richest of creams. She sprayed on her favorite perfume, pulled her hair off her face into a tight ponytail, and dressed in her sexiest short dress and highest black heels. She left her cottage and walked up the path toward the side gate that would lead her to the front gate and on to adventure.

Rose was standing outside when she passed.

"You look like a whore," she said.

"I plan to act like one," Elle said.

"Well, at least no one can say you're a tease," Rose said, and she headed indoors.

Leslie had spent the week in and out of the hospital having tests to ensure that she was healthy enough to have her breasts and womb removed. She remarked on the irony of the situation to one of the nurses who, having been on her feet for twelve hours straight, wasn't interested in irony—all she cared about was getting the necessary bloods so that she could move on to the next patient and so on until her shift was over.

Jim had asked Leslie if she wanted him to go with her, but she had politely and firmly told him no. He had a job and a life of his own, and it wasn't as though she hadn't been going to medical checkups on her own for the past eighteen years. She was in the waiting area reading a pamphlet on reconstructive surgery and picking at some trail mix when a tall, bald man in his late forties sat down beside her. He nodded hello and opened a newspaper. They both sat reading for ten minutes or so before he closed his newspaper and asked her if she had the time.

She looked at her watch. "Just after three," she said.

He sighed. "I've been here since seven this morning."

"Hell," she said.

"Hell," he agreed, and he smiled at her a big wide smile and she wondered how he could smile with such warmth and how he could carry himself with such cheer when it was obvious he had cancer and was going through chemotherapy.

"I'm Mark," he said, and he put out his hand. "It's nice to meet you."

"Leslie," she said, and she shook his hand.

"Are you a patient or family/friend?"

"Patient. Are you starting chemo or near the end?"

"That obvious?" he said, rubbing his freshly shaved head.

"It's not the bald head—it's the color of your skin."

"Ah," he said, nodding. "Off-putting."

"Familiar," she said.

"Do you mind me asking why you're here, seeing as your hair is your own and your skin looks good too?"

"Thanks."

"You're welcome."

Leslie thought about lying or at the very least avoiding the question, but she didn't know the man, and aside from Jim she hadn't spoken to anyone about her radical plans, and so she was honest.

"I'm having my breasts and womb removed in a few months to avoid getting cancer."

"You're joking."

"No."

"To avoid getting cancer?"

"I have the gene."

"But that doesn't mean you'll get it."

"I've lost my entire family and my youth to cancer. I'm not willing to lose any more."

"Except your breasts and womb."

She laughed. "Except for them."

"Well," he said, "I've lost both balls."

Leslie was as taken aback by his honesty as he had been by hers. "Ouch," she said.

He grinned at her. "Could be worse. I could have my balls and no penis."

"True," she said. "That would suck."

They both laughed.

"Yes, it would," he said.

"So how does that work?"

"You mean sex?"

She couldn't believe that she was engaging in such an intimate conversation with a stranger, but she nodded her head to indicate that yes, she did mean sex.

"I can still orgasm, apparently, haven't tried it yet. Obviously I can't get anyone pregnant, and I'll need to inject hormones every few weeks."

"Ah, it'll be pretty much the same for me."

"I see you're thinking about reconstruction," he said, looking at the pamphlet.

She nodded.

"They offered me fake balls."

"Really? Did you take them?"

"No, too weird."

"I don't know what to do," she said.

"Then just take one step at a time," he said.

After a pause she said, "Mark?"

"Yes?"

"Are you married?"

"Divorced."

"Kids?"

"Two boys, twelve and ten."

"Is the cancer gone?"

"That's what they tell me," he said.

"Would you like to go to an art exhibition with me tomorrow night?"

"I'd love to," he said.

"Good," she said, "excellent."

They swapped numbers and soon after that she was called into her doctor's office, and the doctor couldn't help but wonder why she had a stupid grin on her face while he was talking her through the radical procedures she was facing.

Tom fought with Jeanette on the phone in his car. She was pissed off that he wouldn't allow her to attend the Missing Exhibition, and he couldn't understand why on earth she'd want to be there or how she thought her presence would be appropriate.

"It's appropriate because I'm the one sleeping beside you in bed."

"That is why it is so very inappropriate, Jeanette."

"It's not like I'm going to advertise myself. I'll stay quiet; I'll bring Davey and I'll pretend you're my friend and he's my boyfriend."

"No."

"So that's it?"

"Yes, that's it."

"Don't expect me to be waiting for you when you get home."

"Okay."

"Bastard!"

She hung up and Tom drove on, wondering how he had allowed himself to get into such a stupid and dangerous situation with a young woman who had a schoolgirl crush on him. *I'm so sorry, Alexandra. If only you'd come home to me, this nightmare would end.*

He pulled up outside his mother-in-law's house and beeped. She appeared at the door, and he ran up the path and put his arm around her shoulders.

"You look beautiful," he said.

She smiled at him. "You're a liar but I appreciate it."

Alexandra's father had decided not to attend the exhibition. He didn't feel comfortable in arty circles. Instead he would spend the evening as he always did, with his friends in the pub avoiding his new reality. Alexandra's sister, Kate, and brother, Eamonn, were attending with their spouses and traveling separately.

Tom helped Breda into the car and walked around to his side, got in, and took off down the road.

"It's very exciting," Breda said, "all this good work in Alexandra's name."

Tom agreed. Jane had been very pleased with the media interest, and when Elle had insisted that any proceeds earned would go to the National Missing Persons Bureau, it had been a major coup for them and a news story worthy of reporting. The fact that Jack Lukeman was taking time out of his busy touring schedule to come and play led to further interest, including a TV magazine show that wished to film a song from Jack and an interview with

Tom. He was pretty sick at the notion of having to talk to a camera, but Breda assured him he would be great and that Alexandra would be so proud.

Jane was waiting at the door. She greeted Tom and Breda with hugs and ushered them inside. They were early enough to see the pieces hanging from the wall without interruption. Breda stood in front of the painting of her daughter for the longest time. Silent tears rolled down her hollow cheeks. Tom took her hand.

"I still feel her," she said. "She's still with us."

"I know," Tom said, but he didn't know, and every time he ventured into the dark place, he left it hoping she was gone rather than enduring ongoing torture.

Leslie appeared with Mark a few minutes later. Jane welcomed them both and then asked Mark to excuse Leslie for a minute.

Leslie followed her into the back room.

"What is it with you and bald men?" Jane said.

"Is that why I'm back here?"

"No. Elle's missing. I was hoping you had talked to her today."

"No. I haven't. I don't believe it."

"The press is relying on her being here." Jane was starting to freak out. "I can't let everybody down now."

"You're not letting anyone down, bloody Elle is. I'll kill her."

Just then Elle appeared in her short dress and high heels. "Kill who?"

Jane let out a sigh of relief. "Where were you?"

"I have no idea. On a boat and a long way from land, if that helps."

"You nearly gave Jane a heart attack," Leslie said.

"Sorry, Jane. Sorry, Leslie."

"Don't be smart," Leslie said.

Elle hugged her. "I met a boy and I liked him. Of course he's gone now, sailing away on the high seas as we speak."

"Well, good," Leslie said, "good for you. Now go home, change out of the dominatrix gear, and have a wash while you're at it."

Elle saluted, and Tom was given the job of driving her home to wash and change before the exhibition.

Jane introduced Breda to Leslie and explained who she was and what she had done to help them find Alexandra. Breda was very grateful, Leslie humbled, and Mark incredibly impressed by his altruistic new friend.

Then Eamonn, Kate, and their spouses arrived, and Jane welcomed them and offered them wine and watched as they migrated toward the picture of their sister. Eamonn and Kate stood together, shoulders touching, looking into Alexandra's eyes. When they turned to face the crowd, Kate's eyes were damp and Eamonn looked like he was in physical pain.

Mark wasn't drinking, so Leslie merely sipped on a glass of wine. She asked him if he felt well enough to stay, and he said that he did. She told him she wouldn't ask him again so if he wanted to go he had a mouth and he could tell her. He liked that she didn't fuss over him. Dominic appeared with Kurt and Irene in tow. Jane was delighted to see her son and wondered what had brought about his sudden interest in one of Elle's exhibitions.

"What you and Elle are doing for your friend, well, it's really cool, Mum," he said.

"Yeah, Jane," Irene said. "Every girl could do with a friend like you."

Jane was taken aback. "Thank you."

She was still a little miffed, as Kurt had known about the show for months and he'd never seemed particularly interested or impressed before.

"Dad showed us pictures of you and Alexandra when you were our age," Kurt said.

"Can't believe you were a Megadeth fan," Irene said. "I love Megadeth."

Jane looked at Dominic. "What's this?" she asked, feigning a smile.

"Your mother wasn't half sexy in her day," said Dominic.

"Too much, Dad," Kurt said, "seriously, too, too much."

Irene explained that Dominic had shown them the pictures of the Megadeth concert in Antrim that they'd gone to one year before Kurt was born. Jane remembered the pictures: she was smoking and straddling Dominic, and Alexandra was drinking from a bottle of cider and giving the camera the finger.

Kurt nudged his mother and grinned at her and followed Irene to the drinks counter. They picked up a glass of wine each and raised them to her. She turned to Dominic and shook her head.

"What were you thinking?" she said.

"What do you mean?"

"Showing them those pictures."

"Why wouldn't I? They are part of our past."

"Kurt sees me and you and cigarettes and booze and—"

"And he'll run off and get his girlfriend pregnant?"

"Don't make fun of me!"

"I would never do that. Look, all I'm saying is your life isn't his life, so just relax."

"It's not him I'm worried about." Jane pointed to Irene, who was rubbing the back of Kurt's neck and whispering in his ear. "It's her."

"What will be, will be, Janey."

"Easy for you to say," she said, and went to talk to a representative of the National Missing Persons Bureau.

Jack Lukeman arrived on schedule. He was dressed head to

toe in black and his long coat swung behind him. Leslie greeted him with a hug and introduced him to Jane.

He put his hand out and she shook it. He cupped her hand, tipped his head to the side, and viewed her as though he was viewing a painting. She blushed. He grinned and let her hand go. "Nice to meet you, Jane."

Jane told him how lovely it was to meet him and about the many times she'd seen him play, the where and when, how she had gotten there, whom she had gone with, and how fantastic each show had been. Jack nodded as though he cared.

Leslie sighed and shook her head. "Jesus, Jane, as if he gives a shit."

Jack laughed a giddy, dirty laugh and put his arm around Leslie.

"Sorry," Jane said.

"You'll have to excuse her," he said. "She doesn't mix well."

Later Jack and his guitarist played an acoustic set, surrounded by paintings of the Missing, to a captivated crowd. They sat on chairs under a painting of Alexandra. The guitar player strummed gently and Jack leaned forward, closed his eyes, and sang "Metropolis Blue" into his microphone.

Sometimes I ask myself how did I get here?
Country boy with no change for his fares and city girls
are so expensive.
I wanna go back to the girl that I love, I would go back
there if I could.
I know I should. I need you. My lips ache for your kiss.
I need you and not this hungriness.
I just spend my time hanging around here with the boys, drink-
ing whiskey drinking beer,

*Fool I was thought adventure was near, those easy thrills are so
elusive I fear.*
*My heart sings for the one that I love. I would go back there if I
could, I know I should.*
I need you, my tune lacks your melody.
I need you, my eyes no longer see.
*I am floating like an autumn leaf, on the whim of a
breeze I float*
*I would give almost anything, a thousand jewels, an enchanted
view, a billion poems but I'm a fool.*
*I can barely write a note but we live in hope. I need you
for all eternity.*
I need you, you are you my destiny. I need you. I need you.

The audience was silent as though in church and clapped and
cheered only when Jack opened his eyes and smiled. Tom wiped
tears from his eyes. The TV cameras rolled. Elle was back, clean
and in a subdued black outfit, standing quietly and respectfully to
the side with Jane. When Jack had finished his set and the photographers were snapping and the crowd was clapping, she leaned
in toward Jane and whispered, "We've done well, Janey."

And Jane looked at Alexandra's mother smiling a genuine
smile and her sister and brother clapping and charmed by the talented Mr. Lukeman, who had managed to make them forget their
loss if only for a few minutes. She caught Tom's eye, and they
smiled at each other. She turned to Leslie, who was laughing with
the latest bald man in her life, and Jane felt happy.

Jane was about to go to bed when the doorbell rang. She looked
through the peephole and it revealed Dominic. She thought about

ignoring him, but he pushed on the buzzer again and held it down. She opened the door.

"Go away."

He held the door open. "Please let me in."

She let him in.

He sat on the sofa and hugged a cushion. "I think my marriage is over."

"I'm sorry to hear that."

"The bitch just kicked me out of my own house. I mean, is that even legal?"

"Well, it's her house too."

"My arse it is! I've had that house ten years—we've only known each other five minutes."

"Which begs the question as to why you married her in the first place."

"She was pregnant. She lost the baby at eleven weeks."

Jane was shocked. She hadn't ever guessed.

"As soon as I found out, I proposed, because I didn't want to be the same fucker I was to you. I wanted to be a good dad, a good man, but I suppose it wasn't meant to be."

"I'm really sorry." She sat down beside him.

"Don't say anything," he said, "just kiss me."

"Dominic."

"Please, Janey."

And so she kissed him and she straddled him like she had done so many years ago at the Megadeth concert, and they had sex on her recently re-covered sofa.

After he came and the condom was quickly disposed of, they sat together and he looked into her eyes and asked her, "Do you think we should try for another baby?"

For a second she thought he was talking about him and her,

but then the truth dawned. He was talking about his wife, the woman he had married, baby or no baby, and something inside her died. She stood up and fixed her skirt and asked him to leave.

"But I've nowhere to go," he said.

"I don't care."

"But I don't understand."

"I loved you for all these years. I was in love with you, but no more."

She walked him to her front door. She handed him his shoes. She bade him good night. She closed the door and walked to her bedroom, and once in bed she covered her head. She didn't cry because she had done that too many times before. Instead she just lay there and embraced the pain in her heart and told herself, *enough now.*

Elle had smiled for photographers and made nice with the interviewer. She had shaken Jack L's hand and they had posed together. When her work was done, she joined her pals Fiona and Lori at a private party in a club she used to frequent.

"Well, if it isn't Elmore," one partygoer said. "Long time no see!" Two air kisses followed. Elle signed all her paintings "Elmore," but only the biggest assholes within her circle referred to her as anything but Elle.

She moved through the club and toward the pool table where some guys were playing, and she sat on the sofa nearby, and a waitress took her drink order. She drank and watched the guys play. One guy in particular interested her. When he finished his game she asked him to join her and had a drink waiting for him.

"I'd really like to have sex with you," she said.

"I'd like that too," he said.

"Of course you would."

"Are you playing with me?"

"Absolutely not. Tell me, do you like doing it outdoors?"

"It depends," he said. "What have you got in mind?"

"Come with me," she said, and he followed her through the club, outside, and down the street. They crossed the road and as they approached the police station he began to wonder about her, but she pressed a finger to her lips and when the coast was clear she opened the gate that led to the back of the station.

He pulled away from her. "You're insane," he said.

He heard some noise out front and she pulled him onto the ground under a window through which he had seen five or six men and women, some sitting at desks, some roaming around, one at the coffee machine, and another kicking the fax machine.

"We can't," he said, but she could tell that he was excited because he was leaning against her, and so she unzipped his pants and released him. After that there was no going back, and if any of the officers had taken a moment or two to look up and out the window, they would have seen a white, freckled bass player's ass appear intermittently. Afterward, invigorated, she returned to the club, where she joined Fiona in the loo for a few lines of coke. She drank shots with Lori, and as it was a celebration she paid for six or seven bottles of champagne for all twenty of her new best friends.

Kurt woke up around seven. He yawned, stretched, scratched his balls over his boxer shorts, and headed into the main bathroom. He peed, shook himself off, and flushed. It was when he turned around to leave that he saw Elle. She was lying in a bath filled with water. She was completely naked, her lips were purple, and she was either asleep or dead.

Kurt roared. "Mum! Mum! Mum!"

Jane woke up with a start. Kurt was still roaring. She jumped out of bed and followed his yells to the bathroom, where he had remained frozen.

"Oh my God," Jane cried. "Oh my God, Elle!" She ran to her sister and touched her cold skin and shook her hard.

Elle's eyes opened, and she yawned.

"What's happening?" she asked.

"Oh Jesus," Jane said, and sank to her knees. "I thought you were dead."

"I am really cold," Elle said, realizing that she was in a bath of freezing water.

Kurt exhaled and sat on the toilet seat. "Holy shit, Elle."

Jane asked Kurt for a towel. The only one he could find there was a hand towel, which he handed to his mother. She responded with a dirty look.

"Come on, Elle, time to get out," Jane said.

"I can't seem to move my legs," Elle said, and she giggled.

Jane looked at Kurt.

"Oh no," he said, because lifting his naked aunt out of the bath was above and beyond the call of duty.

"I need your help," Jane insisted. "I have to get her out now."

Kurt nodded at his mother and walked over to the bath, flexing his neck and trying not to focus on his aunt's bush. Elle gave him her hand and smiled at him, and her purple lips partially stuck to her teeth. Jane took the other arm, and together they pulled Elle up.

Kurt closed his eyes when he felt his aunt's breast against his chest. "Oh Mum, this is so wrong."

Elle giggled again.

"Here," Jane said, "I'll take her from the front, you go around—"

"Don't even say it," he said.

Jane and Kurt pulled Elle out of the bath, and while Jane held her up Kurt ran to the towel warmer and piled his arms high with bath towels. Jane wrapped Elle in a towel, and Kurt helped his mother carry her into Jane's room. Once she was dry and safely snuggled in bed with the electric blanket on, Jane went to the kitchen and boiled the kettle to make some tea for Elle.

Kurt followed his mum into the kitchen.

"Are you okay?" Jane asked her son.

"My eyes, Mum, my eyes!" he said, covering his eyes and pretending to be blinded.

He was playacting, so Jane relaxed, content that he wouldn't be scarred for life.

"I'm sorry, Kurt. You shouldn't have had to deal with that."

"It's fine, Mum. If it ever happens again I'm moving to France, but it's fine." He was smiling, which suggested he was joking, and after his coming into skin-on-skin contact with his naked aunt that was the best she could hope for.

"I got lucky with you," she said, and Kurt blushed just like his mother often did.

"Whatever," he said.

"Kurt?"

"Yeah."

"Don't you think it's a bit weird that Irene didn't wake up?"

"She wears earplugs. She says I snore like a pig and you should have had my adenoids out when I was a kid."

"How does she hear you snore from the spare room?"

"Oh crap!" He grinned and held up his hands. "She's on the pill, I wear condoms, and I'm turning eighteen in two weeks."

Jane sighed. "I give up."

"About time." He waved her away and headed back to bed to sleep off the image of his aunt's tits and ass.

Jane handed Elle the tea. It was too hot, burning her frozen hands, so Jane kept hold of it and fed it to a shivering Elle until it was gone.

"What's going on, Elle?"

"Just wanted a bath, Janey."

"You could have frozen to death."

"I was just really tired. Big night."

"Did you take something?"

Elle nodded. "I was having a good time—but I won't do it again."

"Do I need to call Dr. Griffin?"

Elle shook her head. "No. I'm just cold, that's all."

Jane sighed and tucked the blanket up under her sister's chin. "What am I going to do with you, girly girl?"

"Just love me, Jane, even though I don't deserve it," Elle said, and then she turned around and fell fast asleep.

Jane sat in the room, touching her sister's hand every few minutes, until she returned to a normal temperature. She turned off the electric blanket and the light and then made her way to the kitchen.

Through the intercom she heard Rose calling.

"Jane, Jane, Jane! It's your mother!"

Jane put her hands over her ears, and if she hadn't been scared of frightening her son for the second time that morning, she would have screamed until her voice was gone.

9

"No Goodbyes"

I love you now as I loved you then
but it's time to save our prayers,
it's time to say amen.

Jack L, *Metropolis Blue*

May 2008

Breda went to Mass every day and had done so for well over thirty years. Every morning she would wake at seven; she'd wash, dress, and drink a cup of tea; and then she would put on her hat and coat and walk a mile down the road to her local church in time for the eight o'clock service. Over the years she had noticed the church becoming emptier and emptier. The young people had all but disappeared and all that was left were a handful of old men and women, most of whom were waiting patiently for the Lord to call them home.

Breda was early, so she knelt and put her hands together and looked up at the statue of Jesus hanging on the cross. She said an

Our Father and then some Hail Marys and a Glory Be after that. The church was empty. Her knees were hurting her and she felt tired and cold. She leaned on the pew and pulled herself into a sitting position, then joined her hands again and waited for the priest and the few last souls seeking solace or saving to join her.

"Dear God," she said, "I look at Your son on the cross, I see the nails in His hands and feet, the thorns on His head, the blood in His eyes, the wound in His side, and I'd trade places with Him in an instant if You would just give me my Alexandra back. This burden is too great and I can't carry on much longer. I'm begging You as your servant, have pity on me. Show her the way home. I'm leaving now." She got up and bowed before the altar. "I won't be back tomorrow or the next day or the day after that. The day she comes home, that's when You'll see me here again." She walked out of the church, and although bargaining with or indeed threatening the Lord was slightly unnerving, Breda felt that He had left her with no choice.

Kurt woke up to Jane, Rose, Elle, and Irene singing "Happy Birthday" at the end of his bed. He grinned because his grandmother was wearing a party hat with 18 written on it, and Elle was draped in a banner that read 18, LEGAL, AND PISSED ALREADY. Irene was bouncing up and down and blowing on a horn. His mum was standing in between them holding a cake with candles blazing and, of course, she was fighting tears. She always cried at every birthday and every milestone, so it was only a matter of time. He smiled, rubbed the sleep from his eyes, and sat up.

Jane made her way around the bed. "Blow," she said.

Kurt blew out the candles in one go. Elle, Rose, and Irene clapped.

Jane leaned in and kissed his cheek. "Eighteen," she said, and she burst into tears.

A big breakfast of steak and chips awaited him when he was showered and dressed. He sat wearing his birthday hat, munching on his favorite food while his mother, aunt, gran, and girlfriend fussed around him. Jane made Rose and Elle some toast while they sat at the table with the birthday boy.

Rose was the first to slide a present across the table. He looked at the envelope and grinned.

"So far I like it," he said, and he opened it. Eighteen one-hundred-euro notes fell out. "This is too much."

She tapped his hand. "It's enough to take you and Irene on a sun holiday after your exams."

"No way," he said.

"Oh my God!" said Irene.

"Apparently it's a rite of passage," Rose said.

"Mum?" he said, waiting for her to veto the trip.

"I've heard that Greece is pretty special," she said.

"No way!" he said.

"Oh my God!" Irene said again.

He leaped up from his seat and dragged his grandmother off her chair and hugged her, and she held him tight for a few moments before letting go.

"You're such a good boy," she said.

Irene jumped up and down on the spot, saying, "Thank you, thank you!" over and over again.

Elle was next. She walked into the hall and came back in with a large box wrapped in red paper. Kurt tore at the wrapping. He opened the box and lifted out a helmet.

"A helmet?" he said, and Elle grinned and turned to Jane, who sighed and pointed to the garden.

Kurt stood up and looked out the window and saw his dad straddling a motorbike. Dominic grinned and waved. Kurt looked at his mother. "No way!" he said, shaking his head.

"Please, I'm begging you to be careful!" Jane said.

"No way!" Kurt shouted, and the back door was open and he was standing beside his dad in two seconds flat.

Dominic handed him the keys and they hugged, and Dominic pointed to his mother and told him that the bike was from both of them, and Kurt ran back in the back door and hugged Jane. She burst into tears again, but this time it wasn't a result of oversentimentality but instead disbelief that Dominic had managed to talk her into buying her baby boy a death trap. Elle handed him the helmet. He hugged her and ran back out to his dad. Together they examined every inch of the bike.

"A Suzuki Bandit 600!" Kurt said. "Holy crap, a Suzuki Bandit 600!"

Jane closed the door and left them to it. Rose kissed her on the cheek.

"What was that for?" Jane asked, a little taken aback.

"Bravery. You're learning to let go, and that's good."

Jane sat down at the table. "Yeah, I suppose it is. Of course if he kills or maims himself I'll hate myself forever."

"You won't be alone," Rose said, and she made her way back to her basement apartment.

Elle and Jane went outside and sat on the steps and watched Kurt take off down the road as Dominic waved him off. Dominic turned and smiled at Jane. She returned his smile before getting up and going inside. Elle walked to where Dominic stood watching his son disappear down the road.

"What did you do to Jane?" she asked him.

"I married someone else," he said.

"She's finished loving you."

"She is."

"It had to happen sometime."

"Yes, it did," he said. "It's truly amazing she loved me at all."

"Yeah, well, the Moore women aren't the brightest when it comes to love," Elle said, and she walked to the gate that took her through the garden and to her little cottage.

Dominic found Jane loading the washing machine.

"Big day," he said.

"It is."

"Our son is a man."

"And still just a boy."

He sat at the table and turned his chair to face her. "Is that why you forgave me so easily? Because you knew I was still just a boy?"

"I forgave you because if someone had given *me* a way out, I would have taken it," she said.

"You're the best person I know," he said.

"Please don't try and sweet-talk me, because it's not fair," she said, sitting down on the floor.

"I'm not and I know. I know. I've been really selfish."

"I let you think I was fine with being friends."

"But I knew better," he said. "And I feel like a prick."

"Well, feeling like a prick isn't exactly unfamiliar territory for you."

"No. It isn't. What are we going to do, Janey?"

"Well, we're going to be parents to a pretty cool kid, you're going to work on your marriage, and I'm going to get a life."

"You're the best person I know," he said again. "You're kind and selfless and cool and funny and sometimes weird and dangerous and I really, really wish I loved you the way you loved me."

"I know you do," she said.

"And I will never cross the line again."

"No, you won't."

"But I don't want to lose your friendship."

"Okay," she said. "Let's just take it one day at a time."

He left soon after, and Jane closed her eyes and felt the pain pulse through her. *It's over.*

Because Kurt's eighteenth birthday fell only a few weeks before his Leaving Certificate exams, he agreed that he'd defer his party until afterward, and so when he returned from his bike ride, he grabbed his books, told his mum that he loved her, and went to school.

Elle went back to bed for a few hours and then met Leslie in the underwear department in Arnotts. She had promised to help her pick out sexy underwear for a date with the Ball-less Wonder, which was what Elle had christened Mark.

"What are we looking for?" Elle said.

"Something sexy."

"Well, obviously something sexy. You don't want to look like his mother—he has enough problems getting a stiffy as it is."

"Yes, that's exactly what I need to hear, thanks so much."

"All right, how about racy red?"

"No."

"Why not?"

"Because I'm not a racy-red person."

"Well, what are you?" Elle asked.

"I'm a sports bra and shorts person."

"Well, that's just not sexy, Leslie."

"Which is why I've brought you."

"Fine, then, you have to listen to me and do what I say or I'm going home."

"Fine," Leslie said, "but if you make me look like a hooker I'm leaving."

Having argued, debated, reflected, and conceded, Leslie finally purchased a black lace set. The bra was padded and lifted her in all the right places, and the pants were shorts as opposed to the G-string Elle had initially suggested.

She bought Elle lunch to celebrate.

Elle was surprised that Leslie was rushing into a relationship with a man who was recovering from cancer and so was interested to hear her reasoning. Leslie admitted that she was worried she was making a big mistake, but she felt a level of comfort with Mark that she hadn't felt with another man in a very long time.

"What about Jim?" Elle asked.

"Jim is my sister's husband."

"*Was* her husband. Your sister died a long time ago."

"And?"

"And he's a very nice man and he cares about you. He's a little on the short side, but you must admit those dimples are to die for."

"You're sick," Leslie said.

"I am not."

"He's my—"

Elle put her finger against Leslie's lips. "He's your friend, that's all."

Leslie saw it differently, and when Elle saw that she was becoming increasingly uncomfortable she returned to the subject of Mark.

"Why the rush?" Elle asked.

"I've known him three weeks."

"Exactly."

"You sleep with people you've met in restrooms, for God's sake!"

"Don't make me sorry for sharing my adventures with you. Besides, we're not talking about me, we're talking about you, a woman who hasn't had sex with anything that wasn't battery operated for eighteen years."

"So?" Leslie said.

"So, I'm curious as to what the rush is."

"I'm having surgery on the first of July."

"What kind of surgery?"

"A prophylactic bilateral mastectomy and laparoscopic hysterectomy."

"A what and what?"

Leslie explained the procedures to an open-mouthed Elle.

"How long have you known about this?" Elle asked.

"Pretty much since we met."

"Why are you only mentioning it now?"

"It didn't come up."

"That's the kind of thing you bring up."

"Well, I'm sorry," Leslie said. "This friendship thing is still new to me."

"You're forgiven. But only because you're having your tits lopped off."

"Charming!" Leslie said, and she laughed a little.

Following Leslie's admission, it was clear to Elle why she was in such a rush to have sex with an actual man, and a ball-less one at that. She wanted to experience it with all her bits just one last time. Elle wished her friend good luck and told her she would expect her call the very next day with full details. Leslie had no intention of providing her with anything like the full details, but she agreed just so Elle would let her go home. She had much to do before Mark arrived.

An hour before he was due, the house was clean and she was

washed, dressed, and looking good, even if she thought so herself. She had thought about cooking, but she wasn't a cook and so it seemed like a much better idea to just order in when he came. That way he could pick what he wanted and there would be no chance of him enduring a bad meal.

Jim phoned half an hour before Mark was due.

"Well?" he said.

"Well what?"

"Are you excited?"

"None of your business," she said, beginning to regret telling him about Mark at all. "Go away."

"Ah, come on, I'm sitting alone watching a DVD about two homeless drug addicts."

"Okay," she said. "Do you think I should play music or is that really corny?"

"No, it's not corny—definitely play music. What have you got?"

"Lots of stuff."

"Okay, what do you feel like listening to?"

"I don't know."

"Think."

"I can't, I'm too nervous."

"Okay, go over to your CD rack, close your eyes, and pick something."

"I don't have a CD rack. I buy all my music online."

"What do you do that for?"

"Because I no longer live in the year 1983," she said.

"Fine. So close your eyes and click on a song or do whatever it is you do to listen to music."

"Okay. Can I go now?"

"Yes," he said. "And, Leslie?"

"What?"

"Enjoy yourself."

"Thanks."

She hung up the phone and went over to her computer and clicked onto her media player. She closed her eyes and dragged the mouse along the various tracks listed, stopped, and clicked, and Alanis Morissette's "In Praise of the Vulnerable Man" started to play. *Apt.*

She sat holding her cat and waited for Mark to come.

Tom opened the door and found Trish, his liaison officer, standing outside. The house call was unscheduled, and so his heart started to race and his palms were instantly damp. If he'd allowed himself to, he would have begun to shake.

"Calm down, we haven't found her," she warned.

He followed her to the sitting room. They sat.

"*Crimeline* is going to do a reconstruction."

"Okay," he said. "It looks like Alexandra has captured the media's imagination. Finally."

"Finally." She nodded. "It's good news, Tom."

"I know."

"You should thank your friends. Without them . . ."

"She'd just be a number."

"Never just a number," she said, "but media interest always helps—just keeping her face out there helps."

She left soon after, and Tom picked up the phone and called Jane. He told her the good news, and they agreed to an impromptu celebration even though Elle and Leslie were unavailable. He offered to cook and she agreed to bring the wine, and so at eight fifteen she knocked on his door.

It was the first time Jane had visited Tom in his home, and it felt so strange being greeted by pictures of the adult Alexandra, the woman she didn't know. In the sitting room there were photos of their wedding day. Alexandra had made a beautiful bride, even in the shot when she stuck out her tongue at the photographer. Tom poured wine and they clinked glasses as it was customary to do. He thanked her once again and told her how grateful he was, and she told him to shut up and that he was boring her. It was true that media interest in the disappearance of Alexandra Kavanagh had increased considerably since their little exhibition, but they were a long way from finding her.

Tom once again put all his hopes in the one basket.

"This will work," he said.

"Please don't get too excited. It's only a reconstruction. It's good news but that's all."

"I know."

"You're contradicting yourself."

"I don't care. I'm happy."

The exhibition had been a great success insofar as the critics were happy, Alexandra's plight and the plight of many others had been given a little time in the spotlight, and they had made some money for the charity.

Originally Elle had put the painting of Alexandra aside for Tom or Alexandra's family pending Tom's decision, but only five of the twelve paintings had sold and a buyer had offered a great deal of money for Alexandra. Now Jane found herself in the uncomfortable position of having to approach Tom on the matter. If the money had been going into the Moore family business, there was no way she would have sold Alexandra, but because the sales were in aid of charity she felt obliged to earn as much money as possible. It had been a shock to her that the paintings failed to sell out, because Elle had been a surefire seller for a long time. Jane had begun to notice a slowdown in sales with some of her other artists, but she had put it down to various reasons and now she was wondering whether or not a change was going to come. This concerned her because while she had banked her money and scrimped and saved, her little sister had gone through money like there was no tomorrow.

Over dinner she broached the subject of the painting with Tom.

"Definitely sell it," he said.

"Oh great. I'm so glad you feel that way."

"To be honest, it's a bit of a relief. It was just too sad."

"I understand," she said.

"Do you ever wonder about fate?"

"Not really."

"I do," he said. "I think about that night in the lift and what would have happened if I'd taken the stairs or decided to give the gig a miss. If I'd gone home with my little bag of leaflets, I think I'd have lost the will and I'd be gone."

"Don't say that."

"It's true."

After dinner they sat in the sitting room and Jane told Tom about Kurt's birthday present of a motorbike and how she'd wrestled with it. Dominic had finally broken her, but she feared that she might now never sleep again. He laughed and told her she'd find a way—after all, he had. He didn't mention the way he'd found was getting pissed.

At the end of the night she thanked him for a really nice evening and one she had needed badly. He was getting her coat when the doorbell rang. Thinking it was her taxi, she answered it.

A girl stood in the doorway, looking quizzically at her.

"Who are you?" the girl asked.

"I'm a friend," Jane said. The girl's aggressive tone put her on edge.

"Jeanette, go on into the kitchen and I'll join you in a moment," Tom warned.

"No," Jeanette said, and it was apparent she'd been drinking. "I'm Jeanette, Tom's girlfriend," she said, and she put her hand out to shake Jane's.

Jane got such a fright she shook Jeanette's hand and told her it was lovely to meet her. This took the wind out of Jeanette's sails. Her aggression dissipated and she told Jane it was nice to meet her too, and all the while Tom was biting his lip and praying he was dreaming while at the same time trying to work out a plausible lie to salvage the situation.

"Jeanette, please, go wait for me in the kitchen," he begged.

Jeanette said good-bye to Jane, who was still smiling like a simpleton, and went into the kitchen, closing the door behind her.

"Jane—" Tom attempted to explain, but Jane just shook her head.

"No."

She walked out of his open front door, and he followed her to the gate.

"You don't understand," he said.

"Oh, I understand," she said. "You're a man, and men are self-centred, lying, cheating bastards. I thought you were different. I thought you were decent. But you're just like the rest of them."

"Jane—"

"Don't 'Jane' me!" she said, and now she was crying. "In fact you're worse than the rest of them because you pretend to be better, you pretend to give a shit!"

"I do!" he shouted.

"Your wife is missing, she's alone and lost or hurt or hurting or dying or dead, and what are you doing? You're fucking, that's what you're doing."

She moved to open the gate and he grabbed her arm. "Please," he said.

"Go fuck your girlfriend," she said, "and let me worry about my old friend!" She pulled her arm away and ran to the taxi that had arrived.

Tom watched her disappear.

He walked inside his house, grabbed Jeanette's coat from the banister, and went into the kitchen. He wrapped it around her shoulders and pushed her through the hall and front door and closed the door in her face without saying one word. She banged on his window and door for a few minutes, then gave up. She knew that whatever sweetness they had once shared had turned sour.

The next night she'd tell her friends all about it over dinner, and they'd tell her he was a user and a jerk and that she was too good for him anyway because he was a broken man.

"Throw him on the pyre and light a match," Davey would say, and Jeanette would laugh and decide that although she would miss him, she wouldn't miss his problems, and so she'd drink to finding a man her own age—sexy, funny, uncomplicated, and without a tragic past.

When Leslie didn't call, Elle decided to visit her in her apartment. She buzzed, Leslie let her in, and she bounded up the stairs. She sat with the cat while Leslie looked for some tea bags because Elle was attempting to cut down on coffee.

"Well?" Elle asked.

"He didn't come."

"Well, he probably couldn't. I mean, I'm not a doctor but, sperm lives in balls and he is ball-less—ergo no come."

"I mean he didn't turn up."

"Oh. What happened?"

"About an hour after he was due he phoned and told me he was sorry but that he wasn't ready," Leslie said, dropping a tea bag into a mug of boiling water.

Elle preferred it when the bag was placed in the teacup before the boiling water, but she wasn't about to argue.

"Sorry," Elle said.

"The man has lost his wife, his kids, and his balls all in the space of a year. He's just finished chemo. I was mad to think anything could happen."

"Not mad. You were just trying to open yourself up, and maybe you rushed it with Mark, but that's okay. Next time will be better."

Leslie smiled at her new friend, because what she said was true. Leslie had rushed into something with Mark. She had been so desperate to move on and to be with someone who really understood what she was going through, and it had all been a little too simple. The poor man had his own issues, his battles to win and lose. Elle was right, next time it would be better because next time she'd know better. *I'm not ready and that's okay.*

"How's Jim?" Elle asked.

"Do not bring Jim into this," Leslie warned.

Elle put her hands up. "Okay, Miss Touchy."

"I am not Miss Touchy!"

After Elle left most of her tea in the cup and Leslie was fortified with a nice hot coffee, they decided to take advantage of the bright, warm day by going for a stroll in Phoenix Park. Leslie was at her mailbox when Deborah from Apartment 8A entered the main door. Deborah had managed to maintain a safe distance from Leslie since the cat shit incident. She mumbled hello.

"Well, hello, Deborah," Leslie said loudly.

"Hi," Deborah said.

"Yes, this is my friend Elle. Say hello to my friend, Deborah."

"Hi," Deborah said again.

Elle grinned. She'd heard the story more than once because for some reason Deborah's misguided concern for Leslie had really hit a nerve.

"You see, Deborah, loners don't have friends."

Deborah nodded and looked around to see if there was anyone around who could possibly save her if Leslie decided to physically attack.

"I'm going now," Deborah said, and she made her way to the lift.

"Lovely seeing you!" Leslie called.

Deborah disappeared into the lift.

"You need help," Elle said.

"Yes," Leslie said, "I really do."

They took a stroll in the park and ended up in the zoo and enjoyed a perfectly charming day together that both women would remember with fondness for a very long time.

On May 29, 2008, the television show *Crimeline* featured a reconstruction of Alexandra's last movements. In the week that had passed, Tom had attempted to call Jane, but she didn't pick up the phone, nor did she respond to his messages. In one of those unanswered messages he reminded Jane of the date and time of the show and he once again thanked her for all her support and help getting him this far along the track. Then he apologized for not being a better man. Jane had listened to his message a number of times, and her anger turned to regret and embarrassment because as much as she was disappointed that Tom had turned out to be a human being with actual faults, the person she was really shouting at that night was Dominic. Of course, that was Jane's problem. She couldn't scream and shout at Dominic. Because she had always been so desperate to win his love she never allowed him to see who she really was and how messed up and sad and lonely and sometimes bitter and hateful she could be. Because to show him that would be to go against the image of cool, great, kind, anything-goes Jane, the Jane she had spent the last eighteen years creating for Dominic and Dominic alone. She took out her pain and aggression on Tom—poor, desperate, haunted Tom—and she felt really sick about it.

The only silver lining was that she hadn't told Elle or Leslie about her encounter with Tom's whore. Her reasoning had simply been that she didn't want them to be as disappointed in him as she was. She didn't want them to stop searching for her friend just because her husband was a selfish dick. But now it dawned on her that neither Leslie nor Elle would have been as disappointed as she was because neither of them was a silly, stupid romantic, and while she had seen Tom as some sort of hero, they merely saw him as a man.

The night of the reconstruction she sat in her sitting room with Elle and Rose, and even Kurt and Irene took a break from pretending to study so that they could all follow Alexandra into the ether and, with any luck, beyond. She had thought about calling Tom just before the show aired, but she didn't have the nerve, so she left it.

Breda sat on her favorite green-velvet chair surrounded by her family—Eamonn and Frankie, Kate and Owen. Even their five-year-old, Ciara, was sitting there quietly waiting to see Auntie Alexandra, or at least the actress who would be playing her.

Alexandra's father smoked a cigarette in the garden and then came inside and sat down in the midst of his family, finally about to face what had gone so wrong.

Despite Breda's invite, Tom watched it alone.

An actress with brown hair, dressed in black trousers and a black shirt with a large bow and carrying a black tote bag, appeared in the doorway of Alexandra's home. The camera followed her walking along her street. An actress in her midfifties was brushing the step at No. 14. Mrs. Murphy had been asked if she'd like to play herself but she had been too shy and had felt an actress would be better. The fake Mrs. Murphy called out to the fake Alexandra, saying what a lovely day it was. The fake Alexandra agreed that it was perfect, and she walked on toward the station and through the turnstiles and stood waiting for the DART. The same three teenagers who had seen the real Alexandra sing James Morrison badly had agreed to be part of the reconstruction to win cool points—the eleven months had done wonders for their skin, especially the girl's. The fake Alexandra started to sing James Morrison's "The Last Goodbye" badly. The teenagers acted as though they were laughing, and one of the boys even slapped his thigh. The fake Alexandra stuck out her tongue and they pretended to laugh harder, ensuring that the camera moved away from them quickly. When the DART arrived, she stepped onto it and sat beside an actor in his midfifties. Across the way an actress in her forties was looking out the window. The camera returned to the fake Alexandra and fake old man. He asked her to wake him at Tara Street if he slept. She agreed. There was a shot of the DART moving along the track before a return to the inside shot. The DART pulled into Tara Street Station and the fake Alexandra nudged the old man and told him it was time to get off. He got off, and she jumped out of the DART and followed him and handed him a bag. He thanked her and she returned to the train. The fake stranger sitting opposite, who had been looking out the window when the fake Alexandra had gotten on the train, grinned at her and told her that her own dad was as bad. The fake Alexandra mentioned that the doddery old man had been sweet, and then they looked away from each other and out the windows. Another shot of the DART on tracks and Dalkey Station appeared. Inside again, the fake Alexandra picked up her bag and stood up and fixed her clothes before disembarking. She made her way through the station and out into the sunshine. She continued straight on to the main street and took the left at the end of the street; after that she took a right and then another left, and after that the fake Alexandra faded from the screen and was gone. The presenter appeared in front of the screen showing an empty street in Dalkey. He reminded the viewers of the date and time of the incident. He reminded them of the woman's name and reiterated what she had been wearing, her height and weight. He asked people to cast their minds back to that day.

"The twenty-first of June 2007—a bright, warm day, a day when Alexandra Kavanagh née Walsh, daughter, sister, friend, and wife, turned a corner in Dalkey and vanished from plain sight. Someone knows something. If you're that someone, please call." He gave the hotline number and the e-mail and postal addresses, and then he moved on to a robbery in Carlow.

Jane, Elle, Kurt, Irene, and even Rose sat quietly. Rose was the first to get up to leave, shaking her head and sighing.

"She was a cheeky pup in her day, but nobody deserves that," she said, and she made her way back to her basement apartment and to a well-needed drink.

Irene and Kurt made their excuses and returned to their studies. Elle and Jane sat together in the dark. "Wanna go to the pub?" Elle asked.

"I'll get my bag," Jane said.

Tom sat alone in his sitting room, ignoring the sounds of the texts buzzing on his phone. He drank from his whiskey glass and prayed that the someone who knew something would phone the hotline, because he wasn't sure how much longer he could hold on.

Alexandra's father cupped his face in his hands and cried like a baby. This distracted Eamonn, Kate, and their spouses from Breda, and while they soothed and calmed him Breda stood up quietly and, unseen, walked up to her bedroom and took off her cardigan and folded it on the bed. She pulled down her duvet and she got into her bed, and except to go to the toilet, that was where she stayed.

10

"Lost in Limbo"

Here we are blind but trying to see
and here we are speechless but trying to sing,
and here we are paralysed but trying to tango,
lost in limbo.

Jack L, *Broken Songs*

June 2008

Jane was doing her accounts in the gallery. When she looked up from her computer screen it was just in time to see an extremely glamorous woman in her late forties enter the premises. It was a hot day but the woman wore gloves anyway, and she took one off as soon as she entered.

"Jane Moore?" she said.

"Yes?"

"I'm Martha, Irene's mother."

"Oh," Jane said, standing, "hello."

"Hello," she said and smiled a wide smile, revealing perfect porcelain teeth. "I thought it was about time we met."

"Okay," Jane said.

Martha pulled a chair that was resting against the wall up to Jane's table and sat down. Jane put her hand out to shake Martha's but she didn't seem to notice it, so Jane sat.

"Well," Martha said, "Irene is so enchanted by you I honestly don't know who she has a bigger crush on—you or your son."

Jane had no idea how to respond to the woman's statement or her passive-aggressive tone, so she remained silent. Martha took another moment to remove her second glove.

"It seems she is determined to stay with you," she said, "but then how could I compete with a party house where anything goes?"

She again smiled a wide smile, and Jane could feel her temper rising and her face twisting, the way her mother's did before she spewed bile.

Martha's smile remained fixed. "So I was hoping you'd give me some tips on how to get her to come home."

"I wasn't aware you'd noticed she'd gone," Jane said in a tone that matched her mother's at her very snottiest, "but then, you were preoccupied with a boy young enough to be your son. I guess mine isn't the only party house in town."

"Funny," Martha said. "I suppose you think I'm a bad mother because I needed to take some time out to recover from a broken marriage. I suppose you think that you're a better mother than me."

"I do and I am," Jane said, channeling Rose.

"Oh really. I know that you're allowing them to sleep together under your roof, allowing them to drive around on a motorbike together, and don't think I don't know about the drinking."

"In case you failed to notice, your daughter had a birthday in February, and as they're both eighteen, everything I let them do, they're entitled to do. I also feed them, clean up after them, listen to them, encourage them, and watch over them, so if you ever want to come into my gallery again it will be with the intention of thanking me for caring for Irene. Understand?"

"You know, I met your mother once at a bridge club. She was a nasty bitch and you're exactly like her."

"I'll take that as a compliment," Jane said. "Now get out."

Martha stood up. "My daughter belongs with me." Her bitchy I'm-better-than-you façade was slipping. "How the hell can I compete with you?"

"I don't know how to help you, Martha, and to be honest you haven't inspired me to want to," Jane said.

Martha walked out, leaving Jane to stare after her.

What an ungrateful tart.

It turned out that Martha had split with her boy toy, and in his absence she missed her daughter. A few days earlier she had approached Irene about coming home and Irene had told her she was happy where she was and didn't want to move as it was so close to her exams. Martha had tried everything in her emotional arsenal to encourage her daughter to return home, but Irene was adamant that she was happy, safe, and secure, and that it was nice to be in a house where she was cared for. Martha had shouted that Irene was ungrateful and cruel to use the past few months against her, but Irene insisted that Martha had always been the kind of mother who had been absent whether she was there or not.

"It's not your fault, Mum. You are what you are."

Martha was selfish, the whole world revolved around her, but despite these failings she was also kind and charming and fun to be around, and Irene wasn't angry at her mum, she wasn't venomous, she didn't want to cause her pain. All she wanted to do was stay with her boyfriend and Jane until her exams.

"And then?" Martha had said.

"And then I don't know."

"Please come home to me then."

"No, Mum, I'm going to Greece with Kurt."

"For how long?"

"A couple of weeks."

"And then?"

"And then you'll probably be back together with whatever his name is or someone else."

"Irene," Martha said, "that's not true."

"Of course it's true," Irene said. "You can't be alone, and that's the only reason you want me home."

"Not fair."

"Totally fair. But it's okay—I understand. I'm terrified of heights; you're terrified of being alone. We all have our issues." She kissed her mother's cheek. "I love you, Mum."

Shortly after, Martha watched her peel off down the street on the back of Kurt's motorbike and instead of thinking about what her daughter had said, instead of realizing that the girl had a point and that she needed to change if she wanted their relationship to change, she thought about Jane Moore and what a stupid bitch she was for turning her daughter against her.

Leslie had three weeks to go before her operation, and the gravity of her situation was starting to take its toll on her. Sleep deprivation made her cranky and she couldn't help but focus on the mutilation her poor body would soon endure. She got out of the shower, wiped the steam from the mirror, and looked at herself, resting the palm of her hand on her stomach. With her other hand she cupped her left breast. She squeezed her breasts together, she tried to flatten them down, and then she held on to the sink and she screamed and screamed and screamed, and when Elle knocked at her door she was lying in the fetal position on the floor, crying for all that she was about to lose. When Leslie eventually opened the door, wearing nothing but her robe, she pretended that she was fine but Elle wasn't fooled even for a second.

"Get dressed," she said.

"No."

"Get dressed."

"No."

"Leslie."

"Elle."

"Get fucking dressed."

"No fucking way."

Elle grinned, and Leslie couldn't help but smile a little too.

When dressed, Leslie wanted to know what Elle had planned, but all she would say was that they were going on a drive. Leslie really didn't feel like driving, but Elle was adamant that she needed to run away from herself.

"You can't run away from yourself," Leslie said.

"Of course you can," Elle said. "You'll see."

It was a hot day and Elle had no idea where they were heading, so she pointed the car in a direction and just kept going. She put the top down and music on and ordered Leslie to lie back and allow the breeze to fill her lungs and play with her hair. Spending time with Leslie had reminded Elle how short and precious life was, and she felt a great need to make the absolute most of every second before she moved on.

After they had been driving for over an hour, Leslie voiced concern as to when they'd reach their destination.

"We'll know when we know," Elle said.

Leslie sighed deeply and shook her head to signal to her friend that she wasn't happy, then lay back, and when the wind caught her hair she smiled.

The sunshine made every town and village they passed seem prettier, the grass greener, the flowers more colorful, the people friendlier, and the world a little kinder and better. Elle and Leslie were warm, content, and looking forward to reaching their destination, wherever it might be. When two hours had passed and they were still driving, Leslie wondered whether they would make it back home and Elle assured her that they wouldn't. Leslie argued that she hadn't got a change of clothes or a toothbrush and, most important, that she hadn't left food out for her cat.

"We can buy what we need and ring Deborah—she'll care for the cat," said Elle.

"You are joking?"

"No, I'm not joking. I know she makes you a little crazy, but face facts. Deborah was right about you. You were a weirdo cat-loving loner who could potentially drop dead and rot."

"Excuse me?"

"You're excused," Elle said, "because that's not who you are anymore, so forgive and forget and ask her to feed your cat."

"What about a key, smart-ass?"

"Knowing you, you have one hidden somewhere in the building."

"How did you know that?"

"Because you're paranoid like Jane, which means you're one of those 'in case of' people and you're such an unfriendly cow there's no way you gave it to a neighbor."

"It's under the carpet to the left of my door."

Elle raised her hand. "There you go, then."

Leslie rang directory inquiries and asked for Deborah James's phone number.

They connected her, and Deborah answered immediately, "Ashley?"

"No, it's Leslie."

"Leslie who?"

"Leslie, the weirdo cat-loving loner with the potential to drop dead and rot."

"Oh," Deborah said, "you."

"Look, I know this is out of the blue, but I need a favor."

"Go on."

"I'm not going to make it home and I haven't left out any food for my cat. I'd really appreciate it if you'd feed her for me."

"Really?"

"Yes," Leslie said, "really."

"Key?" Deborah said.

"Under the carpet to the left-hand side of my door."

"Hmmmmm."

"Well?"

"Okay. I'll feed your cat."

"Thank you."

"Um-hum."

"And Deborah?"

"Yeah?"

"If you poke around, I'll know."

"Don't push it, cat lady."

"Okay," Leslie said, and she hung up. "Sorted," she said to Elle, and she lay back in her seat, breathed in deeply, and stretched her arms in the air.

Elle saw the castle in the distance and told Leslie that it was calling to her. It turned out to be a hotel. She drove up the winding road that led to the large wooden door. Leslie jumped out and looked around at the manicured gardens and shielded her eyes from the sun while she examined the turrets.

"Perfect," she said, and she followed Elle into the lobby.

Elle booked them in and they headed up to their room, which was a deep yellow color and dotted with pictures and small paintings that were rubbish according to Elle. The twin beds were covered with blankets, the top ones flowery, and in contrast the headboards were covered in gingham. Two pink chairs rested at the ends of the beds, and both women agreed the decor was vomit inducing and yet it suited the place perfectly. A white wood-framed window revealed the most beautiful view of gardens that seemed to roll into the sea. Although it was summer, the hotel was all but empty. Leslie and Elle lunched alone in the grand dining room, and when Leslie's mind drifted away, Elle brought her back with talk of a swim. Leslie wasn't too sure as she'd had two glasses of wine, but Elle assured her that the wine would only serve to heighten the experience.

"We've no swimsuits."

"We don't need swimsuits."

"I'm not getting into the sea in my knickers."

"Me neither," Elle said with a grin.

And before Leslie knew it she was following Elle across the lawns and through trees and toward the sea. Elle stripped as soon as she hit the water's edge and threw her clothes behind her and ran full steam ahead into the water. Leslie called after her, but she was gone and swimming, powering through the water like a shark chasing its prey. The sun glistened on the water, making it sparkle, and she was so tempted to feel its softness on her skin. She looked around and there was no one to be seen. *To hell with it*. She stripped and ran as fast as she'd ever run into the freezing water and disappeared under it only to come up spluttering and with her hair all over her face and in her eyes and mouth.

"Holy shit! The cold!" she roared.

Elle laughed and told her to swim and she did, and although she wasn't the powerhouse in the water that her friend was, she swam and swam until the cold turned to warmth and she could stop and enjoy the water swirling around her body.

Elle swam up to her. "Nothing quite like the freedom," she said, "is there?"

"No. There isn't."

They were bobbing along and planning the evening ahead when Leslie spotted a boat in the distance. Mortified, she alerted Elle and was about to make a dash for the shore when Elle grabbed her arm and told her to relax. The boat was coming closer and Leslie could see that there were two men on board.

"Relax? I'm naked!"

"So?" Elle said, and she winked. "Time to get your tits out for the boys."

"Excuse me?"

Elle laughed, and then she kicked and pushed herself out of the water, revealing her breasts, and the men whistled, and she waved and looked to Leslie, who was cringing.

"It's now or never," she said.

Leslie thought about it for a split second, and before she knew it she was revealing her naked breasts to an appreciative audience of two. They wolf-whistled and clapped, and she was laughing and lapping it up, and when she turned to Elle and caught her eye they both registered that they were sharing in a perfect high. They turned away from the men and swam to the shore and ran out and shook themselves off. They covered themselves, and the boys waved, and they responded.

When they had dressed, Leslie lay on the sand in a wet T-shirt and leggings and turned to her friend. "Thanks," she said.

"My pleasure," Elle said, and they both grew silent and stared into the blue sky.

When it got dark, they ventured to the local pub. It was a tiny spit-on-the-floor place with wooden pews for seats and rickety tables leveled by coasters. They enjoyed a couple of drinks before the two men from the boat appeared, and of course Elle was delighted to see them and immediately invited them to join them. Leslie was mortified, the high-on-adventure feeling she'd experienced earlier turning to embarrassment and awkwardness, but Elle was having none of it. The men were both in their early thirties. They were fishing for a few days and roaming from port to port. They introduced themselves as Adrian and Keith. Adrian was tall and broad and he had mousy brown hair, tousled, and stubble on his face. He reminded Leslie of Grizzly Adams. Keith was slightly taller and leaner than his friend. He had long hair tied at the nape of his neck and big brown eyes just like Vincent's except they were not framed by Vincent's thick lashes. The two men sat with their drinks in hand and Elle chatted with them as though she'd known them all her life.

"What about you?" Adrian asked Leslie.

"She's too embarrassed to talk," Elle explained when Leslie left him hanging.

"Why?"

"She's not used to exposing herself to strangers," Elle said.

"And you are?" Keith asked, and Elle laughed but failed to respond to his question.

"Well, trust me, Leslie," Adrian said, "you have nothing to be embarrassed about."

Leslie drained her glass. "Thanks," she said.

By the time the four of them were kicked out of the pub they were friends, laughing and joking and pushing one another down the street under a bright white moon. Adrian put his arm around Leslie's shoulders and she examined it for a second before relaxing against him.

"Adrian?"

"Yes?" he said.

"Would you like to have sex with me?"

"Yes, yes, and yes again," he said.

"Oh good," she said, "that's a big relief."

They walked together to the boat, and Keith and Elle kept walking, leaving them to it.

"How do you feel about a bed in a castle?" Elle asked.

"Sounds like bliss," he said.

"You haven't seen the décor."

They walked on, arm in arm.

"I'm not having sex with you," she said.

"Okay," he said.

"I find you attractive and funny, and ordinarily I would but I'm very tired and today has been perfect and I'd like to sleep now," she said.

"Okay," he said, and they walked into her room together and she kissed him good night and they jumped into the single beds and were asleep within minutes.

Leslie was standing in the middle of a bobbing boat wondering what she was doing. She heard the toilet light go off. The door opened and Adrian appeared. He walked up to her and she waited for him to kiss her. He fixed her hair and touched her face with his hand; he cupped her chin and leaned in and his lips hovered close to hers, and she wished to Christ he'd get on with kissing her because her legs were going to go from under her if she wasn't careful. And when he did kiss her, a deep, wet, soft kiss, she closed her eyes and thought, *This beats the shit out of batteries.*

They made love once, then twice, and after that she told him about her surgery and he kissed her breasts and placed his hand on her stomach as she had done that morning and a lifetime ago, and he told her that she was beautiful and that she would always be beautiful, and she cried and he held her, and when she was done crying he kissed her and they made love again.

On the morning that Kurt and Irene's Leaving Cert exams started, Jane was as nervous as if it were her own future on the line. Kurt found schoolwork easy—he was like his mother that way. Irene had to work a bit harder, but she was happy to do just enough to qualify for Nursing. He was determined to get Medicine. Jane laid out a huge breakfast to feed the pair of them, and when Irene was first into the kitchen Jane pulled out a chair for her.

"Sit," she ordered.

"I'm not that hungry, Jane."

"You need food," Jane said, and she began piling pancakes onto a plate.

As Kurt was still in the shower and they had time alone together, Jane asked Irene why she wanted to be a nurse.

"Because Kurt wants Medicine," she said. "And even if I studied day and night for forty years I wouldn't get Medicine."

"Kurt is your reason?"

"Kurt and I want to go to Trinity."

"But what if you hate it?"

"As long as we're together I'll love it."

"I hope you're right. Otherwise you're going to be cleaning vomit for the rest of your life because of a boy you knew when you were seventeen."

Irene laughed. "You're so funny, Jane!"

Kurt appeared, and they kissed, and Jane began to wonder where time was going.

Her son and his girlfriend enjoyed their hearty breakfast while Jane cleaned around them.

"Do you have enough pens?"

"Mum, you bought us about five thousand. Relax."

"Okay, double-check your bags for calculators."

"Have them," Irene said.

Jane put down the tea towel, reached into her bag and took out a twenty-euro note and put it on the table between them.

"Buy some lunch—oh crap," Jane said. "Batteries. I forgot batteries."

"What do you need batteries for?" Kurt asked.

"The calculators."

"They're solar," Irene said, and she giggled.

"Oh, right, of course they are."

"Jane?" Irene said.

"What?"

"If you didn't have Kurt, would you have gone to college?"

Kurt looked up from his food. It was a question he'd never thought to ask his mother.

"I was thinking about Medicine," she said.

"You never said!" Kurt exclaimed.

"Well, it was just an idea. After all, I didn't sit for the exams. I had you two weeks before them."

"I think you would have been a cool doctor," Irene said.

Jane smiled and blushed a little. "Thanks, Irene."

"Yeah, Mum," Kurt said, "you would have been cool."

"Thanks, son."

"It's a pity you were such a big slut," he said, and he winked at her the way his dad did when he said something outrageous and thought it was funny.

Irene and Kurt burst out laughing and high-fived, and Jane couldn't help but laugh along with them. *Cheeky little bastard.*

Midway through the exams, when Irene and Kurt had a day off, Martha invited her daughter and her boyfriend to lunch. Kurt regarded Irene's mother with suspicion, but Irene begged him to join them, so he did, and he was really glad he had. Martha had reviewed the situation she found herself in with her daughter and decided the only way back into her daughter's good graces would be to buy her way back in, and so at the end of an expensive lunch she handed her daughter an envelope.

It contained two InterRail tickets.

"What's this?" Irene asked.

"It's a month's traveling through Europe," Martha said.

"But we're going to Greece," Kurt said.

"For two weeks," she said, "and then you're going to Europe for a month." She smiled her big porcelain-toothed smile. *Anything the Moores can do I can do better.*

"No way!" Kurt said.

"Oh my God!" Irene shouted.

They hugged each other, and then Irene hugged her mother,

and Kurt shook her hand awkwardly, but when he moved in for a hug, they bumped and Martha pushed him off. "You're welcome," Martha said.

Twenty minutes after that, Kurt witnessed his girlfriend's mother manipulate her into coming back home on her return from Europe, and as much as he wanted to say something he kept quiet because Irene looked so happy.

At first Jane was unhappy with the notion of her child backpacking around Europe, so she called Dominic and they arranged to meet for lunch to discuss it. The rain had been coming down in buckets for three days straight. Jane battled her way into the restaurant and shook the rain off. Dominic was waiting. They kissed and it was slightly awkward, but both pretended not to notice. She got to business straightaway.

"That bitch thinks she's so clever."

"Or maybe she just wanted to do something nice for her daughter."

"She's getting back at me."

"Really? Don't you think you're being a bit paranoid?"

"No, I don't." She sighed. "She's saying in no uncertain terms that if she can't have her daughter, I can't have my son."

"I think you're being hysterical," he said, and she made that twisted face that made her look like her mother, so he backed down. "Or not—you're right and she's a bitch from hell, but at least Kurt gets to do something great."

"It's too much," she argued. "He's never been away from home for longer than a week, and that was with supervision, and now nearly an entire summer!"

"He's eighteen," Dominic reminded her.

"I know, but—"

"But nothing. My brothers did it, I did it, Brick and Mint did it, and we all came home safe and sound."

"Times have changed," she argued.

"Times are always changing. He's not going to war. All he's doing is strapping a bag on his back and going out into the world to have a blast."

"Did you have a blast?"

"Time of my life," he said.

"Alexandra spent two weeks in the Canaries with Siobhan Wilson and Christina Benson. She came home burned alive and with beads in her hair. She said it was the best time of her life."

"Who are they?"

"They were in our class."

"I don't remember them. What was she doing with them?"

"Oh, I don't know, Dominic. Maybe it was because her best friend was sleep deprived, knee-deep in nappies, and on the verge of a nervous breakdown."

"Oh yeah," he said, "sorry."

"So you think I should just let him go?" she asked then.

"I think that if you are really honest with yourself, you have no choice."

"God, I hate that woman!"

"I don't know—maybe you should thank her."

"For what?"

"Kurt's seeing you in a different light. He appreciates you in a way he didn't in the past."

"What do you mean?"

"I mean he's seeing you through his girlfriend's eyes, and as a mother you beat that Martha bitch hands down."

"Yes, I do," she said, and she smiled. "I can live with that."

• • •

It was true. Since his girlfriend had moved into his home, Kurt had come to appreciate his mother more.

"You're lucky," Irene told him one day in his room, "you just don't know how lucky you are."

"Easy for you to say."

"No. Not easy. I live with a woman who doesn't seem to notice if I'm there or not, and as for my dad, the last time I saw him was over three months ago. Your mum lives for you."

"Yeah, well, maybe that's the problem."

"That's not the problem, Kurt. The problem is she gave up her future for you and now you're scared she'll want to keep you."

"Bollocks," he said.

"Okay," she said.

"You're so full of shit, Irene," he said, and she laughed.

"Fine," she said. "Maybe I'm wrong, but it's a thought."

Irene was wrong, but it made Kurt think. A whole new world was opening up in front of him—opportunity, his first foray into adulthood, leaving home, university, making his own decisions, living his own life. He was so excited about his future and was counting down the days until he and Irene were on a flight and leaving their childhood behind for good. And eighteen years ago his mum had been standing in the same kitchen, but instead of holding a bag full of pens and a solar calculator she had been holding a baby, and instead of planning trips abroad, preparing for college and a life without Rose, she had been stuck in the rut she still found herself in eighteen years later.

Two days after their exams finished and with packs on their backs, Irene and Kurt made their way down the front steps and toward Jane, who was holding the car doors open. Elle sat on the wall, wearing sunglasses even though it was dull and raining. Rose emerged from her basement flat and stood by her door. Kurt put his bag in the trunk and went back to kiss his grandmother. She hugged him tight.

"Stay safe," she said. "Life is hard enough without you disappearing on me."

"It's only six weeks, Gran," he said.

"Six weeks is a lifetime, my darling. Live well."

"I will."

She let him go and watched him hug Elle, who took the opportunity to slip him an extra few euros.

"You don't have to do that," he said.

"I do," she said.

Irene got into the car and waved at Rose and Elle, and Kurt joined her. Jane got into the driver's seat and started the car, and Elle waved one final time, and they were gone. Rose went inside, and Elle sat on the wall smoking a cigarette and wearing her sunglasses despite the rain.

Jane had felt bad about the ways things had ended with Tom for a number of weeks, and when she eventually got the confidence to call him, she left a message apologizing for blowing up. She asked him to call her and told him once again she was sorry.

Tom had listened to the message, but he was too embarrassed, too ashamed, to call her back. In the few weeks that had passed he had found himself missing her. He missed her smile and the way she twisted her face when she wasn't happy. He missed her laugh and her calm and caring nature. He missed the devil side of her because just when you thought she was a total pushover, she pushed back, and by God she pushed hard. He liked that. He liked that she was formidable, just like Alexandra, and it made sense that they had once been best friends because in a way they were similar.

Jane missed Tom so much it interrupted her thoughts. She'd be on the phone to a buyer and she'd think of him and lose her concentration. She'd be parking the car and she'd stop dead in the middle of the car park just to remember a moment they'd shared, and only when someone beeped would she resume normal operations. She'd find herself thinking about him and worrying about him, and at night she lay awake wondering what he was doing, where he had been, where he was going, and whether or not she'd ever see him again.

Jane woke up early on June 21 and was up and out before eight. She knocked on Tom's door a little after eight forty-five, and when he didn't answer she pressed the doorbell and held it down until she heard him stamp down the stairs.

He opened the door roughly and, with a big sleepy head and wearing boxer shorts and a GO WEST T-shirt, he yelled, "What?" Then he wiped his eyes, focused, and saw who it was. "Jane."

"Tom," she said and pushed past him into the house. He followed her into his kitchen, where she set about finding the coffee.

"Second shelf on the left," he said.

She located it and made some.

"What are you doing here?" he asked.

"We're going to spend the day together," she told him.

"No."

"Yes."

"Jane, I don't want this."

"Want what? You don't want to spend the anniversary of your wife's disappearance with the woman who recently called you a fucking bastard? Fair enough, but tell me, what do you want to do?"

"I don't remember you exactly calling me a fucking bastard."

"Must have been in my head," she said.

He sat down at his counter. "I was thinking I'd stay in bed."

"No," she said, "out of the question."

"What do you want me to do?"

"I want you to come to Dalkey with me."

"You're joking."

"I think we should walk the streets she walked, and I think we should talk and reminisce, and then maybe we could get some lunch, and after that we'll hand out some of those flyers you keep in that black bag of yours by the door, and maybe we'll make our way into town and we'll stay there until it gets dark and this day is over."

Tom thought about it for a moment or two, then nodded. He went up to his bedroom and came down dressed and ready.

They walked together through the village of Dalkey, and as they walked they handed flyers to anyone who would take them.

After a while Jane decided to broach the subject they had both been avoiding.

"I'm sorry. I shouldn't have said those things."

"You were right," he said, "perfectly right."

"I was taking out my own frustrations on you," she said, "and while I'm never going to be able to comprehend how a man who loves his wife as much as you love Alexandra could possibly be with that woman, I'm still on your side."

"Alexandra's gone," he said, "and I miss her so much I ache, and I'm so terrified that I swear it's brought me to the brink of insanity and I'm just holding on, and for a while that woman helped me do that. I'm not making excuses. I'm just telling you the way it is."

"Okay," she said, "and again, I'm sorry." She handed a flyer to a woman pushing a pram. The woman looked at it for a second and then crumpled it right in front of them. "What a cow," Jane said, and Tom pushed her ahead.

"I ended it with Jeanette," he said. "Actually, if I'm honest, I treated her pretty poorly."

"What did you do?"

"I pushed her out the door and slammed it in her face two minutes after you left."

"Oh, that is a poor show."

"I blame you," he said, and he grinned.

"That's funny," she said.

There had been no developments since the reconstruction had aired. The police had received a number of calls after the show, but none of them had panned out. Tom was at a loss as to what to do next, and part of him wished that he could just let go.

"How about we get a drink?" he said.

"Love to," she said.

Tom put the flyers back into the black bag, and together they walked to the pub.

On the last day of June, Leslie sat up in her hospital bed. The nurse had just taken blood and the trainee doctor had just taken her history for the tenth time. She was asked if she wanted something to help her sleep, but she declined—she wanted to spend as much time with her breasts and womb as possible. She was wearing a nightshirt that Jane had bought for her, and under her bed were slippers from Elle. She moisturized her face and put balm on her lips. When the woman across the way tried to make eye contact, she pretended to read a magazine, and when the woman disappeared into the toilet, she jumped out and pulled the curtain around her bed.

The woman in the bed opposite watched the clock, waiting for visiting hour, but Leslie didn't expect any visitors because she had been adamant that she wanted to be alone.

Jim was the first to appear from behind the curtain with a bag of fruit and a bottle of 7UP raised high.

"I told you not to come."

"I wouldn't have expected you to say anything else," he said, and he sat on the chair by her bed.

"I can't believe you are ignoring my express wishes."

Jane called out Leslie's name, and Jim opened the curtain. "She's here," he said, and he turned back to Leslie. "Looks like I'm not the only one."

Jane appeared with a Brown Thomas bag filled with moisturizer, perfume, and a pair of candles. "They're from Elle too," she said, "and I know it's weird to give you candles, but they smell so good."

Leslie sighed. "Thank you."

Elle appeared, going on about the toilets. "My God, where are we, Basra? There was blood on the floor. Make sure you wear your slippers everywhere."

Leslie nodded that she would, and Jim got up and pulled two more chairs over so that the girls could sit, and just as they sat, Tom appeared with a brown bag full of sweets and mints.

"Oh for God's sake," Leslie said, and she smiled and shook her head. "What are you doing here?"

"Why wouldn't I come?" he said. "After everything you've done for me."

Elle got up and let him sit down, and she sat at the end of the bed. Jane introduced Tom to Jim, and they chatted happily about the building trade dying on its feet. Jim had read an interesting article on the subject, and he was interested to hear Tom's point of view. Tom explained he had closed up shop at the end of '07 and he was happy to see the back of his business.

"So what are you doing now?" Jim asked.

"Well, aside from looking for my wife, nothing."

"What would you like to do?"

Tom thought about it and shook his head. "I have no idea."

"Well," Jim said, "the world is your oyster."

"I suppose it is."

Jane and Elle fussed over Leslie, and she pretended she didn't like it, but she couldn't conceal her joy.

"When this is done," Elle said, "and when you're feeling better, we'll do something fun."

"Can't wait."

"And you know that if things are a little bleak in the hospice, there is plenty of room at my place," Jane said. "The house is so empty without Kurt and Irene."

Leslie couldn't believe Jane's kindness. It took her by surprise, and looking around at the people she now had in her life moved her to tears.

Elle squeezed her hand. "You're not alone anymore, pal."

"I know," she said. She wiped away her tears and opened the bag of chocolate. "Who wants chocolate?"

They all dug in, and even though Leslie couldn't eat, she felt full.

11

"Simple and True"

Like a rainbow after a shower
I don't regret a day, not one single hour.
Ah bring on the bigger things I can't help but follow,
without you by my side my heart would be hollow.

Jack L, *Universe*

July 2008

Breda had refused to get out of bed since the television reconstruction of Alexandra's disappearance. Her daughter Kate
gave her sponge baths, and her husband sat with her and encouraged her to eat the food that Kate and Eamonn's wife, Frankie,
took turns to cook and deliver. She'd take a few bites but only
when her husband pleaded with her and only to satisfy him. It was
not Breda's intent to starve herself or to cause pain to the people
she loved, and if she could have summoned the mental and physical strength to get up, she would have.

"Look, love, it's shepherd's pie," Ben Walsh said to his wife, raising the fork toward her mouth. "Frankie made it according to your own recipe."

Breda closed her eyes and opened her mouth, the food fell in, and Ben cleaned off the tiny amount that fell out with a tea towel. She didn't chew. Instead it just sat in her mouth until it had melted enough for her to swallow.

"Eamonn's downstairs. Would you like to see him?"

She blinked a few times, and he wondered if her eyes were dry or whether she was now resorting to communication through the medium of eye movement.

"Kate will be over tonight with fresh clothes, and she'll help you wash," Ben said, "and I'll be downstairs, so maybe afterward you could come down and join us for a while. I can put a duvet on the sofa. What do you think, love?"

Breda closed her eyes and then opened them and nodded slightly.

Ben smiled at her. "Great, great stuff. I'll tell the kids."

He took the tray off the bed and walked out, closing the door behind him.

Breda lay there motionless, waiting for sleep to come.

Ben joined Eamonn downstairs. Eamonn hung up from a call and turned to his dad. Taking the tray from him, he noticed that the shepherd's pie was not even half eaten.

"We need to get a doctor out here," he said.

"I know," Ben said. "We will."

"When?"

"When your mammy says it's okay."

"Dad, my mother is in no fit state to decide that."

"She's just sad, son."

"No, Dad. She *was* just sad; now it's more sinister."

Ben walked outside and lit a cigarette. Eamonn followed him, grabbed a plastic deck chair and sat beside him.

"You can't hide from this, Dad," he said. "You could hide from Alexandra, but not this."

Ben stayed silent because his son was right. He had hidden from the reality of the loss of his daughter for months. He had pushed her away into a tiny corner of his mind because to think about her and to allow himself to feel the emotions he had felt those first few weeks would have been unbearable. His pain turned to anger, and in the absence of an aggressor he had turned on Tom. He had loathed him since that day over a year before when Alexandra had walked out her door and vanished. He had decided that even if Tom had been working when they lost her and even if he had loved Alexandra, his love hadn't been enough to keep her safe. He didn't care that it was cruel and unkind to blame the man who'd driven himself half mad to find her, because the only time he had felt better in the past year was when he was making Tom feel worse. Eamonn coped by pretending that Alexandra hadn't been as happy as she had pretended to be and that mentally she hadn't been capable of accepting her life as it was. She had forfeited a career she'd worked hard to succeed in for a baby that never came. She had tried hormone injections and four rounds of IVF, acupuncture, herbs, tonics; she had given up smoking, joined a gym, changed her eating habits; and although she had maintained a happy and casual façade, he had known she was lying, he had known that she was desperate to be a mother, and he had known that every single month and every negative test was eating away at his sister until there was little of the real her left. At least that's what he told himself, because it was easier to believe that she had chosen to walk away from her own life or even that she'd thrown herself over Dalkey pier than to face the horrifying alternatives. And so again, while he didn't hold the same anger as his father, there was a large part of him that held Tom accountable for the loss of his sister. The difference between Eamonn and his father was that since the reconstruction and Breda's subsequent withdrawal, Ben had realized, while sitting on plastic chairs in their back garden, that Tom was as helpless in the disappearance of Alexandra as he now found himself in the face of his wife's mysterious illness. All the anger that he'd built up to protect himself from true suffering was slowly dissipating, the pain was slowly returning, and he now found himself experiencing the darkness that Tom had been experiencing all along.

"Call the doctor," he said to his son after the longest time, "and call Tom."

"What are we calling him for?" Eamonn said.

"Because your mammy's fond of him and he'll come," Ben said.

Eamonn nodded and walked inside with his phone to his ear, leaving his father alone to smoke and to breathe through the pain that finally he allowed himself to feel.

Tom arrived just as Kate was leaving. She hugged him and thanked him for coming, and he told her he was delighted to have been asked. He had attempted to make contact with Breda a few times within the previous five weeks but had been told it would be better to stay away. Ben came out from the sitting room, and much to Tom's surprise he offered his hand. Tom shook it.

"I owe you an apology," he said. "Alexandra, well, it wasn't your fault any more than mine or her mammy's. It was just something terrible that happened."

Tom didn't know what to say. His hands shook and his lip trembled. "Thank you."

Ben slapped his back. "She's upstairs. The doctor's been here and he gave her something to sleep, but she's been awake awhile and I know she'd love to see you."

Tom walked up the stairs to Breda's room. It was lit by one lamp by the side of her bed. The room smelled of fresh blankets, and Breda smelled of Kate's perfume. She was thinner than ever and her veins stood out more. He sat in the chair by her bed and took her hand in his. She looked at him, but he wondered if she saw him at all.

"I've missed you," he said, "and I'm not the only one."

She tried to smile—it was the least she could do for poor Tom, who was kind enough to visit with her.

"I'm scared," he said after a minute or two. "I'm scared that you let your mind go to the dark place and that you got stuck there. Did you get stuck there, Breda?"

Tears welled in her eyes and she nodded.

"You need to come back," he said. "You need to be strong, because we can't lose you too."

"I'm sorry," she mumbled, and even her mumble sounded raspy.

"Don't be sorry. Just come back."

"I can't," she said.

"Why not?"

" 'The sacrifices of God are a broken spirit; a broken and contrite heart, O God, you will not despise.' "

"I don't understand. What does that mean?"

"It means if a broken spirit pleases God, that is what I'll give Him."

"Breda, you lying here is not going to bring Alexandra back."

"Maybe it will," she said, and she licked her dry lips.

"This is madness."

"No," she said. "This is all I can do. I have no choice. My body feels broken, but as sad as I am, my mind is strong."

"You have to talk to your family."

She blinked and inhaled and licked her dry lips again. "They don't understand."

"*I* don't understand."

She attempted to grip his hand with hers. "I can't be expected to go on."

"You'll get help now," he said.

She nodded, but she knew that it was too late, that nothing and no one could help her now.

"Whatever the doctor says, you'll do," he said.

She blinked.

"You'll be okay," he said, "and we will find her."

Breda blinked again because she had said all that she was going to say.

Leslie woke up in her ward. It took awhile for her to come around, and when she did, the effects of morphine made the back of her head feel like it was being swallowed by her bed. She thought about attempting to sit up, but she couldn't even garner the strength to move her head so that she could look down at herself. Through the narcotic-induced mist she could feel pain, but not enough to call for someone or seek attention. Her head and heart were both heavy, her insides desecrated, her breasts gone, and she didn't realize it but her finger was pressing down on a button administering morphine and her bed was quickly beginning to feel like a tomb and she heard herself screaming.

Ah for fuck's sake, is this how I'm going to die?

The nurse appeared quickly and removed Leslie's finger from the button and attempted to settle her. "Just relax, everything went well, you're in good hands," she said.

"The fucking bed is swallowing me!" Leslie screamed.

"The bed is not swallowing you."

"Save me, you fuckfaced motherfucking fucker!" Leslie said, and the woman in the bed opposite laughed.

"Okay, everything's fine, I've got you," the nurse said calmly.

"I am dying. I've been dying all my fucking life!"

"You're not dying."

"Has anyone ever told you that you look like a frog?"

The woman in the bed opposite put her hand over her mouth to stop herself from laughing.

"It's the meds talking," the nurse said to the woman, who was clearly enjoying the meds talking and was looking forward to hearing more from them.

"Nurse?"

"Yes, Leslie."

"I've gone blind."

"No, love, you've just closed your eyes."

Leslie fell into a deep sleep after that and didn't wake up for twelve hours. When she did wake, she had absolutely no memory of the incident ever having taken place.

Jim was the first person she remembered who visited. He was reading a newspaper when she woke.

"What's going on?" she asked.

"President Sarkozy has decided to postpone a trip to Ireland to discuss the EU Lisbon Treaty."

"Oh," she said, "I forgot to vote."

"Well, you had other things on your mind."

"Yeah," she said, and suddenly she felt like crying. Her face still felt a little numb, so she didn't realize that she actually was.

"You're going to be all over the place," he said. "It's perfectly normal."

"Nothing about this is normal," she said.

"In a few weeks you're going to feel so much better."

"But I'm going to look so much worse."

"No," he said, "you're going to look like a new woman, a woman with a massive weight taken off her shoulders."

"I'll have no breasts," she said. "I haven't even looked yet. I'm too scared."

"Take your time, allow yourself to heal, be kind to yourself, and then when the time comes if you're not happy, you can get implants."

"Like Pamela Anderson."

"No. Most definitely not like Pamela Anderson."

Leslie would have laughed, but she was too sore. The drains coming out of her stomach and chest had blood and pus spewing into bottles, and it was as uncomfortable as it was unsightly. When the nurse fixed Leslie's bedsheets, the sheet covering a bottle fell away, revealing its horrible contents to Jim, but if he saw it, it certainly didn't faze him. Of course he had witnessed that and more, even if it had been more than ten years before.

After he left, Leslie was sick in a bowl for an hour, every part of her ached, and with every retch her newly stitched skin pulled and burned. When the woman with the cart asked her if she wanted some toast, Leslie pointed to the bowl before leaning in for another spew.

"Say no more, my dear," the woman said. "I'll catch you on the way back."

• • •

Elle waited until the third day before visiting her friend. She did this because when she checked Google, a website told her that day two following an operation was the worst day, and she didn't want to make Leslie's life harder than it already was. She arrived with grapes, magazines, and a book about self-discovery. She was on her own because Jane had to meet their accountant. She was nervous and wasn't sure about what she should say, and for once she was quiet.

"Are you all right?" Leslie asked.

"Shouldn't I be asking you that?"

"Yes." Leslie smiled.

"I didn't sleep," Elle admitted. "I couldn't make my mind stop."

"I've been there."

"Sometimes it feels like my mind is on a treadmill and I'm trying to reach the Stop button but I can't and with every second that passes I feel like I'm about to fall off."

"What kind of things do you think about?" Leslie asked, glad that they weren't talking about the operation.

"Oh, I don't know—work, Jane, Kurt, me, a woman in the Sudan lying on a dusty floor dying of AIDS as we speak; I think about her and how bloody unfair it is. A horse found slashed to pieces, starved and burned, and I think about that poor gentle animal's suffering. A young boy age sixteen stabbed in London on his way home from a football match; I think about him and the family he's left behind. A woman who is promised a new life only to be consigned to a life of sexual slavery; I think about her and the hell she endures day in and day out. I think about Alexandra and where she could be and what has been done to her, and I think about you and how sad your life has been, all that you've lost and all that you've missed out on. I think about how brave you are, and dignified and kind. I think that if I could be like anyone in the world it would be you, and I think flat-chested women are huge on the catwalk right now, that kind of thing," Elle said, and she smiled at her friend.

"Jesus, that's a lot of thinking."

"Yeah, too much."

"Elle, I like your way of thinking. Now pass me a grape and tell me a story."

Elle did as she was told and stayed until the nurse kicked her out an hour later.

Dominic walked into his hotel and was passing the bar when Elle called his name. He turned to her and said hello before looking to see if she was on her own. He approached her, and she asked him to join her as she was having something quick to eat following her visit with Leslie. He agreed and ordered coffee.

"What are you doing here?" she asked.

"Same as you."

"Really? Why do you have a hotel key card in your front pocket then?"

"Okay," he said, "you've caught me, but don't tell Jane."

"Tell Jane what?"

Dominic explained that his wife had thrown him out of their house for a second time in two months over a week ago. He was resigned to the fact that his marriage was over, but not to the fact that he was in a hotel while she was in his house.

"So take it back."

"My solicitor says—"

"Screw your solicitor. It's your house, so take it back."

"How?"

"What do you mean how? Go home, pack up her stuff, throw her out, and change the locks."

"What if she's already changed the locks?"

"Go home, break in, pack up her stuff, throw her out, and change the locks."

"You're serious."

"Absolutely."

"But what if she calls the police?"

"The deeds are in your name. Besides, they'll consider it a domestic dispute and as long as nobody throws a punch you're home free."

"I can't be involved in a domestic dispute. I'm a bank manager."

Elle laughed at the absurdity of his rationale. "I hate to break it to you, Dominic, but the *Herald* isn't parked outside your door waiting for something to report."

Dominic thought about it for a minute or two and was really warming to the idea.

"Will you come with me?" he said.

Elle rubbed her hands together. "I thought you'd never ask."

Bella's car was not in the driveway. They parked two doors down on Dominic's insistence, then Elle made her way to the door and he hid behind a tree in front of the house. Elle knocked and waited. After a minute or two she signaled to Dominic that all was clear. He emerged from behind the tree and fumbled for his house key. He breathed deeply, put the key in the lock and turned it; the door remained shut.

"Damn it," he said.

"Relax," Elle counseled. "Follow me."

They walked around to the back of the house, and Elle picked up a rock and took off her jacket and wrapped the rock in it.

"The French doors are double glazed," Dominic said, still looking around.

"Yeah, but the window in the downstairs loo isn't."

"It's too small."

"Too small for you, fat boy."

"I'm not fat."

"Do you have an alarm?" Elle said.

"Yes."

"Would she have changed the code?"

"I don't know if she'd even know how."

"If she has, what would she change it to?"

"I don't know. Actually, I do know—she has a terrible memory so all her cards are the same number: 6666."

"Fine." She hit the glass with the rock encased in her jacket, and it cracked. She hit it again and it smashed.

The alarm went off. She cleared away all the jagged pieces of glass by chipping away with the rock. She stopped only when Dominic almost shrieked hello to his neighbor Rachel Jameson.

"Forgotten your key, Dominic?" she said.

"Oh, yes, can you believe it?" he said, and Elle thought he might have a heart attack there and then.

"Always the way," she said.

Elle mouthed "always the way" and laughed a little. Dominic gave her a kick. When Rachel went indoors, Elle took a leg up from Dominic and climbed in through the window. She ran to the alarm and keyed in 6666, and it stopped.

"What a moron," she said as she opened the front door.

Dominic sprinted in and shut the door with a swing.

"Take that, bitch!" he said, and he giggled like a girl.

"We're not there yet," Elle warned. "Call a local twenty-four-hour window repair and tell them you'll give them a tip of a hundred euro if they get here and fix the window within thirty minutes. And do the same with a locksmith."

Dominic did as he was told, and Elle went upstairs, armed with a suitcase she found under the stairs, and started to clear Bella's things. Dominic made his way around the house bagging anything and everything that was Bella's. He kept checking his watch and was alarmed to discover he was sweating profusely. Elle was behaving as though she was accustomed to breaking and entering.

"Don't be so dramatic, Dominic; this is your house," she said when he commented on her calm demeanor.

The window guy made it in fifteen minutes and had the window fitted in another ten. Dominic paid him in full and shut the door with another swing. The locksmith followed ten minutes later and was gone within thirty minutes. Dominic hopped, skipped, and jumped up the stairs to where Elle was bagging the last of Bella's clothes.

"I think I love you," he said.

"Yeah, well, hold your horses," Elle said. "Next we need to send her packing."

Dominic carried Bella's cases down the stairs and parked them beside the front door. Elle checked the clock. It was just after nine.

"What now?" he said.

"Now we wait," she replied.

They didn't have to wait long. Ten minutes later Bella's car drove into the driveway. Elle's heart was racing and, despite her cool façade, it had been since she had broken the window. Dominic gulped and braced himself. The key went into the lock and came out, went in again and came out. Bella stepped back from the door and looked at the house as though it would provide some sort of answer. She went back to the door and tried her key again.

She walked around the back of the house and checked the French doors. She cupped her eyes and looked into the empty kitchen. Dominic and Elle waited with bated breath in the sitting room. Bella came around the front of the house once more, stepped over plants, and looked in the sitting-room window. When she saw Dominic and Elle, she banged on the window and shouted.

Elle went over to the window and opened it slightly.

"What can I do for you?" she said.

"You can let me into my house!" Bella shouted.

"But this isn't your house. This is Dominic's house. I know this because I knew him when he bought it, and my nephew has spent every weekend in it since he was four years old. You, on the other hand, have been here for five minutes. I trust in that time he didn't sign over the deed? No, I didn't think so."

"Who do you think you are?"

"Me, I'm someone who pays her own way. You want out of the marriage with Dominic, and to be fair no one blames you for that, but take what's yours. This house is not yours."

While Elle was talking, Dominic was placing Bella's bags outside the front door. He closed the door and gave Elle the thumbs-up.

"Take care of yourself," she said, and she closed the window.

"We'll see about that," Bella said, and she stamped through the plants and retrieved her cases, got into her car, and drove away.

Dominic stood at the window, agog. "I can't believe we just did that."

Elle danced her way around the sitting room. "That was fun."

Dominic opened a bottle of wine to celebrate and insisted Elle join him. They clinked glasses and relived the break-in and laughed and drank, and just when the night couldn't get any stranger, Dominic told Elle she was amazing. Then he leaned in and kissed her, and she responded, and twenty minutes later Elle was sitting on top of Bella's soon-to-be ex-husband in Bella's ex-bed.

Jane took it upon herself to move Leslie to her hospice, and so twelve days after Leslie's operation she gently guided her to her car and helped her sit. She was in a quandary as to whether or not Leslie should wear the seat belt, but Leslie insisted it would be fine if she held it away from herself.

Leslie was quiet in the car, and Jane understood that she didn't want to chat, and so she put on the radio and they listened to a morning talk show. When they were close to the place, Jane rang ahead so that a nurse with a wheelchair met them at the door. The nurse wheeled Leslie inside and Jane followed with her bags. She was brought to a private room, and the nurse helped her into bed and explained how to work the remote control, informed her of mealtimes, and said that someone would be around with pain medication in three hours. Leslie grunted and nodded, and the nurse left.

"Well," Jane said, "that all sounds good."

"Does it?"

"What can I do?"

"Nothing," Leslie said. "Nobody can do anything."

"Elle's been Googling this—it's normal to feel depressed."

"I know. She told me."

"I wish I could help."

"Me too."

"Jim will be here later."

"What's that supposed to mean?" Leslie said, thinking she was hinting at romance the way Elle often did.

"It means that Jim will be here later."

"Oh."

"Would you like me to help you wash?" Jane said.

"You want to see how I've been butchered?"

Jane was horrified that she would think that. "No. God, absolutely no, no, no!"

She was so horrified and so embarrassed and so red that it actually made Leslie smile.

"I'm sorry," Leslie said.

"God Almighty, Leslie," Jane said, sitting down, "my life is hard enough without you . . ." She trailed off and shook her head. "Life is hard enough."

After that Leslie did ask for her help. She hadn't had her bandages changed in five days, and she wanted to do it herself, but she needed help.

"Are you sure?" Jane asked.

"Yes. Are you sure?"

"I offered, didn't I?" Jane said.

She helped Leslie into the bathroom and sat her on the toilet. Jane filled the sink with warm soapy water and then helped Leslie take off her pajama top. The bandages were wrapped tightly around her, and Jane quickly found the fastenings. She slowly and gently began to unravel them. Leslie held the front of them, with her hand protecting and concealing the area as it was exposed.

When the final bandage was unraveled, Leslie dropped her hand and revealed the indents and angry slashes where her breasts had used to be. There were holes from the drains, and one was slightly septic. Leslie's eyes filled, her nose ran, and her lips pursed.

"Seeing is believing," she said as she wiped her eyes. "It's bad, isn't it?"

"It's still healing."

"It's still horrible."

"Look, it is awful, but then I've an ass that looks like it's made of cheese."

"At least you're honest," Leslie said.

"Well, I'm a pretty bad liar, and you're not the kind of person who's easily patronized."

"Do you think I should get implants?" Leslie asked.

"That's your decision."

"Would you?"

"Yes," Jane said. "I probably would."

"It's not an easy decision."

"Neither is opting to have a double mastectomy and a hysterectomy."

Leslie sighed. "With or without breasts, I'll never be whole now."

"Wombs are overrated. They can get you into all kinds of trouble."

Leslie laughed. "I'll think about it."

"Good." Jane squeezed the sponge and gently cleaned around the wounds as Leslie took in her new shape in the mirror.

Tom was sitting on her steps when Jane returned from the hospice. She got out of the car, and he took the bag of Leslie's washing from her.

"I've got some news," he said, "about Alexandra."

Jane stopped in her tracks. "What?"

"They found her wedding ring."

"Where?"

"In a market in Wexford."

"What does it mean?"

"I don't know."

"But it's something," she said.

"Yeah." He smiled. "It's something."

She hugged him, and he dropped the bags and hugged her back, and from inside her flat Rose watched them hold on to each other tightly, and even from a distance she recognized the look in her daughter's eyes.

"Oh Janey, another unobtainable man! At least you're focking consistent."

12

The summer days grow longer but life gets shorter
the heart starts growing cold.
If you remain a loner you gotta take a chance,
get up and dance, you know the song.

Jack L, *Broken Songs*

August 2008

Jane missed Kurt more than she could ever have predicted. Every few days she'd find herself standing in his room, looking around but afraid to touch anything in case he noticed and freaked out upon his return. One day she lay on his bed and, staring up at the ceiling, thought about where he was and what he was doing and what kind of time he was having. *Is every day a new adventure? Will he be sorry to come home? Will he come home? Oh Jesus, he'll definitely come home, won't he? Calm down, Jane. He's on holiday, he hasn't emigrated. Jesus Christ, what if he emigrates?*

Jane felt a great emptiness in her house and heart since his departure. She missed Irene too, because even though she'd been part of their household for a short time, she had made her mark. Jane understood that Kurt's extended holiday was merely preparing her for the day he'd leave home for good. She prayed he would get Medicine in Dublin because he had applied to Cork, Galway, and Belfast as backups. If he didn't get Medicine in Dublin, he'd be gone from home sooner rather than later, and the permanent loss of her son was too great to contemplate.

As the days passed into weeks, Jane also noticed an uneasiness creeping into her mind. All the thoughts of fleeing home that she had long ago put to the back of her mind began pushing themselves forward. *If he goes, I could go. If he's starting his new life, I could start mine. I could sell this house, I could put Rose into a home where she wouldn't be allowed to drink herself to death, and I could set Elle up in a cottage in a pretty place somewhere inspirational, somewhere other than down the end of her sister's garden. I could take my life back.*

As much as these thoughts excited Jane, she didn't dwell on them long, because to take her life back would be to put everyone else's in a spin, and poor old Janey wasn't capable of deliberately upsetting her nearest and dearest. Besides, they needed her. It was unspoken but accepted in the family that Rose would be dead and Elle would be in some sort of state-run facility and most likely a prison without Jane's presence, patience, and care.

In the early days of Kurt's life, Jane had remained at home because she had no money and nowhere else to go, and although her mother did not provide any kind of assistance when it came to caring for the baby, she did feed them. Those first few years of Kurt's life were the hardest and most miserable in Jane's life, but they also ensured that she and Kurt became the center of each other's universe.

When he was four and in school and Elle's talent had been fully recognized, Jane made a decision to learn the business. This was because, according to Rose, a number of people had queued up "to take advantage of Elle," and after Rose had driven them away, Elle was left unrepresented and desperate. Jane combed the streets of Dublin looking for a gallery owner to take her on for four mornings a week, and when one day she walked into a small gallery near Clanwilliam Street, a man in his sixties greeted her with a warm smile, and she knew even before they spoke that she had a job. Initially he told her he had no work, but she pressed him and told him as long as he was prepared to teach her everything he knew, she would work for him for free for a full year. He laughed, believing she was joking, but she was deadly serious, and as long as he didn't mind that she left by midday he had himself some free labor.

Albert liked Jane from the first moment he saw her, and being a man who spent a great deal of his time alone since his beloved wife died, he was thrilled by the notion of company. He was also happy to pass on his knowledge, and luckily for Jane he was a teacher capable of making learning fascinating. Jane had been working with Albert one month before she brought him Elle's paintings. He was blown away, and after Jane read a book on PR they had a showing that, thanks to a few tips from the book and Elle having a genuinely interesting angle to encourage media interest, was packed and a huge success. Jane had been working with Albert only four months when she received her first paycheck, and they continued to work together further for five years and were as close as father and daughter when Albert passed away one cold autumn evening. Albert and his lovely wife never had any children and he was the youngest of his generation, all his family and pals having gone before him, and so he left his business and home to the girl who had brought light and challenges into his final years. As it turned out, Albert's gift of a home and business couldn't have come at a better time because Rose had refinanced her house and hadn't paid the mortgage in a year, and the bank was set to take their home from them. Because Rose liked to stick her head in the sand and because she was arrogant enough to think that the bank would wait for her to decide when she was good and ready to get the job necessary to make repayments, Jane took over. She sold Albert's house and used the money to buy her mother's home from her. At first Rose screamed and roared at Jane for trying to steal her house, but when Jane's solicitor explained to Rose in no uncertain terms that if Jane didn't take over the mortgage Rose would be homeless and that in buying her out Jane would be paying her over €100,000 in cash, Rose became far more amenable. There was enough money left to fix up the basement flat, which Rose had let go to rack and ruin, and when the contracts were signed and the money changed hands she became the owner of a large Georgian property, complete with garden cottage, at the age of twenty-seven. By the time Jane was thirty she had sold the small gallery that Albert had left her and moved into a bigger premises and named it after him. Since then Jane had run a successful business, and some would say that if it hadn't been for her, Elle might not have done half as well. But now, despite owning her own home and running a successful business, Jane wondered whether or not there was something more to life. She thought about all the things she had wanted to do, medicine being one thing, traveling being another. She'd never been out of the country longer than two weeks and never farther than a beach resort complete with a kiddies' club in Europe. As a girl she had dreamed of adventure: trekking in Brazilian rain forests, surfing off the coast of Mexico, going on safari in Kenya. And although her desire to get into medicine when she was a teenager had been tempered by her desire to get into Dominic's pants, over the years she had grieved her lost opportunity because she knew that given the chance she would have made a good doctor, and God knew she had the patience. *Maybe I could still do it? Don't be a dick, Jane, you're ancient.*

Jane's intermittent thoughts of escape were always interrupted by Rose or Elle. Rose was still suffering with stomach problems, but of course she wouldn't admit it because to do so would be to accept that she had to lay off the booze, and she had no intention of ever doing that.

"We all have our crutches, Jane," she said.

"Yeah, but most people's crutches don't cripple them."

"I disagree."

Every now and then Rose would clutch her stomach and breathe deeply.

"What can I do?" Jane asked.

"You can distract me."

Jane stood up and broke into an Irish dance.

"Yes, very funny, Janey, you really should have your own sit-com."

Jane sat down.

"Why don't you tell me about Tom?" Rose said.

"What about him?"

"Well, how is he getting on? Have they found anyone who knows anything about the wedding ring?"

"They sourced it to a guy from Kent, who said he bought it from a man from Clare, and when they knocked his door down he said that he bought it in a flea market in Rathmines. He had thought it would make a nice ring for his girlfriend, but she got confused, thought he was asking her to marry him, and when she noticed that it was engraved with Alexandra's name, she thought he was a cheapskate and broke up with him."

"Well, how did it get into a flea market?"

"The owner swears she doesn't know. She has receipts and a paper trail for everything else she's ever bought or sold. It's like someone just left it there."

"And what does Tom think?"

"He thinks it's hopeful; maybe she's leaving us a clue how to find her."

"Balls. She's dead, long dead."

"Rose, please don't say that."

"Oh don't be ridiculous, Janey. Of course she's dead! And if Tom was honest with himself he'd say so, and you can be sure the police have mentioned the likelihood on more than one occasion."

"Let's just stop talking."

"You like him, don't you?"

"What?"

"Tom—you like him."

"He's a lovely man."

"Don't play coy with me, Jane Moore."

"Oh for God's sake, Rose!" Jane got up from her chair and turned to leave.

"You be careful—you've been a gobshit with men for far too long."

"It's 'gobshite,' Rose—the word you're looking for is 'gobshite,' with an 'e.'"

"You say tomato, Janey, and the point still stands: don't be an eejit all your life. And judging by the dark circles and lines around your eyes, you're not going to be pretty for much longer. So if you want a man, get your skates on."

Jane slammed Rose's front door. *God, I hate that horrible old woman!*

Four weeks into her hospice stay, Leslie was battling depression. Her surgeon had warned her that it was a possibility and explained the reasons why, but reason was hard to hold on to when everything inside her was screaming. She didn't feel like talking, and when she could no longer sleep she just sat staring at the TV with a remote in her hand. Elle would sit with her, and sometimes she'd talk and sometimes she'd say nothing at all. Jane tried little tricks to brighten the place up, including colored balloons, a big cuddly toy, and scented candles. Tom told jokes, which Jane laughed at. Mostly they were jokes that Alexandra had told him. She loved jokes, and once she heard one she stored it and could regurgitate it verbatim at will. He wasn't good at telling jokes and often forgot the punch line, and so it wasn't necessarily the depression that prevented Leslie from laughing. Jim came in every second day. He'd fluff her pillows even if she didn't want him to, and he'd fix the bed and poke around her locker, which annoyed her so much she'd be forced to talk to him.

"Will you just leave it be?"

"No, you've an apple in there and it's gone off."

"Just leave it."

"No." He threw the offending fruit in the wastebasket. "I might clean your sink."

"The cleaners will do it."

"Yeah, well, they're not here right now and if you won't talk to me . . ."

"What do you want to talk about?" She sighed deeply, indicating she was not amused by his neediness.

"I don't know. How about flash floods?"

"Flash floods?"

"In Clonee, can you believe it? Cars were floating down the M50."

"Well, it has pissed rain day and night for the past month."

"I hate the rain," he said, looking out at the dark gray sky and the rain hitting the window.

"Yeah."

"I was thinking about going away. A week in the sun before the end of September maybe."

"Good."

"We could rent a car."

"We?"

"You could get some sun on that sickly body of yours."

"Thanks very much."

"You could walk on the sand and soak up the sun, eat well, sleep because you're tired and not because you've taken a bucket-load of sleeping tablets."

"Stop monitoring me."

"We could go to Greece or Spain or France—I bet it will still be nice there."

"You really want to go on holiday with me?" she asked.

"We're friends, aren't we?"

She nodded.

"And we both need something to look forward to."

She nodded.

"So when you're feeling better and when your hormones are adjusted, we'll go."

"Maybe," she said.

"Maybe is good enough for now."

After that she slipped away from him again, but he was happy enough to have elicited some chat and on the matter of a holiday a maybe was better than an outright no.

Tom was beginning to realize that he needed to fill his days with more than checking the Finding Alexandra and Jack Lukeman sites and hounding his liaison officer. His business was dead and buried, and the way things were starting to shape up for his competitors he was glad to be out of it. He'd heard through the grapevine that demand for new buildings was disappearing at a shocking rate. One builder he knew was close to bankruptcy and another was barely treading water. Once his accountant had finalized his tax and VAT for the end of the business year, he had money in the bank, and because he'd only rented his offices, he was free and clear. Getting back into the business of building was certainly not something he could consider in the current climate, and he wasn't really qualified for anything else, having left school at sixteen to work with his dad on sites around Dublin. Tom's mother suffered from dementia, and unfortunately for her and her family it took hold when she was young, and so from when Tom was ten she had no idea who he was. His father couldn't care for her, so he put her into the best home that money could buy. The problem was he couldn't pay for the home and for him and Tom at the same time. That was when Tom left school, and together they worked to pay the bills. At night Tom would watch TV and his father would drink, and that went on for four years, when he died of cirrhosis of the liver. There was a year to go on the mortgage, and Tom paid it off and sold the house and started his business. He and Jane had discussed their similar backgrounds one night over dinner. She told him about the father she had lost to heart failure, and she didn't need to tell him about her drunken mother because he'd met her. She talked about leaving school to have Kurt and how Albert had given her her life back. He talked about his poor mother who had lost her mind long before she lost her life, and his dad who, unlike Jane's mother, was a falling-down drunk incapable of stopping once he started and capable of disappearing for days on end. He talked about school too and admitted that at the time he had been delighted to leave, not having been one of the most academic of students and not having had any lofty career ambitions, but in the years since he had developed a keen interest in human rights.

"I know it sounds weird," he said. "A bit hippy-dippy for a developer."

"I think the fact that you're using the term 'hippy-dippy' is weirder."

Jane confided in him about her fear of living in that big house without her son.

"It's totally understandable," he said.

"It keeps me awake."

"You need to start living for you again."

"I think you need to take some of your own advice," she said.

Tom stayed quiet for a moment. "Yes, there's a part of me that knows you're right."

Jane had told him about her doomed love for Dominic as part of the apology for roaring at him the night she found him with Jeanette. He asked her about him now to change the subject.

"His marriage is over," she said.

"He told you?"

"No, Elle did. He's staying away."

"Good."

"Yeah," she said. "It is actually, the first time in thirteen years I've a break from my son and his father."

"And you're not the slightest bit interested in how he is?"

"Nope," she said. "I'm moving on."

"Good for you."

"What about Jeanette?"

"Oh don't! I'm so embarrassed."

"Trust me, I know how that feels."

After they ate they walked together on Grafton Street. They stopped in front of a band playing for coins and listened to them for a while, and then they pottered on. Initially they were looking for a taxi, but as the rain had finally stopped and they were entertaining each other, they ended up walking all the way to Jane's. She asked him in.

"I shouldn't," he said, looking at his watch. "It's getting late."

"Okay," she said, "good night."

"Good night."

They both stood there rooted to the spot.

"We'll do it again soon," he said.

"Great."

"Okay."

"Okay."

Tom bit his lip and Jane exhaled, and in that moment they were so close to kissing and yet so far from it. They heard the knocking and they both turned to see Rose tapping the glass. When she got their attention, she wagged her finger and pointed at Tom and gave him the finger. Jane and Tom laughed at the crazy drunk, and thankfully the moment passed.

Elle knocked on Dominic's front door. He opened it and grinned. She walked inside, and he grabbed her by the ass. She slapped his hand, and then she ran to his bedroom with him hot on her heels. He gave chase around the bed, which she jumped over, and she ran down the hall into the spare room and around a chair. He tried to grab her, but she bobbed and weaved and ran to the box-room, where he cornered her. They were both breathing heavily, and Dominic pinned her to the wall.

"We shouldn't be doing this," he said.

"That's why it feels so good," she said, and he kissed her and pulled at her panties, and she jumped on his hips, and if it hadn't been for his bad back they would have finished up there but instead he finished lying flat on the floor. Afterward, when she'd returned from her shower and he was still lying there, she wondered if he was going to be okay.

"Fine," he said, trying to make light of it.

"Good," she said, "get up."

He sighed and she helped him up. He rubbed his back and took two painkillers with water.

"You're going to be the death of me," he said.

"That's nothing to what Jane would do to you if she found out."

"But she won't," he said with alarm. "You won't tell her."

"No. I have as much to lose as you, if not more."

Elle sat down at Dominic's kitchen table and poured salt on it.

"So why are we doing this?" he asked. "And don't say for fun."

"Because I'm compulsive and you'd swing a leg over anything that moves."

Afterward, when she'd gone and he was cleaning salt from his table with one hand and rubbing the small of his back with the other, he promised himself faithfully that he would not sleep with Elle again.

. . .

Leslie came out of the hospice on a Tuesday. Jim had the summer off from lecturing, so he offered to drive her home. Her spirits had picked up a little and she was looking forward to seeing her cat.

Deborah was in Leslie's apartment cleaning out the kitty litter.

"Welcome home," Deborah said, and she seemed genuinely glad to see her, but then again she had been feeding and cleaning up after a cat for nearly a month, and she hated cats the way some people hated iguanas.

"Thanks," Leslie said, and she sat down on her sofa, because getting out of the car, walking to the lift, standing in the lift, and walking from the lift to the apartment had felt like a ten-mile hike.

The cat jumped up on the sofa and rubbed herself against Leslie and purred. Leslie rubbed the cat's head and looked around at her apartment. It was good to be home.

Deborah finished cleaning the tray and made her excuses to leave. "It's good to have you back," she said again.

"It's good to be back."

When she'd gone, Leslie lay on the sofa and Jim made tea.

"Will you come out with me on Sunday?" he asked.

"Where?"

"Surprise."

"I hate surprises."

"Indulge me."

"Why should I indulge you? I'm the one who's just been mutilated."

"Will you stop saying that?"

"It's true."

He wasn't getting anywhere, so he decided to start again. "Will you come out with me on Sunday?"

"Where?"

"Leslie!"

"Tell me where."

"It's a garden center."

She sat up slowly because even though she'd spent five and a half weeks lying in bed it still hurt to move.

"A garden center?"

"Yes."

"I may be in menopause, but I'm not in my seventies."

"It has a really good restaurant and the forecast is positive for once. The gardens are beautiful."

"I'd rather just stay in."

"Please."

"Oh." She sighed heavily. "Fine, we'll go to your poxy gardens."

"Great. And Leslie?"

"What?"

"You're going to love it." He grinned and winked at her.

She made a face. "I'll be the one to decide that, shorty!" She laughed a little. She loved calling Jim names, and he didn't seem to mind in the slightest.

Sunday arrived, and Jim picked Leslie up at midday. The car radio was on. Jack Lukeman was talking to a DJ about his upcoming shows.

"Oh shit," she said. "I forgot to post them on the Web."

"Do it later."

"No, can't." She opened the door. "Wait here—it will only take five minutes."

"Leslie, I don't want to be late."

"Trust me, the garden center will go on without us."

Fifteen minutes later Jim appeared in the doorway, and he was not happy.

"Move," he said.

"Two seconds," she said.

"One, two," he said, and he shut her laptop.

"Ah come on!"

"Get to the car!" he shouted, and he pointed.

"Right. Fine. Keep your high heels on."

They were twenty minutes late. Jim was having a nightmare trying to find a parking space and he kept swearing, which was unlike him, and Leslie was beginning to wonder what the hell he was rushing for. When they finally found a parking space, he practically ran into the restaurant with Leslie following behind slowly and muttering that he was a pain in the ass.

She saw John first. Beside him his daughter, Sarah, was eating a burger and opposite them was a woman Leslie didn't recognize. John glanced up and saw Leslie, then stood, pushing his chair back. Sarah looked up at her father and followed his eye line to where Leslie stood.

John was completely gray and his face was so lined it made Gordon Ramsay look Botoxed, and even though Sarah was sitting, Leslie could tell she was tall, like her mother, Nora. She had her dark complexion.

Jim grabbed her hand and pulled her toward the table.

John put his hand out to shake hers and she took it.

"It's lovely to see you, Leslie," he said.

"Good to see you, John."

"And you know Sarah," he said, "although the last time you saw her she was only five."

"Hi, Leslie," the teenager said.

"Hi, Sarah."

"This is my wife, Claire."

Claire offered her hand and Leslie shook it.

"It's great to finally meet you," Claire said.

Jim pushed a speechless Leslie onto a chair.

"I hope you don't mind," John said. "We were starving, so we went ahead and ordered."

"No," Leslie said, "not at all."

Jim went off to get them some food, and she was left with Nora's husband, her daughter, and John's wife, and she hadn't a clue what to say.

"I didn't know that Jim had kept in touch with you," she said after a while.

"Yeah," John said. "Together in the trenches and all that."

"I suppose," she said.

"Jim told us about your operation," Claire said. "Very brave."

"Thank you."

"If you think I'm doing what she's done, you're mad," Sarah said to her father.

"Sarah!" he warned.

"You've been tested?" Leslie asked her niece.

"Not yet," Sarah said. "Don't want to know."

"That's crazy," Claire said.

"We keep telling her it's for her own good," John said.

"I understand how she feels." Leslie smiled at her sister's child, who was a stranger to her.

Sarah smiled back, glad that someone at least had uttered those exact words.

Jim returned with food, and Leslie nibbled on it and listened to Sarah talk about her life, her hopes and dreams.

"Law, definitely law," she said. "Dad says I could win an argument with Bono on the topic of his choice."

"Like Nora," Leslie said.

"Very like Nora," John said.

"If I don't get law I'm going to repeat until I do get it," Sarah said.

"Good for you," Leslie said.

"What do you do?" Sarah asked.

"I'm a webmaster."

"Cool. What kind of websites?"

"All kinds."

"Would I know of any?"

"A few gyms, a radio station—"

"Which one?"

"It's a country one that specializes in folk."

"Oh."

"Jack Lukeman."

"The singer?"

"Yeah."

"Wow, I love him!"

"Really?" Leslie said. "I could take you to a gig if you'd like."

"Backstage?"

"I'm sure I could arrange something."

"Can I take my pal?"

"Absolutely."

"Cool."

"Is that okay, John?" Leslie asked.

"It's great," he said and he smiled at Jim, who was sitting with a big smug grin on his face.

"Hey, Leslie?" Sarah said.

"Yes?"

"You don't know U2, do you?"

"No."

"Okay, worth a try."

On the way home Jim was still wearing his smug expression.

"I don't know what you're so smug about—that little surprise of yours could have gone very wrong."

"But it didn't."

"Thanks," she said.

"That's what family's for."

"Is that what we are?"

"I like to think so," he said.

"I'm pretty selfish."

"What makes you think that?"

"I cut out John, Sarah, and you because I thought I was doing you all a favor, but the truth is I was just protecting myself."

"How do you work that out?"

"Sarah is going through what I went through. She faces the same challenges. I should have been there for her."

"So you'll be there for her now."

"Yeah. I will."

"Nora would be happy," he said.

"Yes, I think she would," she said, lying back. "And, Jim, let's do as you said—let's get away to the sun in September."

"Ha ha! That's the spirit!"

When Leslie went to bed that night she thought about Jane, Elle, Tom, Jim, John, Sarah, Claire, and even Deborah. She had so many people in her life who cared and wanted to care. She no longer felt alone.

13

*I've been biding my time I ain't that gone
maybe one or two or three or four or five or six too many
but it eases my mind and loosens my tongue,
so come on, sister, won't you take my hand,
be my Alice I'll be Wonderland.*

Jack L, *Universe*

September 2008

The plane was late, which was typical. Jane paced the arrivals area from one end to the other. As the area was about half a mile long, Elle spotted her only every five minutes or so. Elle sat and read a magazine and drank a wheatgrass shot, hoping it would negate the damage she'd been doing to herself recently. Elle was on a binge, and every other night she'd be found in a nightclub dancing on a table, her top optional. She was living on a diet of champagne and morning fry-ups, and when Rose questioned her on her late comings and goings she merely replied that life was too short.

Jane appeared and asked the time and then she was gone. Elle flipped the page, and there was a shot of Vincent and his bride, and he was holding her tummy, and she knew the woman was pregnant before she even read the caption because the bloody pose was so obvious. She wasn't even showing and had just had her twelve-week scan. *I hope she loses it.* She turned the page. She started to read an article about being kind to feet, but the interview with Vincent was calling to her.

Read me.

No. Go away.

You want to know what I'm doing and how happy I am.

I do not. I hope you get knocked down by a bus and dragged for a really long time.

You want me to confirm that I'm in a perfect happy relationship and that the reason we didn't work was you and not me. I'm stable and you're a lunatic. You need to read it. You need to understand that I'm so much better off without you.

"Fuck you, Vincent!" she screamed to a room full of strangers.

The woman beside her with two toddlers picked up three bags, hung them on a double stroller, and with a child holding on to each side of the pram scurried to a place far away from the vulgar mental case. Elle put her explosion down to excessive tiredness and promised herself that she would have a bath later and then an early night.

Minutes later Jane returned and flopped down beside her sister. "I think I've just walked about ten miles. Where the hell are they?"

They were more than an hour late, and after her walk Jane was hungry. She turned to her sister to ask if she'd like to join her for a bit of lunch upstairs, then spied Martha arriving. Martha spotted her immediately and waved wildly and bared that awful sinister Osmonds-on-acid smile.

"Oh no," Jane said.

"What?" Elle said.

"That woman, Irene's mother."

Elle looked around and saw her approaching and rubbed her hands together. "Oh yeah, playtime."

"Elle," Jane warned, "play nice."

"Absolutely," Elle said, shaking her head to suggest that she was planning on doing absolutely the opposite.

"Jane," Martha said and air-kissed her, "you look so refreshed after a couple of months without a teenager in the house."

"Martha," Jane said, subdued and refusing to respond to her stupid redundant and annoying air-kiss or her barbed compliment. "This is my sister, Elle."

Elle grinned and remained in her seat. "I've heard so much about you," she said.

Martha sat in the seat opposite and removed her gloves. "All good, I hope."

"Nope, all bad I'm afraid," Elle said, smiling.

"Well," Martha said, "aren't you hilarious."

"I try." Elle smiled. "So, Martha, how are things with the kid you were screwing? Back together yet, or has he moved on to Betty White? I hear she's a real goer."

Martha got up and walked away without a word.

"You're welcome!" Elle called after her as a grin spread across Jane's face.

"Who's Betty White?" Jane said.

"One of the *Golden Girls*."

"I used to love *The Golden Girls*. Which one was Betty White?"

"Rose."

"Ah, that's right, a pleasant Rose. God, I wish she'd been our mother."

Elle nudged her. "Jane."

"Yeah?"

"Look." Elle pointed to the arrivals gate and to her nephew, brown as a berry, his blond locks bleached white. He was waving.

Jane's heart soared as she jumped to her feet and ran to him, managing to hurdle a suitcase in the process. They met at the barrier, and he dropped his bags, and they hugged and hugged and hugged.

"It's good to be back, Mum."

"Oh God, I missed you!" she said, and her eyes were full and of course she was crying because she always cried.

Elle was next to give her nephew a hug. "You look good," she said. "Better be careful or Irene's mother will make a move."

Kurt laughed and looked back at Irene, whose reunion with her mother was slightly tamer and colder. Her mother air-kissed her and made her stand back so that she could look at her, and then she squeezed her for a second or so. Kurt turned to his mother and shook his head.

"Poor Irene," he said. "I'd hate to be going back to that."

Irene ran over to Jane and Elle and hugged them both far more warmly than she had her own mother.

"We had a ball—we'd do it again in the morning. Can you believe how well Kurt did in his exams? When we got our results we were sitting at a beach bar. Incredible. Can you believe he's got Medicine and I'm going to be a nurse? I just scraped by, thank God. Oh Jane, this summer was the best time in our lives!"

"I can't wait to hear all about it," Jane said.

"I have to go," Irene said, and she seemed a little sad.

"I understand," Jane said. "Come for dinner tomorrow night."

"Great. I'll have some photos by then."

She kissed Kurt and ran off to join her mother, who was waiting by the door.

"Are you hungry?" Jane asked Kurt.

"I'd eat a scabby leg," he said.

"I'll take that as a yes. Did I tell you how proud I am?"

"About a million times, Mum."

She put her arm around her son and together they walked to the airport restaurant, with Elle in tow pushing the cart carrying his bags.

Dominic arrived at Jane's just after six. He ran up the steps, and Kurt was waiting by the door. They hugged warmly and Dominic messed Kurt's bleached curls. "Jesus, son, albinos have darker hair!"

"Thanks, Dad."

"Great to have you home."

"Sorry about Bella," Kurt said as they walked into the kitchen.

"Never mind." Dominic smiled at Jane. "Long time no see, stranger."

She nodded. "Good to see you, Dominic."

She was hoping her heart wouldn't flutter. She hadn't seen him in just over two months. She had not missed him once and had told herself categorically and in no uncertain terms that she was to stop loving him. She did feel a flutter—*Damn you, Jane*—and her pulse did race a little, and although this disappointed her, she managed to work out in those few seconds that even if she was still attracted to Dominic she didn't love him. She had been glad of the distance, she had enjoyed it, and so she could live with a flutter now and then because they were only friends and that suited her just fine.

Jane cooked a family dinner to include Rose. Elle had made her excuses because Leslie needed help with something she wasn't at liberty to divulge.

Rose promised to be on her best behavior around Dominic.

"I'm not a child, Jane. You don't have to monitor my behavior."

"Of course I do, Rose. You have the capacity to insult someone with a mere look. I just want this to be nice for Kurt."

"And don't you think I want it to be nice for Kurt? He is my grandson."

"Fine, fine, but I'm warning you—do not bring up Bella."

"Hmmmmmm," Rose said.

At dinner Kurt talked about the various Greek islands he'd been to; he talked about Paris, Milan, Rome, Barcelona, and Amsterdam, at which point he shared a little knowing grin with his dad.

"I saw that," Jane said.

"What?" Kurt said innocently.

"Don't play dumb with me."

"What are you talking about?" Rose said.

"Nothing," Jane said.

"Sex and drugs on every corner, Gran," Kurt said.

"Well, do you hear that, Janey? Maybe you should get yourself to Amsterdam. God knows you could do with something to lift both your mood and your skirt."

"Rose!" Jane screamed in exasperation, but Kurt and Dominic were holding themselves, they found it so funny.

Rose grinned at her daughter, who mouthed the words "You are dead, old woman."

During dessert Kurt talked excitedly about doing Medicine at Trinity. He couldn't believe he had gotten the scores necessary, because study was so boring that mostly he'd just played computer games.

"Your mother was like that," Rose said. "When Janey was seven she got one of those kids' encyclopedias that were so popular in the eighties. She read it in a week and I swear you could ask that kid any question and she'd know the answer. Remarkable, really."

"My God, Rose, that's the first nice thing I've heard you say about Jane ever," Dominic said.

"I stated a fact, Dominic, and anyway, how's your wife?"

"Rose!" Jane warned.

"She left me," he said.

"Good for her," Rose said. "I'd like to propose a toast to Bella—may she find herself a half-decent husband next time around!"

"That's it! One more word from you and you're going back to the basement," Jane said.

Kurt leaned back on his chair. "I really missed this," he said. "I love you, Gran."

"I love you too, darling."

They clinked glasses, and he drank his beer and she inhaled her wine, and it was just like he'd never been away.

Leslie walked out of the dressing room feeling monumentally self-conscious. She was wearing a red bikini bottom and a matching red flowing top picked out by Elle. Elle had also picked out a wide-brimmed white hat, but Leslie had refused to wear it.

"Well," she said, gesturing to the bottom and top, "can you see?"

"No, I can't see," Elle said. "You look lovely. I told you red is your color."

Leslie looked at herself in the mirror. The top had enough material to conceal the fact that she had no breasts, and instead she just looked flat-chested.

"Try it on in green," Elle said.

"It will look the same," Leslie argued.

"No, it will be a different color and that changes the outfit utterly," Elle said.

Leslie went back into the dressing room. Elle's phone buzzed and it was a text from Dominic. «Just had dinner at Jane's. Feel like shit. What are we doing?????» She put the phone back in her bag. Leslie appeared in the same outfit in green.

"Looks good," Elle said. "Buy them both."

"Really? I feel so exposed."

"You're going to be on a beach, not at the opera. Buy the clothes, please."

"Okay." Leslie took one last look at herself and secretly she was pleased. Although without clothes her body was broken, with clothes she looked quite good for her age. *I can do this.*

They spent another hour buying a holiday wardrobe for Leslie, then stopped off for coffee and a toasted sandwich in a coffee shop that Elle hadn't been to since she was a student.

"It's a bit grotty, isn't it?" Leslie said.

"That's character."

Leslie sat on a bench and pushed the table toward Elle and fixed herself in the seat. "Since when has filth become character?" She pointed to a large cobweb in the corner.

"It's a cobweb, Leslie, not a dangling bucket of shit."

"And there goes my appetite."

They were finishing their coffee when Elle confided what she was doing with Dominic.

"Two more coffees, please," Leslie said to the waiter. "You are insane. Why would you do that?"

"I don't know. I can't help it. It makes me feel . . ."

"Feel what?" Leslie asked.

"It makes me feel, full stop."

"Well, stop feeling because it will end in tears."

"It was easy when Kurt was away, but now he's back and that means that Dominic is back in Jane's life. When Kurt was away we could pretend that it didn't matter."

"So stop."

"So Jim's all packed and ready for this sun holiday, is he?" Elle asked.

"Don't change the subject."

"Excited, I bet."

"Stop what you are doing," Leslie said.

"I know, I know," Elle said. "Stop what you're doing with your nephew's father, you hillbilly lunatic."

"Well, that wasn't exactly where I was going, but close enough."

Leslie was leaving for her sun holiday with Jim the next day, and she was anxious about what she would wear, how she would look, how she'd feel, whether or not it was too soon, and how they would get on. She had thought many times about pulling out, but it had actually been Deborah who managed to talk her around one day when they met in the lobby.

"Why the face?" Deborah asked.

"I was born with it."

"Oh ha ha ha. What's wrong with you?"

"I'm having second thoughts about going on holiday."

Leslie got into the lift. Deborah followed her and pushed the button for their floor.

"You're going," Deborah said.

"I'm scared," said Leslie, "not to mention sore, tired, and itchy."

Deborah's demeanor softened. "You've been through a lot. You deserve to have fun."

"But will it be fun?"

"I have no idea," Deborah said, "but it will definitely beat sitting in that apartment of yours and staring at four walls."

Leslie sighed. "I don't do that so much anymore."

"Not as much, but you still do it."

"I'll go, then."

"I think you should."

"So you'll still mind the cat?"

"Yes, I'll mind the stupid cat."

"Will you be nice to her and give her at least one hug a day?"

"I'll be nice as in I won't kick her when I see her, but I will not hug her."

"Will you let her rub against your leg?"

"Fine. I'll let her rub against my leg."

"Good," Leslie said. "I'll bring you back something special."

"It better cost more than twenty euros."

Leslie laughed and entered her apartment.

Jim picked her up in his car and they drove to the long-term car park and got a bus to the terminal. Leslie checked her handbag for her passport and tickets so many times that Jim took them off her. They put their bags through and went straight to their gate, where they had time for a small lunch.

Leslie was extremely nervous and kept tapping her fingers on the table.

Jim placed his hand on hers. "Relax," he said, "we are going to have a great time."

"I can't," she said. "I've just remembered I hate flying."

Jim laughed at her and promised that if she got too nervous he'd share his stash of Valium.

"Why do you have Valium?"

"Oh, the doctor gave them to me after Imelda died."

"That was over ten years ago."

"Yeah but pills don't go off, do they?"

"I think they do, Jim."

"Oh."

"Still, give me one anyway."

"Are you sure?"

"Positive."

"Okay, but only one."

"Fine," she said.

He opened his bag and tapped a few Valium into his hand, she grabbed two and swallowed them without water, and an hour later she floated onto the plane.

Jane spent the day with the party organizers. The tent had arrived and was being erected in the back garden. Rose had spent much of the morning shouting at the men to watch her various plants. The booze had arrived and the catering team had set up a good-sized bar. The dance floor had lights flashing around it, and the DJ arrived good and early to do a sound check. Dominic kept Kurt entertained for the day because although his belated eighteenth birthday party was no surprise, Jane wanted everything to be perfect when he walked through the door. Irene arrived late in the afternoon to see if there was anything she could help with, but Jane was pretty happy that everything was right on track, and instead they enjoyed coffee on the patio together because thankfully in September it had stopped raining. They talked about the party plans, and Irene was so excited she broke into a clap every now and again. When they were all talked out on the party theme, Jane broached the subject of how Irene was getting on at home.

"It's good," she said.

"You can come back here anytime."

"Thanks, Jane. I know you don't think much of my mum, but she's not half as bad as you think."

"I'm sure you're right."

"She doesn't make a good first impression."

Or a second, Jane thought.

"She was painfully shy up to her early twenties, so sometimes when she's nervous she overcompensates. She was really upset when we got back from the airport."

"I'm sorry."

"She thinks everyone is laughing at her. She feels foolish. She was married to my dad for twenty-five years, he meets someone online, and she's a laughingstock. It's hard for her."

"She's not a laughingstock."

"I wish she believed that."

"She'll recover."

"What makes you think that?"

"Because people do."

"I hope so," Irene said. "I hate seeing her so sad. That guy might have been a user, but at least he was a distraction."

"I really like you, Irene."

"I really like you too, Jane, but next time you meet my mum, go easy on her."

"Promise."

"And Elle?"

"I'll hold her back."

Piped music played from eight onward, people started to arrive around nine, the caterers served drinks to anyone with a passable fake ID, and the kids were going through canapés like there was no tomorrow. Jane was dressed and ready to join the guests, but she waited for her son and his dad. They arrived just before ten. The place was full, lights were flashing, and the music was rocking. Kurt jigged down the steps into his back garden, where his friends were sitting around drinking and having a ball. The group of his closest friends all howled when he approached, and they bent over with arms stretched in honor of his excellent party. He played it cool, kissing his girlfriend and slapping his pals' hands. Jane watched from the kitchen window with Dominic over her shoulder.

"You've done a pretty good job there," he said.

"Despite myself."

"You're always so hard on yourself."

"He's special, isn't he?"

"I think so."

"My heart is full," she said.

Tom appeared behind Dominic with a large boxed present, and Jane spotted his reflection through the glass.

"Tom!" She turned to him. "Thanks for coming."

"Wouldn't have missed it."

She hugged him. "You didn't need to bring a present."

"Yeah, well, I hope he likes it," Tom said while maintaining eye contact with Dominic.

"I'm Dominic." Dominic offered his hand.

"Tom." Tom took Dominic's hand and shook it.

"I was really sorry to hear about Alexandra," Dominic said, putting his arm around Jane. "She was a good friend to us."

"She was a good friend to *me*—she hated you," Jane said.

Tom laughed.

"Only toward the end," Dominic said.

"No," Jane said, shaking her head, "way before that. She thought you were a vain stuck-up brat."

"I'm leaving now," Dominic said. "It was nice to meet you, Tom."

"You too."

Tom turned and smiled at Jane, and Dominic noticed a look in her eye that had once been reserved for him. He walked down into the garden and said hello to a few of Kurt's friends, and once he made sure the caterers were happy and all was well, he snuck down to Elle's cottage and knocked on her door.

Tom and Jane mingled with Kurt's friends, and when she asked him to dance he was horrified and she made fun of him until he relented. Two minutes on the floor and she agreed that it had been a bad idea. They sat and watched Kurt and Irene dance wildly around the floor with their hands in the air.

"It seems like a lifetime ago," he said.

"For me it was a lifetime, Kurt's lifetime."

"Alexandra was so desperate for a baby. We tried everything. I wanted to just skip it all and adopt, but she was determined to have her own. She wanted to feel life inside her."

"Yeah, well, it was a long time ago, but I hated it. The sickness, the constipation—my God, no one tells you about that—the gas, the heartburn, the backache, the pressure on your bladder . . . oh, the hemorrhoids, and did I mention the heartburn?"

"Yes." He laughed. "You paint such a beautiful picture."

"I don't remember enjoying one bit of my pregnancy and, if I'm honest, the first year or two of Kurt's life were from hell, but after that something inside me clicked. It took its time to click, but when it did I could never go back to a time without him, you know?"

"No," he said, "but I'd like to experience that someday."

Alexandra had been missing sixty-four weeks and three days and it was the first day that Tom had expressed a wish for the future, and it was a future in which he envisaged himself with Jane and not his wife. The thought was momentary but profound.

Jane wasn't living inside of Tom's head and so didn't perceive the juggernaut of emotions that had borne down on him with that statement and the accompanying vision that he hid so well.

"I just don't know if I could do it again," she said, staring at her son mooning a friend. "My God, I have no idea how I did it the first time."

"You're a great mother, despite forgetting him outside a shop when he was a baby and threatening to beat up his bully."

"And don't forget breaking my toe when I was kicking down his door—that was an especially proud moment."

"How could I? That image will last a lifetime."

The clock turned to midnight, and the caterer approached Jane and asked her to step outside. Standing there, with a cake the size of a shopping center, was Dominic.

Elle was lighting the eighteen candles. The lighter had run out, and she kept shaking it and cursing. "We should have just got the one and the eight. Eighteen actual candles are so tacky."

"I want to see him blow out eighteen candles," Jane said, and she grabbed the lighter from Elle and shook it hard. She got a few more lit, and then she began lighting one off the other.

"My back is breaking," Dominic said.

When all eighteen candles were lit, Elle signaled to the DJ and he played "Happy Birthday," and Dominic and Jane walked in holding the cake. Kurt was left standing in the middle of the dance floor alone as all his friends abandoned him. He covered his face and then blew out his candles. Everybody clapped, and Jane and Dominic took the cake over to the side, where the caterer started to cut it.

"This is where we decipher who's drunk and who's stoned," Dominic said. "Cake eaters, stoned; non–cake eaters, pissed."

"Don't be ridiculous," she said.

"You're such a square, Janey," Elle said, gorging on cake. "Yum," she said, and she giggled.

After midnight everything got a little crazy. Jane was surrounded by sixty drunk teenagers and was feeling a little worse for wear herself. Tom was on his fifth whiskey, and even though there was plenty of food he wouldn't touch any of it.

"Do you want to get some air?" she asked when the tent got so hot there was steam coming off the teenagers' heads.

"Yes, please."

They walked outside into the cool air.

"That's better," he said. "You know, I'd love a cup of coffee."

"I'd love a cup of tea," she admitted, "but I haven't seen Elle in a while, so first I just want to make sure she's okay."

"You mean you're checking up on her."

"Did you see how much wine she was pouring down her throat? It was like looking at Rose."

"Where is Rose?"

"Her pal's house. She doesn't like groups of teenagers—says they bring out the devil in one another."

"Right." Tom headed up to the house to put the kettle on.

Elle's light was on, so Jane walked inside. The kitchen was empty, as was the sitting room. She called out and heard movement coming from the bedroom. To make sure that Elle wasn't getting sick, she opened the door and saw Dominic attempt to cover his face with the duvet. Elle just sat there as though Dominic wasn't in the bed beside her, hiding when he'd already been seen.

"Hi, Janey," Elle said.

"I don't believe it."

Dominic took the duvet down from his face. "I'm sorry."

"You don't mind, do you, Janey?" Elle said. "You're over him, you've moved on."

"Shut up, Elle."

"Jane, look . . ."

"Shut up, Dominic."

"Janey, relax!" Elle said.

"I'm finished with both of you," Jane said. "Completely and utterly finished."

"What does that mean?" Elle said.

"It means that you are on your own."

She closed the door and walked out of the cottage and through the garden past all the drunken teenagers, two of whom were puking in her mother's rosebushes and one of whom was taking a pee on the graves of Elle's dead gerbils, Jeffrey, Jessica, Judy, and Jimmy. She walked into her kitchen, and Tom was waiting with fresh coffee and tea and was surprised when she slammed the door. She covered her face and then her mouth, and then she sniffed and sat down.

"What happened?"

"Dominic and my sister happened."

"They were together?"

"Yes, Tom, they were together in bed postcoitus."

"I'm sorry."

"Everybody is always sorry. Don't you get pissed off with people being sorry?"

"Yeah, I do."

"Me too. I am so fucking sick of being sorry, feeling sorry, and having people feel sorry for me."

"Me too."

"Dominic is an asshole, he can't help it, I've always known and I've always put up with it. But Elle, it's not her. Elle may be a lot of things, but she has always been kind, never cruel, and this is cruel—she doesn't even like him."

"Drink some tea."

"I don't fucking want any fucking tea."

"That's two 'fucking's in the space of three seconds. I think you need some tea."

"I'm sorry, I'm really sorry."

"It's okay, you're just upset."

"I don't love him."

"I know."

"I just don't understand why Elle would do that."

"I don't know what to tell you."

"I'm finished with her. I have picked up after her since she was a kid, I've put her ahead of me every step of the way. I didn't ask for much, in fact I don't remember ever asking for or wanting anything but Dominic. She knew what she was doing. So I'm finished with her."

Tom handed her the tea. "You'll feel better in the morning."

She shook her head. "No, I won't."

"It's going to be fine," he said.

"How could she do that?" she said.

And it was then that she burst into tears and sobbed and rattled in Tom's arms until she was empty, and when she stopped crying he kissed her and it took her aback, especially as he was in such close proximity and she had puffy eyes, tear-burned cheeks, and, she suspected, a runny nose. It felt really nice and so she kissed him, and then they were both kissing each other for a minute or two or ten, and then he pulled away and under his breath he said he was sorry.

"Yeah," she said, and she sniffled a little. "Of course you are."

He walked out of the kitchen and out of her house, leaving Jane alone staring out at her son and his pals having the time of their lives. She walked into her bedroom and locked the door and laid her head on her pillow and cried into it until it caused her actual physical pain to continue. *Where the hell did it all go wrong?*

Two days after Kurt's party, Leslie returned home from holiday. She was tanned and relaxed and even happy. Despite being sore, tired, itchy, and sometimes emotional, she'd had the time of her life. They laid on the beach, and while she slept under the sun her body and mind healed themselves. They drank wine in the evenings, ate beautiful food while looking at beautiful scenery, and armed with the clothes carefully chosen by Elle she didn't feel odd or weird or freakish once.

In fact she felt good, especially when she caught the eye of a few locals, and one particular waiter attempted to chat her up every time Jim left the table.

She enjoyed Jim's company, they had fun together, it was easy and freeing, they talked when they had something to say and other times they just relaxed in silence. Leslie's mood had improved one hundred percent, she felt better, she looked better, the hormones were obviously kicking in, and a confidence she hadn't known she had was coming to the fore. Jim called it "survivor's confidence." She liked that. She liked Jim, and he was more than family. Leslie Sheehan was falling in love.

14

"I've Been Raining"

*I've been raining I've been pouring
there's a hole in my roof I've been ignoring
I've been washed up idle and wasted.
I know my luck is going to change
I can almost taste it.*

Jack L, *Broken Songs*

October 2008

After weeks and weeks of doctor visits and referrals, Breda was hospitalized. Two days later her husband, Ben, her son, Eamonn, and her daughter Kate were called into a consultant's office and told that she had end-stage colon cancer. Ben didn't understand what the doctor was saying and so he repeated the words a few times, looking at his daughter and son. Kate cried and Eamonn got angry.

"She's been sick for months. How the hell was this not picked up?" Eamonn said, banging his fist on the table.

"Eamonn, calm down," Ben said.

The consultant had no answer. "It should have been picked up," he said.

"Is that all you can say?" Eamonn said.

"I can't answer for the other doctors you've seen. I can only tell you what I've found. I will say this: I reviewed your mother's medical history and only last year she had a clean bill of health, which means the cancer has spread in a very short period of time."

"How do we fix her?" Ben asked.

"All we can offer is palliative care."

"Palliative?" Ben said.

"She's dying, Dad," Kate said.

"Don't say that, Kate," he said.

"How long does she have?" Eamonn asked in a whisper.

"Six to eight weeks," the consultant said.

"Ah no," Ben said, "this isn't happening."

"I'm very sorry, Mr. Walsh," the consultant said.

"No." Ben shook his head. "I can't have this—we lost our daughter only a year ago—I can't have this."

"We will make her as comfortable as possible."

Ben stood up and walked out into the corridor. He looked for the exit sign that would take him outside. He was halfway down the corridor when he stopped and held himself and sobbed so loud and so hard that a nurse came to assist him. She guided him to a chair and waited with him until his family came to find him.

Ben sat in a big red armchair pulled up close to the bed, and when he wasn't sleeping he was holding Breda's hand. His daughter and son took turns badgering him to eat or drink or take a walk or shower or sleep. He said no every time. He washed with antibacterial soap in the disabled bathroom two doors down from his wife's room, Kate brought clean clothes, and he changed in the toilet cubicle. He ate a sandwich in the chair, and sometimes Frankie and Eamonn arrived with some warm stew. They hadn't told Breda she was dying, but Ben knew that deep down she was aware of her situation. She didn't talk much. The medication made her sleep a lot, and the Breda he knew had all but disappeared. So he watched his wife lie still and wondered where her mind was—was she happy or sad, scared or at peace, did she even really know he was there, could she feel his hand, would she come back around and talk to him and did she even want to?

Kate would talk to her, telling her about what was happening and complaining that after an entire summer of rain it was still raining and even for October she couldn't believe how cold and miserable it was. She told her about the liaison officer's latest report on Alexandra, and unfortunately there wasn't much news there: the ring seemed to lead only to a dead end. She talked about Owen's job and how as a member of the management team he had been forced to let some people go because the company was starting to cut back. She brushed Breda's hair and put moisturizer on her face and Vaseline on her lips. She washed her nightgowns and made sure that she had water even though she wasn't awake to drink it, because she would be thirsty when she came back.

Eamonn always stood just inside the door leaning against the wall, watching his mum and waiting for a sign. He was quiet, speaking only when necessary, to answer a question or to ask the doctor or nurse for a status report.

Tom came and went, and it was hard because although Kate

was kind and Ben's attitude to him had softened, Breda had been the only member of the Walsh family never to blame or suspect him in the loss of Alexandra. She maintained his tenuous link with the Walshes, and in her absence he felt like an outsider rather than family, but in deference to her he went anyway.

Things had been slightly awkward between Tom and Jane since the kiss, but when Kate phoned him with Breda's news, she was the first one he called. Initially she was hesitant; he could hear it in her voice, so he didn't beat around the bush.

"Breda has cancer," he said.

"Oh Tom, I'm so sorry to hear that."

"She's dying."

"Oh my God!"

"They say she's only got six to eight weeks."

"Oh Tom, that's awful!"

"I can't believe it."

"I'm so sorry."

"I thought you were fucking sick of listening to people say fucking sorry," he said in jest, and all the tension that had built up that night dissolved.

"Let's just leave it at that, shall we?"

"I'd love to."

"What can I do for Breda?"

"Absolutely nothing."

"God, Tom, I really am so sorry to hear that."

"I know, I know you're fond of her."

"Poor Mr. Walsh!"

"Are you going to call Ben 'Mr. Walsh' till the day you die?"

"Probably." She sighed. "How's Eamonn?"

"Annoyed."

"Nothing new there, then."

"For once I don't blame him."

"I wish I could do something for her," she said.

"Me too."

They agreed to meet for coffee the next day. Jane put down the phone, and Kurt was standing behind her when she turned.

"What's going on?" she asked.

"I'd like to ask you the same thing."

"What are you talking about?"

"Dad says he's not welcome here anymore. What the hell?"

"He's not, and you don't want to know," she said, walking from the sitting room to the kitchen.

"I really do," he said, following her.

"Do you want coffee?"

"Yes." He sat down.

She boiled the kettle and scooped the coffee into the percolator and stood at the counter, tapping her fingers on it. Kurt waited at the table with his hands in his hair.

"Mum?" he said when the kettle was just about boiled.

"It's complicated."

"I'm not twelve."

She poured the water into the percolator, put the top on, and grabbed two cups. She placed the percolator and cups on the table and sat. Kurt leaned back on his chair, opened the fridge door, and grabbed the milk.

"Well?" he said.

"He slept with Elle," she said.

"Elle, your sister, my aunt?" he said, pointing to her and then to himself.

"Yes."

"What the fuck?"

"Language, Kurt."

"No, seriously, Mum, what the fuck?" Kurt stood up and paced. "Why? Jesus, they don't even like each other that much."

"I don't know."

"When?"

"It doesn't matter."

"It matters."

"Your birthday party."

"Oh man!" He sat down. "No wonder Dad's been acting strange."

"I'm sorry, Kurt, but I don't want to see him again."

"I know you love him, Mum," Kurt said.

Jane blushed so red she was embarrassed by her embarrassment. Her eyes filled and stung.

"I'm really sorry, Mum."

"Thanks," Jane said, and she pulled herself together.

"What about Elle?" He hadn't seen her in well over a week, but that didn't mean a thing as she often disappeared for that long and longer.

"She's not welcome here either."

"But she lives down the back of the garden."

"And that's where she can stay."

"Okay. What about me?"

"I don't understand the question."

"I hate what they did to you, but he's my dad."

"And I don't expect you to take sides," Jane said. "You're an adult now. You're starting college next week. You can still have a great relationship with your dad, just one that doesn't involve me."

"Okay, but I promise I'm going to give him such shit for this."

"I appreciate that." Jane smiled at her son. "If you throw in a kick in the nuts I'd appreciate that too."

Kurt practiced swinging his leg. "Consider it done. And, Mum, he isn't good enough for you."

Jane's eyes filled up again. "Thanks, son."

Kurt left the kitchen, and Jane sighed and thought to herself that even if she was about to turn thirty-seven and she was alone, at least she had Kurt, for a while anyway.

She walked to the sink and poured the coffee that they hadn't touched down the drain, and when Elle appeared and stared at her through her kitchen window, Jane ducked.

Jesus, Jane, get a grip.

She stood up and left the room.

Elle deeply regretted her actions with Dominic. As soon as they were caught, their affair was over. There was no discussion, no debate, and no good-bye. After Jane vacated Elle's room, they sat in the bed in silence, allowing her words to sink in. They both knew Jane well enough to hear in her voice the hurt and damage they'd caused, and they both knew her well enough to know that she was serious when she said she was done with them. They both had realized that in that moment their happy family was no more. Jane was the glue that held them all together, and the glue had become unstuck. Elle got out of bed and got dressed, and Dominic followed suit. She walked into her sitting room, closed the door, and cuddled up on the sofa with her favorite blanket, and he left without a word. Since then she had kept out of Jane's way because after sleeping with the love of Jane's life, adhering to her request to stay away was the least she could do.

She missed Jane in her life instantly. Jane was one of the very few people she talked to every day, and Jane was the one who took care of her when she was sick, when she was well, when

she didn't want her to, and when she needed her to. Jane was
Elle's world, and without Jane Elle's world was incredibly empty.
Four days after Kurt's party, Jane sent Elle a business letter ceasing their working arrangement, withdrawing as Elle's agent, and
providing her with names of other agents and galleries she could
work with. Elle was devastated. Jane knew that she was a ditz
with business, and so ceasing their working relationship was the
final straw and it meant that Jane was absolutely adamant that
she wanted nothing more to do with her. For the first time in her
life, Elle had done something so bad that there was no coming
back from it. Jane had been forgiving her all her life, but Elle
had crossed the line.

Leslie arrived at her cottage to go for a planned walk in a
nearby park. Leslie asked if she should nip up to the main house
to ask Jane if she wished to join them, and Elle broke into tears.

"What happened?" Leslie said, hands on hips.

"She found us together."

"Oh no. You cannot be serious."

"At Kurt's birthday, here in my bedroom."

"Oh Elle, you stupid, stupid girl!"

"I know, I know I'm stupid. I'm an idiot, a selfish little liar,
twisted in the head." She was banging her head with her fist hard,
so hard that Leslie had to grab her hand and hold it tight.

"Okay," she said. "Calm down and sit down and stop banging
your head."

Elle sat and wrung her hands. "I've really hurt her, Leslie. I've
really hurt her."

"She'll get over it. It might not be today or tomorrow, but I
promise she will get over it."

"She hates me."

"Well, now she needs to, so let her."

"But I can't cope on my own."

"You're twenty-six. In two months you're going to be twenty-seven. You are old enough and capable enough to take care of yourself."

Elle shook her head. "Not without Jane."

"Yes, without Jane," Leslie said in her strictest voice. "It's time for you to find your own way because, Elle, if you think living in the back of your sister's garden is a permanent arrangement, you're wrong. Things change—if anyone knows that, I do."

"Let's walk." Elle got up from her chair, desperate to change her scenery and the subject.

"Okay." Leslie put on her coat.

Elle walked to the door and stood outside waiting for Leslie.

"Elle," Leslie said.

"Yeah?"

"Your coat."

Elle looked at herself and realized she was standing outside in the cold in a T-shirt.

"Oh," she said, and she took her coat from Leslie and put it on. "Let's go," she said.

Leslie pulled the door shut and wondered whether Elle would truly be lost without Jane.

The first night Elle had slept with Dominic, she had gone home and into her studio and started painting. The theme was sin, and she used a lot of reds and blacks and purples, and there was a girl succumbing to a man with the devil in his eyes. She liked it, and so as the month and her affair carried on, she painted more like it. She hadn't shown them to Jane before the letter, and afterward she wasn't sure what she would do or where she would go, and so she just kept painting. Lori called her two days before the Ken Browne exhibition in Albert's Gallery and asked her if she would be attending.

"I'm barred," she said.

"Don't be an ass. Your sister owns the place."

"She barred me."

"For what?"

"For sleeping with Kurt's dad."

"Christ, Elle, what are you like?"

"A whore, a slut, a selfish, twisted little bitch."

"It was a rhetorical question," Lori said, "and besides, you have to come. I'm hearing a lot of good things about this guy, and you know Jane is all business—she won't make a scene, not in the gallery."

"Okay," Elle said, "I'll go."

She decided to go for two reasons, the first being that she had heard that Ken Browne was an artist worth watching and the second being that she hoped that Jane would see how sorry she was and find it in her heart to forgive her.

On the evening of the exhibition, she met Lori in a pub down the road from the gallery and they had a drink to calm their nerves.

"This is actually quite exciting," Lori said. "There's a whole new edge to the event."

Elle just hoped that Jane would be okay with her turning up. They waited until they knew the gallery would be busy. Jane was rushing around and the artist was talking to patrons and friends, every now and then stopping to have his photo taken. Lori spotted someone she knew and ran off to talk to him, leaving Elle standing alone. She walked over to a painting and stood in front of it for a long time. It was so beautiful it made her want to cry. She stared at the color on canvas, the deep browns, the burnt orange, the translucent white against the brightest blue, and what she saw was scorched earth, and she could feel the heat, and under the brightest blue sky in her mind's eye she saw a beginning of all things.

The woman beside her was just as taken by the painting. For her it didn't evoke the dawn of creation, but it did match her couch.

Elle moved on to the next and then the next, and every painting spoke to her and told her its story. They were celestial, brave, and beautiful. She could hear each voice individually calling to her from the canvas. *This is real art.* The one that had made her want to cry called out, *This is talent. This has heart and soul. You'll never paint like this. You'll never evoke the emotions these paintings evoke. You are a pretender and soon you'll be found out. Without Jane you are just a jumped-up cartoonist.*

"Shut up," she said.

The woman beside her looked her up and down.

"I wasn't talking to you," she said, and she walked away.

Jane appeared behind her. "Go home, Elle," she said.

"Please, can we talk?"

"I'm working, and even if I wasn't I have nothing to say to you and there is nothing that you can say."

Elle left, and Lori didn't notice because she was too busy bowing before Ken Browne.

Elle went home. She walked into her studio and dragged all her finished paintings into the garden. "You're shit," she said. "You're shit, shit, shit! It's all shit!"

She piled them high and doused them in whiskey, then lit

a match and threw it, and the lot went up in flames. She stood watching.

The flames and smoke alerted Kurt and Rose at the same time. Kurt saw his aunt standing far too close to the fire and ran out into the garden and pulled Elle away from the flames.

"Your work! What are you doing to your beautiful work?"

"It's ugly," she said. "It's all so fucking ugly."

Rose grabbed her garden hose and trailed it to where she could point it and douse the flames. Elle watched her put the fire out while being held back by Kurt. When Rose finished and there was only smoldering wood left, she turned to her grandson.

"Put Elle to bed and then come and tell me what the hell is going on around here."

Kurt nodded and took Elle into her cottage. Rose made her way to her basement apartment and waited for Kurt to make sense of Elle's latest episode.

The day after Ken Browne's exhibition, Rose Moore walked up the steps from her basement to the main house and used her key to get inside. Jane was vacuuming the landing upstairs and stopped when she saw Rose. It wasn't feeding time, and there was no special reason for Rose to be out of her chair and up in the main house, so Jane was concerned.

"What's wrong?" she said.

Rather than shout up the stairs, Rose ignored her daughter and walked to the kitchen. Jane parked the vacuum, came downstairs, and followed her in.

"What's wrong?" she repeated.

Rose sat down on one of Jane's kitchen chairs with a groan. "Well, seeing as you asked, *you* are."

"I'm wrong?"

"Yes," Rose said, "you are."

"About what, Rose?" Jane said in a tone that suggested she wasn't in the mood for her mother's madness.

"You know what your sister's like. She acts before she thinks—she's impetuous, highly charged, a slave to her emotions—and that's what makes her so special."

"Sleeping with the father of your sister's child is not special. It's cruel."

"Because of what, Jane? Because you love Dominic? Do you honestly for one moment think that your love for Dominic was real?"

"Yes, I do."

"Bullshit," Rose said. "Dominic was just the best time you ever had, that's all."

"And whose fault is that?" Jane shouted.

"Oh here we go again! I'm the bad mother who stole your future. I'm the one who made you have a baby and then I made you raise him. You're just a victim of my bad decisions."

"I didn't say that."

"You didn't have to—you've said it all before. And maybe if I had my time again I would have considered getting that abortion and maybe I wouldn't. And, yes, I am a bad mother. There, I said it. Are you happy now?"

Jane didn't know what to say. She was shell-shocked, so she said nothing.

"I should have been more supportive. I regret that. I did punish you, Jane. I punished you because I was so angry at all that potential lost. I should have helped you more. Especially that time when—"

"Don't say it," Jane said, and then she sat silently because Rose's apology had taken the wind out of her sails.

"Do you remember when you stopped calling me 'Mum'?" Rose said.

"The day we received Principal Reynolds's letter and you told me I couldn't go back to school."

"No," Rose said, "that was the day you decided to call me 'Rose,' but long after that you'd let 'Mum' slip once or even twice a day. It used to amuse me because every time you said the *M* word you'd almost kick yourself." She stopped talking, but Jane knew she wasn't finished. Rose moved in her chair and tapped the table twice. "The day you stopped calling me 'Mum' was the day you walked into the police station with Kurt in your arms and asked if they would take either him or you because if they didn't you'd kill him."

"Stop it," Jane said. "You promised we'd never talk about it."

"They took him, and you went hysterical so they took you to the hospital and the doctors sedated you."

"I don't want to talk about it!" Jane shouted.

"Social Services was called, and when they asked me if we had any history of depression in the family, I said no."

"So what? I was just so tired, his colic was so bad for so long, and he wouldn't stop crying!"

"I lied," Rose said. "My daughter was sedated and my grand-son was in the care of social workers and all I could think about was making sure no one found out."

"Found out what?"

"About your dad."

"What about my dad?"

"Oh Janey, he was so clever—just as you are! Did you know that he was one of the country's top mathematicians? He had such a great mind. Sometimes he was so happy, the life and soul of every party and everyone loved him, and sometimes he was so sad that he found moving his head hard."

"Why are you telling me this?"

"He didn't have a heart attack, Janey," Rose said. "He hanged himself."

"No."

"He hanged himself with your jump rope."

"No. You're lying."

"People didn't talk about it in those days; it just wasn't something you talked about," Rose said, pale and tired. "I blamed you and Elle." She laughed a bitter laugh. "For the longest time I told myself if you hadn't left the bloody jump rope out he would never have left us and you were the oldest so you should have known better. Of course that was madness because it wasn't your fault— you were just a little girl."

"Why are you telling me this?"

"I'm telling you because I can't keep making the same mistakes over and over again."

"I don't understand."

"You got your dad's brain. Elle got his temperament."

"What are you saying, Rose?" Jane said angrily.

"I'm saying that when I look at my youngest daughter, I see her father," Rose said, and tears ran down her face. "I'm saying that you have to forgive her, care for her, protect her from the world and herself the way I should have protected your dad."

Jane stood up and put her hands on her head. "There is nothing wrong with Elle."

Rose stood up and wiped her face with her sleeve. She straightened and took a moment to collect her thoughts. "It's a lot to take in," she said. "I'll leave it with you."

She walked out, leaving her older daughter both astonished and utterly devastated.

Two weeks had passed since they had returned from their holiday, and Leslie decided to tell Jim how she felt. She would have sought advice from either Jane or Elle, but as they were both locked in combat she decided that honesty was the best policy and if Jim was going to shoot her down it was best he do it before she fell too hard. She put on a cute little vest top and matching briefs that Elle had helped her pick out and then slipped on a pretty black cowlneck jersey dress and some heels. She applied makeup and fixed her pixie haircut. She put on some music and poured wine, and at seven thirty on the dot her doorbell rang.

Jim brought flowers and she accepted them gratefully. He complimented her on the smell coming from the oven, and she didn't tell him that it was premade lamb tagine that she was simply heating up.

She handed him a glass of wine, and he sat at the table while she served the food.

"You look nice tonight," he said.

"Thanks," she said. "I bought the dress yesterday."

"It suits you."

She put his plate of food in front of him and a plate in front of herself, and she sat.

"Eat up," she said.

"No need to ask twice. I'm starving."

They ate in silence.

"Is there something wrong?" he said.

"No, why do you ask?"

"Well, usually you are carrying on about something or someone."

"That's not true," she said, "and anyway, you've been here five minutes and you haven't mentioned one single article you've read today."

"Well, now that you mention it, I was reading the details of the government bank-guarantee scheme earlier. I tell you, Leslie, people just don't realize how close this country came to bankruptcy a few weeks ago. The good times are officially over."

"Don't say that! I've only just started to leave the apartment," she said, and he laughed.

"Well, right about now I think your apartment is the best place to be," he said, and she smiled.

She'd forgotten to buy dessert, so they enjoyed coffee on the sofa. She was wondering when and how she'd break the news of her love for him when he put his coffee down and reached into his jacket pocket.

"I have something I thought you might like to see."

"Oh," she said and put her coffee on the floor. "What is it?" She didn't notice her cat shove her face into the coffee, lick her lips, and turn on her heel, raising her tail high in the air. She was focusing on Jim digging in his pocket.

"Here it is," he said.

"What is it?"

He smoothed it out and handed it to her. "It's a letter from Imelda."

"Imelda. My dead sister Imelda?"

"One and the same."

"To me?" she said, pointing at herself.

284 • Anna McPartlin

"No, to me, but it's about you. Go on—read it."

She opened the letter, and part of her wanted to read it and part of her didn't and she was totally thrown. *Why did he bring this tonight?* She began to silently read it.

Dear Jim,

    It's time to talk about Leslie. We both know she's stubborn and cut off, and we both know why. When I'm gone you'll be all she has left in this world and I know it's a big ask, but please look out for her . . .

She looked up at Jim. "What is this?"

"Just read it," he said.

    We've talked about you remarrying, and you know I want you to find someone to love and to love you. I want you to have a great new life that doesn't include overcrowded hospitals, dismissive doctors, overworked nurses, and cancer. I want you to find someone strong and healthy, someone you can go on an adventure with, someone you can make love to, someone who doesn't cause you anguish and pain. Every time I see your face it hurts because for the first time I see that in loving you I've been selfish and I understand why Leslie is the way she is . . .

"I'm not that person anymore," Leslie said. "I'm trying to change. Why are you bringing me back in time like this?"

"Just read on," he said.

    Leslie is a better person than me. I know you're probably guffawing at that as you read, but it's true. She's watched her entire family die of cancer, and when we were both diagnosed with the

dodgy gene after Nora's death she made the decision not to cause
pain to others the way Nora caused pain to John and Sarah and I'm
causing pain to you . . .

"She's praising me, but I was so stupid, so wasteful," Leslie
said. "She was right. I was wrong."

Before cancer she was smart and funny, kind and caring, and
she still is to me. Without her care I wouldn't have coped. I know
sometimes she calls you names, but trust me, she knows you're not a
monkey, so when she calls you an ass picker, ignore it and be kind . . .

Leslie laughed. "I'd forgotten I used to call you an ass picker."
"And I've tried to," he said, and he smiled.

I thought she was being defeatist. I thought that we'd suffered
enough as a family and that we'd both survive. So I made plans
and fell in love and for a while we had a great life but then that
dodgy gene kicked in. Now I see you look almost as ill as I feel, and I
realize that my sister Leslie knew exactly what she was doing when
she broke up with Simon and all but closed off. I watched her
disappear from her own life. I thought she was insane back then,
but it makes sense now. She put the pain of others before her own.
She watched John and Sarah suffer after Nora, and she'll watch you
suffering after me, and although she pretends not to like you, she
does, and it will hurt her and it will also confirm for her that she
is right to remain alone, waiting for a diagnosis that may never
come . . .

Suddenly Leslie felt the tide of sadness returning. "She always
knew me better than I knew myself," she said.

I'm her last family and friend, she hasn't even let herself get to know her niece, and so when I'm gone she'll have no one and that haunts me. Please go and live your life but all that I ask is that every now and again, no matter how rude or uninviting she may seem, call her, talk to her, be her friend even if she fails to be yours, because she has been there for me, for Mum, for Dad and Nora, and I can't stand the idea that after everything she's been through she should live or die alone ...

Leslie put her hand to her mouth and looked from the letter to Jim and back to the letter. She shook her head. "This is why you're nice to me. It's because Imelda asked you to be. You don't have any feelings for me. You have feelings for her. I'm so stupid."

Jim looked confused. "I just found the letter. I thought you'd like to know how your sister felt about you, that's all."

"Well, now I know," she said, "and I'm actually quite tired, so if you wouldn't mind I'd like to say good night."

"We were having a nice time," he said, startled and dismayed. "I shouldn't have given you the letter."

"No," she said, "I'm really glad you did. It's cleared something up for me, so thanks and good night."

Jim was standing outside Leslie's apartment with the door slammed in his face before he had time to work out what had happened, and only when he was halfway home did the realization dawn that Leslie had totally misread his intentions.

Leslie lay in bed with her cat and read the last piece of the letter.

I know I say it all the time and in all my little notes and letters about this and that, but time is running out and I need you to know

that it's been a privilege to be your wife. And although I feel selfish for all the pain I've caused you, I know I've brought happiness too, so hang on to that and forgive me because even knowing what I know now I'd love and marry you again. I suppose Leslie would say I was a selfish truffle-sniffler, but I can die with that.
Yours,
Imelda

Leslie let the letter drop from her hand and closed her eyes. *I'm such a fool. Jim has no real interest in me. And why would he want me, anyway? I'm half a woman. I'm such a silly, silly fool.*

Tom opened the door and was surprised to see Jane, red-eyed and tearful.

"Are you alone?" she said.

"Yes."

"Good."

"Why?"

"Because I want you to take me to bed," she said.

"Jane, I think you need to—"

"Are we friends?"

"You know we are."

"So please do what I ask and take me to bed."

He nodded and led her upstairs, and he kissed her mouth and took off her coat, and he took off his shirt and unbuttoned her blouse and kissed her neck, and when his face was wet from her tears he took her over to the bed and sat her down. He handed her a pillow to hug and asked her what was wrong. Jane told him about the time when Kurt was fourteen months old and hadn't stopped crying in a week and everything she did hadn't worked and she thought she was losing her mind and she hated him with a real palpable, seething hatred and thought about killing him more than once, she was so tired. Even when her eyes were black and she was zombielike and skin and bone, not once did her mother relieve her. Not once did she pick up the baby and tell her that it was okay and that she'd take care of the child while Jane got some much-needed sleep. Not once did she offer to babysit so that Jane could go out with her friends, and not once did she tell her that everything was going to be all right.

Jane told Tom about that day she had walked into the police station with her son in her arms.

"I wouldn't have hurt him," she said. "I just needed someone to help me."

"Ah Jane," he said, and he took her in his arms.

He lay down on his bed, and she lay on his chest, and she told him about what Rose had said about her dad and Elle.

"I should have known Dad didn't have a heart attack. I'm so stupid."

"You couldn't have."

"And Elle—Rose has always been so protective of her, it used to drive me insane. I made one mistake and she punished me for years. Elle messes up time and time again and Rose always finds a way of making what she's done seem normal and okay when all the time she knew it wasn't and I should have known. How could I have been so blind?"

"Because Elle seems perfectly fine. If you ask me, she's just a little selfish and a little spoiled."

"No," Jane said. "She disappears for weeks and weeks. She's so exuberant sometimes and then other times she's so pensive, so sad."

"We all get like that—it's called life."

"Then there was China."

"What about China?"

"She was in Hong Kong with her boyfriend. They were in some club and they had a big fight. He told her he wanted their relationship to end, that he wasn't happy anymore and that it was over. He was flying home the next day. Right after that there was an accident. Elle was hit by a car and ended up in a coma for two days. By the time I got there she'd woken up, but she'd broken her left leg and arm. She was fine, but it scared the life out of us. Vincent, that was her boyfriend, he was sitting by her bed and so attentive I thought they were still love's young dream, but one day when we were getting coffee he told me about their fight and said that she jumped out in front of the car on purpose."

"And you didn't believe him."

"She swore she didn't see the car."

"So you believed her."

Jane nodded. "Who jumps in front of cars?" She was crying again. "I should have known. After all, her father hanged himself with jump rope, and me, well, Jesus, I threatened to kill my own child."

"You were just crying out for help."

"And what was she doing?"

"I don't know," he said.

She raised her head and looked at him. "How does it feel not to be the most messed-up person in the room?"

"Pretty good." He smiled at her and wiped away a stray tear.

"Well, that's something, then," she said, and he leaned in and kissed her, and they made love twice before they fell into a sound sleep.

• • •

Elle answered her front door expecting it to be her mother, who had been up and down to her cottage harassing her since Jane had stopped talking to her.

Jane was standing there, pulling her coat in close to her chest.

"Can we talk?" she said.

"Yes, please."

Jane closed the door behind her, and for the first time in her life she had no idea what she was going to say to her sister.

15

"Happy Death"

A happy death is all I want,
to feel that I have loved someone
and did the things I said I'd do
and lived my life true.

Jack L, *Universe*

November 2008

Breda died on a Tuesday morning at nine o'clock, and she was alone. Ben was in the toilet next door, and the rest of her family was in traffic. Eamonn arrived ten minutes after she was pronounced dead, with Frankie running in two seconds later, panting and in need of oxygen. Kate followed five minutes later. But it was too late. Their mother was gone.

"She waited until I left the room," Ben said. "Your mother never liked to make a fuss."

Kate hugged her dad. "I know, Dad."

Kate took Ben outside, and Eamonn sat with Breda for a

while. All the pain was gone from her face, all the ravages of time melted away; her spirit had moved on, and she looked thirty years younger than her years.

"Are you with Alexandra, Mam?" Eamonn said. "Is that why you had to go?" He left soon after, and Breda's body lay in silence.

Tom got off the phone with Kate and rang Jane.

"Breda's gone," he said.

"What can I do?"

"Come to the funeral."

"Oh, I don't know." If she hadn't slept with Tom she wouldn't have had a problem with it, but now attending his mother in-law's funeral seemed in bad taste.

"She liked you."

"Making me feel worse."

"Please come," he said, and Jane knew he badly needed the backup.

"Okay," she agreed.

Kurt came in, threw his bag in the hallway, and stormed into his room. Jane followed him and knocked at his door.

"Go away," he said.

"What's wrong?"

"I just want to be left alone."

"Okay."

She walked down the hall and into the kitchen.

"Jane, Jane, Jane, it's your mother! Jane!"

She picked up the receiver. "Yes, Rose."

"Come down."

"I'm busy."

"I want to talk to you."

"Five minutes."

"You have two."

Jane sat on her mother's sofa, and Rose poured herself a large glass of wine.

"What did Dr. Griffin say?" Rose asked.

Jane had made an appointment to see him in his office the previous day. She sat in his waiting room for well over half an hour because it was flu season, and a few times she thought about bolting. When his receptionist told her to go in, her feet felt like blocks of cement and she had to drag herself to his door.

Dr. Griffin smiled at her, and she sat down.

"What can I do for you, Jane?"

"You can tell me how my father died."

He sat back in his chair and looked at his hands before rubbing his knuckles. "When did she tell you?"

"Twelve days ago. I can give you the hour and the minute too if you'd like."

"I'm sorry, Jane. It must have been a shock."

"You could say that. Why have you never told me?"

"It's not my place, Jane, you know that."

"You were there. You saw him. Rose said you took him down." Tears were welling, but she was refusing to let them fall.

"Your dad had a lot of demons."

"And Elle—does Elle have demons, Dr. Griffin?"

Dr. Griffin sat up. "What do you mean?"

Although Dr. Griffin had been the Moore family's general practitioner for thirty-five years, the family member he'd had least contact with was Elle. In fact, the last time he had seen Elle with any kind of ailment was when she was twelve, so as far as Dr. Griffin was concerned Elle was fit as a flea.

"Rose thinks Elle is like my father."

"In what way?"

"Temperament."

He laughed a little. "Well, that's natural. We all inherit aspects of our parents. You are sometimes like Rose."

"I am not!" Jane said with the greatest alarm.

"The last time I was in your house you threatened to kill her."

"That was just talk."

"Yes, but familiar talk," Dr. Griffin said. "Just because some of Elle's behavior is reminiscent of her father doesn't mean there is a problem."

"She stole her boyfriend's car and burned it out. Then she packed her bags and disappeared for a while. She often disappears. She puts a sign on her door to tell us that she's gone fishing and we just wait for her to come back—sometimes it's days, sometimes weeks. She drinks a lot. Two years ago she nearly overdosed on cocaine, and she promised faithfully she wouldn't do it again. A few months ago my son found her asleep in a freezing-cold bath—she was blue. She said she fell asleep. She throws money away. She has sex with stranger after stranger, and recently she had an affair with Kurt's dad, yet for years she barely tolerated him. Sometimes she behaves like there's no tomorrow and other times she acts as though she can see eternity laid out before her and she can't stand it. She lives her life according to a letter she writes once a year to the bloody Universe. And then there was China."

After Jane had finished telling Dr. Griffin about the incident in China, he was adamant that Elle needed to be referred to a psychiatrist who specialized in diagnosing the kinds of conditions he suspected Elle suffered from.

"Rose doesn't want that," Jane said.

"Rose shouldn't have a say."

"She said that it was only when doctors got involved that Dad hanged himself."

"Your dad was very sick and, no, he didn't get the help he needed in time, but times have changed and I promise you that if you get Elle to agree to see someone, it will help—maybe not immediately, but it will help."

"I'm scared."

"That's perfectly normal."

"How could I have been so blind?"

"Because we see what we want to see."

"Vincent tried to warn me," Jane said. "All the times I called him names and thought he was shallow and stupid, and he was the only one who really saw her."

"It's easier when you're on the outside."

"I don't know what to do."

"Talk to her."

"And say what? 'Hi, Elle, we think you're insane'?"

"No, Jane, talk to her, listen to her, tell her that you care."

"Oh yeah, thanks, she'll love that, bearing in mind she threw a shoe at my TV the one time *Dr. Phil* was on. The Off/On button still sticks."

Jane sat in Rose's basement apartment, and for over an hour they debated what Jane should and shouldn't say to her sister. Rose was adamant that no doctor go near her girl.

"They only make it worse, Jane," Rose said, "and you are so good with her."

"I can't be responsible for her mental well-being, Rose."

Rose slapped her thigh. "Which is exactly why I didn't say anything before. You had enough on your plate. Bloody Dominic! The first time I saw his sniveling face I should have knocked his bloody teeth out. He wouldn't have been so cute then."

"You know, Elle isn't the only one with mental problems in this house." Jane stood up and walked to the door.

"Darling, we are all mad—you, me, stupid bloody Dominic, precious Tom, that poor titless woman, the woman next door, Paddy the postman. There isn't one of us that someone hasn't thought mad at least once."

"Yeah, well, this madwoman is going upstairs."

"Just talk to her, just be good to her!" Rose shouted after her. *Please mind her, Janey, please don't let them take her, because when they come, it only gets worse.*

The funeral took place on Friday. Leslie made her way to Jane's and arrived in time to see Kurt running down the steps with toast in his mouth.

"Hi, Kurt," she said.

"Hi, Wezwee."

I've been called worse, she thought.

He left the door swinging open for her, and she walked inside and called out for Jane. Jane came down the stairs in black. Leslie looked at Jane and then at herself. She was wearing red.

"Is this inappropriate?" she asked.

"No, you're fine."

"Are you sure? We were never particular about wearing black at family funerals, but other people are funny about it, aren't they?"

"You're fine."

She looked up the street outside for Kurt, but he was gone.

"I missed Kurt," she said, following Leslie into the kitchen. "Did he look okay?"

"He was running and spoke with his mouth full—so if that's 'okay' . . ."

"Irene broke up with him."

"Oh," Leslie said. "I'm sorry to hear that. I know you were fond of Irene."

"Yeah, well, I'm fonder of my son. I'm actually a bit pissed off with her, which is stupid and childish, I know. He's devastated."

"He didn't look devastated."

"Well, he is. She told him he studies too much, if you can believe that."

"They are young, and young people break up all the time." Leslie poured herself coffee.

"And I wouldn't mind, but he doesn't study that much at all," Jane said. "Obviously more than when he was in school, but this is university and Medicine, for God's sake! What did she expect?"

"Jane, are you taking Kurt's breakup a little worse than he is?"

"No. Maybe. I don't know. He won't talk to me about it."

"I don't blame him."

Jane poured herself coffee and sat with Leslie.

"I slept with Tom."

Leslie coughed and spit up coffee so that it dribbled a little down her chin. Jane handed her a napkin, she dried her face, and Jane took it off her and aimed for the washing basket behind her, threw it, and landed the shot.

"Tom, the husband of the woman we're looking for, that Tom?" Leslie said.

"That Tom."

"I don't know how to feel about that."

"Me either. I really like him, but I don't know if I actually really like him or if it's because he's unavailable. If my history's anything to go by, it's probably the latter. And then there is the fact that he's married to my childhood best friend, whom he loves and who is missing. And if I'm honest, I think she's dead."

"Hah!" Rose shouted from the doorway. "I knew you thought she was dead all along."

"Rose," Jane said, "have you ever heard of knocking?"

Rose sat down beside Leslie. "How are you feeling?" She pointed at Leslie's chest.

"Fine."

"You're so brave," Rose said. "I would have rather died."

Leslie laughed, and Jane silently thanked God for Leslie's good humor. Rose was determined to go to the funeral even though she hadn't laid eyes on the Walshes in twenty years. Jane had attempted to talk her out of it, but she insisted on paying her last respects to the woman who had taken her daughter on holiday on many occasions in the eighties.

"But you didn't like her," Jane had argued. "You thought she was a holier-than-thou, pain-in-the-ass Bible basher."

"Jane," Rose said, "that really is no way to talk about the dead."

Jane gave up. Rose was in good form—she loved a good funeral.

"Where's Elle?" she asked.

"She's making her own way."

"I'm really glad you've made up," Leslie said. "She was lost without you."

"Do you hear that, Jane?" Rose said. "She was lost without you."

"Shut up, Rose."

"Darling, if you think you're going to bag a man with that kind of attitude, you're wrong. I mean, I know Tom's standards aren't particularly high and he has a penchant for cheeky little bitches, but maybe if you toned it down just a tad you'd have better luck."

Jane groaned. "Just go to the car."

They got to the church on time. Jane sat in the back, but Rose walked halfway up the aisle because she didn't want a pillar blocking her view. Elle joined Leslie and Jane. Elle and Jane's relationship was still a little strained. Although Jane had forgiven her, Elle wasn't sure why, and Jane had decided not to explain her reasoning. Instead she had merely said that blood was thicker than water and that if Elle wanted her to represent her artwork she would, as long as she promised not to set it on fire again.

"I promise," Elle had said.

"Why did you do it?" Jane had asked.

"It wasn't good."

"You didn't have to burn it, Elle."

Elle stayed quiet for a while. "Do you really forgive me, Janey?" she asked.

"Yes."

"Don't you want to hear an explanation?"

"No."

"I'm really sorry."

"I know."

Jane had left then because she felt awkward and still angry, and she needed to talk to Dr. Griffin before she spoke to her sister openly and honestly. And since she'd spoken to Dr. Griffin she'd been biding her time, delaying the inevitable. Jane wasn't ready to face the possibility that Elle had a problem, so how could Elle do so?

They sat quietly, waiting for the church to fill and the Mass to begin. In the front pew Ben Walsh was on the outside; beside him was Kate, her arm linked in his. Next in line was Eamonn, then his wife, Frankie, Kate's husband, Owen, and Tom at the end. There was little or no talking among the main mourners.

Rose made her way back to where her daughters and Leslie were sitting.

"Push in," she said.

"What are you doing?" Jane whispered.

"It's no fun on your own," she said.

Elle grinned and pushed in.

"Push in a bit farther," Rose demanded so that her view would be uninterrupted.

They all pushed in for Rose. She sat down and looked around.

"You'd think for such a Holy Joe she'd have a few more to her funeral," Rose said.

"Mum," Elle said, "don't be such a cow."

"Sorry, darling."

The priest came out and everyone stood, bar Rose. "You won't catch me standing for one of those arrogant church bastards," she whispered under her breath.

For the next forty minutes the priest talked and read the same old passages from the Bible that they always read when a person dies; they said prayers, knelt, stood, sat, knelt, stood, sat, and knelt, stood, and sat some more. Leslie, Elle, and Jane got up and queued to receive Holy Communion. Rose sat where she was. "You won't catch me taking Communion from one of those arrogant church bastards," she whispered under her breath. After Communion and before the priest gave the last blessing, he invited Breda's family to come up to the altar and talk about her. Ben couldn't find it in himself to speak; it was all he could do to stand. Eamonn walked to the altar and took a second or two to compose himself.

"This is the good bit," Rose said.

Leslie, Elle, and Jane ignored her.

Eamonn cleared his throat. "I'd like to thank everyone for coming here today. My mother would have been really pleased with the turnout."

Rose looked around with a face that suggested that maybe Breda would be impressed, but *she* certainly wasn't.

"My mother was a good person. She was kind, caring, giving, friendly, happy most of the time. She wasn't jealous or boastful, she wasn't selfish, and she wasn't hurtful. She believed in God. She believed in prayer, and she came here nearly every day of her life until recently. Most of you know we lost Alexandra in June 2007. My mother believed that God would save her. She believed that He would bring her home. 'She's still with us, Eamonn,' she'd say. 'She'll be home any day, any day now. God will deliver her from evil.' When God didn't deliver her from evil, my mother got so sad and so sick that it made me angry about all that time she'd wasted here, on her knees. But then I thought, what if God couldn't deliver Alexandra because Alexandra was already gone? What if the pain and suffering of my mother's loss were so great that instead of delivering Alexandra from evil He delivered my mother instead? Who knows what's real and what isn't? My mother took comfort in believing in a God that could hear her. I may not be the most religious of people, but today of all days and for her sake I'd like to think He did. Thank you."

Elle was crying, and Jane squeezed her hand. "That was lovely," Elle said.

Leslie was silent but nodded in agreement. Rose blew her nose.

Jane, Leslie, and Elle joined the queue to sympathize with the family.

Jane sympathized with Owen, then Frankie and Eamonn.

"That was really lovely," she said.

"Thanks. I hope she would have liked it," Eamonn said.

"She would have loved it."

Eamonn hugged her. "Every time I see you I think of Alexandra. I miss her, Janey."

"I know you do, Eamonn," Jane said, and her eyes filled. "I miss her too."

She moved on to Kate, who hugged her and thanked her for coming, and then to Ben, whose blue eyes were swimming. "I'm so sorry, Mr. Walsh."

"Thanks, Jane."

She reached Tom and shook his hand, but he drew her into a hug, and they held each other so tightly that Kate and Frankie both noticed. Frankie smiled at them. Jane pulled back.

"I'll see you at the graveyard," she said, and he nodded.

Elle and Leslie were following and shaking hands, and Kate reminded Ben that Elle was the girl who had painted all the pictures of the Missing and that Leslie was behind the Missing Alexandra website.

"Thank you, girls, thank you so much."

They both nodded and told them how sorry they were.

It was odd, but all three women, Jane, Elle, and Leslie, felt like they weren't just at Breda's funeral but at Alexandra's too. They discussed it in the car on the way to the graveyard. Leslie was the first to bring it up, but the two others were quick to agree. Rose congratulated herself for being the only one who had worked out that the woman was dead a long time ago.

"We're not saying she's dead, Rose," Jane said.

"Oh fine, Janey. The funeral felt like it was for both Alexandra and Breda, and yet you're not saying you think she's dead. Are you in the habit of burying the living?"

At the graveyard, they followed the crowd to the plot that would be Breda's final resting place. As they walked in line, the heavens opened and heavy rain fell, drenching them all in seconds.

"Oh for fock sake!" Rose said, and Jane nudged her.

They walked from grave to grave under a dark and forbidding sky.

Eamonn stood over his mother's grave, soaked to the skin, and told the crowd that was gathering around him and his family that his father had chosen the casket his mother would rest in, Kate had chosen the flowers, he'd chosen the readings, and the music would be chosen by Alexandra.

"She loved Jack Lukeman, and this is one of her favorite songs. I know my mother would like it, and it seems appropriate. It's called 'Rooftop Lullaby.'" He nodded at Owen, who pressed Play on the CD player, and everybody stood in silence. Eamonn dropped his head and stared at the coffin in the ground.

> *Mother, is there something in the sky?*
> *Something up there that they hide,*
> *a jewel for me and you,*
> *apple trees with falling fruit.*

Kate held an umbrella over her father's head.

> *Oh Daughter, now I don't know*
> *but I believe that it's beauty beyond words,*
> *it's like a tune that I can't sing*
> *but I've heard it sung by birds.*
> *It's a rooftop lullaby*
> *falling from the sky*
> *sends us to sleep tonight.*
> *It's the apple in your eye*
> *keeps you as sweet as pie*
> *dreaming through the night.*

Kate's husband, Owen, held his umbrella over hers.

Oh Father, now won't you tell me if you know
where does half the moon go
when it's not up in the sky
it disappears before my eyes.

Ben Walsh stood in silence, looking into the middle distance, unable to bring himself to look at the box that held his wife beneath him.

Oh my son, why does morning break each day
why do people pass away?

The rain continued to fall on the people gathered in the graveyard and on the people outside walking by and trying to get on with their day. It fell in the cities and the suburbs. It fell by the coast, and it fell on the mountains and under a dark sky, under dead foliage, and in a forgotten part of the Dublin mountains the rain fell so heavily that the earth slid and moved, and under that dark sky and dead foliage and in that forgotten part of Dublin's mountains, a black high-heel boot poked through.

Oh it's the mystery in truth
it's the innocence in youth
or a rooftop lullaby
falling from the sky
sends us to sleep tonight,
it's the apple in your eye
keeps you as sweet as pie
dreaming through the night.

16

"Crazy"

Life's a little mystery waiting to be solved,
questions they come pouring down with a little
pinch of salt,
forever poised to conquer, forever poised to fall
but every time I close my eyes I hear these voices call.

Jack L, *Metropolis Blue*

December 2008

Leslie had successfully avoided Jim for a month when eventually, through his tenacity and refusal to take no for an answer, she gave in. They walked mostly in silence, engaging in some small talk, and when they found a little bench by the bandstand they sat and watched a young band play to a small group of their teenage friends. Jim told her that he had gone home and felt very stupid the night he had given her Imelda's letter. He further explained that it had not been his intention to suggest that the only reason he was in Leslie's life was that his dead wife had asked him to be. Jim hadn't considered for a moment that Leslie would jump to that conclusion, but having read the letter many times since, he felt a bit of a fool for not having considered the possibility. His intention had been to show Leslie how brave she was and how proud her sister would have been to see her not only surviving but living. He wanted her to know how happy seeing her surviving and living made him. He wanted her to know that he cared for her.

"But you don't love me," Leslie said quietly.

"I think that I do," he said.

"But . . ." Leslie said, sensing the word was coming.

"But you've just gone through a massive life-changing operation."

"It's been five months."

"That's no time."

"You think I'm using you," she said.

"No," he said, "I would never think that."

"You think that we could never have anything because you belong to Imelda."

"No." He shook his head. "I let Imelda go a long time ago."

"But you never remarried."

"The relationships I had didn't work out because of age, distance, incompatibility, and a million and one other reasons that had nothing to do with Imelda."

"Do you think you could really love me?" Leslie asked.

"I do," he said.

"So?"

"So I'm scared. Are you really ready for love?"

"I am," she said.

"Don't just say that, think about it."

"I have."

"Please, think about it again."

"Why?"

"Because I survived losing one Sheehan. I don't think I could survive losing two."

"I'm ready. I'm ready for you. If you'll have me?" she said, and he smiled, showing his dimples, and he kissed her right there on a bench in front of ten teenagers nodding to the worst rock band in the free world.

It was Christmas week, which was always Elle's favorite time of year. She loved walking among the hordes of shoppers and the dancing lights and beautiful window displays. She liked the big twinkling trees and the faux snow and the cold crisp air that reddened her nose.

She'd felt strangely content since she'd spoken with Jane after Breda's funeral. Jane had driven them home, and when her mother had gone to bed for a nap, having nearly drunk the Walshes out of house and home, Jane had made her way down to Elle's cottage and they had sat and talked. Jane told Elle about their father and what he had done, and contrary to Jane's reaction, Elle's was considered and calm because to Elle, her father's actions made perfect sense.

Then Jane approached Elle about her own mental well-being.

"You think that there's something wrong with me?" Elle said, and she laughed.

"I don't know," Jane admitted, "but when I think about things you've done, I worry."

"Like what?"

"You disappear for weeks without a word."

"I'm in my late twenties, I live in my sister's backyard, I'm an artist who requires inspiration, and sometimes I just need to get away."

"You sleep around with God knows who—it's not safe."

"That makes me a slut, not insane."

"You nearly froze to death in the bath."

"Because I was stoned out of my mind."

"You burned out Vincent's car."

"I remember you saying you would have done the same thing at the time."

"Yeah, but I didn't mean it. What about the time you rescued all those dogs from pounds around Dublin and you couldn't care for them?"

"Okay, I was pretty overzealous, but I dare you to go into one of those places and not want to save all the dogs."

"You give away too much money."

"Because I have it and I don't need it."

"You don't have that much, and in case you hadn't noticed, the world has changed in the last year. Money isn't falling from the sky anymore."

"Okay," Elle said, "I'll be more careful."

"You burned your beautiful work."

"It wasn't good. I just couldn't look at it anymore."

"What about China?"

"Ah Jane, it was an accident."

"Vincent swears it wasn't."

"Vincent is a liar."

"He said you could not have missed seeing that car."

"Jane, I was upset, I was crying, it was raining, I didn't see the car. I need glasses, not psychiatric care."

Jane stayed silent and thought about everything her sister made light of.

"I'm just a dick. I'll change. I'll grow up," Elle promised.

"Are you sure there's nothing you're not telling me? Because, Elle, sometimes you look so sad."

"We all get sad."

"I know but . . ."

"But I'm fine."

"You'll come to me if that changes?"

"Absolutely," Elle said, and she saluted Jane.

"Okay."

And since that conversation Jane and Elle had been on really good terms. The incident with Dominic was all but forgotten, and Elle felt a strange lightness, like a weary passenger who knows her journey will soon end.

Elle made her way through town buying the best and most expensive presents she could find. In Brown Thomas she bought a sound system for Kurt that cost over three grand. She went into Weir and bought her sister a pair of diamond earrings valued at five grand. She bought her mother a necklace that cost four grand. She bought Leslie the most beautiful silk dress and had it boxed and paid for it to be delivered on Christmas Eve. She bought Tom an antique desk because it was the kind of thing she thought he'd like, and even though her sister didn't know and he didn't know if they were a couple or if they weren't, they would be someday. She even bought Dominic something. It was a set of golf clubs and a bag. They were far superior to the ones he'd been using since his twenties, and she figured now that his bank was being bailed out by the government and he was facing possible redundancy he'd have plenty of time to golf.

Leslie was waiting for her in the restaurant. They hugged warmly and sat. Once they had ordered, Leslie updated Elle on her love life.

"I told you so," Elle said.

"Nobody likes the 'told-you-so' person."

"So when is he moving in?" Elle asked, knowing it would irk Leslie.

"About a quarter past never," Leslie said. "Living together? For God's sake, Elle!" She shuffled in her seat. "We haven't even slept together yet."

"You are joking?"

"We're taking it slowly."

"Yeah, but Leslie, there's moving slowly and then there's going back in time."

"It's a big deal for me."

"I know."

She sighed. "I still feel . . . 'ugly' is the wrong word . . ."

"Mangled?"

"No."

"Butchered?"

"No, but thanks for bringing that up."

"Unfeminine?"

"Yes," Leslie said, "unfeminine."

"Well," Elle said, "you are sitting here beautifully made up, with your copper pixie hair perfectly coiffed; you've got your fingernails and toenails manicured and painted; you're wearing a sexy Jersey dress to the knee that shows off your great legs, which are finished off perfectly by a pair of black high heels. When I met you over a year ago, you were a human condom in bad shoes. Trust me when I say that you are far more feminine now than you were then."

Leslie smiled, because Elle was right. They were halfway through their main course when Leslie told Elle that she and Jim were thinking about going to Florida for Christmas.

"What do you think?" she asked.

"I think that you should do what makes you happy."

"Then I think I should go."

"I think that's brilliant," Elle said. "I'm so happy for you, and I'm proud of you. You're a fighter, Leslie. Not all of us are."

After lunch, briefly, if only for a second, Leslie thought about Elle's demeanor, and it dawned on her that she seemed altered—calmer, more considered, happier, resigned even. But then Jim waved at her from across the street and she forgot all about Elle.

At home, Elle took great care to ensure that her presents were wrapped perfectly. She took time writing the cards, as she wanted everyone she loved to know how much she loved them.

She put them under the tree that Jane had made Kurt carry in from the car. Elle had pulled out her box of decorations, and she and Jane went through them. Jane held up the papier-mâché angel that she had made when she was ten.

"I can't believe you still have this," she said.

"I love it," Elle said, taking it from her.

"It's horrible."

"It's lovely. It's just too broken—it keeps falling off the tree."

"So throw it out," Kurt said.

"No," Elle said and placed it carefully back into the box.

Rose knocked on the door, and before Elle yelled "Come in!" she was sitting on a chair directing Kurt where to put the figurine of Joseph that Elle always insisted on hanging on the tree.

"Kurt, put him a bit higher than that—after all, he put up with an awful lot."

Kurt wasn't looking forward to Christmas Day. He was back with Irene, and she was determined they spend Christmas with her mother. Kurt had promised his girlfriend that he would make more time for her during crisis talks a week earlier, and so he couldn't back out of her mother's invitation to Christmas lunch without being accused of welching on their agreed terms.

"Just dump her," Rose said with her usual tact.

"I love her, Gran. I don't want to lose her." Then he added with an ironic twist of his mouth, "At least not until I'm over second year."

Jane laughed. "That's your idea of love?"

"You know what I mean," he said, placing a bauble on the tree.

"No," Jane said, "I don't."

"Yeah, well, Mum, when it comes to love you're hardly the greatest example."

"Thank you, son, happy Christmas."

Elle looked around at her family, her mother sitting on the chair sipping from a mug pretending it was tea, her sister and her nephew engaging in some good-natured sniping. Her little cottage was lit up and full of Christmas cheer. Elle felt content. When they left, she went into her bedroom for a nap, and when she closed her eyes she saw her father hanging from the rafters of his home office by Jane's jump rope and under him she saw herself sitting on the floor playing with her dolls. She looked up to watch him swing, and when he stopped she tipped him so that he'd swing again. She had been seeing this image since Jane had told her about their dad, and every time she was alone, eyes open or closed, she saw the same image. In her head she heard him crying and gasping and struggling, gurgling and dying.

I'm sorry, Dad, I should have known, but I know what to do now. You won't be alone anymore. I'm so sorry you waited so long. I'll see you soon.

Then she fell asleep.

• • •

Since their sleeping together that one time, Tom and Jane's relationship had not been defined and neither of them was in a particular rush to do so. They didn't talk about having sex, and both of them were able to put it to the back of their minds so that they could still be friends. Jane and Tom behaved as if that night had never happened. It was Frankie who broached the subject with Tom one day when she met him accidentally in the fruit section of the local supermarket they shared.

"It was nice of Jane to come to Breda's funeral," she said.

"She was fond of her," he said.

"She's fonder of you than Breda."

"Oh Frankie, please don't."

"You like each other," Frankie said, "and that's a good thing."

"And what about Alexandra?"

"Let's get coffee," she said.

They dropped their baskets and went to the coffee shop next door. When they were sitting with coffee in hand, Frankie made the point to her brother-in-law that she had long been dying to make.

"You need to move on."

"Easy for you to say," he said.

"It's not easy for any one of us to say. We all loved Alexandra. But Tom, it's been a year and a half, you know the statistics, and you know what the liaison officer has said time and time again."

"People are found all the time," he said, but it was without the conviction with which he had once spoken.

"Bullshit. Wake up and get off the sofa. You're wasting your life. Start up your company again, or start up another one, or go to college or travel the world or buy a fish shop or join the monks,

314 • Anna McPartlin

but do something, Tom, something other than chasing a ghost."
And while she was waiting for his response, she bit down on her
muffin so hard that she chewed on her tongue. "Ouch! I keep
doing that."

"I do like Jane," Tom said after Frankie had composed herself.

"Good."

"No. Not good."

"Why is it not good?"

"Because I don't know if I could ever love her."

"Well, of course you don't. The first few years Eamonn and I
were together I wasn't sure that I even liked him, let alone loved
him."

"Finding Alexandra will always be at the back of my mind."

"The back of your mind is better than the front."

"If only I knew what happened."

"We might never know."

"How's Ben?" he asked, changing the subject.

"Good days and bad days," she said. "He's staying with Kate,
and you should visit."

"I don't want to intrude."

"You're family."

"Not anymore," he said, and she didn't argue because since
Breda had died it was hard not to feel that Tom's final link with
the Walshes was truly severed.

When he returned home he found a message from Jane.

Hi, Tom, Jane here. Just wanted to invite you to Christmas
dinner. I've got a huge turkey, Rose and Elle will be there, but
please don't hold that against me. Kurt is going to Irene's,
so there will be plenty of food, and we'd love to see you.

Tom sat on his sofa and thought about what he was doing with his life, what he wanted, what he didn't want, where he would go, what he would do, and he didn't have one answer to any of those questions. The only question he didn't have trouble answering was yes to Christmas dinner with the Moores. *Where else would I go?*

Leslie and Jim didn't make it to Florida. Leslie became sick with a very nasty flu that forced her to stay in bed for the duration of the holiday. Because she woke up with the flu on the morning they were due to fly out, she didn't bother to tell anyone that she was staying home. Jim moved in to care for her, and for the first two days she spent most of her time asleep. She woke long enough to have some of the Christmas dinner he had made, but she was miserable, shaking and sweating like a pig, and so she was put back into bed and was asleep again within half an hour. Jim spent the day with Leslie's cat, eating chocolates, drinking beer, and watching classic films, which was his favorite way to spend Christmas anyway.

Elle and Rose were already sitting at the table when Tom arrived. He brought a few bottles of wine and a large Christmas pudding. He and Jane kissed each other on the cheek at the door, and then he followed her into the kitchen.

"Rose," he said, and he leaned in and kissed her cheek.

"Tom," she said.

"I have something for you." He handed her a very expensive bottle of wine.

She instantly recognized it for its taste and worth.

"Tom, you shouldn't have," she said, holding on to the bottle with a viselike grip.

"It was the least I could do. Elle, this is for you." He handed her a book on meditation. "Apparently it's the new cool thing to be doing."

"Thanks," she said.

"Jane, this is for you." He handed her a box with a ribbon.

"But you've already given me wine and a pudding!"

"Open it," he said.

She opened it, and it was a round-the-world itinerary.

"What's this?" she asked.

"I was thinking it was time I saw the world, and I was wondering if you'd like to come with me."

Elle and Rose stayed silent while Jane gawped at the itinerary.

"I can't," she said. "I'd love to, but I can't."

"Why not?" Elle said.

"I have responsibilities," she said.

"I think you should go," Elle said.

Rose stayed quiet.

"It's not today or tomorrow," he said. "I don't even know when I want to go myself, but I just want you to know that if I do go I'd really like you to come with me."

Jane smiled, and Elle nudged Rose, whose face remained frozen.

"Well, that's a lovely gesture," Jane said, and just as she was kissing his cheek for a second time, the doorbell rang.

Jane wondered who was coming to her house during Christmas lunch. It was Dominic.

"What do you want?"

"Just wanted to see Kurt," he said.

"Kurt's at Irene's," Jane said, closing the door.

"Janey," he said, holding the door, "please forgive me, it's Christmas Day."

"You are something else!"

"I know," he said. "But I miss you, I miss Kurt, I miss Elle but not sleeping with her, I miss this house, I miss our odd little family—Jesus, I must be losing my mind because I even miss Rose."

"I heard that!" Rose shouted from the kitchen.

"Come in," Jane said.

Dominic followed Jane into the kitchen, and she set a place for him at the table. Tom stood up and shook his hand.

"Nice to see you again, Tom."

"It's nice to see you," Tom said.

"Elle, it's good to see you," Dominic said.

"You too, Dominic."

"Rose," Dominic said.

"Dominic," Rose said. "I better be careful what I drink today or you might try to throw the leg over me too."

"Well, you watching what you drink would certainly make a nice change."

Jane served dinner, and they all ate happily. Afterward, the men insisted on doing the dishes.

"So," Dominic said to Tom while washing a pot, "you and Jane."

"We're friends."

"Are you gay?"

"You know I'm not."

"Well, you're not just friends."

"We're undefined."

Dominic thought about it for a few minutes. "Good for you."

Later, when everyone was in the sitting room battling over a game of Pictionary, Kurt returned from Irene's complaining that he'd just endured the worst duck dinner ever and that he was starving.

"I mean, who does duck at Christmas? And it was dry as an old deer's—"

"Excuse me?" Rose said.

"Sorry, Gran."

"I should bloody think so!" She pointed at Dominic. "Do you hear that? That's you!"

Dominic went into the kitchen with Kurt and plated up some food and heated it in the microwave, and they sat and ate together again. Rose and Elle decided it was time to leave, Rose so that she could entertain her bridge friends, who were due at nine, and Elle because she was tired.

"It was a perfect day," Elle said to Jane, and Jane hugged her. Elle had been so different since their chat, and she really felt that maybe her mother and the doctor were wrong and Elle was fine after all.

When they'd gone, Tom and Jane sat together on the sofa.

"That was a big gesture," she said, referring to the itinerary.

"It feels kind of silly now."

"Don't be like that."

" 'Here's a piece of paper with lots of countries written on it,' " he said, and he laughed.

"You should do it alone," she said.

"I don't want to."

"You should get away from here and find yourself again."

"I didn't know I was lost."

"Well, you are, and I'd love you to find yourself with me, but I know it's too soon."

"For you or me?"

"Probably for both of us," she said.

He nodded and patted her leg. "I think you're my best friend."

"I'm glad," she said.

Leslie woke up and walked into her sitting room in a drugged haze. Jim was passed out on the sofa with her cat passed out on top of him. She looked at the clock and it was ten oh five p.m. She poured water into a glass and threw some tablets into her mouth and gulped down the water until the glass was empty. As she was passing the counter on her way out of the room, she saw the telephone's message light blinking. She pressed the button, and it was Elle. She sounded sleepy and happy. She sounded at peace.

Hi, Leslie. I know you are in Florida now, and I hope you and Jim are having a good time. He's a good one. I had a silk dress delivered to your house on Christmas Eve. I hope Deborah took it in for you. It's beautiful and really feminine, so when you wear it I hope you think of me . . .

Leslie looked at the box covered in bows that Jim had signed for the previous day but that Leslie hadn't had the will or strength to open. She smiled at her friend's kindness.

I just wanted you to know that I've loved being your friend and joining you on your journey. You inspired me because you grabbed on to life, and that was right for you. I hope that you don't hate me for letting go because that's what is right for me . . .

Leslie's smile faded. *What is she saying?*

Tell Jane that I love her and I always have, and Kurt too, and my mother. Tell them to be happy for me, and please be happy for me too. If I could cut out the part of me that's rotten, I would, but I know that I can't now, and I can't bear to be here anymore. I've left notes for Jane, Mum, and Kurt buried in the back garden. Jane will know where. Forgive me.

"*Jim!*" Leslie screamed.

Jim shot up.

"What's going on?" he asked, sitting up straight and rubbing his eyes like a child.

"Get up, get up, get up!"

He jumped up and followed Leslie into the bedroom.

"What's going on?" he asked again, and he grabbed Leslie, who seemed to be running around in circles with her nightdress half off and her trousers half on. He held her in place. "Calm down," he said.

"Elle's killing herself," she said.

"What?"

"Elle left a message on the answering machine, saying goodbye and to forgive her."

Jim ran into the kitchen and checked the time the message was received. Nine twenty. He looked at the clock on the wall. It read ten twenty.

Leslie was dressed and running around looking for shoes.

"Leslie, stop. Call Jane." He handed her the phone.

"I don't know her number. It's in my mobile." She ran around looking for her mobile, and when she found it in her jacket she pulled it out of the pocket and the battery was dead. "Christ!" she roared. "Fucking hell!" She ran around the apartment looking for her charger and found it in the bedroom. She plugged it in and turned on her phone. "Come on, come on, come on," she said as the phone was taking its sweet time. Jim stood calmly beside her. The phone came on. She dialed Jane's number. It rang out.

"No, no, no!"

She dialed it again. Jane answered.

"Hi, Leslie, sorry—the phone was in the bottom of my bag," Jane said. "Oh my God, how is Florida?"

"Go down to the cottage now!"

"Have you been drinking?" Jane asked.

Tom had his coat on and was ready to leave, and she winked at him.

"Jane, Elle left a message on my machine saying good-bye and that she couldn't be here anymore. She's left notes for you in the garden. She asked us to forgive her. Go down to the—"

Leslie didn't get to finish her sentence. Jane was off and running from the sitting room to the hall into the kitchen. Dominic and Kurt were eating chocolates and drinking coffee. Jane ran past them, wrenched the door open, and ran down the steps and across the garden, passing her mother's witch hazels, her roses, the graves of Jimmy, Jessica, Judy, and Jeffrey, and reached Elle's cottage door. It was locked, so she banged at it, screaming, "Elle, Elle, Elle, it's Jane! Elle, Elle, please answer the door!"

She was pulling at the latch like a madwoman, slapping the door and kicking at it.

Then Tom, Dominic, and Kurt were beside her.

"What's going on?" Dominic said.

"It's Elle, she's killing herself!"

Tom moved her aside and started to kick at the lock. He kicked once, twice, and on the third kick the lock broke and the door swung open. Jane was first in, followed by Tom, Kurt, then

Dominic. She ran into the sitting room and then into the bedroom screaming Elle's name. Elle wasn't in either room. She ran to the bathroom door and it was locked.

"Elle, please, please open the door!"

Tom and Dominic both started to kick the door down. Kurt stood with his hands on his head. The door broke and opened, and Elle was lying in the bath and one hand was dangling over the rim of the bath and her wrist was bleeding. She was conscious and crying but clearly drugged. Jane grabbed her other hand and it wasn't cut. The dangling wrist was bleeding a lot but didn't appear to be bleeding enough to kill her. Then again, nobody in the room actually knew how much blood loss and drug-taking it took to die. Kurt got a clean towel and tied it around her wrist while Tom called an ambulance, Dominic emptied the bath, and he and Jane wrapped Elle in towels.

Elle was sobbing. "I was too scared, Janey," she said. "I was so happy to go, but then I thought, what if it's worse on the other side?"

"It's okay, I've got you now," Jane said, struggling to keep it together. "What did you take, Elle?"

"Lots of things."

"Make her stand up, walk her around," Kurt said from the doorway.

"Are you sure?" Jane said. "I don't want to aggravate the wound."

"Listen to him, he's doing Medicine," Dominic said.

"Yeah, but to be fair, Dad, I saw it in *Almost Famous*." He shrugged. "But honest to God I think it's the right thing to do."

Jane and Dominic lifted Elle out of the bath and walked her into the sitting room. Tom ran outside to guide the ambulance men in from the front. Elle passed out on her second round of the room.

"Elle, Elle, oh please Elle, wake up!"

Rose slept through it all.

Jane went with Elle in the ambulance, and Tom drove Dominic and Kurt to the hospital. Elle was unconscious the whole way.

"She'll be all right," the ambulance man said. "Just a cry for help."

Jane nodded numbly.

Tom, Dominic, and Kurt traveled in absolute silence except for when Tom rang Leslie to tell her where to meet them.

At the hospital, Elle was taken away and Jane returned to the others.

"You should all go home," she said.

"No way, Mum, I'm staying," Kurt said.

"I'm not going anywhere," Dominic said.

"Me either," Tom said.

"She's going to be fine," Jane said. "Honestly, you should go home."

Leslie appeared, coming in through the door, sniffling and coughing and shaking and looking like she needed a bed herself. Jim was behind her carrying a hot-water bottle that he'd made her hold in the car.

"Where is she?" she said.

Jane burst into tears. "If you hadn't been home!"

"Not worth thinking about," Leslie said, hugging her. "I *was* home—that's all that matters."

They sat in chairs waiting for word of Elle's condition. Within forty minutes a doctor came out to tell them that she was bandaged, there was no damage to her artery, and her stomach had been pumped. He said he would talk to Jane in the morning about what would happen next. She thanked him, and Kurt hugged her.

It was after midnight when they all made their way out of the hospital. Tom insisted on driving Dominic, Jane, and Kurt home.

When Dominic got out of the car, he leaned in the window. "If this has anything to do with me, Janey . . ."

"It has nothing to do with you, Dominic."

"Okay, good, I'm glad she's going to be okay," he said, and he walked up his driveway.

When Kurt got out of the car, Jane told him she'd follow him in a minute. When they were alone, she thanked Tom for everything and kissed him, and when she pulled away she smiled at him.

"I really do think you should go away," she said. "Have adventures for both of us." She got out of the car and dragged herself up the steps to her house.

He made it home half an hour later. He fell asleep as soon as he hit the pillow and didn't wake up until his doorbell rang the next morning. He answered it in his robe. His liaison officer was standing outside, clapping her hands together in an attempt to beat the cold out of them.

"Trish?"

Trish nodded, her face saying it all.

"Where?" he said.

"In the Dublin Mountains."

"When?"

"Christmas Eve. A man was walking his dog."

"And you're sure?"

"The dental records match," she said, and she handed Tom the necklace that Alexandra had always worn, the one he had given her for their first wedding anniversary. It was engraved. ALEX, I LOVE YOU. TOM.

"How did she . . . ?" He couldn't bring himself to finish the question.

"We won't know for a while yet," she said gently.

"Who could have done that to her?" he asked.

"Tom, I promise we will do everything to find the person or persons responsible."

"And if you don't?" he said quietly.

"You bury her, you let her go, and you move on," she said sadly.

"It's over."

"It's over."

"Oh God," he cried. "Oh my God, my poor, poor, love!"

Trish knelt in his hall and took his hand. "She's safe now," she said.

17

"Apes & Angels".

The heart runs on hope, my friend, let hope be your horse,
open the tattered maps once more and let's set a course,
gonna fight, gonna fight, gonna fight just to love again.

Jack L, *Broken Songs*

January 2009

When she was stabilized, Elle was moved from the emergency room in St. Vincent's Hospital to St. Patrick's Psychiatric Hospital, where she remained as a voluntary patient for three weeks. It was difficult coming to terms with her illness, but it had also been a long time coming. The doctors were kind and reassuring, and for the first time in a long time she felt safe. She would be on medication for the rest of her life, and she wasn't sure how she felt about that. In fact, Elle wasn't sure how she felt about anything. The doctor explained that it might take time to get the cocktail right, but he promised they'd get there in the end. Elle was scared that she wouldn't be able to paint because she believed absolutely that it was her demons that drove her, inspired her, and elevated her to a place far from the humdrum of normality and numbness. She was told that her talent wouldn't be affected, but she seriously doubted that and knew if it was affected in even the slightest way she would sacrifice her newfound peace once more. But for now she was okay. She'd talk and she'd listen and she'd take their advice on coping skills, stress management, and goal setting—which she did anyway in the form of writing to the Universe—and she'd swallow what she was given even if it made her feel numb, because for now, numb was good.

Rose was beside herself when she woke the morning of St. Stephen's Day to find that Elle had tried to do what her father had succeeded in doing so many years before. She cried and shook and instantly aged, and Jane found herself hugging her and calling her "Mum."

"Don't cry, Mum."

"I thought she'd be okay."

"I know. Me too."

"But I should have known better."

"All we can do is our best, Mum."

"But I didn't do my best, Janey," she cried. "I'm so sorry I've made such a mess."

"It's okay."

"It's not okay!" her mother shouted. "I shouldn't have let this go on for years, I shouldn't have made you responsible for her, and I shouldn't have told you not to involve doctors because it didn't focking *work*! She could have died, Janey. My fault, again my fault!" Rose was trembling and beating her chest.

Jane wasn't sure if she was in shock, cold, or suffering the DTs.

"Dad wasn't your fault, Mum."

"Of course it was. I left him alone and I knew he was in despair, I left him alone because he was in despair, and I left him alone because I was focking sick of it!" Rose was rubbing her hands in an attempt to stop the violent shaking.

Jane had no clue what to say or do—she had never witnessed her mother in such distress, nor had she ever really thought her capable of it.

"When your father died, I was angry and sad and bitter and in such pain, and I left you two girls to fend for yourselves. I know I did and I'm not proud of it, but you, Janey, you took over, you took care of me and your sister, and you did a good job. You're the strong one, Jane, you've always been the strong one. That's why I pushed you so hard, because we need you, we always have."

"I thought you were disappointed in me."

"I'm disappointed in myself—you just remind me of that, that's all," Rose said. "I'm sorry, Janey, I am sorry."

She was sniffling, and Jane felt such an overwhelming warmth for her mother it was unnerving.

"Let's just be kinder to each other," Jane said, and Rose nodded.

Jane held her mother tightly, and when Rose composed herself, Jane took a tissue out of her pocket and dried her eyes.

"I hope you haven't snotted in that," Rose said, and their tender moment was over.

Elle didn't have any visitors during her first week in St. Patrick's, but after that Jane and Rose came most days. At visiting time she'd sit in the glass annex that overlooked a lush garden, and her visitors would join her there. On Rose and Jane's first visit together, Rose was not behaving like herself, much to Elle's confusion.

"This is lovely, isn't it lovely, Jane?" Rose said.

"It's lovely, Rose."

"You look fantastic, really beautiful," Rose said to Elle.

"I look terrible," Elle said, and she looked at Jane for a hint of what was going on in her mother's head.

"No, you're lovely," Rose said. "Isn't she, Jane?"

"No, she's right, she looks terrible," Jane said.

"What's going on?" Elle asked Jane.

"Rose is scared that if we're not nice to you, you'll try to kill yourself again," Jane said, and she wasn't laughing.

Jane was angry and Elle knew it. Rose blushed the way her oldest daughter did on most days but not that day.

"You're angry, Jane. I understand," Elle said.

"You understand?" Jane said, pointing at Elle. "Oh good, because I understand too! I understand that you were desperate and scared and out of your mind—trust me, after two years dealing with a colicky baby I do understand—but what I don't understand is you lying to me. I came to you, I asked you if you needed help and told you I would be there to help you, and you lied and lied and lied. You made me doubt myself, and if you had died you would have made me complicit in it."

"I didn't mean to, I didn't want to, everything was so muddled and unreal and I wanted to be okay. I wanted to be kooky, arty Elmore, the genius painter. I wanted it to be okay to suffer for your art and then it wasn't okay, then the world tipped sideways and I felt like I was barely clinging on. I got tired and all I could focus on was letting go."

Rose was silent and pale.

Jane shook her head. "If you ever try to kill yourself again, I will follow you into the next world and I will kill you again." Jane's tears fell, and she allowed Elle to bear witness to her pain and her broken heart.

"I'm so sorry, Janey."

"Don't be sorry. Just don't do it again."

Rose took Elle's hand in hers, and for the first time she noticed her mother tremble.

"We love you, Miss Elmore, whether you're kooky or crazy or a little bit of both, whether you're an artist or a cafeteria lady we love you, but Janey's right. If you ever put us through that again, hell will be a holiday."

Elle smiled. "Okay, Mum."

"Okay then," Rose said. "Now, Jane, let's get out of this focking kip before I see someone else I know."

Kurt and Irene visited once a week.

"How's Medicine going?" Elle asked one day while they ate roast beef sandwiches that Jane had sent in a picnic basket that also included three types of salad dressing and four types of salad, a large bag of lettuce, and three cupcakes.

"Good," he said. "It's hard, though."

"Too hard," Irene said. "I never see him."

"You're seeing me now," he protested.

"And look where we are! No offense, Elle."

"None taken," Elle said.

"The last time we went out was well before Christmas," Irene complained to Elle. "We're in college, for God's sake; we went out more when we were in school."

"My exams were after Christmas, I've just finished them, and

I told you we can go anywhere you like tonight," Kurt said, clearly annoyed at having to repeat himself.

"Yeah, well, I'm not in the mood tonight."

Kurt raised his hands to heaven. "You see?" he said to Elle.

"Nobody goes out in January, Kurt," Irene said.

Elle decided to change the subject. "So how's Nursing, Irene?"

"Hate it," she said, shaking her head. "I'm thinking about leaving and doing modeling."

Elle looked at Kurt, who raised his eyes to heaven.

"Modeling?"

"Mum has a friend in London. She says I've got great cheek-bones and a good attitude."

"Well, then," Elle said.

"Still," Irene said, "I'm not sure I'd like modeling. I might do a beauty course or something. I'm not really sure, so for the min-ute I'll stick with Nursing, but I swear I will never make a nurse. People are foul."

Leslie came every day except the days she had an appointment with her consultant. She would arrive bringing books or choco-lates or both.

"You can never read enough or eat enough," she said.

"You're too good to me," Elle said.

"You're right, I am," Leslie said, "and as soon as you're well enough, remind me to give you a kick in the hole."

"That's lovely language."

"Isn't it? I heard it coming out of the mouth of a ten-year-old as I was making my way over here."

"Is it possible to be depressed that you're depressed?" Elle asked.

"I'm sure it is. I know I'd be depressed if I was depressed."

"I just wish I could look into the sky and make sense of it all," Elle said.

"The answer to life's problems isn't in the sky," Leslie said. "It's in Jack Lukeman's songs."

Elle smiled. "Really?"

"Absolutely. In fact, 'It's Been Raining' changed my life. Well that, a nosy girl called Deborah, a cat with the shits, a broken lift, and a surgeon."

"So name the song that will change my life."

Leslie thought about it for a moment or two.

"Time's up."

"No," Leslie said, batting her away. "Give me a second." Then she grinned. " 'Universe.' "

" 'Universe,' " Elle said and raised her eyebrows.

Leslie cleared her throat.

"Don't tell me you're going to sing it?"

"I'm better than you," Leslie said. She cleared her throat again and began to sing. *"Oh nothing lasts forever . . ."*

"Dun, dun, dun, dun." Elle sang, imitating the trombone.

Two male patients on their way back from a smoke stopped at the door to enjoy the show..

"You can cry a million rivers . . ." Leslie sang, and she pointed at Elle, who nodded and got ready to imitate a trombone once more.

"Dun, dun, dun, dun . . ."

"You can rage it ain't no sin but it won't change a thing, 'cos nothing lasts forever . . ." Leslie reached out and embraced Elle. "Sing it with me, Elle."

Together they sang: *"There's a universe inside where the two of us can hide and there's nothing to be frightened of, a flash of light a raging star don't you know you're not alone, ah there's nothing to be frightened of."*

A nurse stopped beside the two male patients and looked at the two girls singing with arms wrapped around each other, and she smiled before going about her business. The two patients clapped.

"Thank you, thank you, we're here all week!" Leslie said, and Elle laughed.

They sat silently for a moment or two, then Leslie looked into Elle's eyes.

"Well? Did it work?" she asked.

"You're right—I'm cured," Elle said, and she laughed.

"I hate to say I told you so." Leslie smiled at her friend. "It's going to be all right, you know."

The first chance Jane had after Elle was stabilized, she made her way down toward her mother's rosebushes and the graves of Jessica, Jimmy, Judy, and Jeffrey. She walked the correct distance between them and started digging. Rose and Kurt appeared from their respective doors and went to the spot where Elle had told Leslie she'd left her final good-byes. Kurt and Rose were silent while Jane dug. When they heard the shovel tapping on the tin, Jane turned to face them, and Rose nodded for her to continue. She cleared the soil from the top and picked up the box and shook it off. She opened it, exposing the three notes folded inside. She set it down on the ground and took a lighter out of her pocket. She looked once more to her mother, and she nodded again. Jane leaned down and set the paper alight. It went out, so she lit it again, and when it looked like it was going to go out again Rose reached into her pocket, pulled out a flask, and sprinkled some booze on it, causing it to reignite and burn until there was nothing left.

334 • Anna McPartlin

"Aren't you even curious?" Kurt asked as they made their way back to the house.

"No," Rose and Jane said at exactly the same time.

"I am," he admitted, "a bit."

Rose put her arm around her grandson as they walked. "It wasn't Elle's time to say good-bye, so let's just be grateful for that."

Jane found it hard to get rid of all her anger. The people in St. Patrick's Hospital told her that this was a perfectly natural reaction, and they attempted to explain her sister's mental state to her. Jane found it hard to accept that Elle was unwell. She had been so desperate to believe Elle when she had explained away her symptoms, and now she felt so selfish and stupid.

It was her son who got through to her.

"Mum, you do the best you can but you're not perfect. No one is—except maybe me."

"She could have died," Jane said.

"We all could die any day, and not because we want to. Elle is just like the rest of us."

"Oh yeah, and how's that?"

"Fucked up," Kurt said, and Jane laughed for the first time since Elle had tried to kill herself.

Alexandra was buried on a Sunday morning. The church was packed to the rafters. Tom stood at the top of the church, and next to him was Alexandra's father, her brother and his wife, and her sister and her husband. The priest spoke warmly of Alexandra, her mother, Breda, and the entire Walsh family. He spoke warmly of Tom and his fight to find her. He hoped that Tom could now find peace, as he had no doubt that Alexandra had.

When Leslie told the Jack Lukeman camp that Alexandra had

been found, he offered to sing at her funeral. The family was blown away by his kind gesture, and so he sang Breda Walsh's favorite hymns for the girl who had died on the way to pick up tickets for his show. Tom got up and spoke about his wife—how they had met, how they had fallen in love, the reasons he had loved her, the reasons he would always love her. He spoke about their plans and dreams and disappointments. He spoke about her sense of humor, and he ended it reading from the last note Alexandra ever wrote to him.

"Alexandra always had the last word in our house, so I think it's only right that she gets the last word today.

"Tom,
"When you are shopping can you pick up the following:
Bread
Milk x 2
Water x 4
Spaghetti
Mince (Lean! Make sure it's lean and not the stuff they call lean and charge half price, because it's not lean. I want lean cut right in front of you and I don't care how much it costs.)"

The crowd laughed a little, and Tom read on.

"Tin of tomatoes
Basil
A clove of garlic
Wine, if you don't still have a case or two in the office, and make sure it's not Shiraz. I'm really sick of Shiraz.

"If you want dessert pick something up.

"I'm meeting Sherri for a quick drink at 5. She has the Jack Lukeman tickets so I took money from the kitty to pay for them. I'm taking a ticket for you so if you don't want to go, text me. I'll be home around 6:30. Your aunt called. She's thinking about coming to Dublin next weekend. Try and talk her out of it. I'm exhausted and can't handle running around after her for 48 hours straight. Your aunt is on cocaine. I'm not messing. An intervention is needed."

Again the crowd laughed a little and smiled at the words from a girl who couldn't be boring even writing a shopping list.

"Oh, and dishwashing liquid. And will you please call someone to get the dishwasher fixed?

"OK see you later.
"Love you,
"Alexandra

"P.S. When somebody close to you dies, move seats.
God, I love Jimmy Carr."

The crowd laughed and then they clapped, and Tom looked down to where Jane was sitting beside Leslie, and she nodded and smiled because he'd done her old friend proud.

Tom led the mourners to the graveside, and Jim held Leslie and Jane held on to Elle, who had been allowed out of the hospital to say her own good-bye. Rose stood to the side with Kurt and Irene. Alexandra's family bowed their heads in grief and gratitude that the worst of their suffering was over. Whatever the police investigation might uncover, Alexandra was safe now. The priest anointed the coffin and said his prayers; Jack sang as they lowered her into the ground. When everyone had gone, Tom was left alone staring at the mound of fresh flowers covering his wife, who had been dead well over a year. Jane let the others go to the car and joined him. She slipped her hand in his, and he squeezed it.

"The inquest will take at least a year," he said. "I don't even know if I can bear to hear the details."

"She's at peace now," she said. "That's what matters."

"I hope so," he said. "I'm going to go on that trip."

"Good."

"You're sure you won't come?" He turned to look at her.

"This is something you have to do on your own."

"Too soon."

"Too soon."

And together they walked away from Alexandra's grave and to the waiting cars. Tom stopped and turned to look at the grave one last time.

'If somebody close to you dies, move seats,' you said. So that's what I'll do. I love you.

March 15, 2009

Dear Tom,

As you know, the postmortem revealed that Alexandra died of asphyxiation. What it didn't reveal was that she was a fighter, but you already knew that. Our forensics team found skin cells under her nails, and although this DNA is not currently in our database we believe that it is only a matter of time before we find the person responsible for her death, and when we do, Alexandra will help us put that individual away.

On a personal note, I just want to say that I'm so sorry for your loss. I've never said that out loud and I wanted to. Although I didn't ever meet your wife, through you I came to know and care for her. Trust that no matter how long it takes, we will keep looking and we will get justice for you, for her, and for her family.

Now remember what I said—live your life, you've lost enough.
Sincerest regards,
Trish Lowe
Patricia Lowe
Family Liaison Officer
Clontarf Garda Station

To: tomtheroamer@gmail.com
From: janemovingon@gmail.com
Subject: You're not going to believe what I'm doing

Aug. 20 (3 days ago)

Tom,

It's only been 8 months and it feels like a lifetime has passed since I drove you to the airport. It's been fantastic to keep up with all your adventures through the blog that Leslie set up. Good old Leslie. As you know, she and Jim are engaged, but did you know that she's opting for a breast reconstruction? Probably not. I only heard it through Elle, and she wasn't supposed to say anything. Anyway, I'm delighted for her. How's India? The last time you blogged you had the trots. I hope the situation has resolved itself and you are no longer a slave to your bottom half. Anyway, I'm writing to tell you that I applied to study Medicine as a mature student and I got in!!!!! I know it sounds insane, but the gallery isn't doing a lot of business at the moment and, let's face it, the way things are going we'll probably have to shut our doors in a few months. Elle isn't ready to paint yet, and when she does I think it's healthier for her to work with someone else. I've told her and she agrees. I have money saved, and, besides, I know I'd love doing Medicine. I'm so excited. I'm going to be starting in the College of Surgeons in October, which I'm very relieved about, because Kurt would have had a fit if I joined him at Trinity.

Elle is well. She's taking some time off and she's reading a lot about her condition. She's looking at alternative therapies and Christ knows what else. I swear if she read that painting your ass red and dancing the conga helped she'd do it, but so far so good. She's working with her doctors and she seems happy. I don't really know anymore. I just have to trust that she'll be okay. Maybe when I'm a doctor I can find a cure. I'd put in one of those smiley faces in that people do to suggest they are joking, but I've forgotten how to.

Anyway, I just wanted to tell you my news.

I miss you.
Jane X

To: janemovingon@gmail.com
From: tomtheroamer@gmail.com
Subject: You're not going to believe what I've just done

Aug. 21 (2 days ago)

Jane,

I am so proud of you. I think it's amazing and brave and I know that you can do it because you have proved you are capable of so much. I also know that you will make a fantastic doctor because you're kind and caring, and even when those around you are driving you up the wall (how is Rose, by the way?) you have the patience of a saint. I wish you all the luck in the world, but I know you don't need it.

I left India yesterday. My head and my ass had an argument, and my ass won. I wished I could have stayed on, but honestly the water was killing me. I'm en route to Kenya and I can't wait. I have an old pal living there. He's part of a construction team building houses, so I'm thinking about sticking around there for a while and working with him. It will be good to get my hands dirty again. I hear the Neil Mellon Township Trust is looking for volunteers to build homes in South Africa in March, so I'm going to head that way and give them a hand although I think I have to get sponsorship. Tell you what—if you come out, I'll sponsor you and you can sponsor me. Think about it, ten days can change not just their lives but yours too.

I really miss you too and look forward to the day I see you again.

Tom X

To: janemovingon@gmail.com
From: leslie.sheehan@yahoo.com
Subject: I don't believe you!

Aug. 22 (1 day ago)

Jane,

I just got an e-mail from Tom congratulating me on getting new tits!!!!! I can't believe you told him.

Mortified!
Leslie

To: elmore@gmail.com
From: janemovingon@gmail.com
Subject: I don't believe you!

10:20 P.M. (3 hours ago)

See Leslie's mail. I think I just landed you in it!!!! Sorry.
Jane

To: janemovingon@gmail.com
From: elmore@gmail.com
cc: leslie.sheehan@yahoo.com
Subject: I don't believe you!

1:20 P.M. (1 hour ago)

No problem. These days I blame everything on the medication.
Elle

To: elmore@gmail.com
From: leslie.sheehan@yahoo.com
Subject: I don't believe you!

1:21 P.M.

Elle,

You just cc'd me, so now I know your dirty little tricks!
Leslie

To: leslie.sheehan@yahoo.com
From: elmore@gmail.com
Subject: I don't believe you!

1:21 P.M.

L,

You see, I would never have done that if I wasn't on medication!
xE

READING GROUP GUIDE

Alexandra, Gone

Anna McPartlin

SUMMARY

When Alexandra Kavanagh disappears one afternoon, it changes everything—not just for her husband and family, but for long-lost friends and complete strangers as well. In a strange twist of fate, her husband, Tom; former best friend, Jane; Jane's sister, Elle; and the terse stranger, Leslie, are trapped together in an elevator at a concert. They form an unlikely bond, culminating in a pact to do everything they can to find Alexandra. The three women, however, have problems of their own, which are thrown into sharp relief by their efforts to help Tom Kavanagh find his wife.

Jane is the rock of her family, constantly caring for her teenage son, Kurt; artistic and unstable sister, Elle; and alcoholic mother, Rose. But as she invests more and more in the search for her friend Alexandra, Jane thinks back on her teenage years and begins to wonder what happened to her dreams. Elle, abandoned by her lover and beginning to doubt her artistic talent, struggles in the search for Alexandra and in her unlikely new friendship with the reserved Leslie as her unstable emotional state escalates. Leslie, terrified that she will develop the cancer that has ravaged her family, tries to find her way in the world again after years of self-imposed isolation.

As the search for Alexandra progresses, each person unearths truths—some less welcome than others—that they must face, lest they become lost themselves.

Questions for Discussion

1. At the beginning of the novel, who did you believe was to blame for Alexandra's disappearance? Do you agree that Alexandra is not "the type" to abandon her family and husband? Did you ever suspect Tom?

2. Every New Year's Eve, Elle writes a letter to herself with a list of things she wants to accomplish in the coming year, and digs up the previous year's letter to compare her resolutions with her accomplishments. Do you have your own New Year's ritual? How often do you keep your resolutions?

3. After her sister Imelda's death, Leslie is overwhelmed by her family history. She withdraws from the world until her chance meeting with Tom, Elle, and Jane pulls her back. What would you have done in her place? Is it better to know the possibilities, even if the knowledge leads to fear, or do you agree with her niece that it's better not to know and to just live instead?

4. When did you first realize that there was more to Elle's behavior than simple whimsy or selfishness? How often does creative talent disguise or excuse deeper emotional and/or behavioral problems in our society?

5. Dominic chooses college and a career over a shotgun wedding with Jane in high school. Do you agree with his choice?

Were those truly his only options, or was there a third choice he didn't consider?

6. Irene's mother, Martha, accuses Jane of being overly permissive with Kurt and Irene (allowing them to drink, sleep together, etc.), while Jane believes that Martha is the worse parent because of her extended absences and strained relationship with her daughter. Whom do you agree with? Is it better to have potentially dangerous behavior going on in a safe environment, or should Jane have tried harder to prevent these behaviors?

7. Is Tom's relationship with Jeanette truly "cheating," or is it an understandable error on his part? Is Jane's violent reaction based on true indignation on behalf of the absent Alexandra, or on her growing emotional attachment to Tom?

8. Breda's faith keeps her going in the early months of Alexandra's disappearance, but eventually it wears thin. She tries to make a bargain with God, takes to her bed, and develops a terminal illness, all within a short time span. Are these three things related? If yes, in what ways? Does Breda's faith help her through her time of need, or does it actually make it harder for her to let go?

9. What is the driving force behind Elle and Dominic's affair—her mental illness, the forbidden nature of the entanglement, or something else altogether?

10. When Elle learns that her father committed suicide and that she shares his "temperament," she begins to have visions of joining him, and eventually tries to kill herself. Is her attempt

prompted by her discovery about her father? Could Jane have handled this revelation of family history differently, in a way that perhaps would have led to a different outcome?

11. Leslie, in order to move on with her life free of the fears that have plagued her, elects to have extreme surgery—a hysterectomy and double mastectomy. Would you have done the same? What are your feelings about elective surgeries like these? Are there cases in which they shouldn't be allowed, or should it be entirely up to the patient?

12. At the end of *Alexandra, Gone*, Tom and Jane both get second starts in life—Tom as a traveler and philanthropist, and Jane as a doctor. Would they have had these second chances without the traumatic experiences they went through? Is it easier to change direction after a trauma?

13. Each chapter begins with a verse from one of Jack Lukeman's songs. How did these lyrics influence and enhance your reading of the subsequent chapter?

A Conversation with Anna McPartlin

In your introduction, you mention that Jack Lukeman and his fans were a source of inspiration for this novel, in particular the relationship that the fans develop with Jack and the band without ever knowing them personally. What do you think it is about music that lends itself to creating those kinds of relationships? Do you believe the same thing is possible for authors and readers?

I think people respond to others' talents. I don't think an author can possibly have the same relationship with the reader as a performer—whether it's a good singer, actor, or comedian—has with his or her audience. I've been at gigs that Jack has played and you literally could hear a pin drop, the audience was so enthralled. It was fascinating to witness.

Alexandra, Gone **was originally released in Ireland under the title *So What If I'm Broken*. What led to the title change? Were there other things changed to adapt the book for a U.S. audience? Does the title shift change the book for you, personally?**

I hated the title *So What If I'm Broken,* but my publishers in Ireland really liked it, as did the buyers and retailers, so I didn't get much of a choice. I'm much happier with *Alexandra, Gone.* The title was changed to suit the market, so it gets a little confusing. I find it difficult to keep up, never mind my poor readers!

What led you to choose a missing person as the pivot point of the novel? Have you experienced a disappearance in your own life?

When Maddie McCann went missing while her parents were on holiday in Portugal, like everyone else I was completely horrified, and as time went on I started dreaming of this poor child. Her face was everywhere, and I remember watching out for her and doing a double take whenever I saw a little girl who matched her description. Alexandra came from the feelings Maddie stirred in me.

Art and music are an integral part of *Alexandra, Gone,* and are clearly topics close to your heart. How do these interests inform your writing process? Do you listen to certain musicians, or surround yourself with certain artists' work?

Music informs everything I write. Every book I've written has its own soundtrack. When I get the idea for a novel, I upload between five to ten CDs onto my computer and I listen to them, and only them, until the book is finished. The music is my way in and out of the world I've created.

You start each chapter with a verse from one of Jack Lukeman's songs. Describe the process of putting together the lyrics and the novel.

I listened to all of Jack's albums for six months solid before I even typed one word. Elle came to me during one of his shows. He was performing a capella; it was a heartbreaking song and the audience was still and silent; then he burst into this huge up-tempo big-band song, and the audience started to dance and sing . . . and in my mind Elle was born. The rest of the characters all came from particular songs. Tom comes from "Lost in Limbo," Jane was born with "Keep Dancing," and Leslie comes from "I've Been Raining."

Alexandra, Gone **highlights many complicated issues—mental illness, addiction, cancer, missing persons, and teen pregnancy, to name a few. Which did you plan to address, and which cropped up during the course of your writing? What kind of research was involved to get all the small, essential details?**

I never plan to address any subject or issue. I dream up characters and the story comes from them. I knew the moment I dreamed up Elle that she was bipolar although I never actually diagnose her in the book. I knew that Leslie had lost her entire family to cancer and I knew that Jane was living a kind of half life and that Tom was experiencing a living hell. After that, the story told itself.

Do you lay out your plots beforehand, or are there surprises in the writing process? Did you know from the beginning what had happened to Alexandra?

I have a brief story outline, but because I know my characters inside and out, I know what they are capable of and the decisions they'll make; it makes sense to me to write that way. As a result my stories are character and not plot driven. I had no idea what happened to Alexandra until one day I was midway through the book and Jack's "Rooftop Lullaby" began to play. It's such a sad song. I shed a little tear or two because in that moment, I knew she would be found dead.

The novel shifts viewpoints from character to character, revolving around Jane, Tom, Elle, and Leslie. Which character was the hardest to write? Which was the easiest? Which is your favorite?

Elle was the greatest challenge because I had a lot of research to do before writing her. Her mental struggle needed to feel real so I worked really hard to ensure she didn't become a silly cliché. She's also my favorite character because I worked so hard on her and I feel closest to her.

Who are your influences as a writer?

My single biggest influence is Roddy Doyle. When I read "The Snapper," I fell in love with all his characters and their warmth, and I knew I wanted to write stories just like he does.

Are you working on anything new that you can tell us about?

I'm working on a movie about five kids who break into banks during the Irish matches during the 1990 World Cup. Its working title is *The Football Five*.

ENHANCE YOUR BOOK CLUB

1. Incorporate Jack Lukeman's music into your discussion. Compile a mixed CD using the songs that appear at the beginning of each chapter. Or select a moment in the book when a specific song is playing (e.g., "Taste of Fall" during their entrapment in the elevator, or "Metropolis Blue" at Elle's "missing persons" exhibition) and play the song while rereading the segment. Discuss how listening to the music changes the reading experience.

2. Incorporate artwork into your discussion: visit a local modern art gallery; attend a lecture on modern art; ask group members to bring in works by their favorite artist, modern or otherwise; ask group members to check out a few modern artists and pick the one they feel is most like what they envision for Elle's work.

3. Have each member draft a "resolutions" letter. Share the resolutions, and discuss ways the group can help members achieve their goals.